Was her *dat* pushing Adrian to date her?

"Adrian, I am mortified."

"Why would you be?" He looked at her quizzically, as if he didn't understand her embarrassment. Then Adrian did something she did not expect. He tipped his hat back and started laughing.

"I fail to see what's so funny."

"Come on, Grace. It's not unusual for Amish parents to push their single children into dating. You're aware of that, I'm sure."

"My parents haven't even mentioned that they think I should date."

"Maybe they're giving you time because of Nicole."

"About that…"

"But any man would be blessed to have you for a *fraa*, Grace. As for Nicole…she's a sweet thing. You shouldn't let your decision to raise your cousin's child keep you from dating."

Except Nicole wasn't her cousin's child. And Grace wasn't sure if now was the time or place to share that fact with Adrian…

Vannetta Chapman has published over one hundred articles in Christian family magazines and received over two dozen awards from Romance Writers of America chapter groups. She discovered her love for the Amish while researching her grandfather's birthplace of Albion, Pennsylvania. Her first novel, *A Simple Amish Christmas*, quickly became a bestseller. Chapman lives in Texas Hill Country with her husband.

Rebecca Kertz was first introduced to the Amish when her husband took a job with an Amish construction crew. She enjoyed watching the Amish foreman's children at play and swapping recipes with his wife. Rebecca resides in Delaware with her husband and dog. She has a strong faith in God and feels blessed to have family nearby. Besides writing, she enjoys reading, doing crafts and visiting Lancaster County.

USA TODAY Bestselling Author

VANNETTA CHAPMAN

&

REBECCA KERTZ

A Chance to Heal

2 Uplifting Stories

The Baby Next Door and *Loving Her Amish Neighbor*

LOVE INSPIRED

INSPIRATIONAL ROMANCE

LOVE INSPIRED®

INSPIRATIONAL ROMANCE

Recycling programs
for this product may
not exist in your area.

ISBN-13: 978-1-335-74494-4

A Chance to Heal

Copyright © 2022 by Harlequin Enterprises ULC

The Baby Next Door
First published in 2021. This edition published in 2022.
Copyright © 2021 by Vannetta Chapman

Loving Her Amish Neighbor
First published in 2021. This edition published in 2022.
Copyright © 2021 by Rebecca Kertz

For questions and comments about the quality of this book, please contact us
at CustomerService@Harlequin.com.

Harlequin Enterprises ULC
22 Adelaide St. West, 41st Floor
Toronto, Ontario M5H 4E3, Canada
www.LoveInspired.com

Printed in U.S.A.

CONTENTS

THE BABY NEXT DOOR

Vannetta Chapman

This book is dedicated to Tracy Luscombe,
who loves a good book every bit as much as I do.

Finally, brethren, whatsoever things are true,
whatsoever things are honest, whatsoever things
are just, whatsoever things are pure,
whatsoever things are lovely, whatsoever things
are of good report; if there be any virtue, and
if there be any praise, think on these things.
—*Philippians* 4:8

If you reveal your secrets to the wind,
you should not blame the wind for revealing them
to the trees.
—Khalil Gibran

Chapter One

Goshen, Indiana, was a beautiful place to be in April, but when Grace Troyer glanced out the kitchen window into the eyes of a llama she fought the urge to scream. She wasn't afraid of llamas, but this particular one tended to spit, and it belonged next door, not on her parents' property. Unfortunately, baby Nicole saw the llama at the same time that Grace did. Nicole wasn't particular as to what animal she was petting. She simply called out, "Mine!" and insisted on moving closer.

"*Nein*, baby girl. That is Adrian's llama, and hopefully he will fetch it soon."

"Problem?" Her *mamm* walked into the room, carrying her knitting basket.

Leslie Troyer carried knitting with her wherever she went. "If we're sitting, we're knitting" was her favorite slogan. It should be cross-stitched and hung on the wall, right beside the Golden Rule.

"*Ya*. The problem is Adrian's llama." The beast was nearly six feet tall, with white-and-brown fleece. He was surprisingly fast, much too curious and had a disconcerting way of staring directly into your eyes without blinking.

"It's an odd-looking animal, for sure and certain."

"Mine, *Mamm*. Mine." Nicole struggled to be let down, so Grace put her on the floor.

Only fourteen months old, she had begun pulling up and clinging to things. Grabbing hold of her mother's dress, Nicole looked up, grinned, then plopped on her bottom, executed a quick change of position to all fours and took off toward the front door.

"She'll be walking soon."

"So you keep warning me."

"After that, your life will never be the same."

In Grace's opinion, they'd already passed that point, but no use bringing it up on a beautiful April morning. Instead, she finished rinsing the last of the breakfast dishes, dried her hands and hurried after her daughter.

She walked into the sitting room to find Nicole had pulled herself up to the glass storm door and was high-fiving none other than Adrian Schrock. He'd squatted down so that their heights matched better. Nicole was having a fine old time. She considered Adrian a top-notch playmate.

Grace picked up her *doschder* and pushed open the door, causing Adrian to jump up, then take a step back toward the porch steps. It was, indeed, a fine spring day. The sun shone brightly across the Indiana fields. Flowers colored yellow, red, lavender and even orange had begun popping through the soil that surrounded the porch. Birds were even chirping merrily.

Somehow, all those things did little to elevate Grace's mood. Neither did the sight of her neighbor.

Aaron resettled his straw hat on his head and smiled. *"Gudemariye."*

"Your llama has escaped again."

"Kendrick? *Ya.* I've come to fetch him. He seems to like your place more than mine."

"I don't want that animal over here, Adrian. He spits."

"We're working on that."

"And your peacock was here at daybreak, crying like a child."

"George Eliot said that animals make agreeable friends because 'they ask no questions' and 'pass no criticisms' or something like that. I'm paraphrasing."

"George Eliot?"

"British author. Nineteenth century."

"Yes, I remember reading her in school." Probably the reason that Grace remembered the author was because Eliot was a woman writing under a man's pen name. "But back to my point—I'd like you to try harder to keep your animals on *your* side of the fence."

Instead of responding to her perturbed tone, Adrian laughed. "When you moved back home, I guess you didn't expect to live next to a Plain & Simple Exotic Animal Farm."

Grace could practically hear the capital letters for Adrian's newest name for his farm. She'd yet to see an official sign by the road. No doubt that would be next, attracting even more *Englischers*. Adrian wiggled his eyebrows at Nicole and was in the middle of yet another laugh when he seemed to realize that Grace wasn't amused. She hated to be a wet blanket, but his animals were driving her slightly batty.

"I think of your place as Adrian's Zoo."

"Not a bad name, but it doesn't highlight our Amish heritage enough."

"The point is that I feel like we're living next door to a menagerie of animals."

"Remember when we went to the zoo over in South Bend? When was that, fourth grade? That was quite the trip."

That was part of their problem—she and Adrian shared a history together. To be more precise, they'd attended the same school and church meetings. He'd been two grades ahead of her. They'd never been what you might call close. If he'd been a stranger, she might have been able to be more firm, more brusque. As it was, there was an uneasy familiarity between them that forced her to be polite.

As for the zoo trip, Grace remembered monkeys that screeched and the reptile house that Eli Zook had taken her to, insisting she'd love it. She didn't love it. And when she'd screamed upon seeing the giant boa constrictor, Eli had laughed until he was bent over. Although she'd thought she had a crush on Eli, she'd known he wasn't the one for her at that very moment.

Thirteen years later, and she still hadn't found the one—though, of course, she'd thought she had with Nicole's father. That was a mental path she didn't want to go down this morning. But looking at Adrian, she remembered Eli and it occurred to her that the two should be best friends. They certainly shared similar interests.

"What ever happened to Eli Zook?"

"Eli?"

Nicole had crawled over to Adrian and had pulled up to a standing position by clinging to his pants leg.

"Eli moved to Florida. He operates a gator farm

there, close to Sarasota. Lots of Amish, but *Englisch-ers* come by, as well."

"You two are not normal Amish men."

"Normal is underrated. Isn't it?"

"Up, Aden. Up."

Adrian scooped her up, held her high above his head, then nuzzled her neck. He treated her like one of his pets. Adrian was comfortable with everyone and everything.

"Do you think she'll ever learn to say my name right?"

"Possibly. Can you please catch Kendrick and take him back to your place?"

"Of course. That's why I came over. I was feeding the turtles, and next thing I knew, Kendrick was high-tailing it down my lane. I guess I must have left the gate open again." He kissed Nicole's cheek, then popped her back into Grace's arms. "You should bring baby girl over to see the turtles. They like to sun out on the log in the middle of the pond—anytime after noon."

"We have a pretty busy day planned." Her only plans were laundry and cleaning, but it seemed rude to say that she didn't want to visit his place—between the llamas, emus and wild birds, the place creeped her out a little bit.

As he walked away, Grace wondered for the hundredth time why he wasn't married. It was true that he'd picked a strange profession. She didn't know of a single other Amish man who raised exotic animals. How did that even produce an income to live on? No, Adrian wouldn't be considered excellent marrying material by most young Amish women.

But on the other hand he was fairly young—twenty-five years to her twenty-three. He also looked like the typical Amish male who romance authors wrote about and young Amish women dreamed of—brown hair cut as if a bowl had been placed over his head, eyes the color of caramel and an easy smile.

He was good-looking, if you went for the tall, thin type, which she didn't. Grace was suspicious of people who were too thin. She always felt the urge to feed them.

She hadn't been thin even before Nicole was born, and the baby weight she'd gained during pregnancy hadn't disappeared after Nicole's birth. It didn't matter, she told herself as she carried Nicole back inside. She felt healthy, and she wasn't in the market for a man. If she was, and weight kept them apart, then he was not the kind of man she would want.

What was she talking about?

A man was the reason she was in this situation to begin with. She shook away the memories, again making a mental effort not to dwell on the past this fine day.

"Let's go change the sheets."

In response, Nicole put her head on Grace's shoulder and popped the two forefingers of her right hand into her mouth. As Grace walked up the stairs, she glanced out the living room window in time to see Adrian leading Kendrick the Llama back to his property.

They were the same height. As she watched, Adrian took the hat off his head and set it on the llama, who tolerated such silliness for all of a dozen steps before casting it off. She could practically hear Adrian's laugh from where she stood. Well, she couldn't hear it but she could imagine it. He was a lighthearted fellow, but then his life had been relatively easy. Why wouldn't he be carefree? He hadn't made the kinds of life-altering mistakes that she had.

Only Grace couldn't quite bring herself to think of Nicole as a mistake. She hadn't realized it was possible to love someone so much that your heart literally ached, but when she'd first held her newborn daughter, she'd felt that exact thing—a yearning and satisfaction that seemed to exist at the same time but in tension with one another.

Her life had definitely changed in the eighteen months she'd been effectively exiled to her *aenti*'s home in Ohio. She'd grown up, learned what responsibility really was and abandoned any ideas of a *rumspringa*. She'd become a mother and a woman, putting childish things aside.

She'd returned home to find that her parents' home and the small town of Goshen were much the same as before she'd left. The only dramatic change had been at the property next door. No one had lived on the place as long as she could remember—though when she was a child, someone had leased it and worked the fields. But the fields had lain fallow for a long time.

There wasn't even a house there.

As a child, Grace and her siblings had run through the pastures enjoying games of tag.

She'd been surprised to learn that Adrian had bought the property and begun building his exotic-animal zoo. Since they were outside Goshen city limits, there were no restrictions on what animals he could and couldn't own. She certainly hoped he'd stay away from reptiles. Perhaps she should talk to him about that.

Regardless of Adrian's plans, which were really

none of her business, she was glad to be back in Indiana, in Goshen and in their Plain community.

She was grateful that her parents had allowed her to come home. Grace had realized while staying with her *aenti* in her rather large Mennonite community that she wanted to be Plain, and she wanted to raise Nicole that way. If it meant confessing all of her misdeeds in order to live in Goshen, then she was willing to do exactly that.

The strange thing was that, so far, there had been no one to make a confession to.

She was both relieved and perplexed.

She'd tried a few times to start a conversation with her old school friends—who had quickly changed the subject. Her oldest *schweschdern* had been the one to tell her that people thought Nicole belonged to their cousin in Ohio and that Grace had agreed to raise her. Grace didn't know where they'd come up with that idea, but then again, it was somewhat common for Amish families to take in an extra child or two. It was a bit on the unusual side for a single Amish woman to do so.

It seemed people wanted to believe this alternate truth.

Who was she kidding? It wasn't the truth. It was a lie, whether she'd been the one to tell it or not. She needed to set people straight, but how was she to do that other than taking out an ad in the *Goshen Daily News* or the *Budget*?

She planned to join their church in the fall. In fact, the day before, she'd begun attending the class for new members. Bishop Luke instructed the candidates while the rest of the congregation was singing. They'd have nine meetings total. Grace was by far the oldest in the class. Each week, they would cover two different articles of instruction. Luke had led them through Bible verses explaining what it meant to have faith in God as well as the creation story.

Grace wasn't sure exactly what was coming up in the next meetings, but she hoped to have a chance to share the truth of Nicole's parentage.

While she dreaded doing so, another part of her looked forward to it. She was ready to wipe the slate clean and move on with her life—hers and Nicole's.

If only this could be their life.

If only Nicole's father wouldn't look for her, wouldn't find her.

If only she could relax and feel at home again here in Goshen.

She'd give almost anything for those things to be true. There were days when her mood plummeted, and she thought the heaviness of her sins would pin her to the mattress. She certainly couldn't bring herself to dream of a home and marriage anymore. Those thoughts were like splinters in her heart. *Nein*, she would set her sights lower—a safe home for Nicole, a *gut* place to raise her child, the love and companionship of family. Certainly those things could satisfy the longing in her heart. She was even willing to live next door to the Plain & Simple Exotic Animal Farm, though she certainly wished the owner would keep the animals on his side of the fence.

Adrian whistled all the way home, thinking of the image of Grace and Nicole standing on the front porch. Grace was a nice-looking woman. She had pretty brown eyes that reminded him of freshly baked brownies and blond hair that was exactly the same tint as Kendrick's fur. He didn't understand why she wasn't dating. She'd been back in Goshen for two months. That was enough time to settle back into her parents' home again. The fact that she'd brought Nicole home to raise, well, that just raised her attractiveness in his point of view.

Raising someone else's child, even another relative's, showed she was kind and compassionate.

He'd like to meet a woman like that.

Of course it would have to be a woman who shared his love of animals and nature. Maybe someone who had a bit of a sense of humor. His *mamm* had told him just the other day that "a wife will make or break a household." She was always dropping little proverbs here and there, hoping he'd take the hint.

But Adrian didn't need prodding. He was more than willing to court. The problem was that none of the women he knew seemed willing. True, most were married already. Or too young. The few that were of the right age and single weren't interested in a man who was trying to make a living raising exotic animals.

But it was what he loved, and he felt strongly that God had given him a passion for animals for a reason.

Even though the women in his district couldn't see that.

And Grace Troyer certainly couldn't.

It was a pity, too, because he wouldn't mind courting Grace—except she seemed to have lost her sense of humor and she certainly disliked his "zoo," as she called it.

Back at his place, he tended to his animals and

brushed down the emus. It was midafternoon by the time he headed into town. He needed to pick up some supplies, but his real purpose for going was to stop by and see his friend. George Miller was ten years older than Adrian. He had six children, a wife whose quilts were in high demand and a nice seventy-two-acre farm.

Adrian could tell from the boisterous shouts of children coming from behind the house that George was working on the family garden.

"Little early in the year for tilling."

"Tell my *fraa* that. She's already started the cabbage seeds inside. Says we need to get them in the ground soon."

"I told you not to add that window box to the mud room. It only means extra work for you."

"And yet *gut* food for the table."

"All these rows can't be for cabbage."

"*Nein*—cucumbers, green beans, peppers, tomatoes and potatoes will be added after the cabbage. You know how it is. We're always planting something." George stretched his back until he heard a satisfying pop. "If you came to chat, why don't you help me out while we talk?"

Adrian picked up a hoe and set to work on the next row.

Two of George's oldest children seemed to have the right idea—one was turning over sod and the other was breaking it up. Two others were sitting on the ground, filling pails with dirt, then dumping it back out on their laps. He supposed the youngest two were inside. He felt a prickle of envy and pushed it away. He'd have a family when God was ready for him to have a family. There was no point in worrying over it.

"What are you chewing on over there?"

"Me?"

"You've been standing in the same place since you picked up the hoe."

"Oh. *Ya.*" Adrian focused on moving down the row, matching George's pace. Keeping his hands busy made it easier to share what was weighing on his mind. "I wanted to speak to you about something…about my farm."

"Uh-huh. It's in a nice area—good dirt and tidy farms."

"I want to start a tour out that way."

"I believe you've mentioned as much before." George kept his attention on the ground, but Adrian knew he was grinning. They'd been friends for many years, and they'd had this discussion several times in the last six months.

"Since you're the head of the Goshen Tourism Board…"

"Goshen Plain Tourism Committee—we're simply a branch of the overall tourism board."

"Whatever. When can we start tours to my place?"

George leaned on his hoe and tipped his hat up. "How many animals do you have now?"

"Two llamas, four alpacas, a couple emus, six exotic birds, some rabbits and goats, which aren't exotic but children love to pet them. Plus the turtles and my three-legged dog."

George signaled for him to keep going.

"Half a dozen wild turkeys, and I'm talking to Simon over in Middlebury about purchasing a camel or two."

"Sounds like things are really progressing."

"They are. I've also set up small pens for a petting area."

"I don't think it's enough."

"I could order a bison or a yak."

George shook his head. "You don't need more animals, or maybe you do—I don't know about that. What I'm saying is that you need other stops on your tour."

That was not what Adrian wanted to hear. He'd spoken to his parents and his *schweschdern*. None of them wanted anything to do with a tour business.

"What would you suggest?"

"A place where guests could purchase handmade items."

"Quilts and such?"

"Sure. *Englischers* believe that all Amish women quilt."

"Your wife certainly does. Maybe she would—"

George held up his hand to stop him. "Becca's willing to provide quilts, but there's no room here to show them. You're going to have to find at least two more stops for your tour."

"Old Saul said he'd be willing to show his dairy cows."

"Gut."

"But my family isn't interested."

"You need a stop where they can eat." George again leaned on his hoe. "Have you tried talking to Grace Troyer?"

"She is *definitely* not interested."

"Have you talked to her parents?"

"Why would I do that?"

George used the edge of the hoe to scoop dirt to the

top of the row in front of him. "Grace has been a bit reclusive since she's returned home."

"I wouldn't call her *reclusive*."

"But Leslie and James are much more practical. In fact, if I remember right, Leslie does quite a bit of knitting."

"She does. There are baskets of yarn everywhere."

"And Grace is a *gut* cook, right?"

"She told me once she wanted to go to cooking school."

"An Amish chef?"

"*Ya.* That was when we were kids." He broke up a particularly big clod of dirt. "You're right that she's been different since she's been back. I think it's because of Nicole. It's a big responsibility to take on, raising someone else's child."

George's head jerked up. He studied Adrian, then shook his head as if to dismiss some idea. "She's an excellent cook, and I know for a fact that her parents can use the money. Talk to them. Maybe they can change her mind."

Adrian didn't think anything would change Grace's mind. She'd once been an outgoing, friendly young woman, but she'd changed. Adrian didn't know what had happened while she was away, but he did know that she wasn't interested in helping him create a successful tour business. What Grace wanted more than anything was to be left alone, and an Amish tour stop would be the exact opposite of that.

Looking in her direction for help was bound to be futile.

His heart sank as he thought of his animals and how much it would cost to feed them over the next year. He needed to make some money, and he did not want to go back to work at the nearby RV factory to do that. He wanted to be on his farm with his animals. If that meant confronting Grace Troyer, then that was what he'd have to do.

He could very well lose the farm if he didn't find a way to raise some money. There were annual taxes to pay, not to mention he needed money for his own food and clothing. Then there was the care of his buggy horse, plus the cost of the animals' feed and the occasional veterinary bill. He also had a responsibility to give to the church.

Adrian needed the tours to happen, and he needed them to happen soon. There was simply no way he was going to let Grace stand between him and his dream.

Chapter Two

The next afternoon Grace found Adrian in the enclosed area that was labeled Exotic Birds Aviary. The structure was approximately fifteen feet wide, twelve feet tall and stretched for the length of most Amish homes. It reminded Grace of a large dog run. The walls and roof were made of chicken fencing, which she supposed kept the birds inside. When she'd first arrived home in February, she'd noticed that Adrian had wrapped the entire thing in plastic sheeting. When she asked him, he said it was so that the plants—and the birds—would stay warm. He'd even set up a heating system that used solar panels.

The plastic had since been removed, bright April sunshine was streaming through the fencing, and the smell of spring was in the air.

Grace had read about aviaries before, and she'd always imagined them as being calm, quiet, peaceful places. Adrian's aviary could best be described as chaotic. The birds set to screeching as soon as she walked inside, a three-legged dog bounded past her and several rabbits hopped toward patches of grass.

"Grace, I'm surprised to see you here." Adrian hurried toward her. "Why are you carrying that rolling pin?"

Grace glanced down at her hand. Why *was* she carrying a rolling pin? Well, that was Adrian's fault. He was the reason she wasn't still rolling out pie crusts. "I'm not here for chitchat, Adrian. Why did you talk my parents into being a stop on your tour?"

"Well, now, I saw your *dat* out in the field early this morning and we got to talking. One thing led to another, and I suppose I mentioned that I could use his help."

"You could use his help?"

"Plus, I thought it might be *gut* for them—financially." A rather large yellow-and-green bird landed on his left shoulder, and Adrian jerked his head to the right, as if to give it more space.

"What is that?"

"This? It's a bird."

"I've never seen one like it before." She realized her tone sounded quite accusatory. Well, it was his fault this bird was here, that this entire menagerie of animals was here and that her parents were buying into his absurd tourist plan. She attempted to refocus on her anger, but the bird was making it difficult. It had begun tweeting quite adamantly.

"You probably haven't seen one like it before because it's from Australia."

"You've been to Australia?"

"*Nein.* A woman in Middlebury bought this one as a pet. She had it for nearly four years. Then a few months ago, she moved into an assisted living facility. She couldn't take the bird with her, so she gave it to me."

"Yes, well—"

"They cost nearly four hundred dollars, so I was quite happy to provide her a home."

"That's *wunderbaar*, but—"

"She's a red-rumped parrot."

That stopped Grace in her tracks. "But she's yellow and turquoise."

Adrian side stepped over to what must have been a feeding station. Grace could just make out scraps of fruit and vegetables scattered across it.

"Dolly has red feathers on her back—all red-rumped parrots do."

As if to show off her best feature, Dolly hopped to the feeding station, turned and walked across the platform. Her colors really were quite exquisite, including bright red feathers on her back. Grace was temporarily speechless.

"Why are you holding a rolling pin?"

She looked at Adrian, then Dolly, then the rolling pin.

"Oh, yes. Well, I was baking, but then Mamm mentioned your tour. So I decided I needed to speak to you about it right away. What were you thinking?" She waved the pin in the air. "Why do you have to drag us into your crazy plans?"

"There was no dragging."

"I'm not interested."

"Apparently your parents are."

"That's beside the point." She slapped the pin against her palm as Adrian added a bit of birdseed to the feeding platform. "Are you even listening to me? I don't want my family involved. I don't want Nicole around all those…strangers."

It sounded lame, even to her own ears, but it was the best explanation she could offer at the moment.

Adrian rubbed his chin thoughtfully as he walked over to a giant birdcage full of finches. The cage reached from the floor to the ceiling, was big enough around that she could have stepped into it and was filled with some sort of shrubbery. Only as she stepped closer, she could see it wasn't all shrubbery—there were dozens of finches inside.

Adrian scooped small black birdseed out of a barrel and deposited it into a feeding tube. "Did you know the size of finches range from four to ten inches?"

Grace held up a hand to stop him. She did not need a lecture on finches. "Adrian, I don't want *Englischers* stomping all over our home."

"Well, we're starting in a week, so it'll probably be warm enough to feed them outside."

"That's another thing... Who decided that I would be willing to cook for twenty people?"

"I thought you liked cooking."

She stared down at the rolling pin. Why couldn't she be home rolling out pie crust? Why did she have to have this conversation? "I do like cooking."

"Then, what's the problem?" He stepped closer, and she had the absurd notion that he meant to reach out and touch her. She stepped back and nearly tripped over a large brown rabbit.

"It's hard to explain. You're going to have to take my word for it."

"Oh." Adrian put both hands on his hips and stared at the ground. Kendrick the Llama walked by the aviary, and Adrian glanced up, then whistled. The beast turned to look at him and immediately took off running in the opposite direction.

Instead of being irritated, Adrian smiled as if a small child had accomplished a wonderful feat. "What were we talking about?"

"Tours. *Englischers*. Cooking."

"Right. Well, I suppose if you don't want to do it, I could ask Widow Schwartz."

"Are you kidding me? Did you try one of her biscuits last week? *Nein*. You didn't. I know you didn't, because you appear to still have all your teeth."

Adrian started to laugh, but he stopped himself when he caught the frustrated expression on her face.

"I'm sorry, Grace. I—I… Honestly, I thought you enjoyed cooking."

Grace sighed and shifted her weight from one foot to the other.

An owl flew from the back of the aviary to the front and settled on a dead tree limb Adrian had propped against the fence. "Mac had an injured wing. I found him in the barn loft. I think he'll be ready to fly soon." The owl studiously ignored them, tucking its head under its wing.

"I do enjoy cooking."

"So why are you dead set against this?" Adrian stepped closer, stuck his hands in his pockets and waited.

Adrian was comfortable with conversations filled with long pauses. He made her crazy with his animals and his rescues and his short attention span, but she understood that he was a decent person at heart. It was just that his life seemed so chaotic, and by proximity, it seemed to bring disorder and confusion into her life, as well. The one thing Grace didn't need was chaos. She wanted order and quiet and seclusion.

A tourist group didn't bring with it any of those things.

And she was convinced strangers meant danger for Nicole.

She should have never watched that TV show at her *aenti*'s—it was all about what lengths an advocacy group would go to in order to reunite biological dads with their children, even children the fathers hadn't known about.

She'd tried to contact Kolby once, but she'd reached a dead end when the phone number he'd given her no longer worked. Something told her she probably should have tried harder to find him—perhaps legally she was required to try harder.

Grace suddenly felt immensely weary. It was something that happened on a disturbingly regular basis since she'd had Nicole. Most of the time she was fine, then other times she simply wanted to crawl back into bed and sleep for a week.

"Are you okay?"

"I will be." She made no attempt to hide her grimace. "I'm not happy about this, Adrian. I wish you'd asked me first."

"You would have said no."

"Which is exactly my point."

He motioned toward a bench set back in the corner, under an arch that had a flowering vine of some sort growing on it. She hesitated, then took a seat. Adrian leaned against the owl's dead tree limb, arms and ankles crossed, patiently waiting. When she still didn't speak, he hopped in.

"The truth is that I need the tour group. It costs money to feed all of these animals, and then there's the occasional trip to the veterinarian. Plus I have taxes to pay on this place."

"Surely none of that is a surprise."

"It's not, but in my mind if I did the right thing, if I provided a safe habitat for all these animals, then *Gotte* would provide my needs."

"'My God will supply all your needs.' That's Bishop Luke's favorite verse."

"One of them."

"Life isn't that simple, Adrian."

"What do you mean? Give me an example." His attention was completely on her now—something that was rare and disconcerting.

"I know the Bible says that, and I believe it…"

"But?"

"But you also have to use the brain that *Gotte* gave you. Did you work out a business plan at all when you bought the property? You purchased it while I was away, so I had no idea that I would come home to… this. What were you thinking?"

"Oh, I thought about it quite extensively before making an offer. I examined the property closely and did a lot of reading on animal habitat. This place was a real jewel. No home on the property that took up prime animal space—just the barn, which I needed anyway. More importantly, there's a stream and a pond. I knew there would be plenty of water and that I'd have room to grow some of the food."

"Did you think of where you'd live?"

"I live in the barn."

"I'm aware. But certainly you didn't plan to live in a barn. It just happened, right?"

"Now that you mention it, *ya*. It did. I'd planned to stay with my parents a few more years until my business was established. But there's too much work with the animals. They need me morning, noon and night. The travelling back and forth didn't make sense. So I bought a cot and walled off a small area of the barn."

"That's what I'm talking about. You have to think things through. Otherwise you end up sleeping on a cot in the corner of a decrepit barn."

"I suppose, but in my mind, it's also a balance between thinking and trusting." Two rabbits hopped closer, and he pulled a small carrot from each pocket, squatted down and held the offering out in the flat of his palm.

To Grace's surprise, both rabbits hopped forward and took the carrots from him.

"They trust you."

"They do. And I try to trust *Gotte* in the same way."

Grace couldn't resist rolling her eyes. He sounded like a child. Trust was all *gut* and fine until the baby needed diapers or new clothes or a visit to the doctor.

"Can you tell me what—exactly—bothers you about having a tour group here?"

Adrian's question was like a knife twisting in her heart. How could she explain her fear that Nicole's father would turn up one day? She'd first have to explain that Nicole was her *doschder*, and now wasn't the time for that. She had pie shells to roll out and bake.

"*Nein*. I can't."

"Okay." He said the word slowly, as if he didn't understand. Of course he didn't. How could he?

"When my parents agreed to your plan, they didn't realize what they were getting into."

"They're adults, Grace. I'm sure they understood."

"Mamm's all atwitter about having a way to sell her knitted things."

"Which is *gut*, right?"

"As if she didn't have enough projects going. I think her yarn supply is multiplying, like some sort of fungus."

"Your *dat* liked the idea of a tour group, too. He said you all could use the money."

Grace waved that comment away. Her *dat* didn't fully understand the situation. He didn't even know who Nicole's father was. That might sound strange to some people, but in Amish homes, things were often left unsaid. He'd told her that he loved her and would pray for her and the baby, then he'd promptly shipped her off to Holmes County in Ohio—a virtual mecca of Amish and Mennonite.

Only Grace didn't want to live in Ohio.

She wanted to live and raise her child here.

And she didn't want to do it next to a wildlife farm or in the midst of a tour group.

"We've already sold out our first tour—it's next Tuesday."

Grace pinched the bridge of her nose and squeezed her eyes shut. When she opened them, Adrian was still there, still watching her, still waiting.

"I will cook for your group next week, but I want you to try and find someone else, and I don't mean Widow Schwartz. Try to find someone that won't scare your guests away. Maybe…maybe someone would be willing to come here and cook?"

Even as she said it, she knew the odds were slim. From what she'd heard, Adrian didn't even have a kitchen. He had a two-burner stove and a half-size refrigerator.

Adrian assured her he'd keep asking around, then he thanked her for agreeing to help. He wasn't just mouthing the words, either. That was one thing she knew about Adrian Schrock—he was genuine and always said what was in his heart.

He really was grateful.

Which didn't alleviate her fears about having Nicole around *Englischers* one bit. Well, if Adrian couldn't see her side of things, then she would find ways to encourage him to look elsewhere for a cook.

Maybe her cooking wasn't as good as he thought it was.

Adrian managed to add a camel to his menagerie before the first tour date. The female he purchased was a dromedary, meaning it had only one hump. Simon Lapp in Middlebury had purchased the animal to sell the milk, but after three years, he'd decided it wasn't a cost-effective venture.

"It should have been profitable," he lamented. "Camel milk sells for forty dollars a quart."

Adrian let out a long, low whistle as visions of a fat bank account and the funds to buy more animals popped into his head. "I didn't realize it was worth so much. Why?"

"People with Crohn's disease or diabetes seem to digest it well. That's why I got into the business in the first place. One of my *fraa*'s cousins was having trouble—she has Crohn's disease."

"I'm sorry to hear that, Saul."

"The thing is, no matter how I try, I still can't make a profit."

Adrian's vision of more animals popped like a child's balloon. "Oh."

"The beasts aren't easy to milk, either... Their milk will only let down if the calf is in the next pen, and even then, it only lasts three to four months. Then it's necessary to impregnate the female again."

"So you're out of the camel business?"

"Officially, if you'll take this one."

"What will you do?"

"I'm going back to goats."

Saul hadn't given the camel a name. Adrian couldn't imagine how a person could own an animal for three years without naming it. He immediately named the camel Cinnamon, then ordered a large load of sand to be delivered to his place. He'd already researched the animal's nutritional needs, and he had plenty of hay, which the books recommended, plus small quantities of alfalfa. He wouldn't need to build a hut for shelter until the following winter.

Unfortunately, once delivered to his place Cinnamon wasn't sure about her new digs. She stood in the corner of the fenced area where Adrian had the sand dumped and refused to come close when Adrian called to her. For the first tour, the visitors would have to view her from a distance.

Adrian rose early Tuesday morning and spent most of the day cleaning out pens and making sure the place looked in tip-top shape. Unfortunately, Kendrick escaped again, and he spent an hour locating the llama. He found him half a mile down the road and had to walk him back home. By the time Adrian got back to his place, he barely had time to feed everyone before the tour guests were due to arrive.

He rushed into his home, which was basically a single room on one end of the barn. There was no time for a shower, so instead, he washed up at the kitchen sink and changed into clean clothes. There were twenty people signed up when he'd checked with George, who had arranged transportation from three of the local families. By the time Adrian stepped back outside, Triangle, the cattle dog, was running in a circle and yipping as the buggies pulled up to his gate.

Adrian hurried over and opened the gate, making sure that none of his animals escaped.

The *Englischers* who stepped out of the buggy were wide-eyed and all ears. They'd already been over to Old Saul's, so they'd had a peek at Amish life. Now Adrian was shattering all of those expectations—he was a bachelor, living alone in a barn, raising exotic animals. They'd never heard of such a thing.

He briefly explained that he'd purchased the property a little over a year ago, and he currently had one camel, two llamas, two emus, four alpacas, six exotic birds, rabbits, goats, six wild turkeys and turtles.

"Plus a three-legged dog." A gray-haired man knelt to hold his hand out to the dog.

"That would be Triangle. The vet says he's part cattle dog, and he sort of found me."

"How did a dog happen to find you?" an older woman asked.

"Just showed up, and I couldn't send him away."

"Sounds like my husband—our place looks a little like yours." The man with her immediately started laughing and reaching for his phone to show pictures of their newest rooster.

"You live in the barn?" This came from an older *Englisch* woman who wore a T-shirt that said What Happens with Nana, Stays with Nana.

"*Ya*, though that's only temporary."

"How do you make money off your animals?" an elderly man asked.

"Well, that's why you're here. The price you paid to enjoy this tour helps to purchase the animals' food."

"So why do you do it, if not to make a living?"

"Hopefully one day that will happen. Until then…" Adrian shrugged.

"At least you're not tied to a time clock. That's something to be grateful for, even if you don't have much money."

"Henry David Thoreau agrees with you." When the man looked at him in surprise, Adrian quoted, "I am grateful for what I am and have. My thanksgiving is perpetual."

"Thoreau said that?" The old gent shook his head but smiled. "I've been on Amish tours in Ohio and Pennsylvania…never heard a Plain person quote Thoreau before."

Adrian laughed with them, then invited the guests to stroll around his property and enjoy themselves. "Kendrick the Llama may spit, but he won't bite," he added.

The guests wandered off, chatting and pointing at various animals. Adrian walked over to Seth, who was one of the drivers.

"*Gut* group."

"*Ya*. Thought the old guy was going to drop his teeth when you quoted Thoreau."

"How did it go at Old Saul's?"

"Fine, I suppose. Can't imagine why anyone would want to walk around and look at dairy cows."

"But that's not what they're looking at." Adrian glanced around the farm, taking in the animals and the guests, and smiled in satisfaction. "They're looking at a different life, a life probably very unlike the one they live, and many of them… They're looking into the past, maybe the way their parents or grandparents lived."

He wanted to ask if Seth had talked to Grace or her parents, but Kendrick was stalking the *Englisch* woman wearing a large floppy hat. Adrian took off to save both the woman and her hat, Triangle bounding at his heels.

He spent the next hour talking with his guests about animal habitats, what the various animals ate, and what they needed to feel safe and comfortable. Sometime in the middle of that hour, he relaxed. This was what he'd envisioned years ago. It was what he'd wanted to do for as long as he could remember, and a deep contentment flooded his heart.

When Seth signaled it was time for dinner, they walked next door to the Troyer home.

Grace's *dat* had placed three picnic tables out under the front fir trees. They were adorned with tablecloths and small mason jars filled with wildflowers. It looked as if Grace had come around to his way of thinking. Plainly, she'd gone all out to make their guests feel at home.

When she stepped outside, wearing a fresh white apron over a peach-colored dress, Adrian felt his pulse accelerate. How had he not noticed how pretty Grace was? Holding a basket of freshly baked bread and with Nicole clutching the hem of her dress, he couldn't think of anything that better personified their Amish life than the two of them.

He hurried over to her. "Anything I can do to help?"

"*Ya*. Carry these rolls over to the first table, then come back for the pitchers of water and tea."

For the next twenty minutes, he hurried between the tables and the kitchen. Grace's *mamm* sat at one table and her *dat* sat at the other. There was a place for him at the third. The *Englischers* soon felt comfortable enough to ask questions, and laughter could be heard as the chicken casserole was passed around the table.

Adrian was relaxed and happy and hopeful.

If all the tours went this well, word would get around. They'd soon be filled to capacity both Tuesday and Thursday evenings, and hopefully all involved would be willing to add a third weeknight tour or possibly a Saturday one.

The day had gone better than he could have hoped.

Then he took a bite of the casserole, nearly choked and realized that perhaps things weren't going so well after all.

He attempted to swallow the bite, found he couldn't and reached for his glass of water to wash it down. Had Grace dumped the entire box of salt in the casserole? He tried another bite and found it no better.

Adrian's temper rarely showed itself. He couldn't remember the last time something had caused his pulse to rocket, his muscles to quiver and a red tint to descend over his vision.

And yet all of those things were happening as he tried to understand how Grace could have done this.

What would possess her to stoop to sabotage?

And what was he going to do about it?

Chapter Three

"I'm sure I don't know what you're talking about." Grace snatched up a casserole dish that was still half full and strode into the house.

She hoped that would stop him. She hoped that maybe Adrian would go back to his menagerie next door and leave her alone. Why couldn't he concede defeat?

"You purposely made terrible food. How could you do such a thing?"

"Adrian, I have a lot of work to do cleaning these dishes. Perhaps we should talk about this later." Her *mamm* had taken Nicole upstairs for her bath, and her *dat* was checking on the two buggy horses. Unfortunately, that left her alone with Adrian.

"Later? As in, after you poison our next group of guests?"

"Salt is not poison."

"So that's what you did."

She mentally slapped her forehead. The idea was not to confess to Adrian, and honestly—anyone could accidentally add a little too much salt or pepper, or half a bottle of garlic powder.

"I don't understand, is all. How could you do such a thing?"

"Because I don't want *Englischers* traipsing all over our farm. I told you that." She turned on him suddenly, catching him by surprise. The look of confusion on his face tugged at her conscience, but it didn't weaken her resolve. She was doing this for Nicole. She was protecting her child. She needed to stand firm.

"Have you had any success looking for a new dinner stop?"

"I haven't had time to even begin checking into that, what with trying to get the place ready and then spending extra time with Cinnamon, who is not feeling safe in her new pen yet."

Grace did not want to talk about Adrian's camel. Honestly, she felt as if she'd stepped into a scene straight from a Doctor Doolittle movie—one of the few she'd seen as a rebellious teenager.

She stomped outside to grab another armful of dishes, Adrian dogging her heels.

At least he was able to carry quite a few plates at once. Why had they not opted for paper plates? *Englischers* were used to casual dining, but her *mamm* had insisted that anyone eating at her house would eat on a proper plate. She'd claimed it was important that each guest left fully satisfied, which succeeded in making Grace feel even more guilty. Her parents actually wanted the tours to be a success. She was surrounded by people who were determined to make this foolish scheme work.

The only trouble was they didn't realize what was at stake—her *doschder*'s safety.

As she plunged her hands into the dishwater, it occurred to her that perhaps Adrian wasn't her problem. Her problem was that no one understood why she was so against this. Maybe she should talk to someone about her worries, about Nicole and about Nicole's father.

The few times she'd tried to broach the topic, her mother had created a lame excuse to leave the room. Once she'd even muttered *Best to leave the past behind you, dear.*

If only things were that simple.

"Where did you go?"

Grace jumped at the nearness of Adrian's voice, spraying them both with soapy dishwater.

"Sorry."

"It's okay." He accepted the dish towel she handed him and swiped at his shirt. "I know you said you don't want Nicole around strangers, and that you can't explain why, but I want to understand."

Instead of answering, Grace turned back to the tower of dirty dishes, tears stinging her eyes. Why was she so emotional? Because she wanted to talk to someone. She wanted a friend or confidant. She didn't need romance. That had been her mistake to begin with— thinking that Nicole's father could offer her a new and more meaningful life. Romance couldn't do that.

But a friend? A friend was something that she sorely needed. Maybe Adrian could...

What was she thinking?

She was a terrible judge of men.

She could handle this by herself.

So instead of answering Adrian, she took her frustrations out on the dishes, scrubbing them with renewed vigor. To her surprise, Adrian picked up a dish towel and began drying. They worked in silence, until the entire tower of dishes was washed, dried and put away.

When they were nearly done, he stepped next to her—close enough that their shoulders were touching—and said, "Can I have your word that you won't ever do that again? It's not fair to the guests who pay *gut* money for a decent meal."

Of course he was right, which only made her feel worse.

"*Ya*, you have my word."

She wasn't conceding, though. Fine, she'd cook delicious meals, but perhaps she could dissuade this dinner idea another way. She had a few ideas that had kept her tossing and turning the night before. Not that she planned to share those with Adrian. Instead, she smiled up at him, and said, "Or maybe I won't even need to cook again. Maybe you'll find someone else."

Which earned her a frown and a growl.

Ha ha. She was plainly annoying him. Excellent.

By that point, her *dat* had walked through the kitchen, declaring, "Guests wear me out. Think I'll put my feet up and read the *Budget*."

She rolled her eyes. Unfortunately, Adrian caught the expression and started laughing. Leaning closer and lowering his voice, he said, "It's not as if he spent all day cooking."

"What I was thinking exactly."

"Even if it was terrible cooking."

She gave him her most pointed look, tossed her *kapp*

strings over her shoulders and began scrubbing the stove clean. Instead of leaving, Adrian took the dishrag, rinsed it, and began wiping down the table and counters.

"Don't you have animals to look after?"

"*Ya.* I do, but I know cooking can be a lot of work. At least that's what someone once told me."

Grace didn't know how to answer that, so she didn't. His kindness made her feel lousy about the deception. Fortunately, her *mamm* came into the kitchen at that moment.

"Adrian, I'm surprised you're still here."

"Oh, I wanted to help Grace with the cleanup phase."

"Well, I would certainly say today was a success, despite the problem with the casseroles. And Grace, that can happen to anyone. I once added Worcestershire to a dish that called for soy sauce." She pulled out the knitting she kept in a basket and sat at the table. "Yes, I would say that tonight was a real success. I sold quite a few of my knitted pieces, and the money will come in handy. Hopefully, word will spread. This was a *gut* idea, Adrian. Thank you for involving us."

A fresh stream of guilt washed over Grace.

As if reading her mind, her *mamm* added, "And I'm sure Grace will do a better job with the food next time. Probably just nerves."

Adrian rested his back against the counter, crossing his arms. "If you could have seen the old gent's face when he took a bite…"

Why was he always so comfortable in any situation? You'd think he'd been in their kitchen a dozen times, which Grace knew was not the case.

"The bread was *gut*, though. Everyone ate a lot of

that, and most people had two helpings of dessert." Adrian looked at Grace and winked.

Good grief.

She was hoping he'd at least stay angry with her. She was counting on it. How else was she going to convince him to find a different cook?

"I better check on Nicole."

"She's sitting with your *dat* while he reads the paper. Why don't you walk Adrian outside?"

As if he couldn't find his way out. Grace didn't say that, though. Instead, she hung up the dish towel and motioned toward the front room.

She might have been okay with how the day had gone if it had ended there. Yes, she'd done a terrible thing, but no one was hurt and she'd done it for her child. Yes, she was exhausted, but hopefully she was putting this silly tour idea on the buggy lane to shutting down.

Overall, she felt optimistic.

Then they walked through the sitting room.

Nicole was sitting there, curled up next to her *daddi*, forefingers stuck in her mouth. When she saw Adrian, her entire face lit up. "Aden." She held up both hands and began to bounce.

"Look who's still up."

"Up."

Adrian scooped her into his arms. He held her high in the air, and when he brought her down, she snuggled in against his chest and put both arms around his neck, looking over his shoulder at Grace.

She felt as if a knife had ripped through the tissue of her heart. Her baby girl was safe and healthy. She should be grateful for that. Instead, she was reminded that Nicole needed a father—not to provide for her, Grace would do that. Her parents would do that. *Nein*, Nicole needed a father because every little girl should have the love of both parents.

And in that area, Grace had failed miserably.

Adrian didn't see Grace or Nicole at all the next day. He thought about them, though. He puzzled over Grace's desperate attempt to sabotage their *Englischer* tour. In some ways, he felt bad that he'd involved her. But in other ways, he thought it was a healthy thing. Her parents certainly considered the tour a *wunderbaar* idea, and the truth was that he thought Grace needed a little more contact with the outside world. She'd been home two months, and she rarely left the farm unless it was to attend church services.

Nein, he was doing the right thing.

The only issue was convincing Grace of that.

He spent Wednesday and Thursday sprucing up his place. The aviary needed a wider path through the middle so that guests could walk the entire length, and then there was the problem of his new camel. Cinnamon still wasn't feeling at home. He finally earned her trust with treats, then spent an hour brushing her. He'd never brushed a camel before, and he marveled at what an amazing creature she was.

Simon had given him a book on camels. It said the word *camel*, literally translated from the Arabic, meant *beauty*. When Adrian looked into Cinnamon's eyes, he could see why. He also quickly realized that he needed to keep an eye on the water level in her trough. The book claimed that a camel could drink forty gallons at once. He currently filled the animal's trough with a hand pump, so he'd have to monitor the water levels closely.

As he went about those tasks, his mind insisted on turning over the mystery of Grace. He'd never been one to tolerate an unsolved puzzle. As a teenager, he'd once spent an entire week putting together a jigsaw puzzle. His *dat* had bought it at a garage sale. The catch was that there was no box—no picture at all. Adrian had lived and breathed that puzzle for six-and-a-half days until he'd finally put the entire thing together. It had been a cat hanging on to a rope by its little paws, with the words Hang In There written underneath.

He needed to hang in there with Grace. Give her time to change her way of thinking.

Later that afternoon, Seth showed up at his farm with the tour group right on time, leading the line of buggies.

Adrian felt more comfortable with this second group. He didn't stumble over his words as he explained how he'd started the farm and why he provided a home for exotic animals. Kendrick didn't swipe anyone's hat, though he did spit on a gentleman. Fortunately, the man laughed and threatened to spit back. Cinnamon still wouldn't come near enough to be petted, but she did walk closer to the fence of her enclosure.

Overall, he felt that things were going very well.

When they walked over to Grace's place, he was surprised to see there were no picnic tables set up under the trees in front of the house. Grace was waiting for them on the front porch, once again looking as pretty as a picture from a story book. This time, Nicole was in her arms. As the guests gathered around the front porch, she said, "We thought that we'd have dinner to-night near the back of the property by the pond. My *dat* has hooked up the buggy horses to a trailer. You can either ride or walk."

Adrian sidled up close to her and lowered his voice. "A hayride is a *gut* idea. I should have thought of that."

"Well, you can't think of everything."

She gave him a winsome smile, and Adrian had the fleeting thought that something was up.

"Do I need to help you carry things?"

"*Nein.* It's all back there already. Fresh bread, sliced ham, locally made cheese, potato salad and apple pie. There's no chance that I could ruin this meal."

Nicole reached for him, and Adrian pulled her into his arms. He hadn't realized how comforting it was to hold a child. He hadn't really considered himself father material, a worry that had only been reinforced by his lack of success in dating. He was more comfortable around animals than babies—except for Nicole. It felt natural to hold her, perhaps because she came to him so willingly. Adrian didn't know if he'd ever have a family of his own, but he wasn't giving up on the idea. He was still a young man, even though he had turned twenty-five.

Occasionally he realized that he'd like to court someone, that he'd enjoy caring for a family, but invariably he became distracted by his animals and his obligation to them. His animals, his dream of a sanctuary, had taken all of his time and attention. But holding Nicole, it occurred to him that perhaps he should try courting again. So what if previous attempts had been a disaster? Success came to the persistent.

He was so preoccupied with his thoughts, what

Grace was saying to him hadn't quite registered. When she reached to take Nicole from him, he snapped out of his reverie.

"I can carry her."

"She's staying here at the house. Weren't you listening?"

His cheeks heated. "Oh. Guess my mind drifted a bit."

"She missed her nap today and has been a bit cranky."

Nicole waved her arm in the air, laughed, then stuck her fingers in her mouth.

"Do you need to stay with her?"

"*Nein.* Mamm will watch her. Then when the guests come back to see her knitted things, I'll put Nicole to bed."

He nodded as if that made sense.

Grace was being awfully accommodating. Her attitude seemed completely different than two days ago. What had changed her mind? It hadn't been anything he'd said. Adrian was sure of that. She'd looked as petulant when he left on Tuesday evening as she had the day she had showed up at his place with a rolling pin. So what was going on?

She took Nicole inside, then returned with a shawl draped over her shoulders. It was a pretty lavender.

"That's a nice color on you."

"This? *Danki.* Mamm made it—of course." They started off toward the back of the property, walking at a brisk clip to catch up with the guests.

Adrian scratched his jawline, glanced in the direction they were going, then back at Grace. Why was she so happy? Why wasn't she asking him if he'd found another cook for the tour? This was too easy. In his experience, it took a longer amount of time for women to come around to someone else's way of thinking…which he immediately realized was a ridiculous thought. Men could be as stubborn as women.

Better to ask than to wonder. "Say, what's going on?"

"What do you mean?"

"Suddenly you seem on board with this."

"On board with what?"

"You know what I mean, with the tour group."

"Oh, that."

"Yes, that."

Grace increased her pace. How did someone with such small feet walk so fast?

"Tell me you haven't done anything to sabotage tonight's dinner."

"Of course not, Adrian." She smiled up at him sweetly, increasing his nervousness by several degrees. "On the other hand, I can't control everything."

What did that mean? Why was she still smiling? They'd reached the back of the property. She'd put a tablecloth on two old picnic tables and set out a few well-worn quilts by the small pond.

It was perfect. The entire thing was better than he could have imagined. So what was going on? Because for sure and certain, Grace Troyer was up to something.

The guests filled their plates and spread out to eat. His mind registered the fact that there were an awful lot of cut flowers in mason jars—and these weren't the wildflowers like they'd had on the tables on Tuesday. Stepping closer to the picnic table, he saw that they were actually tree blossoms.

They looked nice.

He filled his plate, and took a seat on one of the quilts. Small trays filled with tiny jars of peanut butter and jam were at each place, as well.

He didn't notice the bees at first, didn't understand immediately what was happening. First one guest, then another jumped up and began swatting at the air. By the time the bumblebees had fully invaded their picnic, hovering over the tree blossoms and investigating the peanut butter and jam, they had guests scattered everywhere. At first he couldn't spot Grace, but then he saw her sitting on the other side of the pond.

He couldn't believe it.

He could not accept that she would try to ruin their dinner again. Both hands on his hips, he scowled at her.

And what did Grace do? She shrugged her shoulders, hands held out, palms up. What had she said? *I can't control everything.*

Was he supposed to think this was a random, natural event?

He might not be able to prove it, but he knew the truth. And one way or another, he was going to get to the bottom of her issues. There was no way he was finding another place for his tour groups' dinners now. He'd set her straight about bumblebees and bad cooking and tour groups.

He accepted in that moment that Grace Troyer was not the same sweet young girl he'd gone to school with. She'd changed, and not for the better! Which was all good and fine with him.

He didn't need her to be his friend. He needed her to be his business partner, and he would find a way to make that happen.

After all, what else could she possibly do?

Chapter Four

Grace was out of ideas. She spent most of the weekend brooding over tour groups and *Englischers* and Adrian. Saturday, she scrubbed the house with such vigor that her *mamm* suggested she go easy on the floors or they'd have a hole in them soon. Sunday was a church day, but she couldn't focus on the singing or the sermons, and the new-members' class had only increased her angst. She felt like a fraud sitting among the other younger candidates. She'd already made so many mistakes in her life. How did one start over?

Their lesson had focused on the coming of Christ, something she'd heard about since she was a young girl and believed in with all her heart. She loved to think of heaven and being reunited with loved ones. But some days, heaven seemed a long ways off.

Grace sorely needed instruction on how to navigate the day-to-day of her life. She simply couldn't seem to get her feet underneath her. The service ended, but for Grace, the fellowship afterward was even worse.

All the women her age who also had young children had husbands. They sometimes attempted to draw

Grace into their conversations, but she thought it was more out of pity than a real offer of friendship. The younger girls who didn't have husbands were either dragging out their *rumspringa* or actively on the hunt for a man. She certainly had nothing to add to those discussions.

So for the most part, she kept to herself, helping with both the serving and the cleanup of the meal, and she always found an excuse to leave as early as possible. A few times she caught sight of Adrian. Once he was looking directly at her and talking to his friend George Miller. He offered a small wave, but she pretended not to see. Soon after that, she and Nicole left for home.

Grace was still determined to stop the tours, but she couldn't think of a way to accomplish that. Finally on Monday, her *mamm* recommended that she visit her *schweschder*'s, suggesting that the afternoon away would help her mood, which had admittedly been terrible.

"What's wrong with you?" Georgia was nursing her three-month-old son, Jerome.

Grace missed that closeness with Nicole. Now that her little girl had moved on to drinking from a sippy cup, she realized she should have treasured those moments. Nicole was sitting on the kitchen floor, playing with her cousin Ben. They were very close to the same age.

Georgia prodded her with her foot. "Are you going to answer me?"

"What was the question?"

"Why the somber mood? Why the frowns and sighs? What's wrong with you?"

"I'd tell you if I knew."

She really couldn't blame it all on Adrian and his *Englisch* tours. The tour groups were just bearing the brunt of her bad mood, but underneath those feelings of frustration, she felt deeply unsettled. She had no desire to examine that, so instead, she focused on thwarting Adrian's plans. At least she was aware of her coping strategies. That had to count for something.

"Maybe it's the baby blues. You can have those, even after they're toddlers. I know, because after my oldest started walking I went through a bad patch of it."

"Maybe."

"I'll tell you a funny story to cheer you up." Georgia always had a humorous story to share. There'd been six girls in the house when they were growing up, and she was the comedian of the group. She was also the closest in age to Grace. They'd always been more like friends than *schweschdern*, though even Georgia didn't know who Nicole's father was.

When Grace had first told her she was pregnant— and Georgia was the first person she'd shared that information with—her *schweschder* had enfolded her in a hug and told her not to worry.

"Love will find a way," she'd whispered.

A month later, Grace had been bussed off to live with a Mennonite *aenti* in Ohio.

Georgia resettled her babe at the other breast, then leaned back to tell her story. "Will purchased a dozen goats a month ago. Remember that?"

"Oh, *ya*. You were both quite excited about it."

"We were, though I kept telling him that he needed to reinforce the fencing. You know what Dat always says, if water can get through a fence—"

"Then goats can get through it."

"Exactly. Will kept putting off the fence repairs. I don't know if he didn't want to spend the money on the fencing supplies or simply had other things he'd rather do."

"The goats got through the fence."

"Are you going to let me tell this? It's funnier if I just tell it."

"Fine…" In spite of herself, Grace was interested in the story. She'd heard that goats could be a lot of trouble, which was part of the reason she was so surprised that Adrian had recently acquired eight of the pygmy variety.

They're small, he'd explained. *No trouble at all*.

Georgia raised Jerome to her shoulder and proceeded to rub his back in soft circles. "Will put the goats in the back pasture and assured me they'd be fine. They would try to get out every time one of us went back to check on them or feed them, but Will declared he was smarter than a goat."

"Will is pretty smart. Remember the time he fixed that old windmill?"

"Focus. So I'm on the front porch talking to Bishop Luke when I hear this crying from inside—*mamm, mamm*. That's what it sounded like. Well, from the noise, you would have thought that I had a dozen children instead of four, and of course my girls were in school, so only two were home. Still, I kept hearing their voices—*mamm, mamm*."

Grace pressed her fingertips against her lips. She could see where this was going.

"Those cries were immediately followed by the sound of something crashing—several things crashing. The bishop, he's beginning to look concerned, and finally he says that perhaps I should check on whatever is happening. So I hurry inside, the bishop right behind me. And what do you think I see?"

"Goats."

"Goats." Georgia laughed right along with Grace. Her *schweschder* had always been good-natured. "They were on the table."

"Uh-uh."

"*Ya*. They were on the floor, in the pantry, even under the sink. You wouldn't think a dozen goats could fit in here, but they did."

"Goat," Ben declared from his place on the floor, then banged a wooden spoon against a pot.

"That's not the funniest part. Ben was standing in the middle of the goats, tears streaming down his face. The biggest goat had taken his cookie."

"Goat." Ben rocked up onto all fours and crawled over to his mother, pulling up and resting his cheek against her lap.

"I'm telling you, it's amazing he wasn't traumatized, and praise *Gotte* I had the baby in my arms. Best I could tell, they'd busted through the screen of the back door. I'd left the actual door open because it was such a pretty day. But those goats scattered all over my kitchen, and Ben crying… It's a sight I'll remember even when Ben has children of his own."

Suddenly Grace felt better, because she had an idea how to stop the tours, one that might be seen as Adrian's fault instead of hers. After all, to the best of her knowledge, he had never reinforced his fence around the pasture where he was keeping the new pygmy goats. Also, it just happened to be located on the side of his property that shared a boundary with theirs. In fact, it was very near where they'd had the last picnic.

Which couldn't be a coincidence.

It felt…it felt more like providence.

The next morning, she rose in a better mood. It was true that a tour group—another *full* tour group of twenty people, Adrian had announced gleefully—was coming, but she had a plan that just might work this time.

When Nicole went down for her morning nap, Grace picked up the bowl of vegetable scraps and headed toward the fence line, toward Adrian's pygmy goats.

Thanks to Adrian's enthusiasm and her parents' willingness to listen to anything, she now knew all about pygmy goats.

They grew as tall as fifteen to twenty inches.

Does could weigh thirty-five to fifty pounds. Males usually weighed in at forty to sixty.

Basically, they were the size of a medium dog.

She was prepared not to like them, but there was something about goats that made a person laugh. She squatted at the fence line, feeding them carrot tops, wilted lettuce leaves and cucumber peels. She couldn't stop herself from reaching through the fence and touching their soft fur. Three were gray—ranging from a soft color, like a skein of yarn her mother knitted with, to a dark gray, like storm clouds. Two more were black with white splotches. And the final three reminded her of a box of chocolates her father had bought for Christmas one year—everything from light to medium to dark caramel.

Suddenly she found herself thinking of Adrian's eyes.

Adrian's eyes!

She stood, brushed her hands and checked the gate, which allowed access for her *dat* and Adrian to move more easily between the two properties. Apparently they were now working together on a few projects. The gate wasn't locked, only latched... It would be easy enough to slip it open after the guests arrived.

And really, a goat could do that without her help, if it had the right motivation.

She had more salad scraps in the kitchen.

It was as she was walking back toward the house that she came across her *dat* mending a harness for the workhorses. He smelled of dirt and crops and horses. He smelled like the father who had been there for her all her life. Though he was a man of few words, she understood that he loved her and Nicole, and that he would always provide for them.

"Hold this for me while I mend the strap?"

"Sure."

They worked without talking, a comfortable, peaceful silence, until he'd finished and thanked her. She'd begun to walk away when he called out to her.

"Adrian's a *gut* man."

She turned, cocked her head and waited.

"I know you don't agree with this tour thing. I know it's hard for you."

"That's true, and I have good reasons—"

"I don't need to know why, Grace. The fact that it is hard for you, that's what matters. I'm sorry for that. But this farm needs all the income it can earn... Our family needs all the income we can earn. We won't be passing up *gut* work that the Lord provides for us. That would be wrong, in my opinion." Then he turned back to the harness, having said his piece.

Leaving Grace wondering if she really wanted to follow through with her plan to put a stop to Adrian's tour groups once and for all.

The third tour group could not have gone better. Adrian was growing quite comfortable with talking in front of groups, and the tourists seemed generally interested in his animals. His favorite part, though, was when they wandered off on their own and enjoyed God's creations. That was when he noticed the smiles blooming and the worry lines draining away, as if for a moment at least, they had laid down a burden.

He arrived at Grace's place, surprised to find her *mamm* greeting the group and directing them toward the back pond.

Seth led the group that wanted to walk, while Grace's *dat* helped the others onto the hayride. Adrian held back.

"Something wrong, Adrian?" Grace's *mamm* had always been kind yet to the point. No use trying to beat around the bush with Leslie Troyer.

"I didn't see Grace, and I was wondering if she's *oll recht*."

"Grace is already at the back pasture with Nicole. She wanted to make sure everything was perfect when the *Englischers* arrived."

"Or sabotage it," he muttered under his breath, but Leslie heard him.

If she was offended, she didn't show it. Instead, she walked down the porch steps carrying a large basket of hot rolls. He could smell the yeast and butter, and it caused his stomach to growl.

"Let's walk together."

"I didn't mean to be rude."

"You were only being honest. We both know that the ruined casseroles and bumblebees weren't a mistake."

"If you knew, why didn't you—"

"Stop her?" Leslie shrugged. "First off, I didn't know until after the fact. And secondly, have you ever tried to stop Grace when she has her mind set on something?"

"Then the tours are doomed."

"Maybe not."

"I don't understand why she's so dead set against them. In fact, I'd thought she would welcome a chance to make a little extra income."

"Her *dat* and I certainly do."

"But Grace…"

Leslie stopped, her attention on a week-old calf and the cow that was attending to it. She looked back at him, smiled and continued walking. He hurried to catch up with her. The Troyer women, they were all fast walkers.

"Was I supposed to understand something about Grace, based on that calf?"

"Oh, Adrian." Leslie's smile was genuine, and he couldn't have felt offended if he'd tried. She wasn't laughing at him, he was sure of that, but she was amused at the current situation.

"Grace has five *schweschdern*. Did you know that?"

"I suppose I've never stopped to count."

"And Grace is the youngest and closest to your age… No, maybe Georgia is the closest to your age."

"*Ya*. Georgia and I were in the same grade at school."

"So, six girls. We've been through quite a bit, as far as beaus and husbands and *bopplin*."

"I don't understand."

"My girls all have different personalities, though they are all stubborn to the core. They get that from their *dat*." She smiled at her joke.

They were in sight of the group now, and Leslie stopped, surveyed it, then turned to search his eyes.

"One thing I can tell you for certain is that each of those girls will do anything to protect and care for their children. Just like that cow and calf. It's nature's way. It's *Gotte*'s way."

"Okay, but how does a tour group threaten Nicole?"

"I don't know." She said it simply, and one thing that Adrian understood in that moment was that she wasn't concerned at all. "*Gotte* will take care of Nicole. We can trust He will take care of all of us, but Grace is new at raising a child."

"It's so kind of Grace to raise her cousin's *boppli*." When Leslie gave him an odd look and waited, he crossed and uncrossed his arms. "I... What I mean to say is that I've tried, but it's hard to imagine taking on that kind of responsibility. I mean, I have responsibilities with the animals, but it's not the same."

Leslie glanced toward Grace, then back at Adrian.

He squirmed under her gaze, but he waited. He felt like there was something he needed to understand about this conversation. But he didn't.

"For whatever reason, Grace is being extra careful with Nicole. The thing is... The reason doesn't matter."

"It doesn't?"

"Adrian, I think you've hitched the buggy in front of the horse."

"What?"

She patted his arm. "Stop trying to figure out what Grace is concerned about and just get to know her."

She walked off toward the group that was now once again scattered around the pond and at the picnic tables. Grace was walking from group to group, a pitcher of tea in one hand, holding Nicole on her hip with the other.

Just get to know her.

He had been thinking of Grace as a means to an end. He resisted the urge to slap his forehead with his hand. Basically, he was using her. No wonder she didn't trust him. And the worry about *Englischers* around Nicole? He didn't have to understand that. After all, she was Nicole's *mamm*. She knew what was best for her child.

How arrogant of him to think that he might know more on that topic than she did.

Grace looked up at that moment, and Adrian smiled and waved—as he had done at church. This time instead of ignoring him, she smiled back and nodded, then turned her attention to the *Englischer* who was asking for more tea.

The meal progressed well. The food was delicious. No bees attacked. It was… It was picture-perfect. Adrian began to relax and enjoy himself. He began to wonder about how he might get to know Grace Troyer.

In fact, where was she?

He checked each group but didn't see her. Leslie was watching over Nicole, who was yawning and sticking her two fingers into her mouth. Adrian turned in a circle, looking for Grace, and saw her standing next to the fence line, right before his goats crashed through the gate and made a beeline for the picnic.

Immediately there were pygmy goats everywhere—

in the pond, on the tables, and one was even tugging on an *Englisch* woman's purse. His smallest goat had taken an interest in a tablecloth and was trying to pull it off the table. An *Englisch* man grabbed the other end and proceeded to engage in a bizarre tug-of-war.

Nicole was pointing and laughing.

James and Seth were attempting to herd the goats back toward the fence.

Leslie had grabbed the platter with the coconut cake and was holding it above her head as two of the goats bumped against her legs.

And Grace…

Grace was standing at the fence line, a huge smile on her face.

Chapter Five

It took a half hour to gather up the goats and move them back to their side of the fence. Grace was dismayed to note that the *Englischers* seemed more entertained than perturbed. Several had pulled out their phones and snapped pictures. She even heard one woman say, "I'd heard about these tours. Someone posted on their blog that you could always count on a surprise twist. Wait until I tell my daughters about these goats. What a hoot!"

Her plan had clearly backfired.

Grace expected Adrian to confront her, but although he looked in her direction several times, he didn't seek her out. She was a little disappointed, as she had her defense all ready.

First, he needed a better latch on the gate.

Second, she'd agreed not to sabotage the dinner and she hadn't. The cooking was spot-on.

And third, well, she didn't have a third reason, but she would have come up with one if he'd asked.

He didn't.

He left with Seth after the *Englischers* had tramped

through their house and bought more of her *mamm*'s knitting—receiving blankets and baby booties and small sweaters with matching hats.

"Good thing I have a large amount of items completed already." Her *mamm* glanced up and smiled, then waved the money she was about to put into the mason jar they kept for emergencies. Most of their income went in the bank, what little they had. But the mason jar was the extra-money jar. It paid for birthday gifts and doctors' visits and dinners out. "Two hundred and forty dollars, Grace. It's a real blessing for sure."

How could Grace argue with that?

Adrian didn't stop by that evening or the next morning, but toward dinner on Wednesday, he knocked on the front door. Did she imagine it, or did he purposely show up when they were about to eat? Not that she could blame him. No doubt his cooking skills were limited, and his kitchen—well, it could hardly be called that.

Grace had made a casserole that combined ground beef, cheese and noodles. She served it with a side salad and green beans, and for dessert, she'd made oatmeal pie. As aggravated as she was with him, something in Grace wanted to feed Adrian. Maybe it was her nesting instincts. Maybe it was the fact that he was so tall and thin. If he turned sideways you could look his direction and miss him. Okay, he wasn't that thin, but nearly.

Whatever the reason, she waved him to the seat across from her and hopped up to fetch an extra plate.

Dinner conversation jumped back and forth between the topics of crops, animals and church. No one mentioned tour groups, although it seemed to Grace that they must be on everyone's mind. It was almost as if they were afraid of setting her off.

She wasn't an ogre.

She didn't lash out at people.

Though she had to admit her behavior had been less than stellar. In fact, she wasn't proud of the steps she'd taken to put a stop to the tours. They had seemed necessary at the time. Had they truly been necessary? Had she been wrong? She'd been quite conflicted about her sabotage efforts the evening before as she'd read her Bible. She'd been working her way through the gospels, and the twelfth chapter of Mark seemed to be written specifically to her.

Love thy neighbor as thyself.

That was the problem with the Bible. It was so black-and-white. It didn't leave much room for her justifying her actions. Still, she could defend what she'd done. She was protecting her child. What if Nicole's father showed up, out of the blue, and demanded joint custody? What would she do then?

Nein. She couldn't conceive such a thing.

So what if she added too much salt to a dinner or attracted bees or unleashed goats? No one was hurt by her actions. Perhaps Adrian would grow tired of her antics and find another cook.

The *Englischers* would stop coming by the farm, and Nicole would be safe.

Love thy neighbor as thyself.

She certainly wouldn't want to be served a bad-tasting meal, and some people were afraid of bees. As far as the goats, everyone had been entertained by the little pygmies, which was beside the point. In truth, she was rather ashamed of herself but didn't know what to do about it.

When she began clearing the dishes, Adrian once again dried and put things away as she washed.

"You don't have to do that."

"Help?"

"Yes, help."

"You don't want help?"

"I don't understand why you're standing here in my kitchen holding a dish towel." Her face, neck and ears suddenly felt unbearably hot. She wondered if she was coming down with something. "I don't understand the *why* of it."

"Why what?"

"Why do you want to help me, Adrian? Don't you need to get back to your zoo?"

"Even I grow tired of animals now and then. Their conversation isn't as *gut* as yours."

Which was patently not true. She was a terrible conversationalist. She never knew what to say to a man. They'd already covered the safe topics at dinner. Would Adrian be interested in hearing about Nicole's latest achievements? The way she'd smiled up at Grace when she fetched her from her nap or that she'd patted Grace's face and said "mine"? Had she meant "*mamm*"? Or had she claimed Grace as her own? Why would Adrian want to hear about any of that?

Maybe she was overthinking everything.

She wasn't sure.

Having grown tired of waiting for a response, Adrian nudged her shoulder with his. "I saw that Nicole was standing in the middle of the room earlier—without holding on to a thing."

"Did you see that?" Grace beamed with pleasure, as if she had something to do with Nicole's standing ability. "She's a smart girl."

"Indeed."

"Earlier today, she squatted to pick up a toy."

"Squatted?"

"*Ya*. It's an important milestone, or so my *Milestones for Your Child* book states."

"There's a book called *Milestones for Your Child*?"

"Not my point. Up until then, if she wanted something, she would crawl over, plop down and then drag it toward herself."

"But today she squatted?"

"She did." Grace laughed with him. "Sounds like a small achievement, I know, but it filled my heart with joy. She was holding on to the coffee table, walking around it and laughing, as she does when she thinks she's getting away from something."

"She's a *gut*-natured child."

"And then she saw her baby doll on the floor. She pivoted, squatted and picked up the doll." Grace plunged her hands back into the soapy water. "Children are amazing."

"Indeed they are. Reminds me of Cinnamon."

"My child reminds you of your camel?"

"Hear me out." Adrian brought her up-to-date on how nervous the camel had been when it had first arrived at his farm and the progress they'd made since then. "I believe she was afraid of people, though I have no idea why she would be. Perhaps the man I purchased her from only interacted with her to feed her or milk her. Did I tell you about the milking?"

"*Ya.* I still can't believe it sold for so much. I've never even heard of people drinking camel milk."

"Anyway, at first she'd stand across the pen and stare at me suspiciously. Now, if I'm alone, she trots right over to me."

"How does she get along with the other animals?"

"I believe she's taken a liking to Triangle, my dog."

"I know who Triangle is. That's an odd-looking mutt, but I'll admit he grows on a person."

"She doesn't seem to like Kendrick, though."

"Your llama has bad manners."

"Does not."

"Does Kendrick spit at her?"

"Now that you mention it…"

They again shared a smile, and Grace was suddenly glad that Adrian had stopped by. It was nice to talk to someone other than her parents, and Nicole… She wasn't able to hold up her end of a conversation yet.

Grace had never been good at talking to men. Perhaps that came from being raised with only sisters. She wasn't sure. She did realize now that she'd been very shy as a teen, and she'd dated only in groups. Perhaps that was why she'd fallen for Nicole's father so quickly. He'd paid attention to her in a way that she'd never experienced.

That had immediately been followed by her year in exile.

And now she was home. She was older and more confident in some ways, and she suddenly found that talking to a boy—to a man—didn't seem nearly as intimidating as it once had.

Not that she expected anything to come of it, and maybe that was a plus. Maybe by taking the word *re-*

lationship out of the equation, she was able to relax. She would like to be able to count Adrian as a friend.

Not that it would last. Adrian would eventually marry, and his *fraa* wouldn't want him gallivanting next door to wash dishes with the neighbor. But she was tired of worrying about the future. Perhaps, for just a little while, she could learn to appreciate the moment for what it was.

Adrian hated to ruin the nice conversation he was having with Grace. He could practically feel her relax, and she'd actually smiled a few times. It occurred to him that her life must be lonely here with her parents.

Why didn't she get out more?

Why didn't she date?

He nearly groaned in frustration. He was doing it again—trying to figure out how to fix her life.

Just get to know her.

One thing he understood for certain was how much she cared about Nicole, and that was the reason he'd come to talk to her.

"Would you like to take a walk?"

She looked at him as if he'd sprouted wings. "A walk?"

"It's a nice evening, warmer than it has been." He peered past her, out the window. "*Gut* sunset. Thought we might take Nicole to see some flowers I spied near your front lane."

She continued to look at him questioningly but stammered through a response that seemed more *yes* than *no* and ended with, "Let me fetch our sweaters."

At first they walked slowly down the lane, Nicole toddling between them, each holding one of her hands.

"She's not very fast yet. At this rate, we'll reach the fence line by sunrise." Grace attempted to pick up Nicole, who was having none of it.

She squirmed in her mother's arms, arched her back and said repeatedly, "No, no, no, no." Then she changed her chorus to, "Aden, Aden."

When Adrian reached for her, Grace's eyebrows arched in surprise, but she happily handed her over. "Fair warning—she grows heavier with each step you take."

Adrian was once again struck by how adorable and precious Nicole was. He thought maybe she was small for her age, but what she lacked in weight and height she made up for in attitude. Though she'd plopped her two fingers into her mouth, she pulled them out to shout unintelligible words at various things.

"Any idea what she's saying?"

"Not really."

When they reached the wooden fence that bordered the front lane, he led them to where he'd seen wildflowers—blue violets, Virginia bluebells, and a small white flower his mother called "spring beauties."

"Is it okay to let her down?"

"Sure, *ya*. Maybe she'll wear herself out."

Nicole glanced up at them, then toddled sideways, holding on to the bottom slat of the fence. When she squatted to pick one of the flowers, Adrian and Grace shared a smile.

"She's a pro at that now."

"Indeed."

"Emerson said that 'the earth laughs in flowers.'"

"What does that mean?"

"I don't know, but it comes to mind when I see so

many." Adrian stuck his hands in his pockets, but his arms felt unnatural and awkward. He pulled them back out, then crossed them. Good grief. What was he so nervous about? "Say, Grace. I wanted to talk to you about Nicole."

Which was probably the wrong way to begin the conversation, since Grace instantly froze, the expression on her face one of caution and worry.

"It's nothing bad. It's just that I was thinking about what you said—about not wanting Nicole around *Englischers*."

Still she only looked at him, and he knew then that she was expecting him to argue with her, to tell her how silly she was, to point out the importance of the tours.

He didn't do any of those things.

"My youngest *schweschder*, Lydia, she loves babies. She takes care of her nieces and nephews all the time. I was thinking that I could bring her over on tour nights, and she could stay with Nicole in the house, so she wouldn't have to be out with all the *Englischers*. I'd be happy to pay her out of my portion of the profits."

"Your *schweschder*?"

"Sure. You remember Lydia. Only I guess—" he glanced up at the trees, doing the math "—if she's fourteen, which I'm sure she is, and you're…"

"Twenty-three."

"So you're nine years older, which means you were out of school when she started."

"I know Lydia, Adrian. We all attend the same church meetings."

"Right. Of course."

"And that's a very kind suggestion." She took a

crushed flower that Nicole pushed into her hand. "But why…? Why would you offer to do such a thing?"

"Because you're concerned about Nicole, and I want to ease your mind. If I can."

Grace studied her *doschder*, then turned and looked at Adrian.

"It would help, probably more than you can imagine. I would definitely worry about her less if she was, you know, playing inside."

"Exactly, and Lydia is happy to do it."

"You've asked her already?"

"I suggested that I might know someone who needed her help a couple hours a week. I didn't make any commitment on your part. I wouldn't do that without checking with you first."

Nicole became suddenly mesmerized by a butterfly. She reached a chubby finger out to touch it, laughed when it fluttered up and then back down again. Looking at Grace, she said, "Bird."

"Butterfly." Grace picked her up and kissed her neck, inhaling deeply.

Nicole stared over Grace's shoulder at Adrian, stuck the requisite two fingers in her mouth and watched him solemnly. When Grace turned back toward him, he knew that he'd finally said and done the right thing.

"That was very thoughtful of you, Adrian. *Danki.*"

"Gem gschehne."

"We accept."

"Wunderbaar."

"On one condition."

"Uh-oh."

"I will pay Lydia from *my* earnings." When Adrian

tried to protest, she held up a hand like a traffic cop. "It's only fair, since she'll be watching my *doschder*."

He loved that about Grace. She treated Nicole as her own. He might never know the details of Nicole's birth, but he did know with certainty that the little girl in front of him would never lack for love or family. Grace would see to both of those things.

"All right, but my intent wasn't to lessen what you earn."

"I know that. You want your tours to be a success."

"Yup."

"Which means no more cooking mishaps."

"Your last meal was delicious." For some reason, he was no longer angry when he thought of that first meal, maybe because that particular fiasco hadn't been repeated.

"No more bees," Grace added.

"Bees don't really scare me."

"And no more goats."

"I have to admit, it was rather funny when Nelly tried to snatch the woman's purse."

"You've named your goats?"

"Well, *ya*. Every animal appreciates…being appreciated." He was suddenly aware of the way the last of the day's light played across Grace's hair. Of course most of it was covered with her *kapp*, but a good bit of the part at the front had escaped.

Why was he surprised that her hair was somewhat curly?

He looked at Nicole, then back at Grace. The two looked very much alike… That must be a coincidence. Well, probably Grace's cousin looked like Grace, so it would make sense that her cousin's baby girl would look like Grace.

He wondered again about that situation. Why had Grace agreed to raise Nicole? Would her natural *mamm* want her back at some point?

"You're too good-natured, Adrian."

"Can a person be too good-natured?"

They were walking back toward the house, the sky afire with orange, purple and blue clouds as the sun set upon what Adrian thought had been a very good day. Which had nothing to do with the woman and child walking beside him. It was more that the conflict in his life had suddenly dissipated. Adrian wasn't a fan of conflict. That might be why he sought the company of animals and occasionally avoided people.

Animals were predictable—except for the goats and possibly Cinnamon. Kendrick could be a challenge at times. Mostly, though, he understood why his animals did what they did. Cinnamon hadn't been properly socialized. Kendrick was a little bored. Animals were fairly easy creatures to figure out.

People, on the other hand, were much harder to read. He often didn't understand why they acted the way that they did. But Grace? Grace he could understand. Regardless the reason for her raising Nicole, there was no doubt that she dearly loved the child.

They'd nearly reached the porch steps when he thought to thank her for dinner.

"You don't have to thank me, Adrian. I would have cooked anyway."

"Still, it was nice of you to share." He shifted a sleepy Nicole to his other arm. "I love my farm, and living in the barn isn't a problem, but you know what I really miss?"

Grace shook her head, then ran her fingers up and down her *kapp* strings and waited, almost as if she were interested. He took that as a positive sign and pushed on.

"Ice cream."

"Ice cream?"

"*Ya.* I have a small refrigerator but no freezer." He rubbed a hand over his jaw. "A pint of Ben & Jerry's would hit the spot."

"Ben and Jerry's? You go for the good stuff, then."

"I do. Salted Caramel Almond is my absolute favorite." He slipped Nicole into her arms, and for a moment, they were standing closer than they ever had, close enough that he could smell shampoo and soap and the freshness of the spring evening that seemed to have settled on Grace. She glanced up at him, a smile playing on her lips.

"That's a real tragedy, Adrian."

"It is."

"Maybe you should build a house someday."

"Or at least purchase a proper refrigerator."

Her laughter did more to lift his spirits than a dozen pints of ice cream. As he walked back to his place, it occurred to him that caring for God's animals was all good and fine, but people needed the companionship of other people.

The question was whether he was willing to do anything about it.

His mood sank at that thought. Every woman he'd tried to date had quickly pointed out that he spent too much time and money on animals, that he didn't live

in a proper house, that he had his priorities wrong.
Women didn't understand him. If he ever found someone who did, he would probably have to compromise,
make some changes to his life.

Was he willing to do that?

Things were finally going well.

Which was why it would be ridiculous to entertain
the idea of courting anyone now. Maybe in a few years.
Maybe when he'd built a proper house, with a proper
refrigerator, with a freezer that could hold several pints
of Ben & Jerry's ice cream.

Chapter Six

The next day's tour went perfectly. Grace actually enjoyed cooking the meal, the tourists were pleasant, and her *mamm* once again sold quite a few items—including some market bags and prayer shawls she'd quickly knitted up. She also sold a couple of lap quilts that Grace's oldest *schweschder* had sent over. Greta was a very talented quilter, something Grace had never mastered. Oh, she could attend a frolic and do her part, but she didn't put fabrics together the way that Greta did. Her *schweschder* had a real gift.

But more than all those things, Grace was happy about having Lydia to look after Nicole. Lydia was sitting on the floor playing with her *doschder* when Grace left to oversee the dinner, and she was rocking her in a chair in the bedroom when she returned. The two seemed to have bonded instantly.

Lydia was thin, nearly as tall as Grace and wore glasses with blue frames. The fact that she carried a book in the pocket of her apron made Grace laugh.

"There's always time to read when you're waiting on someone," Lydia explained.

Grace couldn't have asked for the evening to have gone better. She still wasn't convinced that *Englisch* tours were something they should be doing. It continued to feel odd turning their home into a commercial venture, but since her parents had already made up their minds, she might as well get on board.

Then the next morning, Nicole woke in a fussy mood.

"Maybe she's teething again," her *mamm* suggested.

But she wasn't teething. That was always accompanied by excessive drooling. Grace had even sewn up some bibs to put on her during those times. This was different. Nicole whimpered, didn't want any of her toys, wouldn't even look at her *daddi*, who always made her smile, and insisted on Grace sitting down to hold her.

"You know what they say." Her *mamm* was knitting a new baby blanket at breakneck speed. She'd just cast it on that morning, and she had already progressed a good twelve inches. The colors were a soft, variegated baby blue, yellow and pink.

"I'm afraid I don't."

"Cleaning, quilting, cooking… Those things will wait."

"They will?"

"But the years when you can hold your child in your lap, those will pass in the blink of an eye."

By midafternoon, Nicole's cheeks were two red spots and she was tugging at her ear.

"Best take her in to the doctor," her *mamm* suggested.

"Do you think it's that serious?"

"Fevers usually rise at night, and the poor thing

seems so miserable." Her *mamm* stored her knitting needles, pressed a hand to Nicole's cheek, then kissed her softly on the top of her head. "I'll go and ask your *dat* to ready the buggy."

Her *mamm* drove and Grace held Nicole in her arms. The day was overcast with a slight drizzle, and the temps had turned cooler once again. Grace had rather enjoyed the week of warm, sunny days. Now the skies seemed to reflect her feelings—worry pressing down on her heart as the clouds pressed down over the fields. She knew the weather and her mood wouldn't last, but for the moment, she was practically overwhelmed by concern and sadness and fear.

"Do you think it's serious?"

"It could be many things, Grace. Doc Amanda will know what to do."

Doc Amanda had been Grace's doctor. She'd set up practice in the Goshen community before Grace was born, which meant the woman had to be getting up in age. Grace hadn't had a need to see her since returning home, though she had called and made Nicole's fifteen-month appointment for the following month. The pediatrician in Ohio had been a young man whose office was a bit austere. Although he seemed like a good doctor, and Grace had faithfully taken Nicole for her checkups, she'd never felt completely comfortable there.

So she walked into Doctor Amanda's office with some hesitancy. It didn't last long. There were low tables with toys for children, new magazines for harried parents, even a coffee center set up behind a counter with a sign that read Help Yourself.

They had been waiting only a half hour when the

nurse called Nicole's name. As Grace juggled her purse, diaper bag and child, her *mamm* stood and pushed a wad of bills into her hands. "From the mason jar."

"But *Mamm*..."

"That's what the emergency money is for, Grace. Now go."

She expected to wait a long time in the small examining room. The walls were decorated with growth charts and animal pictures, which immediately reminded her of Adrian. But Nicole wasn't interested in measuring her height or looking at animals. She sat curled up on Grace's lap, her fingers in her mouth, an occasional whimper escaping her lips.

The nurse popped into the room with a bright smile. She wore scrubs covered with rainbows and unicorns, and her hair was pulled back into a high ponytail. She asked the standard questions, entered the information into a tablet, then took Nicole's temperature, which was a disturbingly high 102.

Ten minutes later, Doc Amanda tapped on the door. She walked in, placed the tablet on the counter and walked over to a sink to wash her hands. Once she'd dried them, she pulled a chair up in front of Grace so that they were sitting knee to knee.

"It's good to see you, Grace. It's been a while."

"A long while."

"And this must be Nicole."

"We have her fifteen-month appointment in a few weeks for her vaccinations."

"I'm glad to hear you're keeping up with those."

"When she started running a fever, I thought I should bring her in today. She's...she's not well."

"You did the right thing." Doc Amanda turned her

attention to Nicole. "Hey, baby girl. Want to play with my stethoscope?"

Nicole buried her face in Grace's dress, and Doc Amanda was easily able to pop the tip of her instrument into Nicole's ear.

"Definitely an ear infection."

"*Ya?* But you can give her something?"

"I can, and I will. Let's check the other side first."

Which was a little trickier. Nicole didn't want to turn her head and immediately began crying and murmuring, "No, Mamm. No."

"Two-word sentences. Very good."

Doc Amanda finally managed to take a peek in the other ear, then listened to her breathing and looked into her eyes.

"The left ear has an infection. The right one looks a bit irritated, so she could be getting an infection there, as well. Don't be surprised if you see her pulling on both. A little medicine should fix Nicole right up. Let's try the pink stuff."

"Pink stuff?"

"Amoxicillin. My kids call it the pink stuff." She tapped something into the tablet. "What pharmacy do you use?"

"I haven't needed one."

Doc Amanda looked up from the tablet. "You moved away for a while."

Grace wasn't exactly surprised that she knew. Doc Amanda was the pediatrician most Amish families in the area used, and little went unnoticed in a small town. But Grace realized there was an opportunity here, and honestly, she was ready to be truthful with someone.

"Yes. I moved to Ohio while I was pregnant with

Nicole. My family thought it was best if I stayed with an *aenti*."

"Well, it's good to have you back."

"Danki."

"And it's good to meet Nicole. She's a beautiful child. She looks a lot like you."

Why did those words send a surge of joy through Grace's heart? It was silly, really. Of course a child would look like her mother, though Grace had often wondered if Nicole looked more like her or her father. It was difficult to tell when you were so close to someone, and there was no one she could ask, since no one knew that Nicole was hers.

She was suddenly glad that she'd been honest with Doctor Amanda. It helped that someone knew her situation and didn't judge her.

The doctor was still tapping on the tablet. "Goshen has grown a bit in the last few years."

"It certainly has."

"We have several pharmacies—the biggest is at the Walmart."

"That's on the opposite side of town from where we live."

"How about Meijers grocery store?"

"Yes, that would be better. I could pick up some other items while I'm there."

Doctor Amanda stood and plucked a handout from the counter where she'd washed her hands. "Here's a sheet on reducing fever in toddlers. You'll want to pick up something for that, as well. She should be feeling better in twenty-four to forty-eight hours. If not, come back and see me again, or you could call and we'll prescribe a stronger antibiotic. I like to start with the pink stuff, and it usually works."

"Danki."

"You're very welcome, and I look forward to spending a little more time with Nicole when she comes in for her regular checkup."

Nicole was still burning with fever and pulling on her ear, but now they had a plan. That made Grace feel immeasurably better. As she paid with the wad of bills her mother had pressed into her hand, it wasn't lost on her that they had extra money largely due to Adrian. Because of the tours, she didn't have to worry how much the medicine cost or whether she should buy one bag of diapers or two at the store.

Many people thought that all Amish babies wore only cloth diapers, and certainly she did use cloth when it made sense to do so. But when they were at church or out in public, she popped on a disposable. Her *mamm* waited on a bench at the front of the supermarket with Nicole as Grace gathered up supplies, including a few things they needed in the grocery section.

She was on her way to the checkout line when she passed the ice cream freezers.

Ice cream.

What was it Adrian had said he liked?

She backtracked and hunted around until she came away with a pint of Salted Caramel Almond. Then she added a vanilla to share with her *mamm* and Nicole, and Chunky Monkey for her *dat.* Three pints of ice cream was a splurge, but suddenly she felt like celebrating.

After all, she had the money for it in her pocket.

She had the medicine for her daughter in her purse.

And she had Adrian's tours to thank for both.

* * *

It was Monday morning when Adrian learned that Nicole was sick. He was helping Grace's *dat* mow the area around the back pond, which was where their guests apparently enjoyed dinner the most. The recent light rains they'd had seemed to have caused the grass to grow a foot. Everything was green and spring-like, and Adrian was thinking of how much he was looking forward to their next tour group, when James pulled him out of his daydreams.

"Leslie might be cooking tomorrow's meal."

"Why's that?"

"Baby girl has been sick—she had an ear infection."

"Is she okay? Does Grace need anything? Does Nicole need—?"

James held up his hand to stop the flood of questions. "The first medicine didn't work, so Doc Amanda called out something stronger. It's been a tough few days for both Grace and Nicole, for all of us, really. When the baby doesn't sleep, no one sleeps."

"I had no idea." In that moment, Adrian realized it wasn't the tour group he'd been looking forward to as much as it was seeing Grace again.

He'd spent quite a bit of time thinking about their walk to the fence line. He'd reached the conclusion that he'd like to be friends—close friends—with Grace. Nothing romantic, of course. He knew zilch about courting a woman, and he wasn't really in the right place to do so from a financial standpoint. But friendship? That he was ready for.

"Is there anything I can do?"

"Nicole was better this morning, but poor Grace.

After three nights of very little sleep, she's a bit of a mess."

"I guess so."

"She's finding out what it means to be a *mamm*—fortunately, the good outweighs the bad, which is one reason we all have so many children."

"I guess. I mean, I'm sure Nicole is a great kid. It's just that I don't have any experience in that area."

"You have nieces and nephews."

"True, though I suspect that's drastically different from having your own."

"What are you waiting for?"

Adrian looked up from the mowed grass that he was raking out of the picnic area. For a moment, he was confused by the question, then he realized that James was asking him why he wasn't married, why he hadn't started a family. "I'm not sure what I'm waiting for. The right time? The right person?"

James laughed. "In my experience, the right time is now."

"I don't know…"

"As for the right person, that's often someone you already know, but simply have to look at in a different light."

Wait a minute… Was he dropping a hint?

Did Grace's *dat* want him to court her?

Before he could think of how to ask either of those questions, James had started up the diesel-powered weed eater again and was proceeding around the pond.

Adrian spent the rest of the time he was doing yard work with his thoughts bouncing around in his head. On the one hand, he was consumed with concern for Grace and Nicole. On the other hand, he was puzzled.

Why had James brought up families and marriage? Both were distracting thoughts, which he couldn't shake even after he went back to his place. He found himself dumping bird food in Kendrick's feed bucket and trying to groom Cinnamon with a dog brush.

You could have knocked him over with a feather duster when Grace showed up at his place an hour before sunset.

"Is Nicole okay?"

"*Ya*. She's much better." Grace was holding something in her hands, a paper bag from the grocery store, but she seemed to have forgotten about it. "Thank you for the wildflowers you left on the front porch."

"Your *dat* shared that it's been a hard few nights."

"Indeed. I thought teething was difficult, but it's nothing compared to ear infections."

"You're certain Nicole is better?"

"I am. The second antibiotic that Doc Amanda sent out worked wonders."

Adrian crossed his arms and leaned against the wall of his barn. "I went to Doc Amanda when I was a child."

"So did I."

"Hard to believe she's still practicing."

"I know, right?"

"Whatcha got there?" He nodded toward the bag in her hands.

"Oh. This." She thrust it toward him. "I bought you something."

"For me?"

"Uh-huh."

He pulled out the pint of Ben & Jerry's. "Oh, man.

This will hit the spot. Let me run inside and grab two spoons."

"Oh, I didn't mean—"

But Adrian didn't hear the rest. He ducked into his barn, jogged to the tiny kitchen at the end of his living area and snagged two spoons. By the time he made it back outside, Grace was sitting on the bench, her head back against the wall and her eyes closed.

"You must be beat."

She opened one eye and glanced at him, then shrugged and resumed her nap. The sun was nearing the horizon, and like during the walk they'd taken just a few nights before, it was dropping its rays across her. She reminded him of a cat sleeping in the sun, and he started to laugh.

"What's so funny?" Grace kept her eyes closed and her face tilted upturned toward the sun.

"Just thinking how you remind me of a cat, in more ways than one."

"Is that so?"

"Sure. You're sleeping in the sun."

"It's comfortable here. And quiet."

He sat beside her, placed the bag between them on the bench and the ice cream on top of the bag. "If you're cross with someone, you tend to hiss."

"I do not hiss." She didn't look at him, but now she was smiling, too.

"And you take care of Nicole with as much love and attention as our old barn cat used to take care of her litter."

"I don't know whether I should feel complimented or offended."

"Oh, it's a compliment, for sure and certain." He

popped the top off the pint, stuck a spoon in and took the first bite. "Mmm, so rich and creamy. Don't you want some?"

"Ice cream is probably the last thing I need. All that sugar will keep me awake when I need to go home and sleep."

"The second bite is even better than the first."

"Though now that you mention it..." She sat up and accepted the spoon he was holding out to her. The expression on her face after the first bite was pure bliss.

"There's a reason it's my favorite."

"I've never had... What is this again?"

"Salted Caramel Almond. Hey, wait. How'd you just so happen to have a pint of my favorite ice cream?"

Now she shifted uncomfortably on the bench and was suddenly completely focused on digging out one more spoonful.

"Grace, did you buy this just for me?"

She put a huge spoonful in her mouth. "Can't talk. Mouth full."

"You did buy it for me. Just the other night we were discussing how I didn't have a freezer, and I said—"

She licked the spoon clean, reminding him again of a cat. Finally, she glanced at him and smiled. "You said that you loved Salted Caramel Almond."

"I can't believe you remembered."

"When Nicole first started running a fever, and I was so worried, all I could think of was getting her well." She dug out another spoonful, ate it, then stood, brushed her apron smooth, and finally looked at him. "Mamm had given me this wad of money from our emergency jar. That's a jar that we—"

"I know what an emergency jar is, Grace. My family has one, too."

"As I was leaving Doc Amanda's office and paid the bill, then went to pick up the medicine, I realized what a blessing it was not to have to worry about money at a time like that."

"You don't ever have to worry about money. Any number of people from our church will help if you need it, including myself."

"I realize that's probably true."

"It is true." He'd finished the pint of ice cream. He set it on the bench next to their spoons. And that simple sight, two spoons next to an empty pint of ice cream, reminded him of what James Troyer had said earlier.

What was he waiting for?

Did he need to look at the woman standing in front of him in a different light?

"So when I went by the store to get her prescription—this was the first prescription, the pink medicine, which didn't help Nicole much—I thought of you."

"You thought of me?" He stood and stepped closer.

Instead of stepping back, she glanced up at him and smiled. It was maybe the first easy smile he'd seen from her. Maybe that was what exhaustion did—helped you to drop all pretenses.

"Well, *danki*. That was very kind."

"But I ate half of it," she teased.

"Maybe a quarter."

"Okay, a third."

"Guess we'll have to buy another." He moved beside her, and they both turned to look at the colorful display in the sky to the west.

"We have a habit of watching sunsets together."

"You can bring me ice cream anytime." He bumped his shoulder against hers, wishing he was brave enough to reach for her hand.

At that very moment, Triangle jogged around the corner, holding a squirrel in his mouth.

"Ew."

"Just bringing us a gift." Adrian picked up a dustpan leaning against the wall of his barn, then squatted down in front of the dog. "Good boy."

Triangle dropped the squirrel into the dustpan, then flopped onto the dirt, panting and looking for all the world as if he was quite pleased with himself.

"Guess I need to dispose of this. If you're not too tired…"

"*Nein*, I've been trapped inside for four days."

"…want to go with me? We can stop and pet Cinnamon."

"I can think of nothing I'd like to do more than pet your camel."

Which was how they ended up walking across his place, on a perfect spring evening, as the sun set on another day.

Adrian wasn't thinking about animals or ice cream or even whether or not he should reach for Grace's hand. Instead, he was thinking of what her father had said.

The right time is now. As for the right person, that's often someone you just have to look at in a different light.

Which really left him with only two questions.

Was he falling for Grace Troyer?

And if he was, what was he going to do about it?

Chapter Seven

The next day was the first time in a week that Nicole finally acted like her old self. She smiled when Grace first went in her room, ate all of her breakfast and squealed with delight when Kendrick the Llama paused in his daily run to look in their kitchen window.

Grace felt good about leaving her *doschder* with Adrian's *schweschder* Lydia, and the evening's tour group was one of their most enjoyable yet. Now that she wasn't working against Adrian, against the tour's success, she could actually enjoy planning and preparing each meal. It was fun to cook for *Englischers* who claimed that Grace's homemade bread was wonderful and the fresh cheese they bought from down the road tastier than any they'd ever had before.

Grace was limited only by what she could serve in a picnic setting. She had a lot of ideas, and suddenly a part of her was once again that young girl who'd dreamed of being a chef. Moreover, she didn't have to skimp on ingredients because she had the money to spend and she knew that she'd more than earn it back.

Nicole plopped down, clapped her hands and hollered, "Lydee," when she saw Adrian's *schweschder*.

Her *mamm* once again sold another dozen items, further depleting her inventory.

Everything was going well. It made no sense that she woke on Friday restless and out of sorts.

"Your mood is probably caused by our beautiful weather."

"Shouldn't the weather make me feel better?"

"Not when you've been stuck in this house for a week."

"*Gut* point."

"I heard Adrian say he was going to be working in his vegetable garden. Why don't you go and help him? You could take Nicole with you. Some time outside would do you both good."

Grace knew that she could go out and work in their own garden, but perhaps her *mamm* was wanting some time alone. She could certainly understand that. So she packed a sippy cup and snack for Nicole, grabbed an old blanket, put on Nicole's lavender sweater and *kapp*, then tucked everything—including her *doschder*—into the stroller. They'd have to go down the lane and around by the road, but perhaps the walk was just what she needed.

And her mood did improve as she made her way over to Adrian's place. She found him on his knees in the garden next to the barn. Or what might have been a garden. It was hard to tell, with all the plants scattered around.

"What happened?"

"Hey." Adrian smiled up at them, blocking the sun with a hand. "I didn't hear you come up."

"What happened to your vegetables?"

"Ah…" He turned to survey the torn-up plants and demolished rows. "Goats."

"But…it's fenced. How'd they get in here?"

"I guess I left the gate open. I hear I should fix the latches on my gates."

There wasn't much she could say to that, since she'd definitely been a bad example to the very same goats. So instead of chiding him, she laid the blanket out under the shade of a nearby tree, plopped Nicole onto it and scattered a few toys around her.

"I'll help."

If Adrian was surprised, he hid it well. Within a half hour, they had a good amount of the vegetables replanted, though she wasn't entirely sure if they'd survive.

"Why don't they eat them, once they pull them up?"

"There's no understanding a goat. My only guess is they have a short attention span."

It felt good to work her fingers in the soil, and Grace realized that it was nice to be somewhere different. She spent entirely too much time on her parents' farm. Perhaps she should start going into town once a week.

Or maybe she needed friends.

That was probably it.

"You're focusing awfully hard over there."

"*Ya.* Just thinking that it feels good to be away from our place for a little while."

"I remember feeling that way when I was still staying at my parents' farm."

"You did?"

"Sure. I guess it's something about living in the same place after you're grown."

"Well, I might as well get used to that, because I'm not moving anywhere anytime soon." Grace glanced over at Nicole, who was still happily sitting on the blanket, playing with her toys. Usually she'd be scrambling about, but the recent illness seemed to have left her with less energy. Or perhaps it was getting close to nap time. "Baby girl will be raised in the same house I was."

"You don't know that."

"Pretty much, I do."

"So you're saying you'll never marry?"

Grace had been tenderly replanting a tomato plant that had been ripped up by its roots. She sat back on her ankles and studied him. "I'm not sure that marriage is in my future, Adrian."

"Because of Nicole?"

"Because of her…and other things."

"Oh. Well, a wise man once said to me—"

"What wise man?"

"Your *dat*."

"Oh?"

"He said something to the effect that we need to stop waiting for the right time."

Grace suddenly wished the ground would open up and swallow her. Could things get more embarrassing? Was her *dat* actually pushing Adrian to date her?

"We?"

"And then he said that sometimes we just have to look at someone we already know in a different light."

"Adrian, I am mortified."

"Why would you be?" He looked at her quizzically, as if he didn't understand her embarrassment. Then he did something she did not expect. He tipped his hat back and started laughing.

"I fail to see what's so funny."

"Come on, Grace. It's not unusual for Amish parents to push their single children into dating. You're aware of that, I'm sure."

"My parents haven't even mentioned that they think I should date."

"Maybe they're giving you time because of Nicole."

"About that…"

"But any man would be blessed to have you for a *fraa*, Grace. As for Nicole… She's a sweet *boppli*. You shouldn't let your decision to raise your cousin's child keep you from dating."

Except Nicole wasn't her cousin's child, and Grace wasn't sure if now was the time or place to share that important fact with Adrian.

Did her parents truly think it was time for her to date? Were they ready for her to get out from underfoot?

Why would her *dat* say such a thing to Adrian, the one person Grace considered a friend?

Adrian was a *gut* person, but she didn't think he was ready to be a husband or a *dat*. It took only one look at his garden to see that. He couldn't even remember to close the gate. His family would starve! As for the animals… She looked up as Dolly settled a few feet from them. The red-rumped parrot squawked something unintelligible and then commenced preening herself.

Adrian actually responded with a similar squawk, then looked at Grace and smiled.

It would take a patient woman, indeed, to agree

to live in Adrian's menagerie. It would take someone completely smitten with him!

She wished him the very best in finding a woman to set up housekeeping in his barn. Was Adrian looking for a *fraa*? She felt the sudden and painful loss of his friendship like an ache in her stomach, which was ridiculous... He was kneeling six feet from her.

But it would happen.

Eventually some woman would take a shine to Adrian Schrock, and she'd lose the one friend she had in Goshen. What was the point in growing close to someone, in developing real friendships, when life seemed to rip them away? Wouldn't she be better off learning to be happy alone?

She'd thought herself in love with Kolby, then he'd vanished.

She'd finally learned to trust Adrian as a friend—nothing more—but he, too, would one day be pulled from her world. Her mood sank to even lower than it had been earlier that morning. Tears stung her eyes, and she vowed not to let them spill down her cheeks. What was wrong with her? Why was she so emotional? And would someone please tell her how could she learn to rein in her feelings?

Adrian wasn't sure what he'd said to upset Grace, but she'd gone suddenly quiet on him. She sat there patting the dirt around a plant that she'd already finished with, her head ducked so that he couldn't see her expression. Her shoulders were hunched, and she reminded him of a turtle that had gone into hiding.

Why?

What had happened while they were working in the garden?

He waited for a few moments to no avail. Grace was completely focused on tapping down the earth around the plant.

Perhaps she needed a distraction from whatever was bothering her. He moved over to her row, picked up a bell pepper plant and plopped it into the ground.

"I've decided to farm organically."

"Excuse me?" She looked up at him with an expression that suggested he was wearing his suspenders backward.

"Organic farming. Surely you've heard of it."

"I guess."

"I've decided to do it. I even visited the library and checked out a few books on the subject. Did you know there's an Amish man in Ohio who has founded an organization—?"

"Hang on." Grace had been kneeling in front of the plants, but now she sat down, her legs crossed like a child. "I know what organic farming is. You're saying that you don't plan to use any fertilizers or pesticides."

"*Ya*. That pretty much sums it up."

"But why?" She shook her head as if she needed to free it from a bothersome thought. "You have more work here with all these animals than any one man can possibly handle."

Kendrick picked that moment to dash down one of the rows of vegetables, sidestepping onto the plants. Adrian jumped up, shooed the beast out of the garden area and closed the gate. When he walked back over to Grace, she still hadn't moved and she certainly hadn't reset any more of his plants.

"Where were we?"

"I was helping you replant until I found out you're not going to fertilize, which means the plants won't grow, so why bother?"

"Of course they'll grow. Plants don't have to be drowned in chemical fertilizers. They just need the right balance of nutrition. Zook says so in his book. Did you know that eggshells worked into the soil can provide needed calcium?"

"Do you eat eggs? Because I don't see any chickens here."

"Well, not often. Mainly when I'm at my folks. But I could buy a few chickens, and then I'd have eggs to eat. I could save the shells and put them on my plants. It's not that difficult to figure out, Grace."

"What is wrong with using regular fertilizer?"

He glanced up at the sky, trying to remember what he'd read the night before, then snapped his fingers. "Mahatma Gandhi said something to the effect that a *gut* man is a friend of all living things."

"You're quoting Gandhi now?"

"What's wrong with that?"

"It has nothing to do with whether or not to use fertilizer." She crossed her arms in front of her chest. "Changing the subject doesn't prove your point."

"I'm not changing the subject and I don't have to prove my point. Fertilizers and pesticides are not natural."

"Not natural?"

"*Nein.* They're both made in a laboratory, not in a field. I don't want to put any of those chemicals on my plants."

"Do you want to eat?"

"Ha ha. *Gut* one. You made a joke there."

She stood and brushed dirt off the back of her dress. "Actually, I was serious. I think I should be going home now."

Adrian jumped up to follow her. "Why are you so peevish today?"

"Peevish?"

"Irritable?"

"I'm irritable?"

The look she gave him caused Adrian to wish he'd simply let her go without a word. Now she'd stopped, hands on her hips, staring him down—though she had to look up to do so, since he was taller than her.

He brushed his hands against his pants leg, unable to look her in the eye. Why did he suddenly feel embarrassed, like he needed to apologize? He hadn't done anything wrong. He'd only shared his own opinion about natural farming on his place. "I don't know what I said earlier to change your mood."

Instead of answering, she turned her head and stared out in the direction of his camel.

"And the organic farming—I was just making conversation. I thought you'd be interested, especially in light of Nicole and all."

"What does this have to do with Nicole?" She turned to face him and skewered him with a pointed look.

"I'd think you'd want to feed her *gut* food—food free of chemicals."

"You're saying I feed my child poison?"

Adrian had a sudden and overwhelming urge to go brush his camel. Cinnamon was always glad to see him, enjoyed his attention, and she never argued. But instead of walking away, he fumbled around, looking for an answer that would wipe the angry expression off Grace's face. "I didn't say you feed Nicole poison, but I guess you could see it that way."

"But your way—organic farming, which you've probably studied all of three days—is the right way?"

"Natural is better, yes." Now he felt his temper flaring. He liked Grace, and he liked it when things were smooth and comfortable between them, but right was right and wrong was wrong. Unfortunately, he decided to voice that thought. "Right is right whether you like it or not."

"What did you say?"

"I said right is right and wrong is wrong."

"Oh, Adrian." She closed her eyes, and an expression that resembled amusement passed over her face. When she opened her eyes, she stepped closer, and to his surprise, she put a hand on each of his shoulders. "I remember what it's like to be your age."

"I'm older than you."

"There was a time when I, too, was quite sure of myself."

"I can show you the book on organic farming." He shifted from one foot to the other, uncomfortable with how close she was and the look of pity in her eyes.

"There was a time when I was convinced that I knew what was right and what was wrong—a time when I had had no doubts." She shook her head in a mournful way, walked over to Nicole and set about picking up her things.

"If you know what's right, why would you doubt it?"

She didn't answer right away. Instead, she clasped Nicole closer, whispered in her ear, straightened her *kapp*, smoothed down her dress. Those things seemed to calm her. When she looked up again, the anger and frustration had been replaced by a calm certainty. She stuffed the bag of toys and the quilt into the back of the stroller, then added Nicole, who waved her arms at Adrian.

He waved back—and waited.

Finally Grace answered his question. "To doubt is normal. We doubt because we're imperfect and we make mistakes. We doubt because life isn't that simple."

She searched his eyes for something, again shook her head as if she were sorely aggrieved, then she turned and hurried down his lane, back to her parents' farm. Adrian stood there, watching her retreating figure and feeling the loss of something that he didn't quite understand. He didn't know what had just happened. He certainly didn't know what he'd done to set her off, but he did understand that Grace was not talking about farming—or at least not only farming.

He felt a nudge on his shoulder and turned to look into Kendrick's eyes. He reached up and rubbed the llama between his ears, which was exactly what Kendrick wanted. He really should stick to animals. They at least made sense to him.

For the next hour, no matter how he tried, he couldn't keep his mind on the animals. He finished his chores, thinking the entire time about Grace's brown eyes— eyes that reminded him of cocoa and coffee and chocolate, all things he loved. He thought of Grace staring up at him. What had she been trying to tell him? He was still puzzled over that.

He walked outside and looked over at the Troyer farmhouse.

He should go over there now and talk to her.

Nein.

The last thing she wanted was to see him.

So instead of going next door, he hitched up his gelding, Socks, and headed out to George's place. He found his friend in the barn, having already finished dinner.

"Does Becca know you're hiding out here?"

"*Ya.* She understands I need an hour to myself."

"I imagine she's the one who could use some private time, what with six *kinner* to care for."

"Normally I would agree with you, but her *schweschder* who lives in Wisconsin is visiting for a few days. My being out here gives them plenty of time to chat." George drew a pipe out of his pocket and began packing it with fresh tobacco, something with a sweet scent to it. Once he had it going, he motioned outside. They settled in chairs under the barn's eave.

"I don't understand women." Adrian had meant to tiptoe up to the subject, but the words popped out as soon as they were seated.

"Any woman in particular?"

"Grace."

"Ah."

"What does that mean?"

Instead of answering, George motioned for him to continue, so Adrian did. He laid out the entire, inexplicable afternoon. With each detail, the smile on George's face broadened.

"I don't understand what you find so amusing."

"*Youngies.*"

"Please. I'm twenty-five."

"Uh-huh, but in matters of courting, you're a bit behind."

"Thank you for the insight, though it's most definitely not what I need to hear today."

"You're out of sorts. Probably a full day of splitting wood will put you in a better frame of mind."

"You want me to split wood? It's almost May. I won't need wood for months."

"True, but it's something that requires your complete attention and uses up a bunch of nervous energy."

"I don't have nervous energy. What do I have to be nervous about? I didn't do anything." He forced himself to stop jiggling his leg.

George studied his pipe for a moment, then stood and said, "Walk with me."

Adrian had five *bruders* and five *schweschdern*. He was squarely in the middle of eleven children. He loved his family, but he'd never gone to his *bruders* for advice. They weren't close in that way. He felt closer to George than he did to his own family. Maybe that was normal. He wasn't sure, but he followed George across to the pasture fence, interested in what he was about to say.

"I've a mind to give you some advice about women, if you're interested in hearing what I have to say."

"Sure, *ya*, but just so we're clear, Grace and I are friends—only friends."

"Okay. Let's leave that alone for a minute."

Which was a rather odd thing to say, in Adrian's opinion. Before he could correct him, George was speaking again.

"Three things." He ticked them off on his fingers for emphasis. "Number one—it's not always about you."

"What's not always about me?"

"Anything. A mood. A look. A perceived slight. Maybe the baby was teething that day. Maybe she feels a little blue because something she was working on didn't turn out quite right."

"Last week, Grace was making a cake that she claims fell. You'd have thought someone died. I don't even know what that means. Cake is cake. Right? How can it fall?"

"Number two. Don't go too fast."

"Go where too fast?"

"For a man, things can be simpler." George pointed to his field with the stem of his pipe. "Say you need to plow that field. You hitch up the team and plow it. Simple. But for a woman, there's more things to consider. Maybe she wants the vegetable garden planted, because she's worried about having enough vegetables to put back for winter. Maybe she was planning on going to town, but now she can't because you're in the field and there's no one to watch the *kinner*. Maybe—"

"Maybe she doesn't know a thing about organic farming."

"Whatever. The point is, step back and give her some time."

"Okay. That makes sense."

"Number three. Don't go too slow."

"Seems to contradict your second point, which was don't go too fast."

George nodded as if that was his intent—to contradict himself. "A man and a woman can start out as friends, but if you stay there too long, if you don't act on your feelings, then you can miss an opportunity to grow closer."

The sun was setting, splashing a kaleidoscope of colors across the sky. Adrian didn't understand how sunsets worked any more than he understood women. "I'm not saying I have those kind of feelings for Grace, but hypothetically…"

"Yes, yes, let's keep this hypothetical." George didn't laugh outright, but he looked as if he wanted to.

"How would I act on those feelings?"

"Hypothetically…" George grinned, then pushed on. "You could start by bringing her flowers, maybe help her with a chore or ask her out to dinner."

"I can't afford a dinner in town."

"Ice cream, then. Whatever. You're missing the point. Show her your romantic intentions, because once you fall firmly in the friend category, it's hard for her to see you differently."

"But as I said, we are just friends."

"Now. But do you always want to be just friends? Or do you think that you might one day be interested… romantically…in Grace?"

"I hadn't thought that far ahead."

"Uh-huh. That's plain enough."

If anyone else had said it, Adrian would have been offended, but as they turned and walked back toward his buggy, Adrian realized that George was trying to help. At least he wasn't laughing at him—not outright. The entire thing was embarrassing enough.

He climbed up into his buggy and was about to close the door when George stayed it with his hand. "One more thing. In many ways, women want the same thing men do. They want to be appreciated, listened to and valued. They're different from us in some ways—

maybe even in how they relate to the world, but they're also the same."

Adrian resisted the urge to drop his head into his hands. Different but the same? Don't go too fast, but don't go too slow? Where did the madness end? And why couldn't women be as easy to care for as animals?

Because that was one thing Adrian had realized in the midst of George's advice. He very much cared about Grace. He wasn't sure if it was only as a friend or something more, but he knew that when things weren't right between them, he felt unsettled.

Now he had some ideas for how to get things back on a solid footing.

At least he thought he did.

Chapter Eight

On Saturday, Grace made up her mind to stop thinking about Adrian. It wasn't as if she wasn't busy. She had a child to raise, tour dinners to plan and… And nothing.

That was it.

Those two things were the entirety of her life.

Maybe she'd start a new hobby. She could learn to knit. Unfortunately, she tended to purl when she was supposed to knit and knit when she was supposed to purl. She often lost count and had to frog things out, and when that happened, she might as well start over because she could not thread the stitches back onto the needle.

She could clean. She'd always been good at that.

Grace's *schweschder* had picked up Nicole for a playdate with her *kinder*, so Grace had the entire day to herself. She decided to give the kitchen a good solid cleaning. She started with the oven. The brown stuff on the bottom that she had to scrub off somehow reminded her of Adrian's garden.

So what if he wanted to organically farm?

That was his business, not hers.

In the same way it wasn't her business if he let his animals wander through his vegetable garden to graze every day.

And living in a stinky old barn? That was his choice.

None of it had anything to do with her.

The calendar in the kitchen declared it was the first of May. Wasn't May the best month of the year? She should take advantage of the fine weather, but instead, after finishing in the kitchen, she attacked the rest of the house as if it hadn't been properly cleaned since winter. She and her mother had already done the spring cleaning a month earlier, though that fact didn't slow her down one bit. She beat rugs, mopped floors, scoured the two bathrooms, even took the stiff outdoor broom to the front porch.

Fortunately, her *mamm* was too busy knitting scarves and mittens for the *Englisch* tourists to notice her frenzied energy, and her *dat* was busy out in the barn.

And where was she? Stuck at home, cleaning an already clean house.

Grace whacked at the cobwebs on the porch.

The first of May, and she was stuck at home because she had no social life at all.

Turning the porch rockers over, she knocked dust off the bottom.

Soon it would be summer, and what did she have to look forward to? More tours. More cooking. More cleaning.

Her life was an endless cycle of sameness.

It was at that unfortunate moment of self-pity that Adrian pulled into the driveway, his horse, Socks, tossing his head and his dog, Triangle, sitting up smartly on the front seat.

Adrian was the last person she needed to see today, especially after their argument the previous afternoon. She almost fled inside, but hadn't she done that just the day before? She'd run off rather than deal with his stubborn tunnel vision.

She personally hated it in novels when the main character ran from the room. Grace did read the occasional novel that she borrowed from the library. Some Christian romances her *schweschder* passed on to her. Georgia was always scouring garage sales for books, which she purchased four for a dollar or a dime a piece. They did come in handy on those nights when Grace was teething and wanted rocking. One couldn't knit while rocking a baby, but one could certainly read.

In those stories, when the main character inevitably turned and fled for whatever reason, Grace always wanted to shout "stand your ground!" Perhaps it was time she followed her own advice.

Instead of getting out of the buggy, Adrian pulled it around in the circle, stopping so that he could hang his arm and head out the window and speak to her. "I was just headed to town."

"Okay." She aimed for nonchalant but wasn't sure she was pulling it off. Must be nice to be able to gallivant off to town whenever one felt the urge.

"I wondered if you needed anything."

That was considerate of him to ask. If there was one thing that Adrian was *gut* at, it was thinking of others.

"Or maybe you'd like to come along?"

She glanced down at her dirty clothes.

As if he could read her mind, Adrian added, "Triangle and I aren't in any hurry."

She needed to change, and she did want to go to town. Suddenly she could think of nothing she'd rather do than get off this farm for an hour. Now wasn't the time to be too proud to accept an invitation.

"Give me ten minutes." She dashed into the house, splashed some water on her face, tidied up her hair, repinned her *kapp*, changed into one of her three weekday dresses, then took it off and put on her Sunday dress, then took it off and put back on her weekday dress. The sunglasses at least made her look as if she were heading somewhere special. She snagged her purse and hurried to the kitchen to tell her *mamm* where she was going, but her *mamm* wasn't there.

Then she heard voices and looked outside to see her *mamm* petting Triangle.

"It really is amazing that he gets around so well."

"The vet said he was born this way, so I suppose it's all he's ever known."

Who else but Adrian would adopt a three-legged dog?

Five minutes later, they were headed down the lane and Grace's mood had lightened considerably.

"Why are you headed to town?"

He didn't answer right away. Finally, he turned to her and grinned. "No real reason. Guess I need some time away from my place."

"I can relate to that."

"Funny how you can love your home and still need time away."

"Exactly. I woke with so much excess energy that I was cleaning the bottom of rocking chairs."

"Wow."

"I know."

The sun was shining, the day was pleasantly warm, and Triangle now sat on the seat in between them, watching through the front window with a smile on his face.

"Anywhere in particular you'd like to go?"

Suddenly Grace realized that she did want to go somewhere in particular. She wanted to stop by the fabric store and purchase material for a new dress for Nicole. She wanted to check in at the dry goods store to see if they had the yarn her *mamm* had ordered. She wanted to go by the library. She blurted all that out to Adrian in one long, rambling sentence.

"All *gut* ideas." Adrian smiled at her, then allowed Socks to accelerate into a nice trot.

Why had she mentioned the library? She didn't really need to look at one of their cookbooks. She had a dozen *gut* cookbooks at home that she'd been using for years. She'd like to browse through something new, though—not that recipes changed much. Still, it felt as if her cooking was in a rut, rather like her life. She suddenly—desperately—needed to cook something different for their tour group. As for Adrian, he probably wanted to check out more books on organic farming, but that didn't bother Grace as much as it might have the night before.

Because she was going to town on a beautiful spring Saturday.

She was free of all obligations for at least the next three hours.

And she was with a friend.

For now, all that was enough.

They spent the next couple of hours enjoying the day. Only once did Adrian throw out a crazy quote he'd read recently—this one by William Wordsworth. "The flower that smells the sweetest is shy and lowly."

"You have some strange reading material, Adrian."

"*Ya?* I guess I do." He glanced at her sheepishly.

Somewhere along the way, Grace was able to forget that she was a single *mamm* who didn't know what she was doing with her life.

When they were at the library, she used the computer to print off half a dozen recipes. Adrian sat beside her, looking up best habitat improvements for a camel.

As they stood in line to pay for the copies she'd made, Adrian nodded toward a shelf of books with a sign that read For Sale—Donations Accepted.

"I guess I could look for my *schweschder*." In the end she chose three books—a picture book for Nicole, a historical romance with a picture of a castle on the front for Georgia and a murder mystery with a drawing of an Amish B&B on the cover for herself.

"Murder mystery? Should I be worried?"

She decided that she liked this more easygoing Adrian. As she thumbed through her purse for money to put in the donation jar, she saw that he'd tucked a slim volume under his arm. When he slipped his dollar in the jar, his hand touched hers, and Grace's heart set off into a gallop.

Then he smiled that goofy grin, and she relaxed.

He was a *gut* friend and a nice neighbor. That was all. Nothing more.

He went next door to the hardware store while she purchased material in the fabric shop. She bought a little extra, deciding that she could make a matching dress and apron for Nicole's baby doll. She glanced at fabric for herself, too, but she truly didn't need a new dress. That could wait. Maybe after a few more weeks of tours.

And there it was again.

The tours. She had extra money in her pocketbook because of the tours, because of Adrian.

When he stopped in front of the local ice cream shop, she insisted on paying.

Adrian chose peanut butter Oreo, and she picked blueberry cheesecake. They carried their cups of ice cream over to one of the picnic tables and sat beside each other. Triangle flopped down in the dirt, his eyes closed, though he cast a glance at them occasionally as if to say "a dog can hope."

She looked over at Adrian, then focused on her ice cream. The sun was warm on her face, and the ice cream was sweet with a splash of tartness. It tasted rich and creamy and good on her tongue. *"Danki."*

"For what?"

"Stopping by my house, asking me to come along, being pleasant company... Take your pick."

"I'm pleasant company?"

"Don't make a thing out of it."

"Wouldn't dream of it." But the smile on his face told her that he was inordinately pleased with the compliment.

She savored another bite, then said, "We get along pretty well as long as we don't talk about anything important."

"So that's the secret." Adrian paused, a spoonful of ice cream nearly at his mouth and a twinkle in his eyes. "I was wondering."

"It's true."

"*Ya*, I suppose." He shrugged, then bumped his shoulder against hers.

Grace popped another spoonful in her mouth. "We're both opinionated people is the problem."

"I'm not opinionated. I'm right."

"Lord, grant me patience."

Adrian laughed, then Grace laughed, and Triangle opened both eyes as if his treat might soon be a real possibility.

"You're a different kind of guy, Adrian."

"Uh-oh. That doesn't sound so great. Let's go back to my being pleasant company."

"No, seriously. You are different. You think differently. You view life…differently."

"Is that bad?"

"*Nein*, but it will take a patient woman to marry you."

"Know anyone who fits that description?"

Grace scrunched her eyes as if trying to remember who might be patient enough to take on such a project. "I'm coming up blank. Maybe you haven't met her yet."

"And maybe I have. Sometimes we have to look at someone we already know in a different light."

"I still can't believe my *dat* said that to you."

"So you disagree?"

"*Nein*. I don't disagree. It's just… Well, I'm not in a place in my life to be thinking about such things." She'd reached the bottom of her cup but had left a few drops for the dog. "Is it all right to give it to him?"

"Milk has sugar, and dogs can't process sugar." He reached into his pocket and retrieved a dog biscuit, then put it into Grace's hand. "Give him this instead."

"You carry dog treats in your pocket?"

"Guilty as charged."

"No wonder he's so devoted to you."

Triangle sat up pretty as could be and cocked his head, waiting for Grace to offer the treat in the palm of her hand. Grace had always thought of dogs as farm animals, good for warning off intruders. Now that she thought about it, Triangle could do both of those things. Triangle hadn't let his disability hinder him.

When she offered him the treat, he politely took it from her, then lay back down and happily devoured it.

They finished their ice creams and tossed the cups in the trash can. Grace realized she wasn't ready for the afternoon to end. She was surprised to find she enjoyed Adrian's company so much—when he wasn't lecturing her about organic farming.

It occurred to her then that Adrian knew things. He had an inquisitive mind, and that wasn't necessarily bad. But when you lived alone, who did you share your ideas and thoughts with? She struggled with that herself. She didn't live alone, but often she felt her parents wouldn't be interested in what she had to say. Their worlds were very different.

Did they care that she'd noticed a small wrinkle near her right eye?

Or that it was two years ago during the first week of May that she'd met Nicole's father?

Or that Nicole had put her chubby little hands on Grace's face and patted her, then said *mine*? Okay, her *mamm* and *dat* would both be interested in that one.

The point was that Adrian had fewer people to talk to than she did—unless you counted Triangle or Kendrick or Dolly. That had to be lonely. Sometimes, when he came across as bossy or arrogant, maybe he was just eager to share an idea.

She thought of his admonition about not giving milk to dogs and smiled to herself.

"Care to share?"

"Share?"

"What you're smiling about."

"Oh…that." She shook her head, thinking there was no way she was going to share what she'd been mulling over. But then it occurred to her that she might as well. What did she have to lose? And it felt good to talk about things, even wayward thoughts that popped out of nowhere.

Perhaps that was what friendship was—the freedom to say what was on your mind. Grace knew that she could use a friend at this point in her life.

The question was whether she dared to open herself up to the man sitting beside her, whether she was willing to take that leap, whether she could risk her heart—because even friendships had the power to hurt and wound.

Her relationship with Kolby had started out as a friendship but then quickly morphed into something else. It had all happened so fast it had made her head spin. She could see that now. She'd never felt so abandoned or alone or unworthy as when she'd realized he'd left town without even a goodbye. He'd left, and she didn't even know where he'd gone. He'd left, and she'd been pregnant with his child.

Kolby had hurt her in ways that might take years to heal.

But it had already been two years. Maybe it was time that she moved past what had happened. Maybe it was time she took a risk and allowed herself to be a friend to someone else. It was frightening, but then being alone wasn't working out so well, either.

Perhaps today was the day to try something different.

Adrian had expected to be nervous around Grace or uncomfortable being alone with her or even anxious to get back to his animals. He hadn't expected to thoroughly enjoy himself. But that was what he'd done all afternoon. The whole reason that he'd thought to invite Grace along to ride with him to town was because of something George had said.

It's not always about you.

Perhaps her frustration the day before had not been about him. Maybe she'd been annoyed with her life in general. A few hours away from the farm tended to clear the cobwebs from his mind, like Grace had been clearing the cobwebs from the bottom of the rockers. When he'd seen her doing that, he'd known that she would agree to go with him. He'd known it was the right thing to do to ask her to go.

Now they were in the buggy, headed back toward home, and Adrian wished the afternoon could last a little longer.

Then he saw her glance at him and smile. So he'd asked what that was about. She took her time mulling over her answer. Finally she angled herself in the seat so that she was facing him.

"I guess I was thinking that you're not necessarily bossy or arrogant."

"Who said I was?"

"Oh, I don't know if anyone said it exactly, but someone sitting here in this buggy might have thought it."

Triangle whined and dropped his head to the seat. Adrian and Grace started laughing at the same time. When her laughter had died away, Grace fiddled with her purse, zipping and unzipping it. "I was thinking that it's just that you know things. You probably read a lot."

"Not much else to do on a farm once the chores are done."

"But lots of people read, Adrian. They read the *Budget*, over and over, like my *dat*."

"Your *dat* is a smart guy. He always knows where to buy the cheapest hay or the best seed."

"Sure. I get that. But you read books like—" she reached toward the pile of packages on the floor of the buggy and retrieved his book "—*Self-Reliance and Other Essays* by Ralph Waldo Emerson. What is this even about?"

"Well, it's essays, which are—you know—shorter writings."

"I know what an essay is."

"I enjoy reading them before bed, because often I'm too tired to read for very long."

"Uh-huh. That makes sense, and maybe I've heard of Ralph Waldo Emerson in school… But that was a lot of years ago, and I've had quite a few sleepless nights since then." She tapped the side of her head. "I might have forgotten a few things."

"Emerson was a philosopher and writer and poet."

"When did he live?"

"Eighteen hundreds."

"Not exactly current stuff."

"I guess, but a lot of what he wrote about transcends the time he wrote it."

"Give me an example."

"Okay." Adrian rubbed his chin, a little surprised that Grace was interested in Emerson. But then why shouldn't she be? She obviously had an intelligent, curious mind. "Emerson believed that all things are connected to God, so all things are divine."

"Like that newly planted field." She nodded toward the west, where an *Englisch* farmer had recently planted his crops.

"Sure."

"Or animals."

"Exactly."

"Or even children."

"*Ya.* I'm not going to pretend I understand his philosophy, but I like to think about how our plain and simple life is connected to the divine, to *Gotte*'s work."

"See? That's what I'm talking about. You know stuff."

"A lot of what I know is useless. Trust me. For example, did you know that the word *camel* in Arabic means *beauty*?"

"I did not know that."

"Now you do."

"And every time I think of Cinnamon, I will now think of it and be reminded of how beautiful she is."

They were nearly to her house. Adrian's mind cast around for some way to postpone taking her down the lane, but he couldn't think of a single excuse. So he turned in, though he called out to Socks, slowing him down a bit.

"When you were telling me about organic farming, I thought you were being a show-off…"

"Not my intent."

"…and naive."

"Always a possibility."

"And then I thought you were judging the way that I'm raising Nicole."

He pulled to a stop in front of the house, next to the buggy that belonged to Georgia. Grace had shared that Georgia had picked up Nicole for a playdate. The fact that her *schweschder* had beat them home meant Grace would be eager to go inside to see her *doschder*. But what she'd said about him judging her… He needed to correct that impression.

Turning in the seat, he looked directly at Grace and fought the urge to reach out and cover her hands with his. He didn't want to ruin this day by being too forward, but neither did he want to go too slow. He settled for reaching forward with one hand and squeezing hers lightly, then letting it go.

"I think you're doing a fantastic job raising Nicole, and I'm amazed at what a kind and generous person you are to even do such a thing. Raising a child that isn't yours? That takes a special kind of person, Grace, and you are special. You're terrific, actually."

She glanced down at her hands, worrying her bottom lip, then began gathering her packages. Had he said something wrong again? Or was she just tired? When she looked up at him, her expression was more solemn. She started to speak, stopped, shook her head, then hopped out of the buggy.

"*Danki*, Adrian. I had a *wunderbaar* time."

And then she was gone, leaving him to wonder if

he'd gone too slow or too fast or if maybe—finally—he'd managed to hit it just right.

He went home and checked on Cinnamon, then made sure the goats hadn't escaped their pasture. Triangle ran at his side. Adrian considered Triangle something of a wonder. When he'd first adopted the dog from the local shelter, he'd stopped by the vet he used for his other animals and asked for advice.

After assessing the area where Triangle's hind leg should have been, the vet had stood and smiled. "Looks to me like your dog was born with only three legs."

"It wasn't an amputation?"

"Nope. There's no scar there."

"Anything special I should do?"

"Keep his weight down. That's probably the most important thing. Exercise is good as is swimming, if you have a pond."

"Thanks, Doc."

"No problem." The vet had walked him out to the counter where a receptionist was waiting to print out Adrian's bill. "No charge today."

"I don't mind paying."

"And I'll be happy to take your money when you bring Triangle back in for his annual vaccinations."

"Danki."

"Thank you for taking a dog that some people would see as damaged. Many people would never have considered doing such a thing." The vet had clapped him on the back, tossed a dog bone to Triangle and gone back to work.

Many people would never have considered doing such a thing.

Those words circled in Adrian's mind as he walked his farm, then went inside and made a simple supper.

Triangle flopped down in his corner of the kitchen, though really the room was too small to be called that. There was a sink, a half refrigerator, a small two-burner stove and a cabinet with a few dishes in it. He had what he needed.

It occurred to him that perhaps the reason that Grace wasn't dating was the same reason that no one had adopted Triangle. Perhaps no one had considered dating her.

Why wouldn't they?

Because of Nicole?

But in Adrian's mind, Nicole only made Grace more appealing. Nicole was evidence of what a caring, kind, selfless person Grace was. Oh, she had a temper, for sure. He'd seen that often enough, but who wanted a perfect *fraa*?

He choked on the bite of sandwich he'd swallowed, and Triangle raised an eyebrow as if to say, "you okay, boss?"

Was he thinking of marrying Grace?

They hadn't even gone on a proper date yet.

But they had shared an afternoon trip to town, and it had gone well. If that was any indication of her feelings for him, then he thought he had a chance.

Marriage was a long way off—if it was even a possibility.

He didn't have much to offer a *fraa*.

But dating was a different thing.

Dating was simply getting to know one another. He could do that. One didn't need a proper kitchen or a lot of money in the bank in order to do that.

Adrian realized he was ready to begin courting, and the one woman he was interested in just happened to live next door.

Chapter Nine

Grace often found herself dreading church, then feeling guilty for having such a bad, unspiritual attitude. The truth was that her conscience bothered her more than ever of late. She wanted to stand at the front of the assembled group and proclaim that Nicole was her *doschder*, but of course that sort of thing simply wasn't done.

During their new members' class, she tried to focus on Bishop Luke's words. He was instructing them about the *Ordnung*, their unwritten rules. The *Ordnung* guided their everyday life. It covered such things as the type of dress they wore. For example, when Grace was a small girl their local *Ordnung* had been changed to allow women's dresses to be made out of fabric with pastel colors—before that most dresses had been gray or dark blue or dark green. Someone wised up to the fact that pastels were a nice color, too, though of course, red and orange and purple fabrics were still out of the question. It wasn't that they thought bold colors were bad, only that they sought to be humble.

A more recent change to their *Ordnung* had been to

allow the gradual adoption of solar power. Some *Englischers* saw that as hypocritical, since they didn't use electrical power. Amish didn't believe in being connected to the grid. They were supposed to live their lives separate, set apart. Could someone live set apart with electricity in their home? Possibly, but with that electricity would come many temptations—television, radio and even the internet.

Solar power, on the other hand, allowed them to be separate but with some of the conveniences of modern life. They still wouldn't have a television or a radio or a computer, but they would be able to charge their tools and batteries, possibly even hook their refrigerator and stove up to it. Solar power would be much simpler and cheaper than propane. Plus solar power was basically free once the panels were set up. The sun was a part of *Gotte*'s creation. The Amish saw it as using *Gotte*'s natural resources.

Personally Grace was in favor of pastel dresses and solar-powered generators. She didn't think putting Nicole in a lavender-colored dress would make her *doschder* overly proud, and she certainly didn't think there was anything wrong with a fan that used batteries charged by the solar-powered generator in their barn.

But it wasn't fabric or fans that Grace thought of as she sat through the prayers and sermons. Instead, she was wrestling with her need to bare her soul.

After the service, she helped in the lunch line. Although many of the women still gave her the cold shoulder, a few women were polite to her. Anna Lapp asked how Nicole's teething was going, but then before Grace could answer, she'd had to run and check on one of her *boppli*. Anna was the same age as Grace, but she'd married at eighteen and now had four *kinner*. Occasionally, Grace thought they might be friends, but Anna didn't seem to have time for such things.

As for the other women, the ones who stopped talking when Grace walked by them, she was trying not to let them ruin her day. Perhaps they weren't even talking about her. Maybe they simply thought she wouldn't be interested in the topic of their conversation.

Or maybe *she* was the topic of their conversation.

There was nothing she could do about it either way.

Bishop Luke paused in front of where she was shuffling pieces of pie to the front of the table. "I hope you enjoyed the new-member class today, Grace."

"*Ya*, I did." She moved Nicole from her right hip to her left. "I'm looking forward to the baptism service."

"Excellent. And remember, if you need to, you're always welcome to bring Nicole to class with you."

But Grace knew that none of the other candidates would be bringing children. She'd learned the oldest among them was nineteen—a full four years younger than she was. Four years seemed like a lifetime to Grace. So instead of taking Nicole with her into the area where they had class each Sunday, she arranged for her *mamm* to look after Nicole while she was meeting with the other candidates.

Still, it was kind of the bishop to offer such a thing.

Or was he trying to tell her something else?

Was he suggesting that she confess her indiscretions to her other classmates?

She was stewing over the conversation when Adrian appeared in front of her. "Come and sit with us when you're done?" He nodded toward George and Becca

Miller who were spread out around the far picnic table with their six children.

"Okay."

"I could take Nicole now, if you'd like."

Before Grace could answer, Nicole lurched toward Adrian, reaching as far as she could and calling out, "Aden, Aden, Aden."

Grace passed Nicole over the table to Adrian. It startled her how natural her child looked in his arms.

"She still can't say my name."

"Don't let it hurt your feelings. Half the time she calls me *mamama*."

Nicole turned in Adrian's arms, pointed at Grace and said, "Mamama."

"See what I mean?" She pushed a piece of apple pie toward Adrian. "Take that with you. She loves apple."

As he walked off with her baby girl, it occurred to her that Adrian would make a *gut dat*. He really should settle down, find a *fraa* and start a family.

Where had those thoughts come from?

Just because he'd taken her to town the day before did not mean he was interested in courting. It also did not mean that he would want a ready-made family.

Grace stayed at the serving table until most of the desserts were gone, then grabbed an empty plate, forked a piece of ham on it, added a spoonful of beans and a piece of fresh bread, and hurried over to where Adrian and his friends were sitting.

She expected to be uncomfortable.

She didn't really know George and Becca Miller that well.

But she found she enjoyed sitting with Adrian's friends and hearing stories about him.

"I mostly hung out with Adrian's older *bruder*." George pushed his plate away and crossed his arms on the table. "Adrian insisted on hanging around the big boys, which used to drive Joseph crazy."

"Grace probably doesn't remember my older *bruder*." Adrian was still holding Nicole. He turned her in his arms so that she was facing the table. Then he handed her a spoon and she proceeded to try to pick up Jell-O and eat it. About one in three times, the jiggly red snack made it into her mouth. "Joseph is ten years older than me, same as George."

"Are you calling me an old man?"

"*Ya.* Come to think of it, I am." Adrian wiped off Nicole's face. "Anyway, Joseph moved to Maine. Left George here to look after me."

"Which is a full-time job, I can tell you." He proceeded to tell how Adrian had decided to turn a cattle trough into a fish tank when he was ten years old. "By the time Joseph figured out what Adrian was doing, the cattle could barely drink out of it, the thing was so full of fish and turtles."

The men turned the conversation to farming, and Becca and Grace talked about children and the coming summer break. "Only two of mine attend this year. But the middle two will start year after next. Then I'll have some time alone with the babies."

Grace couldn't imagine having six children. Some days, she was completely worn-out with just one.

She enjoyed sitting with Becca and George. Even though they were older, she felt she had more in common with them than she did with the girls her age. And she liked learning about Adrian's antics.

They were walking down by the creek, just Grace

and Nicole and Adrian, when she stopped and studied him. "Why don't I remember any of the things George was talking about? We've always gone to the same church, attended the same school…"

"Maybe you have a terrible memory."

She reached out and pushed him. He laughed and put a hand on her elbow, tugging her toward an old rope swing that the older children had ignored in lieu of a game of baseball.

"It's probably because I'm older than you."

"Only two years."

"When you're in school, two years seems like an awful lot."

"I guess. I feel like I should have paid attention better." What would her life have been like if she'd given the time of day to someone like Adrian rather than falling recklessly in love with Nicole's father? But each time regret crossed her mind, she was brought up short. She couldn't make herself wish away the mistakes of her past, not when she looked at Nicole.

They were walking under a stand of trees. Grace glanced up, then looked over at Adrian.

"What?"

"Nothing."

"I suspect it's something."

"Don't you have a quote to share…about the trees?"

"Hmm, let me think." He rubbed his forehead for a few seconds, then snapped his fingers. "I've got it."

"Wordsworth again?" She was teasing him, but actually she was curious.

"Blake."

"As in William Blake, the poet?"

"The same." Adrian pointed to a tall maple tree,

growing off by itself. "Blake said that a fool doesn't see the same tree as a wise man."

"Huh."

"You asked for a quote."

"So it all depends on the eye of the beholder?"

"Maybe. If you're a tree."

Laughing, they walked over to the maple tree with the old rope swing. Adrian nodded toward it and grinned. "Have a seat."

"There?"

"Sure."

"Why?"

"I'll push."

"You'll push me and Nicole?"

"I'm strong. I can handle it."

"Uh-huh. I guess the bigger question is whether the rope can handle it."

The rope held, and she found herself laughing as Adrian pretended to struggle with their weight. The rope creaked and the breeze cooled Grace's brow. Nicole laughed and clapped her hands. It was a rare moment of delight as Grace let go of her worries and stepped, for a moment, outside the endless circle of thoughts that plagued her.

As the afternoon progressed, it became obvious to Grace that Adrian was interested in courting, and she found herself warming to the idea.

True, it made her a bit nauseous to think of letting someone close. Perhaps the fluttery feeling in her stomach should make her run the opposite direction, but then she'd watch Adrian interact with Nicole and her doubts would melt away. Surely a man who could be so kind to a child wouldn't break her heart?

Because that was one of the things that scared her. It had taken her nearly two years to recover from Kolby's rejection. He hadn't rejected Nicole, not really, because he didn't know about her. He was long gone by the time Grace had realized she was pregnant.

How many months had she spent praying he'd come back?

Had she done something wrong, something to drive him away?

Or had he never really cared about her to begin with?

And which was worse?

Adrian and Nicole were pulling wildflowers from the fence line when Grace pulled her attention back to the present. Nicole looked up at Adrian and pushed the flowers toward his nose. Adrian laughed at Nicole's insisting, "Smell, Aden. Smell." Then he looked up at Grace, and in that moment, another part of the ice she'd carefully constructed around her heart began to melt.

Maybe it was time she took a chance.

Maybe it was time for her to trust what her heart was trying to tell her.

Adrian wanted to kiss Grace.

And yet...he didn't.

He was still thinking about George's advice—*don't go too slow, don't go too fast, listen.*

Her parents had gone home while Grace was playing volleyball. He'd never seen her play any game. He'd never seen her so relaxed. He was holding Nicole on the sidelines, cheering on Grace's team, when her parents walked up, looking for their *doschder*.

"I'm happy to give Grace and Nicole a ride home."

Grace's *mamm* thanked him, then sent a knowing look to her *dat*. Perhaps Adrian wasn't being as subtle as he thought he was. He didn't much care. It didn't bother him one bit if people knew that he had feelings for Grace or that he adored Nicole.

When the game was over, Grace collapsed in the grass beside him.

"I should probably get more exercise."

Her hair was sneaking out from the sides of her *kapp*, her face was flushed and sweat glistened on her forehead. In other words, she looked prettier than ever.

It was later, when he was taking her home, that he started thinking about kissing her. Nicole had fallen asleep in Grace's lap. She was curled there, in the last of the day's light, a look of complete relaxation on her face. Why was it that only children slept with such abandon? Adrian kept glancing at them, thinking how glad he was that he'd purchased the farm next to Grace's parents.

Thinking of how good Grace would feel in his arms.

Thinking that he'd been lonely before, maybe for years, but he hadn't realized it.

He wanted to kiss her, but he also realized this was probably one of those moments when he shouldn't go too fast. Grace had spent the entire afternoon with him, and she'd done so in front of all of their church members. That was a big step for her. He was learning that she was a very private person, and also very careful.

So instead of kissing her when he pulled up in front of her house, he set the brake and turned to face her.

"I had a *gut* time today."

"We did, too. *Danki* for, well, for everything."

"I have a question for you, if that's okay."

"Of course." Her eyes widened when he reached for her hand.

He laced his fingers with hers, satisfied at the sight of their hands intertwined. Pulling in a deep breath, he gathered his courage and looked into her beautiful brown eyes. "I care for you, Grace. For you and Nicole. I was wondering… That is, I'd like to ask if—"

She waited, but she didn't look away and she wasn't shaking her head no. He took those as good signs.

"I'd like to court you, if that's okay. If you'd like me to."

She didn't speak for a moment, and then she reached out with her other hand and touched his face. "I'd like that."

"You would?"

"*Ya.*" She pulled her hand away, a look of concern shadowing her smile. "But here's the thing, Adrian."

She glanced down at Nicole, kissed her on the head, then looked up and met his gaze. "Nicole cares about you."

"I care about her."

"In my mind, she thinks of you like an *onkel*—a favorite *onkel*."

"That's *gut*, right?"

"*Ya*, but if this doesn't work, if during our courting we find out that we're not right for each other… I don't want Nicole to lose her favorite *onkel*."

"That's not going to happen, Grace." His voice grew husky at the thought of not being a part of Nicole's life, of Grace's life. He'd only recently admitted how much they brightened his day. He couldn't begin to imagine losing them now. They would be taking a risk by pushing their relationship toward something else. But it was a risk worth taking, and he only needed to convince Grace of that in order for them to move forward. He did understand Grace's worry. What she was saying was about herself as well as Nicole. "We'll always be *gut* friends. You have my word on that."

"Okay." She looked as if she wanted to believe him. "I better get her inside."

He wanted to see her to the door, but she was already struggling out of the buggy, carrying a sleeping Nicole. She hurried up the porch steps, and in the last of the day's light, she turned and waved.

Adrian didn't remember driving home. The next thing he knew, he was standing in the aviary, putting seed into the finch feeder. Triangle had followed him into the birdhouse, and Kendrick was camped outside the door, waiting for his evening snack.

He thought about how not so long ago, Grace had shown up in the aviary, brandishing a rolling pin. She'd been so determined to not be a part of the tours. She'd been so afraid, and he still wasn't sure of what. But she was calmer now. She was on board with the plan to host *Englischers*, and they'd even discussed expanding to an extra tour day. Business-wise, things were going very well.

Who would have thought that they'd end up courting? It sounded like something from the romance novels his youngest *schweschder*, Lydia, occasionally read. In other words, it sounded improbable, but it also felt like *Gotte*'s planning.

All Adrian had to do, if you looked at it that way, was not mess things up.

He spent that night creating a list of improvements he'd like to make around his farm.

Build and install a swing for Nicole. There was a perfect place under the maple tree next to the camel pen. *Reinforce the fencing around the garden.* Maybe even add a few more plants. *Ask Mamm how to put the vegetables up for winter.*

Build a house.

He tapped his pen against the pad of paper, then circled the fourth item. That was the crucial thing. If Grace did fall in love with him, if they decided to marry, he couldn't ask her to live in a barn. The home could be small, but there needed to be space to add on to it. He knew the perfect spot. The drive into his property angled off to the right, where the barn and animal pens were located. But he could grade another drive to the left, where there was a good half acre of land surrounded by trees. It sat up on a small rise and afforded a good view of the rest of the property.

He'd once thought of turning it into a pasture for miniature horses, but horses were happy wherever you put them, as long as they had grazing, a little shade and a trough for water.

But a house needed to be somewhere special.

Because that was where he'd spend the rest of his life with his *fraa* and where they'd raise their children.

But how would he manage to build a house while he was just getting his business off the ground?

How could he afford it?

He didn't bother tallying up the costs. If they decided to marry, he knew a work crew would show up to help build a home. Hopefully he could save enough to pay for the supplies.

He could do that with the tours, especially if they added another day.

Was he thinking way ahead? *Ya.* He was, but it was better than not thinking things through at all, which, if he was honest, had been his mode of operation the last few years. That wasn't good enough for Grace or Nicole, though. He needed to anticipate their needs and be ready with solutions.

Because he cared about them.

He picked up his Bible and turned to where he'd been reading the night before—Proverbs. Solomon was always a *gut* read. "Ponder the path of thy feet, and let all thy ways be established."

Ponder the path of thy feet.

He stared at the page, thinking about how he needed to take more time to do that. Finally his thoughts turned to the look of vulnerability on Grace's face when she'd brought up what might happen if their courting didn't work out. Had she courted before? Had her heart been broken? And now she had to think not just of herself but also of Nicole.

Court Grace.

Spend time with Nicole.

Begin saving for a home.

Those things were more important than his other list. They also seemed pretty simple to him. The only question was what he would do if their courting didn't work. Because he already cared about both Grace and Nicole, more than he would have thought possible. Since he was being honest with himself, it was time to admit that he couldn't imagine his life without them. Even considering such a thing caused sweat to bead up on his brow.

Life without seeing Grace's smile?

Days without hearing Nicole's laugh?

Nein.

That just wasn't possible, so he needed to commit himself fully to winning her heart. The time had come to show Grace how much he cared.

Chapter Ten

The next week flew by for Grace.

On Monday, she took Nicole in for her vaccinations and well-baby visit. Doctor Amanda assured her that Nicole was doing fine in every category.

She was a little ahead in her speech and where she should be as far as grasping objects, walking, even feeding herself.

"Though, more lands on the floor than in her mouth," Grace said.

Doc Amanda smiled. "Every new mother should have a dog to clean up those messes."

Grace thought of Triangle. Nicole loved Adrian's dog, though she'd yet to master his name. It still came out "Angle," but the little dog never failed to make her *doschder* smile.

Nicole's weight was squarely in the middle of the chart.

Her height was below average, but then Grace was only five foot three.

"And her father?" The doctor smiled as she asked, adding another notation on the computer tablet.

"A little taller. I don't know exactly how tall."

The doctor glanced up at her, cocked her head, then set the tablet aside. She was sitting on her little stool that rolled easily around the exam room, and now she scooted closer to the wall, rested her back against it and focused on Grace.

"You're not the first mom to be a single parent, Grace." When Grace only shrugged, the doctor added, "I have at least three children under my care right now—all of them are being raised by single moms."

"Are they Amish children? Are they Amish single moms?"

"No. They're not. Which isn't to say that I haven't had other single moms who were. You have to remember I've been in this community a long time. This isn't a new issue."

"It's definitely new in my family."

"You live with your parents?"

"Ya."

"And how are they reacting to having you and Nicole in their home?"

"Gut. My parents are great, actually. They don't… don't want to talk about what happened before, but they've been very supportive since we moved back." Tears pricked her eyes as she added, "They're kind to me, and they adore Nicole."

Nicole looked up at her name. She'd been playing with a toy the doctor had handed her to test her dexterity skills. Holding up one of the plastic animals that looked like a llama, she said, "Kendrick," and then she plopped it into the correct hole.

Both Grace and the doctor laughed, though Doc Amanda couldn't have known about Adrian's llama.

"I'm happy to hear things are going well with your parents." The doctor picked up her tablet and walked to the door, but she paused and turned back, her hand on the doorknob. "Just remember, the way life is today isn't the way life is always going to be."

And then she was gone, leaving Grace to wonder just what she had meant by that parting statement. But of course she knew. As she drove back to her parents', she wondered if she believed it.

Life was a bit lonely now. Would it always be?

Certainly it was hard at times. Could she hope it would get easier?

And if she were honest with herself, occasionally the future stretched out like a road that continued forever in the distance, never deviating left or right, up or down, just an endless line of sameness—laundry and dishes, cooking and sewing, six days of work followed by a day of rest where she didn't quite fit into any group.

Did she see her life changing for the better?

Adrian believed it was possible.

At times, he seemed naively optimistic to her, as if you could decide a thing and it would just happen. Purchase a farm and turn it into your life's dream. Build a zoo and the animals would come. Fall in love and walk off into the sunset together.

Grace wanted to believe in those things, but it was frightening to get her hopes up. It was actually quite terrifying to allow herself to care again. What if everything went south? She probably wouldn't be any worse off than she had been when she was alone and pregnant, but she didn't want to once again endure that sort of pain. It had been too hard to recover the last time.

Sometimes, feeling nothing was better than making her heart vulnerable.

She just didn't know if she was brave enough to risk that kind of disappointment and rejection again.

What she did know was that when she was with Adrian, life seemed better. The burdens she carried around on her shoulders seemed a bit lighter.

Was that love?

Monday gave way to Tuesday, and she found herself looking forward to the tour guests.

For Tuesday's dinner, she made Swiss Mushroom Chicken and corn fritters, with a fresh salad and black-berry cobbler. There were no leftovers to put up. On Thursday, she cooked bacon-ranch pasta salad with grilled ham sandwiches, and peanut butter fingers for dessert. Several of the women claimed they'd love to buy a cookbook if she had one. Grace had found the recipes in the book from the library, but she'd swapped out a few ingredients and adjusted a few others.

Could she write a cookbook?

How would she even do such a thing?

She would ask Adrian's opinion on Saturday. He would be honest with her, and he was good at weighing the pros and cons of something—though he always tilted toward the pros. He was taking her out to dinner, and her *mamm* had insisted on watching Nicole.

"It's hard to court if you take your child with you."

"But we're a package deal—me and Nicole."

"Of course you are, but trust me, time alone is important for every couple, whether you've just met, are courting or are married. Plus baby girl and I could use some girl time."

"Hey. I'm sitting right here," Grace's *dat* chimed in.

Which caused Nicole to toddle over to her *daddi*, who scooped her up, then set her on his lap and proceeded to read to her from the *Budget* in funny voices, as if it were a children's book.

Adrian had spoken with Grace and her parents about adding more tour dates. They agreed that it needed to be a unanimous decision, made by all involved with the tours. So they scheduled a meeting for Friday afternoon at four o'clock. Grace baked oatmeal bars, made raspberry tea and brewed a fresh pot of coffee. She had never hosted a meeting before, but she was as ready as she was going to be. Adrian's idea to expand to Saturdays sounded good on the surface. In theory, if they went from two tours a week to three, they could increase their profits by 50 percent. But there were still only seven days in a week, and giving up another day might be hard on some of their group. It was best to address all concerns up front.

Old Saul showed up for the meeting fifteen minutes early, which wasn't a problem because he immediately fell into a deep discussion about cows with her *dat*. Seth arrived next, claiming he could barely find the place without a buggy full of tourists. He joined the men out on the porch. Then George Miller arrived, representing the Goshen Plain Tourism Committee. Her *mamm* and *dat* were also sitting in on the meeting. Which left only Adrian. Where was he?

By 4:15 p.m., even her *mamm* was concerned. "Perhaps you should go check on him."

"*Ya. Gut* idea."

Nicole was sitting in her high chair, eating a snack of Cheerios, though a good portion of them were falling to the floor. Grace thought of what the doctor had said, about how it helped to have a dog to clean up such messes. She had to admit it would be helpful to have Triangle there to scoop up the fallen bits.

Yes, that was exactly what she needed—a house dog.

She was probably going a little crazy.

Too much pressure. Too many changes.

But she didn't feel crazy or under pressure, and she was enjoying the changes.

It finally felt like her life, which had been on hold for so long, was moving forward again.

She hurried over to Adrian's. He wasn't in the aviary, and though she knocked on the barn door, no one answered. She even stuck her head inside the barn and shouted, "Yoo-hoo! Anyone home?" All to no avail.

He had to be home. Socks was out grazing in the pasture.

She found him with Cinnamon, holding one of the camel's hooves between his legs and brandishing a large metal file that he was using to grind down her nails.

"What are you doing?"

"Oh. Hi, Grace. I didn't hear you come up."

"What are you doing?" she repeated, her voice rising. When he looked at her blankly, she wanted to shake him. "Did you forget about the meeting?"

He dropped his head, though he still held on to the camel's hoof. "*Ya.* I guess I did."

"Everyone is at my place—waiting."

"Right. Okay. I'll just finish this and—"

"Adrian! Now. You need to come over now." She felt the beginnings of a headache in her left temple. She tried to rein in her frustration, but she was com-

fortable with Adrian now. It was difficult not to share
what was bothering her, and why should she hold back?
He was the one who had called the meeting, and now
he'd forgotten?

"Adrian, how could you?" Her hands went to her
hips of their own accord, as she squinted her eyes at
him. "This was your idea. I made snacks. I cleaned up
the house. I even changed my apron. Now you need to
get over there and lead this meeting!"

Adrian's eyes widened, but instead of becoming de-
fensive, he grinned at her. "You're cute when you're
angry."

"Don't."

"Gives you a little blush to your cheeks."

"Teasing me won't change a thing. I'm still aggravated." But in truth, her heart was racing from the way
he was looking at her, and he seemed to have forgotten
he was holding Cinnamon's hoof.

"I have a sudden urge to kiss you."

"Here? In the middle of Cinnamon's pen?" Now her
face, neck and ears felt impossibly hot. He'd inadvertently hit on something she'd been thinking about—
what it would be like to kiss Adrian Schrock. Instead
of giving in to the embarrassment, she tossed her *kapp*
strings over her shoulders. "You want this to be our
first kiss?"

He was at her side in three long strides. And suddenly she didn't care about tour dates or visitors or
the fact that Cinnamon was staring at them curiously.

He slipped a hand to the back of her neck, tilted her
face up to his and kissed her softly on the lips once,
twice, then a third time. When he stepped back, the
smile on his face made her laugh.

He looked like a child on Christmas morning.

He looked like she felt.

Had she fallen in love with this man? The man who forgot meetings and allowed his goats to pillage his garden and quoted poets? None of that mattered, though. Not really. His shirt was covered with pieces of straw, dirt and camel hair. His pants weren't in any better shape, and his hair looked as if he'd forgotten to comb it.

He was a mess!

So why did Grace's heart lighten as he hurried back down the lane with her?

Honestly, she didn't care if his clothes were dirty— that was part of the life of being a farmer.

As for his hair, if she could get him to sit still, Grace's *mamm* could give him a *gut* haircut. Her *mamm* had been cutting her *dat*'s hair for as long as Grace could remember.

They found everyone assembled on the back porch, enjoying Grace's oatmeal bars and cold drinks. Only Seth seemed particularly put out that they were starting late. "I need to get home and clean up," he explained. "I'm taking Lynda Beachy to the Art in the Park Festival. They're having food trucks, music, even balloons and such for the kids. You should take Nicole, Grace. She'd love it."

"She goes to bed pretty early."

"It's running all weekend, eight in the morning to nine at night."

Adrian winked at her, then said, "Great idea, Seth. Now, let's get you out of here in time for your date."

As Adrian laid out their plan, everyone nodded in agreement. Grace was surprised when every single person was in favor of adding a third day. She'd thought that perhaps they'd be too busy with their various jobs and families.

Old Saul said it made no difference to him or his cows.

Seth said he certainly didn't mind driving another day. "The tips are *gut*, and my buggy horse enjoys the opportunity to show off."

Surprisingly, only her mother voiced any concern at all. "I can't keep up with the demand for my knitted items as it is. They're buying everything I make, which is a *gut* problem but still a problem."

George leaned forward, elbows propped on knees. "Leslie brings up an important point. Growth is something that has to be managed in the tourism market. It's *wunderbaar* that things are going so well with you all, but at the same time, you don't want the quality of the experience you offer to suffer."

He turned to Grace. "Are you sure you won't have trouble cooking for a third day? I can only imagine how much work it is."

"*Nein*. I'm *gut*. I'm actually enjoying it." She thought of her idea to write a cookbook but decided that it wasn't the right time to bring up such a venture. So instead, she said, "Honestly, I usually cook dinner, anyway."

"Yes, but not for twenty people."

Everyone laughed at that, and then George moved on to address her *mamm*'s concerns. "I assume that you're open to selling items made by other women in our community."

"*Ya*. Of course. You know I have your *fraa*'s quilts,

and I have all of my *doschdern* who live in the area knitting in their spare time—which is pretty limited."

"I suggest you put a call out to the community at large. I know for a fact that Donna and Meredith Bontrager have items they'd like to sell. Donna sews a lot, though they're not quilts—more like dolls, things to go on the dining table, pot holders, etcetera. Meredith has started making homemade soaps. Both are small-ticket items, but I think they'd compliment the other things you're selling."

Grace cringed at the mention of Donna and Meredith. Both had been very pointed in their disapproval of Grace, though they had never spoken to her directly. That wasn't their way. They were much more likely to talk behind her back. It was an uncharitable thought, but one she knew to be true. Still, if their items could make the tour a success, she would put aside her reservations. Her *mamm* was already nodding in agreement, so she really didn't have much choice.

"I guess we're done here, then." George stood and reached for his hat, which he plopped on his head. "You have my approval, not that you needed it, and I'll make sure that the larger tourism board is aware that you've expanded the days you're operating."

Grace was surprised when Adrian indicated he had something to say before the group dispersed.

"Some of you had reservations when we started this venture. Some of you I had to badger into giving it a try." Everyone again laughed when Adrian gave a pointed look to Grace. Even she laughed.

Had she really intentionally made a terrible casserole?

Invited bees to a picnic?

Let out Adrian's goats?

"I think we've come together as a *gut* group, and I appreciate each of you. *Danki* for taking this adventure with me, and may *Gotte* bless our endeavors as well as the people that we serve."

Murmurs of "amen" circled the group. Twenty minutes later, everyone was gone. Grace stood on the front porch with Adrian.

"Would you like to stay for dinner?"

"I'd love to, but I have a camel with several filed nails and a few unfiled nails that are probably driving her batty."

Adrian reached for Grace's hand and squeezed it, sending tiny shivers of delight down her arm and reminding her of the kisses they'd shared earlier. She wasn't a *youngie* on her first date, but oh, how her heart soared when he looked at her as he was now.

"I'd like to take you and Nicole to the Art Festival tomorrow. I saw your eyes light up when Seth mentioned it."

"Mamm had offered to watch Nicole, but I think she would enjoy the festival. So yes, we would love to go."

"Pick you up at ten?"

"*Ya.* Ten will be *gut.*"

The afternoon had been almost perfect. The only thing to mar it was the thought of having to work with Donna and Meredith. Later that evening, after Nicole was tucked into her bed and while her *dat* was doing a final check on the animals, Grace broached the subject with her *mamm*.

"I'm worried about including Donna and Meredith in our tour."

"Why is that, dear?"

"Certainly you're aware they aren't the most pleasant people."

"I am aware. Your *schweschder* has shared with me her problems with her in-laws many times."

Grace grimaced. The only thing worse than having to do business with those two women was to have them in your family. She would need to remember to pray for Georgia.

"What, in particular, are you worried about?" Her *mamm* was knitting a baby sweater. The needles were a blur in her hands. This time, she was using a variegated blue color that was quite beautiful.

Grace would like to have a son someday.

She'd like to have a big family.

She didn't want Nicole to be an only child. Most of the time when she thought of courting Adrian, she felt excited about the prospect, but occasionally, she fell into a rut of worrying. What if he decided he didn't want a ready-made family? What if his feelings for Grace weren't what he thought they were? What if he learned the truth about Nicole and rejected them?

She needed to tell him the truth before he heard it from someone else. She'd tried a few times, but the words had lodged in her throat.

"Grace? Would you like to share what's bothering you?"

Grace was working on the doll's dress for Nicole. She'd already finished the dress and apron for her *doschder*, but she wanted to surprise her with the doll's clothes at the same time. Each evening, she waited until Nicole was in bed to pull the project out of her sewing basket.

"Both Donna and Meredith are… *Unkind* is the nicest way to say it."

Her *mamm* raised an eyebrow, encouraging her to go on.

"I think it's because of Nicole, because of the circumstances of her birth. They judge me. Which is fine. I made my mistakes, and I don't mind paying the price for them."

"But…"

"But Nicole shouldn't have to. They shouldn't be rude to her. That's wrong, *Mamm*. That's not what the Bible teaches us."

Her *mamm* tugged on the ball of yarn and continued knitting. "The Bible says many things."

"For example?"

"It says to love your neighbors."

"*Ya*. That's what I mean. They're not loving. I wish you could see the way they treat me."

"I have seen, and it hurts my heart in the same way that seeing someone treat Nicole unkindly hurts yours. But Grace, Christ doesn't tell us to love only the neighbors who are pleasant. We're to treat everyone the way we want to be treated."

"That's not easy to do sometimes."

"You're right."

"And it makes me angry. Donna and Meredith aren't perfect. They have no right to judge me."

"You're right again, but it doesn't change a thing." Her *mamm* paused in her knitting, counted her stitches, then finished the row and stuck the needles into the ball of yarn. Scooting to the edge of the couch, she picked up the family Bible, ran her fingertips over the cover, studied it a moment and then she placed it in Grace's hands. "The answers you're looking for—they're here. But I have to warn you, I've been reading the Bible for many years and I've yet to find any promise that life will always be easy or pleasant or that people will always be kind."

"If this is a pep talk, it's terrible."

"It could be that *Gotte* has put Deborah and Meredith in our path for a reason. Perhaps we're to minister to them."

"That would be like ministering to a snake. I'm more likely to be bit for my trouble than thanked."

"We don't do it to be thanked. We do it because we're commanded to do so."

And with that, her *mamm* stood, kissed her on top of the head and headed out onto the porch to wait for her *dat*. Grace heard them out there almost every evening, usually sharing a hot cup of tea and talking over their day. Grace wanted that. She wanted someone that she could spend the last moments of each evening with as well as the first moments of each morning. She wanted someone who would care for her regardless of her past mistakes.

She honestly didn't know if Adrian was that person.

Her stomach grew queasy when she thought of confessing all to him. She would do it—soon. Not tomorrow, though. Tomorrow, she was taking Nicole to town in her new lavender dress. She scooped up her sewing things, determined to finish the doll's dress before she called it a night and equally determined to put her worries about Deborah and Meredith out of her mind. It was bad enough that she was going to have to deal with them on a weekly basis. There was no point in dragging them into her life earlier than she had to.

Because despite what her *mamm* said, she wasn't sure that they were commanded to tolerate mean people. It seemed to her that she and Nicole were both far better off avoiding them.

Chapter Eleven

Adrian's life took on a fullness and richness that he couldn't have imagined six months before. He'd found what he was missing, and he hadn't even been looking for it.

He'd found Grace and Nicole.

May gave way to June. He continued to take Grace out once a week—sometimes with the baby and sometimes without, though Nicole could hardly be called a baby now. Toward the end of June, yellow became her favorite color. She looked everywhere for it—picking yellow flowers from the roadside, falling in love with lemon slushes and wearing out her yellow crayon. Yellow bananas, baby chicks, corn, butter and daffodils were a few of her favorite things.

She was now walking like a champ and had even recently learned to run. She thought it was quite funny to make her *mamm* chase her, and though Adrian tried to look serious and disapproving, the sight of Grace chasing Nicole through his aviary brought him too much joy. He simply couldn't scold her. In that way, he might make a terrible *dat*, but he was sure he could make up for his lack of sternness another way. Perhaps it was something he could learn. He didn't expect he'd need to be firm with the little girl anytime soon, probably not until Nicole was a *youngie* and needed scolding. Fortunately, he had plenty of time before that would happen.

Grace and Nicole came to visit him nearly every day, and when they didn't, he went to their place. He kissed Grace on a regular basis now. She was still something of a mystery to him. She'd learned to relax when he reached for her hand or kissed her or complimented her, but he had the distinct impression that she was holding a part of herself back.

They spent many summer evenings walking the fields as the sun set and talking about their youth.

"You were the middle child?" She glanced up at him and smiled.

Adrian realized she could melt his heart with that smile. What wouldn't he tell her? What wouldn't he do? They were supposed to be finding out if they were right for one another—that was the purpose of a courting time—but Adrian already knew that the only woman for him was Grace Troyer.

"Can't remember?"

"Huh?"

"I asked if you were the middle child in your family." She bumped her shoulder against his.

"Oh, *ya*. I was square in the middle—five older and five younger."

"What was that like?"

"It seemed normal to me. I've heard middle children can carry a chip on their shoulder—they're not the oldest getting into trouble or the youngest causing parents to realize how quickly time passes." He plucked a weed growing by the fence line, studied it a minute and then stuck it in his mouth. "I never felt that way. To me it was more like being in a litter of pups. There was always someone to play with or drag off to see the latest animal I'd adopted."

"Even then?"

He laughed. "*Ya.* Even then. What about you? I know Georgia and Greta both live in the area."

"They attend different church districts, but they're close enough that we see them every week."

"You have other siblings, though?"

"Sure. Three married and moved away—Gloria, Gwen and Gina."

"Your *mamm* likes the letter G."

"As much as Nicole loves the color yellow."

"And you're the youngest."

"I am." She glanced at him, then looked quickly away.

"Something you want to add to that?"

"Only that being the youngest, well... Sometimes it means you make mistakes that others didn't. My *schweschdern* were already married and out of the house by the time I was a *youngie*."

"I'm sure you did the best you could."

She studied him then, as if to see whether he really meant it. Finally, she said, "I hope you always believe that."

"Of course I do... I will."

They'd been to dinner at both Greta's and Georgia's. Adrian thought both of Grace's *schweschdern* approved of their courting. At least they were polite to him, and their *kinner* were full of questions about his animals.

He and Grace came to know one another's childhood through those long walks. But a wall seemed to appear between them whenever they spoke of their teenage years. Adrian didn't mind admitting the times he'd stepped outside their *Ordnung*. Once when he was fourteen, he'd tried to drive a car and ended up steering it into a ditch. Another time, he thought it was when he was sixteen but really couldn't remember, he'd tried smoking and ended up coughing for an hour.

Grace listened attentively to his stories, but she didn't share any details about her own *rumspringa*.

Adrian thought the whole idea of *rumspringa* had been overemphasized. Without fail, every single tour group asked him about the practice. Many of them had read about it in books or seen it depicted in television shows. He had no idea how accurate those things were. He could speak only to his own experience and that of his siblings. When he explained that *rumspringa* was a time for teens to try the *Englisch* world, to experience what they would vow to give up when they joined the church, the folks in the tour group invariably look baffled.

"So your parents approve of your smoking and drinking?"

"*Nein*. It's not like that. It's more that they want us to experience those things that we're curious about before we give them up. Things like going to a movie in town or driving a car—or yes, even smoking a cigarette. They'd never give us money for cigarettes and if you know how much they cost..." At this point, several *Englischers* would always nod their understanding. "So you understand that it's not like an Amish teen is going to run to town and buy a carton of smokes. There's no way he or she could afford it!"

He'd go on to explain that many of the things that happened during *rumspringa* were normal things for teens, but for Amish, it was more like poking a toe into the *Englisch* world.

"What if a teenager decides they like it? Decides they enjoy movies at the cinema and cell phones?"

"I can't speak for everyone, but in my extended family, you're usually shipped off to a Mennonite *aenti* or *onkel* at that point. Mennonites are very much like Amish but somewhat less strict. So they live there awhile before they make a decision. Of course they can come back anytime they want."

"No shunning?"

"Shunnings are exceedingly rare these days, and I don't mind admitting I'm glad. As our bishop once said, he'd never tell us we can't see or speak with a family member. *Gotte* leads each person in a different way."

"Your bishop sounds pretty progressive."

Adrian had shrugged and turned the topic to his animals. But here and now, speaking with Grace, he thought about those conversations again. Even when they occurred during the meal they fed the tourists, Grace didn't chime in.

She didn't speak of *rumspringa* publicly or privately.

Instead, she'd change the subject or ask him another question.

He hoped that the closer they became, the more comfortable she would feel sharing. But by July, he was beginning to suspect that might not ever happen. Which was okay with him. He loved Grace regardless of what silly antics she'd done during her *rumspringa*.

After all, how bad could it be? She was in the new-member class. She was joining the church.

Then the two letters arrived. One a day after the other.

The first was penned in feminine handwriting and contained a single line. "Ask Grace about Nicole's father."

There was no signature or return address. He'd tossed the letter onto his junk-mail pile, which threatened to topple off the kitchen counter, and given it little thought.

Then the second letter arrived. It was rather more pointed. "You should know why Grace moved to Ohio before you decide to marry her."

That was signed "a friend." Adrian somehow doubted that whoever had penned it was a friend. More than likely, it was someone who was sticking their nose where it didn't belong.

Adrian picked up the stack of junk mail including both letters, which were definitely junk, and carried them out to the old metal barrel where he burned trash. Throwing a match into the can and watching the paper flame, he frowned.

Trash.

That was what those letters were. They were rubbish. He didn't know what motivated people to be nosy. He didn't know why sometimes people—even *gut* people—treated one another poorly. But he did understand it was one of the reasons he was more comfortable with animals.

Take Millie the blind albino donkey he'd recently acquired. Triangle would start barking anytime Millie ended up somewhere she shouldn't be. Even Kendrick treated the donkey kindly—blocking the door to the aviary when Adrian inadvertently left it open. He didn't have to worry about the birds flying out and not returning. They knew where the feeding stations were. He liked leaving the door open so the birds could enjoy the great outdoors.

But a blind donkey in his aviary could create a real mess. Millie might even manage to get hurt. But she never went in, because Kendrick always blocked the way. He would find them in something of a standoff, with Millie trying to push her way in and Kendrick moving left, then right, then left again to impede her progress.

Whenever that happened, Adrian would relocate Millie to her pasture and give Kendrick an extra treat.

Animals seemed to display the very characteristics that were missing in people. Perhaps they were just looking out for their own unusual herd, but shouldn't people do the same? Shouldn't they lift one another up instead of bringing each other down?

Adrian struggled with these questions as he attempted to give Grace the time and space she needed.

The evening after he'd received—and burned—the second letter, he'd gone to see Grace as was his custom when she hadn't stopped by during the day. It was mid-July, and they'd been properly courting more than two months.

He had absolutely no intention of bringing up the letters, but he was irritated by them. As he and Grace sat on the back porch, watching Nicole toddle around her swing set, some of that irritation must have leaked out.

"What's bugging you?" Grace asked.

"Nothing." Then deciding that it was best to be as honest as possible, he added, "Why can't people just do what's right?"

Grace took her eyes off Nicole to study him. "What do you mean? What people? And how are you sure what's right?"

"Just regular people."

"Not very specific."

"Let's say—hypothetically—Plain people."

"Okay. And these Plain people did something wrong?"

"*Ya.* They did." It may have come out more forcefully than he intended, but this was Grace's business they were poking around in. How dare they?

"Maybe they didn't know it was wrong."

"Anyone would."

"Maybe they couldn't help themselves."

"Of course they could help themselves. It's just easier to do the wrong thing, to give in to the wrong impulse. It's easier to pretend you're not Plain and to have a foot in both worlds. That's not how we live, though. That's not how we're supposed to live. We're supposed to be different."

"Oh, come on, Adrian. You're not that uncharitable."

"I'm serious. Just do the right thing."

"Oh, it's that simple, is it? Like when you know that you can't afford another animal, but you adopt a blind donkey anyway?"

"Millie's adjusting quite well…and it's not like that at all. I'm talking about a moral choice where someone intentionally chooses wrong. It could hurt people, and they should be more responsible."

Grace stood up, arms crossed, a tiny frown forming between her eyes. He'd seen that look a few times. Bad things usually followed, but did he pay any heed to that warning in his head? *Nein*. He did not.

"You are not perfect, Adrian Schrock."

"I never said I was."

"Maybe you haven't been in an uncomfortable position, where choosing the wrong thing doesn't seem like a choice at all."

"I have no idea what that means."

"Perhaps you shouldn't be judging people."

"Who put a bee under your *kapp* today?"

Grace's eyes widened. "I do not have a bee under my *kapp*, and I'll thank you not to make fun of me."

"I wasn't making fun, Grace. I was only venting my feelings, is all. Can't a man do that with his girlfriend?"

"He can, but then he risks hearing the other side of an argument—something you don't appear prepared to do."

Adrian felt his pulse accelerate and his body tense. He thought there might be smoke coming out of his ears. He was protecting her, but he couldn't tell Grace that unless he wanted to confess all about the letters. And what good would that do? Now she was mad at him. Some days, women made no sense at all to him. He stood and slapped the hat he'd been holding back on his head.

"Guess I should be going home."

"Fine. Go home."

"You don't seem in the mood for visiting."

"No doubt your animals are better company than I am."

"When you're acting like this... *Ya*, they are."

Which caused Grace's face to turn a charming pink.

She opened her mouth, raised her finger to shake it at him and then Nicole let out a scream that split the summer evening and caused all other concerns to fall away.

Grace was about to set Adrian straight. How could he think that he always knew what was right? He was no better than Deborah and Meredith, who she'd had about enough of. Their under-the-breath comments and superior looks had just about pushed her to the edge of her patience. Adrian wasn't helping things, and it wasn't her fault that he had picked this evening of all evenings to start an ethical debate.

But when she opened her mouth to tell him exactly how wrong he was, Nicole's scream stopped her short.

Where was Nicole?

Grace turned, saw her standing at the base of the yellow slide, covered in mud. How had she…?

There hadn't been rain in over a week.

There wasn't any mud.

And then she was sprinting toward her *doschder*. She scooped her up and slapped at the ants that had covered her arms and legs.

Adrian ran for the water hose and proceeded to squirt the ants off her, revealing dozens of large red welts. Dropping the hose, he said, "I'll get your *dat*'s buggy."

He dashed around the house as her *mamm* came outside to see what was wrong. By the time they'd wrapped Nicole's arms and legs in wet towels, then bundled her up in a summer blanket, Adrian had brought the horse and buggy around.

Grace's *mamm* pushed her purse into her hands.

"Go. Straight to the hospital. We'll bring Adrian's buggy and be right behind you."

Adrian set their mare into a gallop.

"How is she?" Adrian didn't take his eyes off the road.

"I don't know. Nicole, honey. Look at me."

"Is she breathing okay?"

"I think she is."

But in fact, Nicole seemed to be having trouble pulling in a good breath. Was she having an allergic reaction to the ant bites? Or was she breathless from her sobbing? She refused to be consoled. The ride to the hospital seemed to take hours and also seemed to happen instantly. One minute, Grace was standing in the backyard with her baby girl, and the next, they were rushing through the doors of the emergency room.

The next hour was a blur.

She filled out a clipboard full of forms, though she couldn't have told anyone what she wrote on them.

A nurse ushered her through a pair of double doors. She glanced back just once and saw Adrian standing in the middle of the room, his hat in his hands and a lost expression on his face. She wanted to run to him, to feel his arms around her and to apologize for flying off at him. She didn't do any of those things. Instead, she carried Nicole into their assigned room and placed her on the bed.

The nurse asked more questions.

A doctor arrived and examined Nicole. "She's having some difficulty breathing. This happens occasionally with allergic reactions. We'll give her Benadryl through an IV drip. She'll be right as rain in no time."

The nurses were good. They'd dealt with children

many times through many different types of situations. One distracted Nicole with a puppet while another started the IV. The poke of the needle brought more cries from her *doschder*, but then she looked back at the puppet and seemed to forget the ouchie on her arm. The nurse placed a wrap around her arm—perhaps so Nicole wouldn't attempt to mess with the IV. The wrap was decorated with bright flowers, and Nicole touched the yellow ones—alternately crying, hiccupping or calling out, "Yellow, *Mamm*. Yellow."

Grace had no idea how much time had passed when she heard a light tap on the door and looked up to see her mother standing there.

And that was when the tears started.

"It happened so fast. I should have been watching her more closely."

Nicole was curled on her side, now fast asleep. Grace's *mamm* came in and sat down beside her, placing one hand on top of Grace's hand and the other on her cheek. "I'm sorry, Grace. This is what being a mother is about. You can't watch them all the time, and you can't protect them from everything that will hurt them."

"Then it's too hard. Being a *mamm* is too hard. I would rather have all of those ant bites—double the number, even—on me."

"Of course you would, but we don't always have that choice. You did the right thing. You reacted quickly and kept your head on straight."

Grace didn't answer that. Her *mamm* patted her arm, waited a few minutes and finally said, "Do you remember the time that you and Georgia disturbed that beehive and came running inside, screaming as if a pack of wolves was chasing you?"

"I was five."

"You were. Georgia was seven. I blamed myself for that little incident. If only I'd been watching you more closely, if only I'd kept you inside, if only…"

"One stung me on the eyelid." Grace reached up and brushed a finger along the small scar. She hadn't thought of that incident in years. The pain had been sharp and her eye had swollen instantly. She'd feared she would never be able to see again.

"Your eye swelled completely shut. I rushed you to the hospital that day, just like you and Adrian rushed Nicole here tonight."

"And what did the doctors do?"

"They gave you Benadryl in an IV and put a compress on your eye. Georgia had bites on her neck. She walked around for a week with her hands wrapped around her neck if she was outside. I felt like a terrible *mamm*."

"You were a *gut mamm*. You always were."

"*Nein.* I had my days where I was less than that, but I think you girls know how much I love you. That's the true test. Isn't it?"

The doctor walked in and checked Nicole's breathing. After he made a notation on his tablet, he looked at them and smiled. "She's responding well to the Benadryl. We'll want to see her awake and eating before we let her go home."

"So she can go tonight?"

"Sure. She should be home by bedtime."

After the doctor left, her *mamm* pulled out some

knitting—this time, it looked she was making a sweater of light yellow wool.

"For Nicole?"

"Of course."

"But you should be knitting for the *Englisch* tourists."

"If I'm ever too busy to knit for my own *grandkinner*, then I'm too busy."

Grace watched her for a few minutes, then said, "I don't know how you focus."

Her *mamm* smiled, the needles and yarn a blur in her hands. She finished a row, checked her marker, then dropped the knitting back into her bag. "I'll tell you a secret. The reason I love to knit is that it's predictable. Dependable. If I follow the pattern carefully, if I knit when I should knit and purl when I should purl, if I count my stitches, then the thing I'm making turns out correctly every time."

"That does not happen when I knit," Grace admitted, but then she rarely remembered to count her stitches, and she often purled in the wrong place.

"It's comforting to me, for sure and certain." Her *mamm* stared at Nicole for a moment, then looked back at Grace, a smile playing on her lips. "Life isn't predictable in that way. It never has been. Knitting helps me to feel grounded. It helps the crazy days feel... manageable."

Her *mamm* stood, walked over to Nicole and kissed her on the top of the head. She paused when she reached the door and looked back. "Your *dat* and Adrian would like to come in."

"*Ya*, of course."

Her *dat* stayed less than five minutes. It was as if he

needed to see for himself that Nicole was fine, and then he was content to leave the details of her care to Grace.

"Would you like us to wait around until the doctor is ready to dismiss her?"

Grace glanced up at Adrian, and maybe for the first time, she fully realized how much he cared about her and Nicole, because the expression on his face told her that he needed and wanted to be the one to take them home.

"*Nein, dat. Danki*, though. Adrian will bring us home."

Her *dat* nodded, as if that was what he'd expected her to say.

Which left Grace alone in the room with Adrian and her sleeping child. Adrian had purchased a get-well card from the hospital gift shop. The card sported a teddy bear carrying a large bouquet of balloons. "It was the only thing I could find with the color yellow." He placed the card on the little stand holding Nicole's cup and pitcher of water. Then he stepped closer to the bed, bent down and kissed Nicole on the head.

When he met Grace's gaze, she moved her purse off the chair beside hers and motioned toward it. He sat down heavily, with a sigh that seemed to come from the center of his bones.

"I've never been so scared."

"Me, too."

"You acted quickly, Grace. You were—you were amazing."

"You're the one who thought of the water hose." She glanced down at her apron, which had been quite wet but was finally dry. Rubbing her palm over a water stain, she said, *"Danki."*

"For what?"

"Bringing us here. You didn't have to do that. She's not..." Her lips trembled and she pulled the bottom one in, drew a deep breath and pushed forward. "She's not yours, but you reacted as if she was."

He claimed her hand. Adrian liked holding hands, and Grace found great comfort in his touch—in that connection between them.

"Grace, I care about you and Nicole. Maybe more than you know."

She nodded and rested her head against his shoulder. She was suddenly quite exhausted. The clock on the wall assured her it was only eight in the evening, but it felt much later. "I'm sorry," she whispered.

"For what?"

"Arguing with you. Flying off the handle. Losing my patience. Take your pick."

He leaned away, holding her at arm's length. "What? You're not perfect?"

"I most certainly am not."

Adrian pulled her back against his side. "Duly noted." Then he added, "In case you're wondering, I'm not perfect, either."

"Two imperfect people." Grace offered a fake shudder.

"We'll push our way through whatever comes our way."

"Like ant bites."

"Yup."

"And silly arguments."

"Those, too."

They were silent for a moment, but the earlier fight still weighed on her. It all seemed so trivial now. "As you've probably noticed, there are some subjects that are a bit touchy for me."

"Uh-huh."

"Like *rumspringa* and mistakes and not being perfect."

He didn't respond. He simply waited. She loved that about him—his willingness to wait and let her gather her thoughts."

"I made mistakes, Adrian. During my *rumspringa*. There are things...things that you don't know about me." She was too tired to cry. Too tired to protect her secrets.

He didn't move away.

He didn't question her.

Instead, he kissed her on top of the head—it seemed everyone was kissing her head—and whispered, "I love you, Grace."

Then tears did sting her eyes. She closed them, trying to find just the right words to lay out her past. Now was as good a time as any. In fact, it was the perfect time. They were alone. It was quiet. Adrian didn't need to dash off and care for an animal.

But the day's emotional highs and lows had been too much. The adrenaline that had propelled her across the yard to rescue Nicole was gone. She was left with a deep-seated tiredness. Her thoughts circled round and round—Nicole crying, thinking she was covered in mud, seeing ants, Nicole's face looking up in confusion, then the piercing cry. Running toward her. Adrian suddenly at her side with water. The mad dash to town. The doctors and nurses and the yellow get-well card.

Her head nodded and she nearly allowed herself to sleep. She tried to remember what they were talking about. *Rumspringa*. She needed to tell Adrian about her past. She rubbed both hands over her face, stood and fetched a cup of water, then sat down beside him. Still, he waited.

"I need to tell you something."

"Okay."

But it wasn't meant to be, apparently, because for the second time that night, Nicole interrupted them. This time, she was calling for her *mamm* and exclaiming over the "yellow boons" and demanding something to eat because she was hungry.

The nurse bustled into the room carrying a tray with Jell-O and a small box of juice.

The chance to confess all to Adrian slipped away, but Grace would do so. Maybe not in the next hour, maybe not even that night, but she would tell him. Because he mattered, and she didn't want anything to loom between them.

She knew, with complete certainty, that the only way to move forward was to face her past.

Chapter Twelve

The trip to the hospital changed Adrian. He'd understood that he cared for both Grace and Nicole before that mad-dash ride into town. He'd realized he was happier and more at peace when he was around them. But now he accepted that they had changed his life in some fundamental way.

When he woke in the morning, his first thought was of them.

As he worked, he'd toss around ideas of various ways to brighten their day.

When he went to bed at night, they were the last images on his mind.

His life wasn't about himself anymore or even about his animals—though the zoo brought meaning and purpose to his daily work. He loved sharing *Gotte*'s creatures with folks who attended the tours. But they weren't the reason he'd been placed on this world. He was there to love and care for and cherish Grace and Nicole.

Within twenty-four hours of the ant attack, Nicole was back to her old self—toddling around, delighting over any yellow item and proudly showing off her boo-boos. Nicole was the same sweet, precocious child she'd always been.

But Adrian was forever changed, and it seemed that Grace was, as well. There was a softness about her now, as if the wall that had existed between them had finally been breached. Perhaps that was the purpose of hard times. Maybe they brought two people together in ways that a dozen afternoon picnics could not.

The extra tours and additional animals—he'd picked up an injured owl, several axis deer and a miniature pig—claimed much of his attention. He saw Grace every day, but sometimes it was for only a few minutes. He vowed to change that, and soon.

It was time to ask Grace to be his *fraa*. It was past time. Why hadn't he asked six weeks ago? But he'd never asked a woman to marry him. He wasn't exactly sure how it was done. Where would be the best place to ask her, or did that even matter? What was the best way to explain how much she meant to him?

He wasn't *Englisch*. He couldn't simply drive into town, stop at the local jewelry store and buy a diamond ring large enough to represent his love. Amish didn't wear jewelry. But picking a bouquet of wildflowers seemed somewhat inadequate.

He needed someone else's opinion, someone he trusted. George had been helpful, but he wasn't sure how much George understood women. What he needed was a woman's perspective. So five days after the hospital trip, Adrian hitched up his buggy and went to see his *schweschder*, Beth. She was only three years older, and she'd always seemed to understand him in a way that the rest of the family didn't. She'd even understood his need to open an exotic-animal farm. Beth was the one who had told his parents, "*Gotte* put this dream in Adrian's heart. Let Adrian see if he can make a living from it."

He'd sought her advice many times that first year. Now Adrian needed to talk to someone about Grace. He needed to decide if his next step was the right one. He didn't want to go too slow…or too fast.

"Surprised to see you in the middle of the day." Beth was out behind the house hanging laundry on the line.

His six nieces and nephews were scattered about the place. The oldest was five and there were two sets of twins. He didn't know how she handled them all, but everyone seemed happy and healthy. Several came running to hug his legs, or ask if he'd brought any of his animals with him, or demand that he come and see something.

"*Ya, ya.* But let me talk to your *mamm* first."

Beth raised an eyebrow, then motioned to the back porch. The temperature was average for July but still quite hot. She fetched two glasses of iced tea.

"Ice? You're getting all *Englisch* on me."

"Yes, well—the new propane refrigerator we bought has a larger freezer area. I claimed a corner for ice trays. Take a sip. You'll see. It's very cooling."

He drank half the glass in one gulp. "Hits the spot, for sure and certain." Then he pulled off his hat and wiped his brow.

"So what's this thing you need to talk about?"

Beth was good about that. She never wasted time beating around the bush.

"I want to ask Grace to marry me."

"I see."

"I love her."

"Do you now?"

"And I love Nicole. I want them to be my family. I want *kinner* and a home and a *fraa* to share my days, to share my life with."

"Well. That's quite a speech. I believe I need some oatmeal bars to help me digest this news."

She scooped up a child and dropped her in Adrian's lap. Another was yawning and rubbing his eyes, so she carried him inside. "Give me a minute. I'm putting this one down for a nap."

He heard a sleepy "But I'm not tired, *Mamm*" as they walked away.

She returned for the *boppli* that Adrian was holding—the boy had been named Aidan because Beth had thought the infant looked like his *onkel*.

"This one needs to go down, too," she cooed as she reached for the child.

When she returned, she was carrying a plate of oatmeal bars, which the remaining children rushed to consume.

"One each, and I set cups of water on the kitchen table. Take them inside."

Finally, she turned her attention back to Adrian. "I'm happy for you, *bruder*. I really am."

"But?"

"I didn't say *but*."

"And yet I heard one nonetheless."

She didn't answer right away, which was strange for Beth. Usually she knew what she wanted to say and had no problem saying it. Her youngest, who was close to Nicole's age, crawled up into her lap, and she set to rocking the child.

"Grace and Nicole will be a *gut* addition to our family."

"I agree."

"Have you told Mamm and Dat?"

"*Nein*. I haven't even asked Grace yet."

"But you think she'll say yes."

"I hope and pray she will."

Beth nodded as if he'd confirmed everything she'd been thinking. "How much do you and Grace talk?"

"We talk every day."

"*Nein*. I mean…" She waved a hand back toward the kitchen, where they could just make out the sound of her three oldest children talking. "Sometimes it's hard to have a real conversation with *bopplin* around."

Adrian thought about the discussion he'd had with Grace in the hospital. It had seemed she was about to tell him something important, then Nicole had awakened and they'd shifted their attention to her.

"We're both pretty busy," he admitted.

"Daniel and I try to spend a half hour or more on the back porch each evening, no matter how tired we are. We need that time to speak to one another without interruptions."

"Okay."

"Make time to speak with Grace. That would be my advice."

"Okay." This time, he said it more slowly. He wasn't really sure what the big deal was, but he trusted that if Beth said it was important, then it was.

He stood and stretched, then walked down the porch steps.

His nephew Joshua dashed past him before turning around and walking backward. "Come on, Onkel Adrian. You said you'd come take a look."

"Guess I'll go see what that's about."

"Probably a nest he spied in one of the maple trees. Your nephew has your fascination with animals."

"*Gut* to hear." He walked toward Joshua, who had run to the tree and was now lying under it, staring up into its branches, but Beth called him back.

"When you talk to Grace, try to be open."

"Open?"

"Don't be so didactic."

"Didactic?"

"Stop repeating what I say. You know what the word means."

"I'm not didactic."

"You tend toward declarative statements."

"What are you talking about?"

"Don't end every comment or thought with an exclamation point. Try a few question marks." She readjusted the sleeping toddler in her arms. "Sometimes what you think is right isn't right every time in every way."

"That makes no sense!"

"See? A declarative statement. It's one of your faults."

Adrian jerked off his hat and slapped it against his leg. He did not speak in declarative statements. Not all the time anyway.

She smiled at him. "How else could you say what you just said—'that makes no sense'?"

"Um…"

"Try something like 'That doesn't really make sense to me. Could you explain what you mean?'"

Adrian rolled his eyes. "It's not like that between me and Grace. We understand each other."

"Right."

But twenty minutes later, as he was driving back toward his place, he remembered the argument they'd had over *rumspringa* and choosing right from wrong. Had he been didactic then?

He didn't think so.

But maybe...

Well, if he had been, he wouldn't be anymore. He loved Grace, and he was going to tell her so and ask her to marry him. And then he'd listen, and he wouldn't judge.

Perhaps he should make a list of pointers for how to go about having a conversation with her. Just when he thought he'd conquered this courting thing, just when he was feeling confident around Grace, his *schweschder* had to go and throw a stick in his buggy wheel.

Unfortunately, the more he thought about it, the more convinced he became that possibly she had a point.

He could always count on Beth to be honest with him.

The smart thing would be to follow her advice.

He'd reclaimed his good mood by the time he pulled into his lane. He could do this. And hopefully within the next few nights, he'd find time to speak with Grace alone. Then they could begin their life together.

Two days later, Grace received word that Adrian's *dat* had suffered a heart attack.

"They say it was a small one." Beth had stopped by

on her way home from the hospital. "They say it's *gut* we made it to the hospital so quickly."

"It's hard to think of a heart attack as *gut* in any way."

"True, but his cardiologist says very little of the heart muscle was damaged. They put stents in two other arteries and are starting him on blood thinners and statins to lower his cholesterol."

"So, will he be okay?"

"Oh, *ya*. The doctor says he might be plowing the fields again by fall, but he needs to take it easy—stop working ten-hour days."

"Will he do that?"

Beth shrugged. "My *mamm* can be pretty bossy if she needs to be. If the doctor says to shorten his work-day, Mamm will see that he cuts back on the hours he spends in the fields."

Grace thought of her own father. He seemed so healthy. It was hard to conceive that her parents could grow old and develop health problems, though most people did. She had a sudden urge to find them and give them both a big hug.

"Adrian asked me to stop and bring you up-to-date. He's sorry he hasn't been by to visit."

"Oh!" Grace felt her face blush.

Beth's smile grew until her eyes squinted.

Grace felt ridiculous. Why couldn't she control the way her body reacted when someone mentioned Adrian's name? She wasn't a *youngie* anymore. She swiped at hair that had escaped from her *kapp*. "It's no problem. He needs to be there for his family. We understand."

Beth lowered her voice and leaned out the window. "He came to see me about you."

"What?" Grace squeaked. Forcing her voice lower, she asked, "Um…what do you mean?"

"Just needed someone to talk to, I guess. He's been bouncing his feelings and ideas off me for years."

"Oh."

"He cares about you, Grace."

"I see. We…that is I…actually Nicole and I and even my parents, we care about him, too."

Beth picked up the reins and released the brake on the buggy. "Don't worry if you don't see him for a few days."

"Okay."

"Or weeks."

"Weeks?"

"He's going to have his hands full, taking care of those animals on his place while at the same time help-ing at my parents' until our *dat* gets back on his feet."

"Of course."

"But he's thinking about you both, and he'll be by when he can. That was his exact message." She offered a little wave, then called out to the mare.

Grace watched Adrian's *schweschder* disappear down the lane.

He'd talked to Beth about her?

He was thinking of her?

And he'd stop by when he could?

It wasn't the way she'd envisioned the next few weeks going, but then life often threw surprises out in the middle of the road. Surely she could handle a few weeks of not seeing him.

She kept herself busy tending their vegetable garden

and cooking for the tour groups. Seth took over guiding guests through Adrian's farm. Grace sewed more clothes for Nicole, who was growing faster than the green bean vines in the garden. Grace also attended the last of her baptism classes. The final lesson covered excommunication and separation from the church. The topic terrified her. She loved and valued her church. She didn't want to be separated from it.

Bishop Luke explained that this was a last resort.

That they sought to council wayward members first.

That it didn't apply to sins they'd committed before they'd become members.

That no one was perfect.

Still, the entire topic caused a rock to form in Grace's belly. She loved her community, and she always wanted to remain a part of it. Even people like Donna and Meredith were important members. They had a terrible attitude, but the items they sold to the tour groups were quite popular. Perhaps something in their past caused their bitterness. Maybe there was a reason for their distrust of others.

Grace didn't know, but she did know that she'd rather be a part of their church community than not be a part of it.

Perhaps more important, she felt genuine regret that she'd stepped outside *Gotte*'s plan for her life. She loved Nicole. She was grateful for Nicole. Perhaps her *doschder* was *Gotte*'s way of bringing her back into the fold. If she hadn't become pregnant, she might have stayed on that wayward path much longer. Her *doschder* had brought her home to her family, to her church and to Adrian.

Adrian.

She missed him more than she would have thought possible.

Georgia stopped over to drop off a few items she'd knitted. She'd left her children at home with her mother-in-law, and Nicole was down for a nap. It was a good time for the two sisters to talk.

"How are things going with Adrian?"

"*Gut.* I've hardly seen him since his *dat*'s heart attack."

"Will stopped over yesterday to help in the fields. He said that Adrian's *dat* looks much better—his color is healthy and his energy is returning."

"I didn't realize how much I looked forward to Adrian's visits."

They were pulling laundry off the line, folding it and placing it in large wicker baskets. As Grace pulled off a sheet, Georgia unpinned the other end. They folded it in half, then Georgia walked toward her and matched the ends together.

"I should have told him." Grace's words were soft but certain. She'd missed an important opportunity at the hospital. Let that be a lesson to her—do the important thing when you can. Don't put it off. Don't think you'll have time tomorrow. "I wish I had talked to him already."

"About?"

"Nicole…and Kolby."

"So, tell him."

"It's harder now. It feels like…sort of like I've been lying to him all this time."

"I guess you have and you haven't. They say a lie of omission is the same as any other lie."

"Thanks. That's helpful."

"Just tell him. What's the worst that could happen?"

They finished folding the sheet, and Grace placed it in the basket.

"He could decide he doesn't want to be with a woman like me."

"A woman like you?"

"One who's made a mistake." There, she'd said it! Why was it so hard to talk about such things?

Georgia finished folding a towel, then sat down in one of the lawn chairs and patted the one next to her. Grace joined her, suddenly too tired to unpin another piece of laundry. She still had those days, where she felt fine one minute and exhausted the next. Maybe she did have the baby blues, or maybe holding such a big secret in her heart was taking its toll.

"You want to tell Adrian the truth?"

"I do. I want to tell everyone. I want everyone to know that Nicole is my *doschder*."

"Okay. My advice is to start with Adrian. He deserves to hear it first."

"And if he rejects me?"

"Grace, if he rejects you, then he's not the man *Gotte* intended for you to spend your life with. Better to know now how he responds, before your feelings grow even more." She reached forward and brushed Grace's *kapp* string to the back. "There will always be some people who judge."

"Like Deborah and Meredith."

"Yes. Exactly. We're not responsible for those people or their reactions."

"But what does that mean?"

"It means you should live your life the way you

think you're supposed to live it, and stop worrying about other people."

"Right."

"Talk to Adrian."

"I will."

"Soon."

"Okay."

Grace felt immeasurably better making that promise to Georgia. No more procrastinating. No more acting like a child. It was time to move forward, hopefully with Adrian, but even if it meant doing so without him, she needed to move forward. Being stuck was worse than having to move in a different direction.

She was ready.

Then Adrian's *dat* had a slight setback. He returned to the hospital, though they released him after three days. He'd tried to do too much too fast. Adrian would be needed there at the family farm a little longer.

Two weeks passed, then three. August arrived and the day of her baptism drew nearer.

Then the rains began.

Chapter Thirteen

Goshen, Indiana, received an average of four inches of rain each month during the summer. Grace knew this, because her *dat*—like most farmers—found the topic of weather and rain and averages to be fascinating. Her *dat* was quite happy when they received five days straight of solid rain.

"*Gut* for the crops," he reminded her when she stood by the window, frowning out at the clouds.

"Yes, but not so *gut* for little girls." Grace thought that she'd never view rain the same again after having a cooped-up eighteen-month-old to contend with.

Grace had woke on Friday morning to the sound of more rain hitting the windowpanes. "Great," she murmured, and pulled the quilt up to her chin. But soon she heard her *mamm* downstairs in the kitchen, and then Nicole called out from her room across the hall. It was time to face another day trapped in this house.

Which meant facing another day when she probably wouldn't see Adrian. No doubt this rain was causing a lot of havoc with his exotic animals. As far as she knew, he'd started work on an ark.

They had breakfast, Grace cleaned the house a bit, then she and her *mamm* pulled out their needlework, but Grace couldn't concentrate. She was attempting a sweater in yellow for Nicole, but something had gone terribly wrong with the sleeves. She sighed and set about pulling out the last few rows she'd knitted.

They ate lunch.

Knitted some more.

She read a few picture books to Nicole.

The rain finally slowed to a soft drip, certainly less than the downpour they'd endured all morning. No doubt another round of heavy rain was coming. Though the clock read two in the afternoon, it seemed more like dusk outside. Grace had pulled the pillows off her bed and scattered them on top of a blanket in the kitchen in front of the large window. Nicole sat there like a queen on her throne, playing with her baby doll and talking to her in a whisper.

"You should go and check on him." Her *mamm* pushed a cup of coffee into her hands. "After you drink this. You look as if you could use a little caffeine."

Grace sipped the coffee, which was delicious. Unfortunately, it did nothing to mitigate the restlessness coursing through her veins.

"This storm system has to move on eventually."

"Indeed. But until then, it helps to get out whenever it eases up, as it has now."

"You want me to walk over to Adrian's…in this weather?"

"It's plenty warm enough. Wear my rain boots and a light sweater. Oh, and take the umbrella." She hesitated, then added, "Trust me, you'll feel better if you talk to him. You haven't seen him since he finished up working his *dat*'s fields."

Grace looked fully at her *mamm* then, and in that moment, she knew that her *mamm* had guessed her feelings for Adrian. She'd never been good at hiding such things.

Now her *mamm* squeezed her hand and said, "Baby girl is about to go down for a nap."

Sure enough, Nicole was now lying on the blanket, fingers stuck in her mouth, baby doll clutched close to her side.

"You won't even need to move her."

"Exactly. Now go, and tell Adrian to come over here for dinner. He probably hasn't had a good meal since this rain started five days ago."

By the time Grace had fetched a sweater—taking ten minutes to decide between the blue or dark green, and finally opting for the blue, hoping it helped her complexion to look less pale—found an umbrella and donned her *mamm*'s rain boots, Nicole was fast asleep.

Her *mamm* had poured coffee into a thermos. Now she handed it to Nicole along with a lunch pail. "Fresh peanut butter bars in there." Stepping closer, she put a hand on each side of Grace's face and kissed her forehead, then nudged her toward the door.

But she called her back before she stepped outside.

"Do you remember the emergency signal?"

"*Ya*. Um…find a window and put two candles in it."

"One means all is right."

"Two means send help."

"Candles or lanterns. I suspect that Adrian is fine. No doubt he's in that old barn with his animals, but in case there's a problem, we can see the barn from here.

So if you need us, put two lights in the window and I'll send your *dat* right over."

Which pretty much summed up her *mamm*'s attitude toward life. Get on out there. Do what you need or simply want to do. But have a plan ready if things take a turn for the worse.

Grace hurried down the porch steps and to the lane, dodging giant puddles and small rivulets that threatened to turn into streams. It was actually a bit lighter outside than she had thought, though as she looked to the west, she saw darker clouds and knew they were about to get slammed again. She stopped, looked back toward the house and wondered if she should abandon this fool's errand.

But her *mamm* was right. They should check on Adrian.

Plus, Nicole was fine. She needed to stop using her *doschder* as an excuse for avoiding the uncomfortable. She turned and continued toward the main road, made a right, then skirted more puddles as she walked to the lane that led into Adrian's property. No one was out on the road. No cars. No buggies. People were buttoned-down for the storm, and they had been for the entire week now.

Her heartbeat quickened at the thought of seeing Adrian. Did he feel the same way that she did? When had she fallen in love with him? When had she lowered her defenses enough to begin caring for someone?

Perhaps it had been when she'd let the goats out and he hadn't become angry.

Maybe it had happened after Nicole's ear infection, when she'd visited his place and they'd taken that walk and he'd first held her hand. Or perhaps it had been the first time he'd kissed her, when they'd been standing in Cinnamon's pen. She smiled to herself at that memory.

She could see his barn now, but none of the animals came to greet her. In fact, it was eerily deserted, though as she passed the aviary she did hear birdsong.

But where was Adrian?

Where were his animals?

She hadn't realized that his property was lower than theirs. The water here was much deeper, and she was glad she'd worn the rain boots. The barn was on a bit of a hill, and it took her twice as long as usual to even reach it. Turning to look back the way she'd come, she realized that Adrian's place resembled several ponds more than anything else.

She nearly slipped in the mud twice as she made her way up to the main doors. She thought of her *mamm*'s admonition about the emergency signal. Glancing back toward their place, she saw the single battery-operated lantern in the window. Her *mamm* must have placed it there after she left.

She turned back toward the barn and pulled in a deep, cleansing breath. The walk had helped to clear her head. She knew what she needed to do. She needed to tell Adrian how she felt. She needed to find out whether he felt the same. Not knowing was making her crazy. So she murmured a prayer for courage, then raised her hand and knocked on the door, but no one answered. Thinking he couldn't hear her, she pounded on it. Finally, she pushed open the door to the main section of the barn, and when she peered inside she didn't know whether to laugh or run for help.

Cinnamon stood in the main portion of the barn, and the camel seemed twice as big as normal, twice as big as when she was outside in her fenced area. She turned her large head toward Grace, then back toward the bucket of feed.

Kendrick was on the other side of the room, and for once, he seemed subdued. Perhaps the camel had finally settled their score, or maybe there was nowhere for him to run, so he'd decided to behave himself.

Those two animals looked so incongruous together that Grace felt laughter bubble up inside. They pretty much represented Adrian and what he was trying to do here—bring together every strange and diverse animal that needed a home and teach them to coexist.

Grace heard Triangle's bark, and she followed the sound down the north side of the barn, past the stall holding Adrian's buggy horse, who seemed to be sleeping, then back outside and around the corner of the barn. Adrian's barn was what they called a bank barn, meaning it was built into the side of a hill. The top portion of the barn could be driven into with a buggy, and hay or supplies could be easily off-loaded and stored. Farther in, it became a loft that overlooked the bottom portion of the structure.

When she climbed the hill toward where Triangle was apparently having the time of his life, what Grace saw there was something she'd remember for a very long time. Adrian was waving his arms, trying to drive the pygmy goats into the upper section of the barn. Triangle was barking and running in circles. Millie, the blind donkey, stood near Adrian, shadowing his every step. And Dolly the red-rumped parrot sat on the open barn door, squawking as if her voice would help the situation.

Adrian's mouth fell open when he saw her standing there.

"Grace, is everything…is everything okay?"

"*Ya*. Just came to visit."

"Visit?" He glanced at his goats, then back at her, apparently at a loss for what to say.

"What are you doing…with the goats?"

"Oh. These. My *bruder* came by, said I need to move all my animals inside because the worst of the storm is coming."

"Worst?"

"*Ya*, and then he couldn't stay, so I've been moving—" Nelly the pygmy goat dashed past him, then stopped and cried out like a very unhappy child "—trying to move them inside."

"That explains the camel and llama in your barn." She set the thermos and lunch box under the roof hang. "Let me help."

They spent the next thirty minutes together herding goats. They'd manage to get two in and three more would slip out. At one point, they had seven of the eight goats inside the large barn door, and Nelly decided to dash through the middle and scatter everyone. The rain began to fall harder, and Adrian's expression changed from frustrated to desperate.

That look, the one that conveyed how much he loved his crazy collection of animals and how worried he was, convinced Grace they needed to try something different.

"I have an idea," she called out over the wind. She ran over to the lunch pail and pulled out the peanut butter bars, then held them out to Nelly, who immediately ran to where she was standing. But instead of giving the beast the treats, Grace held the bars above her head and walked backward into the barn. Nelly followed Grace, and the other goats followed Nelly.

Dolly flew inside, Triangle circled around behind the slowest goat, and Adrian grabbed her thermos and slammed the barn doors shut.

Grace crumbled up two of the bars and let the pieces fall to the floor. The goats surrounded her, nudging one another, completely focused on the food at her feet.

"You're beautiful. Did you know that?"

"Pardon?" She glanced up, and what she saw in his eyes raised a lump in her throat.

"You're beautiful."

"I'm muddy and wet. We both are." She reached up, found her *kapp* had slipped back, half off her head, and attempted to pull it forward. But her hair was soaked and the *kapp* was soaked, so she pulled it off and wrung the rain out of it. Looking again at Adrian, she shrugged. "Want a peanut butter bar?"

Five minutes later, they sat at the edge of the loft, feet dangling over. It was a funny view, looking down at Kendrick and Cinnamon. The goats, even Nelly, had finally collapsed onto the hay behind them. Dolly the parrot sat atop one of the higher bales of hay, preening herself. Triangle had curled into a ball and was watching them through half-closed eyes.

"Are your other birds going to be okay?"

"Sure. Dolly, she's just used to following me around."

"She's a *gut* bird."

"And beautiful." He nudged his shoulder against hers. "Like you."

"Are you comparing me to a parrot?" Grace laughed

as she pulled her hair over her left shoulder and finger combed the braid out. How had she managed to get so wet?

"It's a compliment."

"One can hope."

"I meant what I said earlier about you being beautiful." Adrian laid a hand over his heart. "Honest."

"Adrian, are you trying to sweet talk me in order to get more peanut butter bars?" She pulled another out of the lunch pail and leaned back, holding it out of his reach.

Which caused Adrian to reach for it, and then they both fell over in the hay, laughing, and Triangle belly crawled closer to lick them on the face.

When she looked up at Adrian, he pushed the hair out of her eyes, then he did what she'd been dreaming about for days. He kissed her—softly at first and then more thoroughly. Grace felt her face flush, wondered if she had mud on her cheeks, then realized she didn't care about any of that. The only thing that mattered was Adrian's fingertips on her face, his lips on hers, his eyes drinking in the sight of her.

And in that moment, Grace did something she hadn't been able to do since the day she'd first learned that she was pregnant with Nicole.

She stopped being scared.

She let go of her regrets.

She allowed herself to be happy.

When Adrian pulled away and sat up, she opened her eyes, looked around, then also popped up beside him.

"What's happening?"

"I don't know." Adrian cocked his ear toward the roof. "I think it's here."

"What's here?"

"The worst part of the storm. The part my *bruder* warned me about."

The rain against the roof was setting up quite a ruckus, and the day outside had turned significantly darker. Funny that she hadn't noticed any of those things while Adrian was kissing her.

"Let's go check it out." He stood and reached for her hand.

Grace froze because it occurred to her that she was doing more than putting her hand in Adrian's. It seemed like she was finally stepping back into the stream of her life, the part that moved forward, the part that would keep her from being alone. Which was all something that up until now she'd dared only to dream of.

It was risky, she realized. She could get hurt again. She didn't believe that Adrian would hurt her. She thought the risk was worth taking.

Adrian stood, waiting, holding out his hand to Grace.

She seemed to hesitate, and he wondered if he'd gone too far. Perhaps he shouldn't have kissed her so boldly. But being around Grace and not kissing her seemed a terrible thing to ask of a guy.

Then Grace slid her hand into his, and she smiled, and something clicked inside of Adrian. Something that was missing had suddenly, undeniably been found as he pulled her to her feet.

The goats were no longer frantic. Even Nelly had calmed down. Hand-in-hand, Adrian and Grace made their way across the loft and down the stairs, into the main part of the barn, and over to the windows.

"Wow." Grace stepped closer and pressed her nose against the window. "That's a crazy amount of rain."

"Ya."

"Are we…are we okay here?"

"Oh, *ya*. This happened before, maybe a year ago. I guess it was when you were gone."

"Your property flooded?"

"Sort of. The barn is on enough of a rise that it doesn't easily take on water, but my *bruder* and I decided to cut some trenches around the barn to make it even more secure."

"I'd wondered about those." Grace again pressed her nose against the window. "It's like there's a moat around your barn."

"Exactly. Timothy said that when considering your land, you have to think like water. Where do you want it to go? Where do you need it to go? And how can you get it there? We worked on those trenches for a few weeks, but as you can see, it was a *gut* idea. The heavier rain should push through in an hour or so."

"Should I be worried about Nicole or my parents?"

Adrian squeezed her hand. "Their place is a little higher than mine, but let's go and see."

He led her back upstairs and to a window that faced her parents' farm. Even through the darkness of the downpour they could see a single light in the kitchen window.

"See? One light means all is fine."

"You know the signal?" She turned and looked up, studying him. He wanted to kiss her again, but he stopped himself when she started laughing. "Of course you know the signal. My *mamm* probably made sure you knew about it the first week you moved here."

"Pretty much."

"We should put one light in the window here so they'll know we're okay."

They found an old battery-operated lantern on the shelf and put it in the window. One home assuring the other that all was fine. One group calling out to the other as if to say you aren't in this alone. And once again, Adrian realized that was what he wanted more than anything else. He wanted Grace right here, by his side, every single day. He wanted her and Nicole to be his family.

"Marry me."

"What?" They were sitting among the pygmy goats, and she had Heidi in her lap. She'd been rubbing the goat's silky ear between her thumb and forefinger. Now she looked up, the expression on her face saying she must have misheard him.

"I love you, Grace. I know... I know things have been crazy the last few weeks. My *dat*'s illness sort of interrupted our courting, but I care about you...about you and Nicole. I want us to be a family."

"Adrian—"

His mouth went suddenly dry when he saw her hesitation, but he'd jumped into it now. There was no backing out, and he didn't want to. He wanted to move forward, into their future, not backward where they had been. So he reached for her hand. "You don't feel the same?"

"I do. I care about you. I care about you very much." She pulled her hand away and resumed petting Heidi. "But there are things...things you don't know about me. Things that I need to tell you because they might change how you feel."

"Then, tell me." He'd been sitting beside her, but now he scooted around in front, so they were knee to knee, so he could look her in the eye. "Tell me anything and everything, but I promise you that it will not change how I feel."

She pulled the goat closer, held it in her arms as if it could give her the courage that she needed, and in that moment, Adrian's heart broke for Grace. What had she been through that frightened her still? And did it have to do with Nicole?

"Nicole isn't my cousin's child."

"Oh." His mind tossed about in an attempt to respond to that. "A friend's? Because it doesn't matter to me. She's your family now, and I want you both to be my family."

"She's my *doschder*, Adrian."

"Of course she is." He felt his head nodding like a bobble head toy. "And I will treat her the same, too."

"Adrian, look at me."

He raised his eyes to hers and waited.

"Nicole is my *doschder*, my flesh and blood. I met a boy...an *Englisch* boy who was working on one of the farms." She bit her lip, glanced down at the goat, then back at Adrian. "I fancied myself in love and he said he cared about me, and I... Well, I made some foolish choices."

A tear slipped down her cheek. Adrian longed to brush it away, but he sensed that if he moved now Grace might run away, run out into the storm and not return. So he waited, though it took every ounce of willpower to do so.

And while he waited, several things slipped into place. He remembered the way that friends and family would look at him when he'd praise Grace for raising another's child. He thought of how Grace's parents doted on Nicole—on their granddaughter. He recalled the moments that he'd seen Grace and Nicole together and how he'd wondered that they favored one another so much. He thought of his *schweschder* warning him to not be didactic, to not judge.

Of course Nicole was Grace's *doschder*.

He'd been blind not to see it, and though it was a testament to her youth and immaturity that she had stepped outside the rules of their *Ordnung*, a wayward teenager wasn't who was sitting in front of him now. The woman he was weathering the current storm with was older, wiser and confident. She was also loving and kind.

"I don't regret my mistakes." She raised her chin defiantly, but her voice... Her voice remained a whisper. "How can I regret those mistakes when the result is Nicole? I can't imagine my life without her."

"Of course you can't." He reached for her hand now, no longer worried about if he was being careful enough. He needed to assure her that this thing, this part of her past, didn't matter. "Nicole is a blessing, Grace...regardless the circumstances she was born under."

"Do you think so?"

"*Ya.* Of course. None of us are perfect." He rubbed his thumb over hers. "The fact that you made a mistake, that you misstepped... Well, it seems to me you paid for that with your time away. And now you're home, with your *doschder*, and I've fallen in love with you."

"What about what you said before, the afternoon that Nicole was attacked by the ants? You spoke quite strongly about not being a hypocrite, about not having a foot in both worlds."

He had said those things. He wanted to slap a palm to his forehead. How could he have been so cold-hearted? How could he have been so sure?

"Because that's exactly what I did, Adrian. And if that makes you think less of me, then our being together can't possibly work."

"It doesn't make me think less of you. How could I ever think less of you?" He looked down, turned her hand over and ran a fingertip across her palm. Then he looked up at her and smiled. "What I said that afternoon, it only proves that I still don't know it all and that I can be wrong. Can you live with that?"

"Of course I can."

She struggled to her feet, and he popped up beside her. But instead of moving into his embrace, she paced away from him, walked back over to the window. The rain was lessening, and the sky had lightened up enough that he could look past her and see the swirling waters racing away from his barn.

"I can't… I can't have everyone believing that Nicole is my cousin. I need to make a confession in front of the church."

He was shaking his head before she finished speaking. "Bishop Luke won't require that. You weren't a member of the church when you became pregnant."

"You're right."

She turned toward him now, looked up into his eyes, and Adrian felt himself falling more thoroughly in love than he'd thought possible.

"Luke has already told me that it's something I don't have to do, but I *want* to do it. I'm tired of living under a pretense, a lie, really. I want people to know that Nicole is my *doschder*, and if that makes them think differently of me—"

"Of us, Grace. You're not in this alone anymore."

"Okay. If they think of us differently or treat us differently in any way—"

"Then it will be their loss."

He pulled her into his arms, kissed her gently and then held her. But Grace wasn't done yet.

"There's something else." She stepped away, pulled him toward a bench. "The reason I was so worried about the tours, about the *Englischers*, is that I'm worried Nicole's father will show up and want custody of her."

"Can he do that?"

"I don't know. I've been afraid to ask anyone."

Adrian ran a hand up and down his jawline. Then he snapped his fingers. "I've got it."

"You've got it?"

"George has an *Englisch* friend who is a lawyer. We'll go to town as soon as we can and ask his advice."

"I'm so afraid of losing my baby."

"You're not going to lose Nicole. You're a *gut mamm*. There's no reason to lose her. As far as her father... It's better that we know what the *Englisch* laws say. We don't want to live with this hanging over us. We don't want to live afraid of what might happen."

"You're right. I know you're right." She covered her face with her hands. "Every time I think of Nicole staying with someone else, with a virtual stranger, I feel sick."

"Hey." Adrian pulled her hands away from her face. "We're in this together, okay? And *Gotte* didn't bring us this far to leave us. He didn't bring you home and put the two of us in each other's paths if there wasn't a way forward. He didn't do all of that only to abandon us now. Right?"

"Yes. Yes, I think you're right. I hope you are."

"The important thing is that we'll go through this together, not just you and me and Nicole, but both of our families, too. We'll stand together, Grace. And we'll find a way through this."

She snuggled into his arms, and Adrian said a silent prayer of gratitude that *Gotte* had brought her into his life. Then he realized she still hadn't answered his question.

He held her at arm's length and asked again. "Do you love me, Grace?"

"I do." Tears shone in her eyes, but she was smiling.

"Will you marry me? Will you and your *doschder* be my family?"

"Yes. Yes, I'll marry you. Nicole and I will be your family."

Chapter Fourteen

The next day the storms had pushed through, and they were able to meet with George's friend, Jason Stromburgh. He seemed to enjoy being a small-town attorney, and he assured them that he could investigate Nicole's father. Finding Kolby would be the first hurdle. Depending on where he was and his response to initial inquiries, they'd decide together how to proceed.

Grace expected to be a bundle of nerves in the days that followed, but she wasn't. Somehow, knowing that she wasn't in this alone, that Adrian was at her side supporting her gave her the courage to believe in herself. She'd handled being alone and pregnant, she'd handled being a single mom, and now she would handle this. *Gotte* would give her the wisdom and strength that she needed. *Gotte* had given her Adrian and Nicole and *gut* parents. She could trust that He wouldn't desert her now.

Six days later, they once again were ushered into Jason Stromburgh's office. He was probably the same age as Grace's father, with gray hair and a slim build.

Like the last time they'd visited his office, he was wearing blue jeans and a snap-button western shirt.

Grace and Adrian sat side by side, with Nicole on Grace's lap. Her baby was a little girl now, a staggering eighteen months old. The days and weeks and months had flown much faster than Grace had thought possible. Certainly it was time to move on from the shadow that Grace had allowed to color her world.

"Good to see you both again. I trust you are well."

They both nodded, and Nicole stuck her fingers in her mouth and buried her face in Grace's dress.

"I suppose you want to skip the chitchat and get right to it." The attorney had a single file centered on the desk in front of him. He opened it, read through the first sheet, then smiled up at them. "I think you're going to like what I found."

Grace couldn't imagine that. She couldn't imagine anything on that sheet of paper that would make her feel happy.

"The person that you thought was Grace's father doesn't exist."

"I don't understand." Grace glanced at Adrian, who also looked confused.

"Kolby Gibson doesn't exist. I checked with the ranch where he supposedly worked."

"I'm sure he did work there. We drove by a couple times. We even stopped in to pick up his pay once."

Stromburgh sat back and steepled his fingers. "Do you remember if he received a check or cash?"

"It was cash."

"Makes sense. Apparently the name he gave to his employer was Kolby Gibson, the same name he gave you. He also told you he was born in Indianapolis and that he was twenty-five years old, correct?"

"*Ya.*"

"There is no public record of a Kolby Gibson who was born in Indianapolis in 1996. I expanded the search by five years in both directions. All that inquiry yielded was one young man who was born in 2001, but he died in a traffic accident five years ago."

They all three looked at Nicole. The Kolby Gibson born in 2001 couldn't have been her father.

"*Nein.* That can't be him."

Stromburgh sat up straighter and closed the folder. "Look, I know you're trying to do the right thing here, but you've met your legal obligation. You've attempted to find Nicole's biological father. The fact that he was working under an alias and that the information he gave you can't be corroborated, it means you're off the hook."

"He can't…" Grace felt suddenly light-headed. Could it possibly be this simple? She looked at Stromburgh, who smiled and waited patiently. Then she glanced at Adrian, who had sat back and breathed out a deep sigh. Finally, she looked down at Nicole, kissed her on top of the head and found her voice. "You're saying he can't come back and ask for his parental rights?"

"No. I don't believe he can. After all, he deceived you, and he made no attempt to follow up after your relationship ended."

Stromburgh tapped his fingers against the desktop. "I admire your desire to pursue due diligence, Miss Troyer. We've done what we can, and you can rest assured that I have been thorough in my investigation. Now, I suggest you move on."

"Move on?"

"If I'm not mistaken, you two are…"

Grace blushed, but Adrian smiled as if he'd just been handed the gift of a lifetime.

"*Ya.* We plan to marry, but Grace wanted to take care of this first."

"Then, I wish you both the best." Stromburgh stood, walked around the desk and shook hands with Adrian and Grace.

Nicole had recovered from her shyness and held out her doll to the attorney, who declared it beautiful. They stopped at the front desk to pay their bill, which was a staggering one hundred twenty dollars for what amounted to less than two hours work. Grace would have gladly paid double that for the peace of mind that Stromburgh's investigation had given her. She counted out the bills—money from the tour groups—and attempted to keep from laughing.

They stepped out into a perfect August afternoon.

"Something funny?" Adrian cupped a hand around her elbow.

"I was just thinking that the tour money helped to pay for the lawyer."

"I've heard those tours can be a real financial blessing for folks willing to participate in them." He ran a hand up and down her arm, then reached for Nicole. "I'm wondering if my two favorite gals would enjoy some ice cream."

"*Ya.* I think ice cream would be perfect."

It was while they were sharing their cups of strawberry and vanilla with Nicole, sitting at a picnic table, that Grace seemed able to speak of what they were to do next.

"Should we talk to my parents first?"

"If that's what you want to do."

"Then yours."

"Okay." Adrian grinned and spooned some strawberry into Nicole's mouth. She made a grab for the spoon, so he let her have it and put a little of his ice cream into an extra cup he'd asked for.

Nicole was quite satisfied to whack the spoon into the cup and laugh, though very little ended up in her mouth.

"You're going to be a *gut dat*."

"I am?"

"Ya."

"More, Adrian. More."

They both stared at Nicole in surprise.

"She said my name right. I can't believe it."

Maybe it was the stress of the last week, but Grace finally lost it. She started laughing and had trouble stopping. She held her stomach and then put her hands to her cheeks to cool them. Adrian watched and waited, his eyes dancing in amusement. She shook her head, pulled in a deep breath and used her napkin to wipe the tears from her eyes.

"She thinks we're funny, Nicole. Can you believe that?"

"What's funny is that she finally…" Laughter threatened to bubble out again, but Grace stopped it by taking a big drink from the cup of water. "Nicole can finally say your name, but it won't be your name for long. Soon she'll be calling you Dat."

"Oh, *ya. Gut* point."

"Much easier to say."

"Has a nice ring to it, too."

As they cleaned up their table and Nicole's hands and face, then climbed back into Adrian's buggy, Grace's mood grew more somber. What she had to do next was something she'd both dreaded and longed to do for over two years. She was finally going to be honest with her parents. And they were going to listen, whether they wanted to hear what she had to say or not.

She could handle their disapproval, but she couldn't handle their not knowing the truth.

When they reached the house, Adrian put his hand on her arm. "I need to go and check on the animals, but I can come back if you like."

"*Nein.* I need to do this on my own."

"All right." He kissed her lips. "I'll be praying that they are receptive to what you have to say."

He hesitated, but then he pushed forward. "What happened to you, that part about Nicole's father lying about his name—"

"Everything. He lied about everything."

Adrian reached toward her, tucked a strand of hair behind her ear. "You didn't deserve that, Grace. Neither you nor Nicole deserve to be treated that way. You deserve to be cherished."

She nodded, tears threatening to fall. But she wasn't going to cry. She was done with crying. She was ready to own up to her past, because she knew with certainty that it was the only way to embrace her future.

She waited to speak with her parents until dinner was finished, the kitchen was cleaned and Nicole was tucked into bed. Her *dat* was perusing the *Budget*, and her *mamm* was knitting at her usual lightning speed when Grace walked into the living room and sat down across from them.

"I would like to speak with you both—if now is a *gut* time."

Her *dat* lowered his paper and, sensing the seriousness of the moment, folded it. Her *mamm* finished counting the row she was on, then pushed her knitting needles into the ball of yarn. It was a little disconcerting, having both of their attention so completely on her.

"Adrian and I have decided to marry." She wasn't sure why that popped out first, but her parents reacted quite enthusiastically—which was to say that her *dat* grinned broadly and her *mamm* rose to give her a hug.

"There's more."

"More?" Now her *dat* looked confused and a tiny bit worried.

"I didn't want our marriage to be built on deception, so I told him about Nicole being my *doschder*. I told him about Nicole's biological *dat*."

"We don't need to go into that, Grace…" Her *dat* reached for the paper, but Grace leaned forward and put her hand on top of his.

"You may not need to hear it, but I need to say it."

Now her *mamm* looked visibly upset. She kept eyeing her knitting as if it could save her. Grace had the urge to snatch it away and tuck it out of sight.

"I know that you've never asked, that you've never really wanted to hear the details." Neither parent interrupted her now. "But as I said, I need to tell you. Two years ago, I met a young man named Kolby Gibson— at least, that's what he said his name was."

"Why do we need to know this, dear?" Her *mamm*

clutched her hands in her lap. "You know we love Nicole—we love you both."

Grace decided the best thing to do was just plow through. "It turns out Kolby Gibson was not his real name. Adrian and I went to an attorney to see if Kolby might have parental rights. He doesn't, because he was working under a false name. He was dating me under a false name. I don't even know who he was…or is."

Her *dat* harrumphed and her *mamm* tsk-tsked.

"The point is that I don't have to worry anymore about him showing up here, about him wanting custody of Nicole. I don't know why I thought he might, but it was just always there, lurking in the back of my mind. Now…now I'm at peace. Now Adrian and I can begin our life together on solid ground."

She waited—partially to catch her breath after such a long speech and partially to give her parents a chance to comment.

They didn't.

"I know I must have disappointed you terribly. I understand now that my actions must have hurt you, and I'm sorry for that." She brushed away a tear. She'd sworn she wouldn't cry, but there were times when her emotions didn't follow orders very well. "And I ask your forgiveness."

Her *dat* looked at her *mamm*, who put her hand over his and squeezed. That image of her hand on his, of the way they were looking at one another, told her how much she had hurt them. She'd thought the past two years were difficult for her, but now she realized how heavy the burden was that they had carried. She felt such grief for that, for what she'd put these two good people through, that it nearly pinned her to the chair.

It was with great effort that she stood, walked over to the coffee table sitting in front of them and perched on the edge of it.

"Can you forgive me?"

"Of course we forgive you, Grace." Her *dat* scooted forward, placed his hand on top of hers. "The more important question—the question that your *mamm* and I have prayed over since you first told us of the pregnancy—is whether you've forgiven yourself."

Tears cascaded down her cheeks, and Grace made no attempt to wipe them away. She realized as she sat there, her parents waiting for her answer, that she *had* forgiven herself—not all at once, not at any particular moment, but day by day as she'd watched Nicole grow, as she'd fallen in love with Adrian, as she'd found God's grace in her prayers.

"*Ya*. I have."

"Then we are happy for you, and you and Adrian have our blessing." Her *mamm* put her hand on top of Grace's *dat*'s, the same hand that sat on top of Grace's.

It was a moment that Grace would always remember, and one that would sustain her through the tough days ahead.

"Things went well, then."

Adrian and Grace were watching Nicole run through his group of goats. She wasn't really running. It was more like lurching from goat to goat, but the goats didn't seem to mind. They'd become quite accustomed to the little girl with the golden curls.

"*Ya*. Better than I'd hoped."

"And it's *gut*—to have that off your chest."

"It is."

"So what's the *but*?"

Grace started to laugh. "You know me pretty well."

"I'm a quick study when it comes to someone I plan to spend the rest of my life with."

"Okay. I'm worried about your parents."

"Don't be." Adrian wished he could fast-forward through the next twelve hours, not because he was worried about the outcome but because he could see how much this pained Grace. He hated to think that anything he might say or do, anything his family might say or do could cause her such concern.

"At least it will be over tonight." Grace sighed dramatically, only she wasn't being dramatic.

She looked as if she was having trouble pulling in a full breath. Adrian rubbed her back in slow circles, as he'd seen her do with Nicole.

"They're excited that you and Nicole are coming for dinner, and I'm pretty sure they've guessed that we're going to announce our intentions to marry."

"The rest will be a surprise, though."

"Maybe not as much as you think." When Grace looked at him in surprise, he squeezed her hand, then nodded toward Nicole. "She looks more like you than you realize."

"True."

"And your leaving town suddenly, then returning with a child... Let's just say it doesn't take a genius to figure things out."

Grace leaned her shoulder against his. "Did you? Figure it out?"

Adrian laughed. "Nope. But now that I look back, when I would mention to my *bruder* or George or my parents how *wunderbaar* you were to raise someone else's child—"

"You did that?"

"Yes, I did, and they'd always give me a look."

"A look?"

"As if I was a bit slow. I didn't understand it then, but now, thinking back… Well, I suspect most everyone had guessed the truth except me."

Grace hopped up and began pacing back and forth in front of him.

"That's going to make it worse—that they already know. They're going to think of me as a liar. I obviously should have done this months ago when I first came home."

Nicole had plopped down on the ground and stuck her fingers in her mouth. Adrian recognized that look. She was sleepy and about to start crying. Best to intervene before she wound herself up. He was at her side in three long strides. When he picked her up, she slipped her arms around his neck and rested her head on his shoulder, and Adrian realized he was a goner. Not only did he love the beautiful woman standing in front of him but he would do absolutely anything for this child.

He walked back over to Grace, who was still worrying her *kapp* strings.

"The people who love you will not judge you, and the people who judge you are not the ones who love you."

"What does that mean?"

"It means that everything will be all right."

"Okay."

"Let's take this baby girl back to your parents' house so she can have her afternoon nap. Tonight's a big night for all of us."

* * *

The evening with Adrian's family went better than he could have hoped. They were barely in the door and seated around the kitchen table when Grace asked if she could speak.

Before she managed to gather her thoughts, Adrian cleared his throat, waited until he had everyone's attention and then he said, "Grace and I, we love each other, and we want to marry."

His parents broke into large smiles.

His youngest *schweschder*, Lydia, squealed in delight.

His older *schweschder* Beth reached over to hug Grace. Her husband congratulated them, and though her *bopplin* were too young to have any idea what was going on, they clapped their hands in delight. Nicole began to bang her spoon against the tray of the high chair they'd sat her in. It was plain as day that she wanted to join in on the celebration. Adrian wanted to enjoy the moment, but he realized that Grace wouldn't be able to do so until she'd had her say.

So he raised his hands, indicating he wasn't finished. "Grace would like to share something with you."

She took her time looking around the table at each person, but when she finally started talking, she addressed her words directly to his parents. "If I'm to be a part of your family, which I hope and pray I am, then I know I must do so honestly. Nicole isn't my cousin, she's my child. I… I met an *Englischer* before I moved away, and I fancied myself in love."

She glanced at Beth, then Adrian, then back to his parents, who were now listening intently. "My parents thought I should move to Ohio while I was pregnant, and then when I returned, everyone just assumed that Nicole was my cousin. I should have set them straight, though, from the beginning, and I'm sorry that I didn't. I'll make a confession at church Sunday, but before I do so publicly, I wanted to share the truth with you… in case it changes the way you feel about…about our marriage."

Adrian's parents shared a look, one he'd seen a thousand times growing up. He knew what it meant. They were on the same page. They'd already discussed the topic at hand. They'd simply been waiting. Now his *mamm* stood, walked around the table and squatted next to Grace's chair.

"We will be proud to have you as a part of our family, you and your *doschder*." Which was all she needed to say in order to lift the burden of worry off Grace's shoulders.

As his *mamm* and Grace hugged, his *dat* stood. "I'd like to pray over this fine meal and also ask a special blessing on these two new additions to our family."

Everyone quieted and bowed their heads, even Nicole, who carefully placed her hands palm to palm as Grace had taught her.

"Heavenly Father, we thank You for this *gut* food and for all of Your provisions. This night, we'd especially like to thank You for bringing Grace and her *doschder*, Nicole, into our family. We ask that You bless this union between Adrian and Grace, that You guide them in all things, and that Your loving arms remain around them through the many years they will share."

Amens resounded vigorously around the table, and then dishes were passed as everyone talked at once. When Grace passed the bowl of mashed potatoes to

Adrian, she met his gaze. In that moment, Adrian understood that this was the one thing that had worried her the most. The confession at church would be difficult, but what she had longed for, what she had needed was the blessing of their families. She could handle whatever happened at church because she would have Adrian, his family and her family supporting her.

Adrian realized there would be times, like this dinner and like the church service the next day, when he wouldn't be able to take a difficult thing out of his *fraa*'s path. But he could walk that path with her, and he was determined to do so.

After dinner when they'd moved to the sitting room, Lydia admitted that she was thrilled. She'd grown quite attached to Nicole. Now, sitting on the floor with the child, she glanced up at Adrian and said, "Guess I won't be paid anymore for babysitting."

"And why is that?"

"Adrian! I don't want to be paid for watching my own niece."

"Huh." He rubbed a hand up and down his face as if he was in deep thought, then snapped his fingers. "Nicole's a bit easier to care for now. It wouldn't hurt for her to be at the dinners with us. Maybe you could keep an eye on Nicole and help with the tourists at the same time."

"I could do that."

"In which case, you'd need to be paid, same as anyone else who helps with the *Englisch* tours."

Lydia smiled and nodded, then said to Nicole, "Let's go see my room. When you come over to stay with us, you can sleep with me."

Nicole slipped her right hand in Lydia's and proceeded to chatter about the baby doll she clutched in her left. As they walked down the hall, Adrian could hear Lydia saying, "*Ya*. You're sure? That's *gut*, Nicole."

Grace smiled at him as he pulled her down on the sofa next to him.

His mother sat across from them, a small quilt that she'd been attaching the binding to in her hands. She didn't pick up her quilting needle, though. Instead, she beamed at Grace and Adrian. "I thought Adrian might never marry."

"Thanks, Mamm."

"And I couldn't ask for a better daughter-in-law, a better granddaughter, than you and Nicole."

Which was exactly what he'd known she would say.

Adrian's father immediately started talking about asking the bishop to schedule a workday to build a home on Adrian's farm. "Can't expect any granddaughter of mine to be raised in a barn." Which had caused everyone to laugh, and suddenly for a brief moment, Adrian entertained the notion that it might actually be that easy.

The moment didn't last long.

Adrian's *schweschder*, Beth, came to the doorway between the kitchen and the sitting room and asked Adrian for his help in the kitchen. Grace was talking wedding plans with his *mamm*, his *dat* had gone out to check on the horses, and Nicole was in the bedroom with Lydia. Adrian shrugged and followed Beth into the other room.

Beth pounced as soon as they were alone in the kitchen.

She'd never been particularly patient...or subtle. That wasn't Beth's way, which was one of the things he liked about her. But the look on her face had him worried. This couldn't be good.

"Can you talk her out of the confession thing? You said yourself that Luke won't require it."

"She's sure it's the right thing to do."

Beth dropped a dish into the soapy dishwater and set about scrubbing it a bit too vigorously. "I think it's a bad idea."

"Why?"

She slipped the plate in the rinse water. He plucked it out and dried it, then set it in the cabinet.

"Because people can be cruel, Adrian. It's your job to protect her from those people."

"Grace is a big girl. She has a mind of her own, and this is what she wants to do. She wants a fresh start—"

"It won't be a fresh start, though. Don't you see? When she first came back—" Beth glanced over her shoulder to confirm they were still alone, then lowered her voice "—some people, a few, were quite unkind about Grace and her situation."

"Ah. You're talking about the gossips in our community."

"It's taken six months for them to finally move on to someone else. This will just stir them up all over again."

"'Better to hold out a helping hand than to point a finger.'"

"Really?" She stopped scrubbing mid-plate. "You're quoting a proverb to me?"

He smiled and patted her clumsily on the shoulder. "I appreciate your concern, but Grace is right about this. I plan to stand beside her and support her, and I know you will, too. As to what other people do… We have no control over that."

She pointed a soapy finger at him. "Just remember I warned you."

"Duly noted."

He thought they were finished with the topic, then Beth added, "Grace will fit right into this family. Stubborn, like everyone else."

"Including you."

His sister mock scowled at him as he walked out of the kitchen. Adrian considered sharing his *schweschder*'s warning with Grace that night as he drove her back home, but he couldn't do it. She was so happy with his family's response to her confession and their announcement. He couldn't ruin this moment for her. Instead, he would pray that the people who Beth had spoken of would have a change of heart. And if they didn't, then he would do what he'd said he'd do.

He'd stand beside Grace.

Chapter Fifteen

The new-members' class had finished the week before, and the next Sunday, each participant was to be baptized. Grace had shared the details of her past with her bishop. He hadn't looked surprised, but he had assured her of *Gotte*'s promise to forgive all who repented.

"Do you repent your past misdeeds, Grace?"

"*Ya*, I do."

It had been as simple as that. It had always been that simple, only she hadn't been ready. Now she was.

She had asked for permission to address the congregation before her baptism, and Bishop Luke had agreed. He seemed to recognize that this was something she needed to do. He'd even given her a list of scripture to study. "And then if you still feel you should speak, of course you may."

Confess your faults one to another...

If we confess our sins, He is faithful and just to forgive us...

And were baptized of him in Jordan, confessing their sins.

Grace understood that by speaking the truth to her

family and Adrian's family and her bishop, she'd fulfilled her duty. But her heart needed to clean the slate. She'd lived under a false pretense for too long.

Sunday morning came, and she remained convinced that a confession was the proper thing to do, the thing she needed to do.

She barely heard the words of the sermon.

And though voices rose in song around her, she found that her mind couldn't focus on the lyrics.

So instead, she prayed, and she waited.

When finally the service was near its conclusion, Bishop Luke stood and addressed the group. As was typically the case, there were about three hundred people gathered on the benches that had been placed outside under the shade of the maple trees. This Sunday, they were at George and Becca Miller's farm, which helped to calm Grace's nerves. They were a kind family, and George had been a good friend to Adrian.

"Our new-member class concluded this week, and I'm happy to share with you that we have eight candidates for baptism."

There were murmurs of "Amen" and "Praise God" and "Hallelujah."

"Before we begin, Grace Troyer would like to share a few words."

It wasn't unheard of for a woman to speak in church. Contrary to what *Englischers* thought, women did have a voice in the workings of the congregation. However, it was unusual for a woman to formally address the entire group. Grace's *mamm* reached for Nicole, but Grace shook her head and carried her *doschder* with her to the front of the congregation.

"I want to thank you—my church family—for being

so kind to me and to my *doschder*, Nicole, since we have returned from Ohio."

There were many nods and smiles, but Grace knew this didn't mean they understood what she was saying. They considered Nicole her *doschder*, but they didn't yet understand that she was her *doschder*. She could have stopped there, but then it wouldn't be a confession. Would it? Grace swallowed, found Adrian's gaze from the men's side of the group and continued.

"Today, before I'm baptized, I want to confess that I stepped outside the lines of our *Ordnung* when I became pregnant with Nicole. I was a single woman, and Nicole's father was an *Englischer*. I should have controlled my emotions and my actions better. I should have acted in a manner that respected the way my parents raised me. My deeds and my words should have been above reproach."

Now she searched the crowd to find her *mamm* and then her *dat*. Her *schweschders* Georgia and Greta, were also there with their families. Technically, they belonged to another church community, but they'd wanted to be there for the celebration of Grace's baptism.

The group as a whole had gone suddenly quiet, as if they were waiting for Grace to offer a better explanation for her actions.

"Moreover, I should have been honest from the day I returned. I have prayed to *Gotte* and sought His forgiveness, and today, before my baptism, I ask for yours."

She noted one, two, maybe three people who refused to meet her gaze, but overall, there were many nods of approval.

Bishop Luke stepped forward. "Now if all the candidates will come to the front, we will celebrate the holy sacrament of baptism."

Grace's *mamm* hurried up to where Grace stood and took Nicole. Grace and the others who were to be baptized sat in chairs that the deacons had placed near the front.

One by one, Bishop Luke and George Miller moved down the row. When they came to Grace, she covered her face with one hand as she'd seen so many before her do. Luke had reminded them of the reason for doing so at their last meeting. *The covering of your face indicates submission and humility to the church.*

George Miller was one of the deacons. He held the bucket of water, which he ladled out into Luke's hands. The bishop poured the water from his hands over Grace's head. He did so once, twice and then a third time. As he did, he prayed for *Gotte*'s blessing on her life, her child and her future.

And in that moment, Grace finally felt cleansed.

She understood that the water wasn't special in and of itself. It was the fact that they were following Christ's example. She was ready to live her life that way—for Nicole, for Adrian and for herself. She was ready to live a life that she wouldn't have to apologize for.

The next hour passed in a blur, with members coming up and congratulating her. Many promised to pray for her and Nicole. Through it all, Adrian stood by her side. They'd decided to wait a month to announce their intention to marry, but it was plain to anyone with eyes to see that they were in love.

They sat with George and Becca as they ate. Together the four spoke of children, summer crops and their future plans.

Grace and Adrian planned to wed in the fall.

George and Becca were expecting their seventh child.

All four were looking forward to attending the summer festival at the park the next weekend. They made plans to meet up and go together.

So this is what it feels like to have friends.

The thought seemed ludicrous, even to Grace. George and Becca had been their friends before her confession. But their kindness touched her heart, as did the kindness of others.

One of the girls she'd attended school with walked up to Grace after she'd finished eating and invited her to attend a sew-in the following week.

"All the *mamms* are working on quilts for the auction for the schoolhouse," Anna Lapp explained. "Your Nicole will be attending before you know it."

She'd squeezed Grace's arm, then pulled her into a hug before hurrying off to stop her son from attempting to climb on top of one of George's goats.

Perhaps the other *mamms* never had excluded her. Maybe Grace had excluded herself.

There were only three people who were rude to her. The first had confronted her when Adrian was standing by her side.

"It's easy to confess a thing, but it's another matter to change your ways," Widow Schwartz had muttered, shaking her head and walking away.

Adrian had pulled her closer to his side, but the widow's words hadn't wounded Grace as much as she had expected. She saw now that Widow Schwartz was simply lonely and perhaps hurting from some past experience that she'd never spoken of to others. Grace understood that sort of pain.

Donna and Meredith Bontrager had turned their backs and refused to speak when Grace and Adrian had put their dishes in the bucket of soapy water. Adrian had wanted to say something, but Grace had touched his arm and nodded toward where the children were playing. "Let's go check on Nicole."

So they had.

She saw no reason to let two bitter women ruin her day. Donna and Meredith had always been gossips. Grace had tried for months to ignore them and not allow their rudeness to sting. She understood now that it was possible she would always be the recipient of their gossip. So be it. She couldn't stop people from talking poorly of her, if they were so inclined.

The day had gone better than she'd hoped.

Most everyone was quite supportive, and the few who weren't kind at least were in the minority. Grace decided she could live with that.

It was while she was putting Nicole down for a nap on a blanket under the maple trees that Deborah King approached her. Grace took in a deep breath and squared her shoulders. Deborah was Georgia's sister-in-law. Grace's *schweschder* had shared once that certain members of the family were quite strict.

Perhaps if Nicole hadn't been lying there, listening with wide eyes, Grace would have ignored the woman's words. Of course Nicole couldn't understand what she was saying, but that wasn't the point to Grace. The point was that it was her job to protect Nicole.

She wasn't going to tolerate anyone being unkind

to her *doschder*, and it was best to set people straight on that now. Anyone who thought they could be hurtful to Nicole would have to go through Grace to do so.

Deborah stopped directly in front of Grace, wagging her finger and frowning. "I would think that you'd have the sense to at least move somewhere else, if not for your own sake, for Nicole's."

Grace froze in the process of handing her daughter her favorite doll, a Plain doll with a lavender dress and white apron. She remembered sewing the clothes for the doll. The way that Nicole had smiled when she'd first showed her the matching dress. Now Nicole accepted the doll, clutched it to her chest and popped her two fingers into her mouth.

Grace stood, straightened her dress and then faced Deborah. "I will thank you to not speak unkindly in front of my *doschder*."

"I was merely being honest and saying what others are thinking."

"Others are welcome to share their concerns with me privately, as you should have done."

"Well, I never…"

"Never what, Deborah? Never made a mistake? Never regretted a moment of weakness? Never wished that you could go back and change something?" Grace's temper rarely flared, but it was in danger of igniting. She pulled in a cleansing breath and remembered Bishop Luke pouring water over her head. She remembered the commitment of her baptism. "The truth is that I wouldn't change that mistake I made—I will gladly carry the burden of the things I've done wrong—since it means I'll have the joy of Nicole in my life."

"Humph." Deborah pulled her purse string over her shoulder and strode away.

And instead of feeling slighted or hurt or sad, Grace had the urge to laugh. She turned back to her baby girl, who pulled her fingers out of her mouth long enough to point and declare, "Adrian."

Grace turned and saw the man she loved walking toward her. She felt the sun's rays on her skin, but it was what was in her heart that sent warmth through her. She'd faced the very worst that could happen, and put it behind her.

Her heart felt lighter, so much lighter.

As Adrian sat beside her on the quilt, she forgot about Widow Schwartz and Donna and Meredith. Instead, she let her thoughts drift over the people who had been kind, over her family and Adrian's.

Gotte had provided them with the people they needed.

All that was left was to walk together into the future that was waiting just over the horizon.

Epilogue

Grace heard the delivery truck pull into their drive. She was moving more slowly these days. Her second child was due in two weeks. By the time she made it to the front porch, the delivery man was pulling away down the lane.

But the box of books were there.

Adrian must have heard the truck, or perhaps he was sticking closer to the house these days. He was certain their child would be born early. "Eager to meet everyone," he'd said the night before. "Especially his big sister."

Which had started Nicole asking a dozen questions.

Would she be able to play with him or her?

Could they share a room?

How did the baby come out?

Would it be like the kittens in the barn?

Nicole had turned four, and questions were her favorite thing.

Adrian scooped Nicole up in his arms and hurried toward the front porch.

"The books?"

"*Ya.*"

"Here. Use my pocket knife." He opened the small knife and handed it to her, handle first. "Careful."

"Of course." She slit the top of the box and let out a small gasp when she saw the covers. She'd seen them before, pictures of them, but this was the first time she'd held a copy.

Plain & Simple Recipes
By Grace Schrock

The front cover showed a picture of their garden, with Nicole squatting and picking cherry tomatoes from a plant. Only the back of her *kapp* and dress showed, and her little hand reaching for the tomatoes. Peeking out of the corner of the cover was Kendrick the Llama—as usual, he was poking his head where it didn't belong.

"It's a beautiful book. I'm so proud of you."

"Pride is a sin," Grace murmured.

"As you're aware, I'm not a perfect man."

"Walk with me to *Mamm*'s?"

"Of course."

Grace tucked one of the copies under her arm, and the three of them walked down the drive, down the lane and next door to her parents'.

Grace remembered returning there when Nicole was just a babe. So much had happened since then—the tours, falling in love with Adrian, sharing the truth about Nicole.

Their marriage.

A new home built by their church community.

The last two years hadn't all been rosy. Adrian's

mamm had suffered a stroke and died a year after they wed.

A tornado had come through the year after that and taken several neighbors' barns.

But those things had brought them closer together. They were a family, and Grace was so grateful for that. They had each another to depend on through the trials and tribulations, and of course, the joys of life. The baby inside her moved, and she covered her belly with her hand.

"Everything okay?" Adrian's voice was low and close to her ear.

Nicole had stopped to pick a yellow flower. Yellow was still her favorite color.

"Everything is *wunderbaar.*" She kissed her husband, then slipped her hand in his. As she did, she thanked *Gotte* for how far He'd brought her, for the way He had knit this family together, for His care and provision. She knew that was one thing she could always depend on—*Gotte*'s provision. No matter what lay ahead, she didn't need to be afraid.

* * * * *

LOVING HER
AMISH NEIGHBOR

Rebecca Kertz

For my husband, Kevin, for his patience,
his kindness and his enduring love.

What time I am afraid, I will trust in thee.
—*Psalms* 56:3

Chapter One

Late springtime, New Berne,
Lancaster County, Pennsylvania

"You be a *gut* girl for your aunt," Lucy Schwartz said as she lifted her four-year-old daughter into her arms for one last hug, something that was getting more difficult with her advancing pregnancy. "I'll be back to get you after supper."

"Why can't I stay with you?" Susie blinked pretty pale blue eyes up at her, eyes so like her father's—Lucy's late husband.

"I have work to do, *dochter*," she explained, her fingers caressing Susie's cheek. "You'll have more fun with *Endie* Nancy and your cousins."

"Come on, Susie!" her cousin Sarah cried as, *kapp* strings flying, she ran toward their big red barn beyond their dirt driveway.

Susie wriggled to get down. "I'll see you later, *Mam*." Blue skirts flipping enough to show her sneakers, she ran after Nancy's daughter. "Hold up, Sarah! I'm coming! Hold up!"

Lucy grinned as her child scampered off. "My Susie's got energy, that's for sure," she said with a chuckle. She turned to her sister-in-law Nancy. "*Danki* for keeping her."

Nancy smiled, watching as the two girls disappeared inside the barn before meeting Lucy's gaze. "We love having her. You know we're always here to help in any way we can."

Blinking rapidly, Lucy nodded. "I appreciate it." Her marriage to Nancy's brother hadn't been a happy one. Still, her sister-in-law had stepped up to help Lucy after Harley had passed on. Her relationship with Nancy had actually improved since Harley's death.

"I need to go home, collect my baked goods and deliver them."

"If you need us to keep her overnight, let us know," Nancy said as she walked with Lucy toward her buggy.

Lucy nodded. "I will." She heard wild cries of joy as Sarah and Susie ran out of the barn. Sarah had a rope wrapped around her waist while Susie held on to the ends behind her, urging her on. "I guess Sarah is the horse this morning," she said with a chuckle.

Nancy laughed. "No doubt Susie will get her turn this afternoon."

Lucy climbed into her buggy and picked up the leathers. "Is there anything you need from the store?"

"*Nay*, but I appreciate you asking."

With a wave, Lucy left the property and headed home. She'd baked various cakes, cookies and pies yesterday and packaged them for sale this morning. There were enough for King's General Store and Peter's Pockets, a dessert shop that catered to tourists wanting a taste of Amish. It would be the perfect place to feature her bakery items.

As she steered the buggy, she thought about the changes in her life since she'd married Harley Schwartz, a widower. The union had been arranged by her father. At nineteen, she hadn't wanted to marry, but her father had made it clear that she'd be left alone to fend for herself otherwise. And then her heart had melted after seeing Susie, Harley's two-week-old daughter. Susie's mother had died in childbirth, and the tiny babe had no mother to love and care for her. For Susie's sake, Lucy had agreed to wed the baby's father.

As if marriage hadn't been enough of a change, Harley had taken her from her Amish community in Indiana and brought her to live in New Berne, Pennsylvania, where she knew no one. She'd been forced to leave her little brother Seth behind and she'd missed him terribly. She still did.

Eventually she and Harley had settled into a comfortable life. Harley had worked and supported them while Lucy kept house and took care of Susie, whom she adored.

A little over four years later, Harley died in a truck accident at his construction job. While their marriage hadn't been ideal—Lucy had wanted more from it—Harley was a good man, and it was a tragedy for him to die at only twenty-nine years old.

The settlement money from Harley's employer helped her make ends meet, but she knew the money wouldn't last forever. With Harley gone five months now, Lucy had to earn a living to support Susie, her unborn child and herself. After Nancy asked her to bring sweets for Visiting Sunday last weekend, Lucy remembered how much her late husband had loved her cakes and pies. Her ability to bake had been the one thing Harley had raved about, and he'd never been one to give compliments to Lucy, the replacement for his beloved dead wife.

Selling baked goods seemed the best way for her to earn money and stay at home raising the children. With that in mind, Lucy had approached several local shops with samples of her baked sweets to pitch the idea of selling her wares on consignment. The shop owners had loved her bakery samples and were happy to do business with her. Today would be her first delivery of her sweets.

The day was bright and balmy, which made it a perfect morning for her errands. Lucy smiled as she passed horses galloping across the paddock of a nearby farm. The warm breeze caressed her face, bringing with it the scents of spring blossoms, new grass and farm animals.

As the steady clip-clop of her horse's shoed hooves hit the pavement, Lucy wondered with a smile if Susie was enjoying herself. Was she playing hide-and-seek or tag with her cousins?

A car came up behind her, and Lucy moved onto the shoulder of the road to allow it to pass. She was just easing back into the lane when a sudden loud rev of an engine alerted her to another motor vehicle approaching from behind. She didn't have time to move to the shoulder again, but instead, held tightly to the reins as she waited for it to pass. Something clipped the back of her buggy hard, startling her, and she cried out. Her mare whinnied and spooked before the animal took off, Lucy holding on for dear life. Her horse and buggy careened off the road and bounced along the embankment as the car zoomed past. Blackie's flight jostled her vehicle. She held on to the leathers as she tried to calm her horse while her right side slammed against the side wall.

Reaching a hand out to brace herself, Lucy bumped her head and felt a jolt along her arm as her buggy jerked and dipped before finally coming to a complete stop in a ditch, tilting to one side. Grabbing the dashboard, she looked up through the windshield. The driver of the black car had sped off, either not caring or not realizing that he'd left the scene of the accident he'd caused.

She took a deep breath, let go of the dash and wrapped the leather reins around her left hand. Her head ached, and pain throbbed down her right side. Lucy cradled her swollen belly with her right hand, gasping with the movement, but the ache in her wrist quickly eased. "We're *oll recht, bubbel.*" She felt no twinges along her abdomen. "You and I are going to be fine."

She had to get out of the buggy. She tried to open the door on her side so she could slide out through the opening but there was no room. And if the vehicle toppled over, she and her baby would be crushed.

She needed help but had no way to call anyone. Some Amish in the country had cell phones for work or emergencies, but it was a luxury Harley had told her they couldn't afford.

Her only hope was for someone to drive by, see her predicament and stop to help.

Lucy closed her eyes and sent up a silent prayer to the Lord for assistance.

She finished with an "amen" and pressed her fingertips to the place on her head she'd been injured. She was startled when her hand came away with blood. Her distress intensified as she worked to figure out her next move. She checked her surroundings, moving carefully so as not to shift the buggy. Blackie stood, seemingly unhurt, still attached to her vehicle. At least her buggy was far enough off the road to avoid being hit again. *Thank You, Lord.*

Lucy frowned. Now what was she going to do? She reevaluated her injuries. Except for a slight headache and the few areas on her side that ached, the only other thing she felt was a throbbing pain along her right arm down through her wrist. She didn't think her injuries were serious. As long as her baby was all right...

Heart beating wildly, she breathed deeply to calm herself then sent up a silent prayer of thanks that Susie was safe with Nancy. Until someone happened along, the only thing she could do was wait. She leaned back against the seat with her eyes closed, praying that her injuries were mild and help would come soon.

The clip-clop of horse hooves on the road behind her caught her attention. Lucy opened her eyes. The sound stopped. Had she imagined it? She prayed that she hadn't.

"Hallo?" a man's voice asked from the street side of the carriage.

Relief hit her hard. Someone had stopped to help. She hadn't imagined the sound of another buggy. She sensed his presence before he appeared at the open window.

His gaze sharpened as he looked inside. "Are you *oll recht?*"

"I think so." Lucy met the man's gaze as he assessed

her condition, his expression filled with concern. He was Amish with dark hair under his straw hat, brown eyes, and a jagged, raised scar across his left cheek. She tried not to stare, focusing instead on the solid maroon color of his long-sleeved shirt and black suspenders that reached over each shoulder.

"I'm Gabriel Fisher. What's your name?"

"Lucy," she said. "Lucy Schwartz."

"Lucy," he said calmly, "I'm going to help you."

She met his concerned gaze. *"Danki."*

"What hurts?"

"Mostly my head and arm." She touched a hand to the side of her head again and saw more blood on her fingers. "I'm bleeding." She swallowed hard as she let go of the reins to rub her belly with her left hand.

He lowered his gaze to where she cradled her abdomen. "Try not to move," he commanded, but his tone was gentle. "Anything else hurt?"

"My right side."

Gabriel nodded. "I need to get you to a doctor."

"I thought about climbing out, but I was afraid the buggy would move and crush me."

"Ja, it looks unstable but I can fix that. Hold on."

She closed her eyes. Why did she feel so tired? Because of her pregnancy or an injury? Lucy wanted nothing more than to lie down and rest. This past year, with her husband's death and with all that had come afterward, had taken a toll.

She no longer heard Gabriel's voice. Her eyes shot open and she looked to where he'd stood. He was gone. Her throat tightened as she started to panic, and she struggled to breathe evenly. "Gabriel?"

Silence.

"Gabriel!"

"I'm here." His voice sounded muffled, as if he lay under her vehicle. "I'm checking the damage to your buggy." His head popped up again in the window on the street side.

"Blackie? My mare? Is she *oll recht*?"

"Amazingly, *ja*." His smile was soft, reassuring. "I'm going to unhitch her and secure her to my buggy. *Ja?*"

She nodded then grimaced at the movement.

"A simple *ja* would do," he said gently. "You mustn't move or you might injure yourself further."

"I'm fine."

"Let's let the doctor decide that, hmm?"

Releasing the reins, Lucy closed her eyes as she sensed him leave her. She felt her rising panic again when he didn't immediately return. "Gabriel?"

"I'm here." His head popped up on her side. "Took care of Blackie." He frowned as his gaze settled on her forehead. "I was on my way home from the lumberyard. I'm going to shore up the buggy on this side with a two-by-six I have in the back of my buggy. It should just about be long enough."

Gabriel disappeared from sight. Lucy took a calming breath and shut her eyes. When she could see him, she felt better. She gasped, startled, and opened her eyes to find him leaning inside the buggy, his head close to her. "I'm going to wedge the board between your buggy and the ground," he said softly. "It hasn't rained all week. The dirt should be hard enough to hold the weight." He studied her with a frown. "Lucy, are you with me?"

She met his worried gaze. "*Ja*, I'm here."

He smiled. "Give me a minute. The carriage may shift a bit. Don't panic. *Ja?*"

"I understand."

"*Gut* girl," he praised.

The buggy shifted, and Lucy instinctively grabbed onto the edge of the seat with both hands. She gasped as pain surged through her right wrist. She fought back tears but held on.

He rose to his feet, peered in at her. "That should hold but it's best if I bring you out the opposite side."

The street side, Lucy thought. The sound of an engine broke the silence. She tensed, locking gazes with Gabriel before he turned to face the approaching vehicle. She detected a harsh, high-pitched sound as if the vehicle was braking hard, and she closed her eyes and prayed. *Please, Lord, save us.* Gabriel was in as much danger as she if her buggy was hit again.

When she opened her eyes, Gabriel was walking away until she could no longer see him. The sound of male voices rumbled in her ears before he returned with an *Englisher.*

"Don't you worry, miss. We'll get you out in a sec." The man was big, gruff and tattooed. He wore a baseball cap with the brim turned backward, a dark T-shirt and jeans. His appearance should have frightened her, but as he smiled at her, she wasn't afraid. "Bert Hadden, miss," he introduced himself as he stood beside Gabriel.

Her attention shifted to Gabriel, who captured her gaze reassuringly. "Gabriel," she whispered.

"I've got you, Lucy," he assured her. "Bert is going to give us some help. He's called someone with a horse trailer to take care of Blackie for us."

"My brother-in-law," Bert explained. "He and I own a farm less than a mile from here." He grinned, displaying stained, uneven teeth, but there was something about him that convinced her he was harmless. "How did this happen?" he asked as Gabriel skirted her vehicle to the other side.

"Blackie got spooked after a car hit the back end of my buggy."

"And the driver didn't stop?"

"*Nay.* He kept going."

"Can you give a description? We need to tell the police."

"She will when she's ready," Gabriel said. "If she remembers what the car looked like." He unlatched the door. "Bert, make sure the buggy is braced well. I've got another two-by-six if we need it."

"Right." Bert grinned at her.

Gabriel slowly climbed into the buggy. The vehicle shifted under his weight, and Lucy inhaled sharply. "Bert?" he called.

"It's fine, Gabe. The board—she's gonna hold." Bert propped his body against the outer wall of the buggy to further brace it.

"Lucy, slide my way if you can," Gabriel urged with one hand extended toward her.

Through every inch she slid her sore body, she fought back tears.

"Stop," he said gently. "Rest easy now. 'Tis *oll recht.* I've got you." He carefully maneuvered closer then paused as if to gauge the seriousness of her injuries. He gave a nod, apparently satisfied that he could move her. "Lucy, lean toward me a little."

She did as he asked. The vehicle rocked a bit. "It's okay," Bert called out. "She's holding steady."

With her gaze focused on Gabriel, Lucy pushed up with her hands to stand, then cried out when a sharp pain in her wrist stopped her. "I'm *oll recht*," she assured him. "Just give me a minute."

"Need help?" Bert asked, his head appearing briefly in the window on Lucy's other side.

"We're fine," Gabriel assured him.

Using only her left hand, Lucy managed to move a few inches closer to Gabriel. She started to rise and nearly fell back onto the seat, but he reached out to steady her.

"I have you." He slipped his arms around then beneath her and lifted her.

"You okay in there?" Bert asked.

"All *gut*. Coming out now." Cradling her against his chest, Gabriel turned and, clearly mindful of her injuries, carried her slowly to the street side of the buggy.

Bert was there as Gabriel was ready to step down with her in his arms. "I can take her."

Gabriel shook his head. "I've got her." She heard his sharp intake of breath and saw him grimace as he stepped down, still carrying her weight. Bert reached out to steady him. With the man's help, Gabriel lowered her to the ground.

"I called 9-1-1," Bert said gruffly.

Flashing lights in the distance with a short burst of a siren drew her attention. The emergency vehicle pulled up and parked in front of Lucy's buggy. Two paramedics got out and ran in their direction with a medical bag. Lucy was unsteady on her feet, and Gabriel held her up with his arm around her. "You should sit," he said worriedly.

She met his gaze. "I'll be *oll recht*."

"I know you will," he whispered in her ear, and his breath against it made her shiver.

"Ma'am, we need to examine you. You need to sit or lie down."

Before she could answer, Gabriel lifted her up into his arms again. "Gabriel!" she gasped. Ignoring her outcry, he carried her to his buggy where he set her in the open doorway.

He stepped back, his expression shuttered. He moved out of the way, and the female EMT took his place.

"Can you tell me what happened?" she asked as she opened her medical bag and pulled out a stethoscope.

"My buggy was hit by a car. I was forced off the road. The driver didn't stop."

The woman nodded as she listened first to her baby bump then to her heart, and finally she placed the listening device to her neck and throat. "Your baby's heartbeat is strong," she said with a smile as she put her medical equipment back in her bag. "You need an ultrasound to be sure he's fine."

Lucy nodded. "All right."

"Where do you hurt?" she asked. "You bumped your head." She examined the injury. "A little cut. Looks like the wound bled, but bleeding's stopped." She checked Lucy's eyes with a small flashlight. "Headache?"

"A little one coming on." Lucy saw the other paramedic talking with her rescuer. "I hit my right side. It hurts but I don't think it's bad. My right arm hurts, but now I think it's my wrist that's injured. I couldn't use it when I tried to push myself up to stand. I had to use my left."

The paramedic grasped her right hand. She gently manipulated her wrist, and Lucy inhaled sharply. "Can you move your fingers?" Lucy did. "Good. Let's check your elbow and shoulder." A moment later she declared, "They look good, as well. You'll need an X-ray, but nothing seems broken. You most likely have a sprained wrist. We'll need to make sure." The woman smiled. "You're lucky, Lucy. I've been on the scene of many buggy accidents, and most have more tragic results."

"I know." She recalled one such terrible accident that had killed a member of her church community back in Indiana, where she'd spent her childhood.

Gabriel bent as if to pick her up again, but she held up her good hand. "I can stand," she assured him. She stared at her buggy. "How bad?"

"Broken axle," he told her quietly. "Body is in good shape, though."

She met his gaze, nodded. "Could have been worse."

Gabriel studied Lucy and the wild beating of his heart subsided a little. When he'd spied the damaged buggy in the ditch, he'd feared the worst. And when he saw she was pregnant, stark terror struck him.

"You'll see a doctor soon," he said reassuringly. He'd worry until he knew for certain that she was all right. She looked at him, her big beautiful blue eyes filled with gratitude, and he shifted uncomfortably.

"An ambulance is on its way," the male paramedic said. "Lucy, you need to go to the emergency room."

As if summoned, flashing lights and the whine of a siren heralded the ambulance's arrival.

"I'd rather go to the clinic down the road. I have a doctor there. She can help me. I promise I'll go to the hospital if she tells me to."

The paramedics exchanged a look.

"We'll take you there by ambulance," the woman insisted. "No arguments."

Lucy nodded. She grabbed on to Gabriel's arm. "Would you go with me?"

"Do you need me to get in touch with your husband?" he asked quietly.

She shook her head, briefly averting her gaze. "I... I'm a widow."

He felt a jolt; he knew what it was to be hurt and alone. "I'm sorry," he said softly. "I'll go if you want me to."

"Danki," she whispered, her blue eyes filling with relief.

"I'll be right back," he said. "Know anyone who can drive my buggy?" After only two months in New Berne, he was familiar with the medical building with doctors' offices and an urgent care facility. He'd become a patient of a neurologist and a burn specialist because of severe injuries he'd suffered during a house fire.

"I'll do it. I know horses," Bert told him. "Drive lots of wagons. I'll be happy to drive it home for you." He smiled. "I'll call my nephew. He can bring me back for my pickup. And I'll arrange for my brother-in-law to bring your horse home in his trailer. What's the address?"

Gabriel looked at Lucy, who gave Bert her address.

He was surprised that she lived about a half mile down the road from him.

"I don't know how to thank you, Bert," Lucy said.

The gruff *Englisher* smiled. "You just did." He shot Gabriel a glance. "You take care of her, and I'll take care of everything else."

The ambulance driver parked and the female EMT swung open the double rear doors. Two ambulance workers pulled out a stretcher and carried it in Lucy's direction.

"Are you sure you want me to go with you?" Gabriel asked.

She nodded. "*Please.* I don't know what I would have done if you hadn't stopped to help me."

The two paramedics helped to lower Lucy onto the stretcher. "Gabriel stays with me," Lucy told him.

It looked as if one of the ambulance workers would object, but then the female medic said, "He can go." The attendants lifted Lucy into the back of the vehicle. They climbed in after her and waited for Gabriel to get in before closing the doors.

When he woke up this morning, Gabriel never thought he'd end up rescuing a woman he'd never met and staying with her while she went to the doctor.

For the first time in a long time, he felt almost... normal. Lucy hadn't been repulsed by his visible burn scar, and it made him feel good.

Chapter Two

~~~

Lucy sensed Gabriel's concern before she met his gaze. He sat so closely beside her in the ambulance that his knees brushed the stretcher the paramedics had insisted they transport her on. "I'm sorry," she murmured.

His brow furrowed as he frowned. "Why?"

Without looking at him, she rubbed along the edge of her hairline with light fingertips. Why had she asked a stranger to come with her to the doctor? She stretched her neck slightly to alleviate the stiffness. Her head didn't hurt as much as it had earlier but it ached between her shoulders. "I shouldn't have asked you to come. Maybe you need to get home."

Was he married? She'd feel bad if he was. But if he were married, wouldn't he have gone home? Closing her eyes, Lucy lay still and took several calming breaths before she opened them again.

"I don't," he said with a lopsided sad smile that tugged at her heartstrings. "I don't need to go home."

Lucy felt emotional and afraid. She was pregnant and an accident victim with a young daughter and no husband to take care of her if she was badly hurt. And now she was relying on a stranger's kindness. "Gabriel," she whispered.

"What is it?" he said, looking concerned. "What's wrong?"

She watched the scenery fly by, thankful the driver at least hadn't put on the siren. "My daughter, Susie, is at my sister-in-law Nancy's *haus*. I was supposed to get her after supper. If I can't make it, will you let Nancy know? She'll take care of Susie if I end up in the hospital." Lucy was worried. What was she going to do about the delivery of her cakes and pies? She didn't want all of that baking to go to waste.

"*Ja*, I'll make sure she knows." His expression softened slightly. "Bert has arranged for your buggy to be moved to a carriage shop. He promised to get in touch with an estimate for repairs." He leaned closer and settled a comforting hand on her shoulder. "Don't worry about your *dochter*. If you give me your sister-in-law's address, I'll take a ride over there to tell her."

"I need to take your vitals," the paramedic said before Lucy could answer.

Straightening, Gabriel withdrew his hand, and Lucy felt the loss as the attendant wrapped a blood pressure cuff around her left arm.

After he took a reading, the man checked her pulse. "Blood pressure and pulse are fine." He shined a tiny flashlight in one eye and then the other. "Pupils are normal and reactive. All good signs."

Reassured, Lucy nodded. "*Danki.*" Her gaze capturing Gabriel's, she saw that he looked relieved. She closed her eyes and settled her good hand on her belly, hoping, praying that her unborn *bubbel* hadn't been affected by the accident. The paramedic strapped a splint onto her right arm to stabilize it.

She felt the stretcher shift as the vehicle slowed then turned.

"We're here," Gabriel said softly.

The ambulance stopped and the rear doors opened. Gabriel climbed out first. She heard the attendant talking with the paramedics who had treated her at the scene. The rolling stretcher was lowered down by the driver and the man who'd ridden in the back with them.

The female paramedic appeared in her vision as she leaned over Lucy to make eye contact. "We'll come inside with you to give them our report." She accepted a clipboard from the man who'd been in the back with them.

As she was wheeled inside, Lucy sent up a silent prayer of thanks for Gabriel and Bert.

Her eyes flew open. "Gabriel, your buggy—"

"Not to worry. I'll call for a car when you're done."

Lucy sighed with relief. For the first time in a long time, she didn't feel alone.

As they entered the clinic, Lucy lost sight of Gabriel. Her chest tightened and she could hear her own heartbeat as she started to panic. Then she caught a glimpse of a wide-brimmed, banded straw hat. With the realization that he'd followed her stretcher, she felt herself begin to calm again. She'd never met Gabriel before today, yet it felt as if she somehow knew him.

Her stretcher stopped moving, and Lucy waited while the paramedics spoke with the receptionist at the front desk. She heard the words "accident" and "hit and run." Gabriel moved closer to her side, leaning over her, and flashed her a reassuring smile. "How are you feeling?" he asked huskily.

"I'm…" Without thinking, she shifted on the stretcher, then winced and clutched her right hand as pain radiated down her arm to her hand beneath the splint.

"Lucy—" He looked at her with alarm, his dark eyes filling with concern.

She breathed through the pain until it subsided. "I'll be fine."

His expression softened. "They'll be taking you in the back in a few minutes."

He glanced toward the front desk and Lucy studied his arresting features.

Her stretcher began to move as an attendant rolled her toward an open doorway. Lucy rose slightly, needing to see Gabriel before she disappeared into a back room. Her panic started to rise again, making it difficult for her to breathe.

"Wait," she heard Gabriel say. Her stretcher stopped moving. Suddenly, she could see him again as he leaned over her, his features warm and filled with emotion. "I'll wait for you here."

"*Danki*, Gabriel." Her eyes felt scratchy.

Fear kept her silent as she was pushed into a small green room. The ambulance attendants transferred her from the stretcher onto an exam table then left her alone. As she took stock of the room, Lucy prayed for the good health of her baby and for the strength she'd need to face the uncertainty of the days ahead.

She closed her eyes, picturing Gabriel's face, his warm brown eyes, his smooth voice telling her she'd be all right. And her fear started to recede. *Gott* would help her, and knowing Gabriel waited for her out front made it easier to focus on the good and not the bad.

The door opened, and Lucy struggled to sit up as two women entered the room.

"Stay still." The soft command came from a pleasant-looking woman dressed in a white lab coat worn over a floor-length floral dress. "Hello, Lucy," she said. "I am Dr. Benjai, and this is Karen. We're going to take a look at you and see how you're doing." While Karen hovered close by, the doctor gently brushed back her hair to check her injured forehead. "I heard you were in an accident. I see you bumped your head and hurt your arm. Tell me what happened."

Gabriel fidgeted in his seat while he waited for what seemed like forever. Was Lucy all right? He abandoned his chair to pace, his anxiety increasing with each step he took. His left leg burned with every movement, but he didn't care. He was more worried that he had injured her further when he'd lifted her from her buggy.

As he reached one end of the room and turned back, he sensed that others inside the waiting room were staring at him, but he didn't care. He resisted the urge to tug down his hat brim in an attempt to hide his face.

He heard the swish of the glass automatic entry doors opening and looked up. Bert had entered the care center, his gaze searching the room. When he saw him, he headed in Gabriel's direction. "Drove your buggy home." He shoved his hair from his forehead, briefly calling attention to his tattooed hand. "Fred tied up the mare by the barn. Made sure she had water before he left."

"Appreciate it," Gabriel said gratefully. "What can I do to repay you?"

Bert looked horrified by the notion. "Nothing, Gabe," he replied, his voice gruff. "Just glad to help." He nodded toward the reception desk. "How is she doing?"

"I haven't heard yet. She said her right side and arm hurt, but otherwise she feels fine."

Bert nodded. "Good thing she's getting checked out, being pregnant and all." He peered through the glass doors, his hand shielding his face from the sunlight. He was grinning as he faced Gabriel. "I called a friend of mine in the towing business. We were able to push the buggy onto his flatbed. It wasn't easy, 'cause there's something wrong with the axle. Told him to bring her to Lapp's place in Happiness." He paused. "You got a cell phone?"

"Nay." He'd been meaning to get one for business reasons. He made toys and wooden crafts to sell on consignment in area shops. Cell phones were never allowed in his former church district in Ohio, but he hadn't been planning to start up a business then so it hadn't mattered. Here it was permitted, but only for work, never personal reasons. And for emergencies. Lucy needed one, too, he thought. She didn't know him, but still he'd have to convince her to get one, especially being pregnant.

"He'll call with an estimate. I'll stop by and let you know what he says." The big man grinned. "I know where you live now."

Surprise made his face flush. Bert thought that he and Lucy were related. He didn't bother to correct him, although he knew he should. It would be too awkward to confess the truth that Lucy and he were strangers after the way he'd stayed by her side.

Something hit him square in the chest. *Because I'm worried about her*, he told himself. He barely knew her, but now he knew she was his neighbor. He'd moved to New Berne two months ago, but except for arranging consignments and delivering his work to stores, he'd kept mainly to himself.

Gabriel was grateful that the large, kind man covered in tattoos had cared for their horses and vehicles. "If there is anything I can do for you…"

Bert waved his hand in dismissal. "Na. I'm good. It was nice meeting you, Gabe. You and Lucy." His hazel eyes held regret. "Wish it'd been under better circumstances."

"Me, too, Bert. I don't know what we would have done without you."

The man actually blushed. "You would have managed."

"Not as well."

Bert nodded as he turned to leave. "You take care of your girl."

"Bert!" Gabriel called after him, ignoring his comment about his relationship with Lucy. "Will you ask Eli Lapp to leave a message for Lucy about her buggy at King's General Store?"

"Will do. I know the place," Bert assured him. He started toward the door then halted. "How're you getting home?"

"I'll call for a car."

Bert handed him a card. "Here's my number. Call me. I'll come back with my car instead of my pickup. It won't take long for me to come."

"Thank you." Grateful, Gabriel tucked the card beneath his suspender strap near the waistband of his pants.

Without the distraction of the Good Samaritan, Gabriel started to pace again. Step by step, he went over everything that had happened since he'd come upon the scene of Lucy's accident. He felt warmth in his chest as he recalled Lucy pleading with him with her eyes as she'd asked him to ride in the ambulance with her. He liked that she'd needed him, but that didn't mean anything. He was simply being neighborly. Of course, before today he hadn't known she was his neighbor.

Gabriel felt the familiar pins and needles in his leg that meant he'd overused it. He took a seat and rubbed his thigh, prepared to wait for as long as it took until Lucy was released and he could take her home. It was close to noon. He was a little hungry, and despite what she was enduring, he wondered if she'd want to eat once she was released. He'd left the house after a quick cup of coffee and a muffin to make two early morning deliveries on the other side of New Berne before restocking his supply of wood for his shop at the lumberyard. He'd been on his way home when he'd spied Lucy's buggy off the road. After Bert took them to Lucy's, he'd take his buggy to pick up sandwiches. It would be the neighborly thing to do.

What would he do if she were admitted to the hospital? First, he'd tell her sister-in-law as promised. It was possible her family would step in to take care of everything while she recovered. If not, he could ask his sister to help care for Lucy's child.

His leg prickled, making him tense up. He took several deep, calming breaths to relax. The pain would get better. It had to. Lucy would be released soon, then he'd ride home with her so she could rest before he headed over to tell her sister-in-law. Everything would be all right. It had to be. If Lucy wanted her daughter home, he could get Susie for her. As long as the burn in his leg didn't worsen.

It had been a long time since he'd prayed or been to church service. Not since before the fire that had taken his parents and his three other siblings. There had been complications with his burns and the skin grafting surgery that he'd needed, which had extended his recovery time in the hospital and at the uncle's house where he and his only surviving sister Emily had lived until Gabriel had sold their family's farm property and moved with her to New Berne. Although he'd been here almost two months, he hadn't been able to bring himself to attend church in his new community yet. He hated the stares, the looks of pity or dismay whenever someone new saw him. But he could pray. Surprised by the strength of his desire to pray, Gabriel closed his eyes and sent up a silent prayer to *Gott* that Lucy was all right.

Just as he was opening his eyes, a door opened, revealing the back area where she had been taken over an hour ago. Lucy came out, walking gingerly on her own with an Ace bandage around her right wrist to her forearm and carrying a small medicine bottle. The cut on her forehead was barely visible.

Relieved, Gabriel got up and approached her. Her blue eyes brightened when she spotted him. He felt a startling tenderness toward her as her mouth curved up when he reached her. "How did you make out?" he asked.

"*Gut. Danki* for waiting."

"I was worried about you." He settled his gaze briefly on her pregnant belly. "Are you ready to go?" he asked gently.

"*Ja*, I'm done." Grimacing, she held up her bandaged wrist. "The doctor said it's not broken but sprained. It should be fine in a couple of days." She settled a hand against her belly, clearly something she did often during her pregnancy. "I'm in *gut* shape, considering."

Gabriel was relieved. "Thanks be to *Gott*," he murmured. He gestured toward the glass entry doors. "Bert's going to give us a ride. Why don't you sit for a minute while I call him?" When Lucy nodded, he helped her into a chair then hurried to ask the receptionist if he could use the phone.

Bert arrived five minutes after Gabriel's call. "I was across the street, picking up a few groceries."

Gabriel thanked him, and Lucy smiled. "That's kind of you," she said.

The man smiled. "I'm parked up front."

"Are you ready to go?" Gabriel asked her.

"*Ja.*" She pushed herself up, wobbled on her feet. He steadied her. "Are you sure you're *oll recht*?"

She beamed at him. "I'm fine."

He slipped his arm through hers and led her through the doors to where Bert had parked his car, a silver four-door sedan. Gabriel instinctively reached to open the car door for her. Lucy glanced back to lock gazes with him. He felt the sharp impact of her bright blue eyes and attempted to smile, but she quickly averted her gaze. Leaning forward, he held the door open to let her pass. As she brushed close to him, he became aware of the scent of vanilla and honey intermingled with a light fragrance unique to Lucy.

Gabriel was conscious of the warmth of her skin as he clasped her arm and lowered her carefully inside.

He couldn't help but notice how her eyes glittered in a pale face as he got into the back seat. "It won't take long to get you home and more comfortable."

She nodded and tentatively touched her right side with her left hand but stopped when she saw him looking.

After a short journey, Bert pulled into Lucy's driveway and parked.

"Thanks, Bert," Gabriel said. He handed him some money. "For gas."

Bert brushed it aside. "Nope. I'm good." He glanced toward Lucy. "You take care of yourself, Lucy."

She smiled at him. "I will."

"You still have my card?" Bert asked.

"*Ja*, I've got it," Gabriel said.

"Call if you need anything."

He got out of the car and then, mindful of her injuries, carefully helped Lucy. Once she was steady on her feet, he leaned into the car's open window. "I appreciate it," Gabriel said.

Lucy started toward the house as Bert drove away. As he turned to follow her, he twisted his ankle, sending shooting pain up his left leg. Not wanting to alarm Lucy, he breathed through it. Following behind her, he rubbed his thigh, relieved as it quickly diminished to a burn and then a prickle.

"Would you like something to drink? I have iced tea, lemonade or something hot if you'd prefer," she said as she unlocked the door and stepped inside. He tried not to hobble as he followed her.

"Are you hungry?" he asked, glad his pain had eased. "Would you like me to get some sandwiches?"

"*Danki* but *nay*. I'm not hungry, but I could drink tea."

He stopped and looked around. Almost every available space was filled with baked goods—cakes, pies, bar and regular cookies. "What's all this?"

Looking tired, Lucy ran a hand across her forehead. "Baked goods," she said. "I've arranged to sell them on consignment at King's General Store and Peter's Pockets. I was supposed to deliver these this morning."

"It smells amazing in here," he said. "I'm sure they'll sell well."

"I hope so." Lucy grabbed the teakettle and filled it with water. She shifted to move it to the stove and wobbled unsteadily on her feet.

Gabriel was quick to take it from her hands. "Sit down, *ja*?" he urged gently as he eased her into the nearest chair. "You had an accident. You need to rest. I'll take care of this for you."

"*Danki,*" she whispered, her face pale. She sat and pushed a few of the packaged bakery items out of the way so there was room at the kitchen table for their tea.

Looking at all the cakes and pies and other baked goods, Gabriel realized they would go to waste if they weren't delivered.

"I can take these for you," he offered casually, gesturing with his hand as he leaned back against the counter facing her. The teakettle whistled, and he turned to take it off the heat. "What do you take in your tea?" When she didn't answer, he looked to find her gaping at him. "What's wrong?"

"Did you just say you'd make my deliveries?"

He hid a grin. "Cups?" he asked, opening cabinet doors. "Here we are." He pulled out two mugs and set them on the counter. "Sugar? Milk?" He faced her.

Lucy hadn't moved. "Why would you offer to make my deliveries?"

"Because you're hurt, and I can." He realized it was true. Because of the scar on his face, he didn't like being around a lot of people. They had a tendency to stare whenever they saw him. He usually made his deliveries early to avoid times when the store was busy, but he would do this for Lucy...because she needed him to. "I make toys and wooden crafts that I sell on consignment, so I understand what you want to do. I have a standing arrangement with both stores, so sit, drink your tea, and then let me do this for you."

He saw her swallow hard. "I don't know what to say." She looked stunned by his offer, which made him feel good.

"How about 'I like sugar in my tea'?"

"Gabriel—"

"Rest, Lucy." He quirked an eyebrow. "Tea bags?"

"In the tin on the counter behind you." She shook her head.

"Milk or cream?"

She scowled. "Just sugar."

Stifling amusement, Gabriel fixed two cups of tea and placed one directly in front of her. He sat down to drink the other one. "As soon as I'm done, I'll start with your deliveries."

***

Watching him as he drank from his mug, Lucy shifted uncomfortably in her chair. He had offered to take her baked goods to the stores! She was relieved that everything wouldn't go to waste but she didn't know what to say. Gabriel Fisher, a man she'd never met before today, had rescued her not once but twice. His generosity was beginning to make her feel off-kilter. He would be making her deliveries after rescuing her from her accident, riding with her in the ambulance and staying to accompany her home. After today, she'd figure out a way to cope on her own while she recovered. She couldn't continue to rely on a stranger, even one she thought she could trust.

"Danki," she whispered as she stared into her steaming mug of tea that he'd fixed for her. She took a sip. "It's…*gut.* Just how I like it."

Gabriel's slow smile made her heart beat harder. "Something we have in common. I drink it the same way."

Sipping from her tea, Lucy studied him. He had taken off his hat and set it on the wall hook by the door. Her gaze settled on the scar on his cheek, and it did nothing to take away from his attractive masculine features. Although he was somewhat closed off, she was so comfortable with him that it felt like he was a friend rather than a stranger. She had to remind herself that she didn't know him.

He glanced up suddenly. "You look tired." He narrowed his gaze. "Do you want your pain medicine?"

She shook her head. "I'm fine."

His chair was perpendicular to hers at the table, and Gabriel moved it closer. "You need to relax and let me handle things for you today," he said, his expression intense as he studied her. "Your head hurts, and you've sprained your wrist."

Lucy blushed and averted her gaze. "I've taken too much of your time. I need to learn to manage on my own."

His heavy sigh drew her attention back to his expression. "What bothers you about accepting help? Or is it just mine that bothers you?"

She felt her cheeks heat. *"Nay,"* she whispered. "I'm grateful for your help, but I can't..." Unable to explain, Lucy stared into her teacup. "I asked too much of you already." She thought of her father, a man who should have loved her but clearly didn't.

She trusted Gabriel. He couldn't let her down if she didn't spend more time with him.

"Lucy."

Jerked from her thoughts, she blinked and met Gabriel's gaze. She had the strongest urge to tell him about her past.

"You're in pain." His voice was gentle, reminding her of things she'd once wanted from marriage but would never have now. "I think you should take one pill." He stood as if to get it for her.

"Nay." Lucy shut her eyes against the concern in his gaze.

"Then finish your tea," he quietly urged. "I'll clean up when we're done so you can nap."

"I don't need a nap."

Gabriel stopped to stare at her and Lucy shifted uncomfortably. "Fine," she said. "I'll rest but I doubt I'll sleep."

His small smirk suggested he thought otherwise.

"What time do we need to leave for Susie?" He arched an eyebrow. "You do want her home, *ja*?"

She sighed, resigned to the fact she needed his help. Again. "About six." Lucy couldn't control a yawn and then shot him a glance.

He continued to watch her with amusement. "I'll be back before then. How far do we have to go?"

She hesitated, concerned about what Nancy might say after seeing her with Gabriel. "You don't have to come back. I can get her. If you hitch up my horse for me, I can take my wagon."

A scowl darkened his features. "You cannot steer a wagon safely with a sprained wrist—and you have to be sore after the accident." His lips firmed. "I'll be here by five thirty."

She knew he was right, but she didn't want to admit it. "Gabriel… I appreciate everything you've done, but—"

"I will be here at five thirty," he repeated firmly, his expression brooking no argument. "You can tell me where to go then."

His intent stare made her back off. "Fine, I'll accept your help, but I'll owe you."

They finished their tea in silence. Lucy again fought the urge to learn more about him, about his past. His scar. The stiffness in his gait she'd noticed, as if he'd struggled to walk, when he'd exited Bert's car and approached the house.

Gabriel stood slowly and collected their dishes. "I enjoyed the tea and the company."

Lucy blushed. "Me, too." To her shock, he carried the mugs to the sink to wash. "You are *not* washing the dishes!"

He captured her gaze over his shoulder. "I will because I *want* to. And it's only two mugs." The retort she would have made died on her lips as he filled up the dish basin then washed the mugs before stacking them in the drying rack. She must have made a sound as he reached for a dish towel, because he faced her with narrowed eyes. "Go rest, Lucy," he urged gently. "I'll dry them, pack up your baked goods, and lock up before I leave."

Lucy had to admit that she did feel tired. Now that she'd enjoyed her tea, it seemed as if the morning had caught up with her, and she'd lost all of her energy. She knew her pregnancy often made her tired, but this exhaustion, she realized, was a direct result of the accident.

A dish towel over his shoulder, Gabriel leaned back against the counter with his arms folded and stared at her. "Go lie down, Lucy."

She sighed. *"Oll recht,"* she grumbled. "I'll go upstairs."

His features softened with approval. "I'll be back at five thirty."

She nodded, grateful that he'd offered to get Susie with her. She wanted her little girl home. Susie's smiles and hugs always made her feel better.

As she climbed the stairs wearily, she could visualize Gabriel drying the mugs then putting them away. He amazed her with everything he'd done for her. Harley had never been that helpful, believing that men's and women's work remained separate. She couldn't find it in herself to blame Harley for the way he was— or for anything that had happened in their relationship. Their marriage had been a convenience, and it had gone fairly well, considering Harley had been grieving his late wife when the two of them had wed. About a month before his death, Harley had softened toward her, and Lucy thought their marriage had become something more. They'd grown close enough to conceive a child. But then Harley had become a different person, bitter and riddled with guilt that he'd betrayed the memory of his beloved late wife.

As she settled in bed under the covers, Lucy smiled as she thought again about Gabriel and his rescuing her. It left her wanting to know more about him.

Chapter Three

Lucy had napped, freshened up, eaten a sandwich and was icing her wrist when she heard the sound of buggy wheels on asphalt filter in through an open window. She removed the ice pack and placed it in the freezer to use again later. Opening the door, she watched with a small smile as Gabriel climbed from his vehicle and approached.

His expression was unreadable as he reached her. "Lucy. I hope you were able to rest."

"Too much, I'm afraid. I slept the afternoon away." She stepped back as he walked into the house.

"You needed it. You'll heal more quickly if you get enough sleep." She knew the exact moment when he noticed her Ace bandage on the table. "Shouldn't you be wearing that?"

"I was following the doctor's orders. Icing it to keep the swelling down."

"Do you need any pain medicine?"

Lucy shook her head. "*Nay*, I feel *oll recht*."

His gaze narrowed as he looked at her. "Take the medicine if you are in pain, Lucy. *Please*. Don't wait until you're hurting, because it will be more difficult for the medicine to work if you do."

She widened her eyes at his entreaty. He was acting like he was worried about her. "*Oll recht*. I'll take it if I need it."

Gabriel gave her a nod of approval. "I made your deliveries. Mary King and John Zook were glad to get them. They'll let you know when they need more."

"*Danki*," she said, blinking rapidly. He had no idea how much he'd helped her by doing that for her. She got herself under control. "If they sell well, then I'll be able to restock and have a good business with them."

"I may be able to help with some of the stores I do business with regularly if you are interested." He didn't wait for her to reply and she was glad, feeling overly emotional. "Are you ready to go?" he asked quietly, as if he'd sensed her mood.

"*Ja*, I miss my *dochter*. I'm not used to her being gone."

"Let me help you with your Ace bandage." He picked it up, ready to put it on for her.

Lucy shook her head. "I'd rather not wear it. I'll put it on after I get back." She bit her lip. "I don't want to worry them," she said.

His brow cleared. "Let's bring it in case you need it, *ja*?" He picked it up, and she scowled at him, which made him arch an eyebrow.

Minutes later, Gabriel helped her into his buggy then skirted the vehicle to the driver's side. "Where are we headed?" he asked as he climbed in.

Lucy reluctantly gave him the address.

Gabriel flashed her a glance. "What's wrong?"

"Nothing."

"Lucy."

"I don't like taking so much of your time and—"

"And?" He waited for her answer.

"My sister-in-law—"

"You don't know how she'll react to me," he said, his voice flat.

"I'm worried about what she'll say when she sees you with me."

"I guess we'll see," Gabriel murmured, pain flashing briefly in his brown eyes before he flicked the reins and urged the horse pulling his buggy toward the road.

It wasn't his looks that would concern Nancy. It was Nancy's reaction to seeing her brother's widow with another man, someone she'd never met.

The scar across Gabriel's face was raised and jagged, and Lucy realized he must have suffered greatly when he'd gotten hurt. She wanted to know how he'd been hurt, but she didn't feel comfortable asking, since they'd met only that morning.

"Gabriel, this isn't about your scar," she said softly. "'Tis because I'm a widow, and Nancy is my late husband's sister."

He shot her a quick glance but didn't say a word, and she wondered if by mentioning his scar she'd made things worse for him instead of better.

Gabriel could feel the tension rise within him as he guided his horse down the lane leading to Lucy's sister-in-law's property. As the residence came into view, he saw two girls and a boy burst out of the side door, laughing as they ran into the yard. They raced in circles before running up the steps to reenter the house.

His jaw felt tight as he anticipated the children's reactions to his face and the ugly burn scar that marred his left cheek. Seeing adults' reactions was bad enough. Children had a tendency to be outspoken and truthful.

"Stay where you are until I can help you get out," he said brusquely.

"Gabriel." Her tone made him hesitate to study her before climbing down. "I don't want them to know about the accident." She seemed on the verge of tears. *"Please,"* she entreated.

"I understand." And he did. "But I can still help you. No one will think any less of you for accepting help." He kept his tone gentle. "'Tis a simple courtesy."

"My husband never…" She looked away. Finally, she inclined her head in agreement, then gazed through the buggy's windshield, staring toward the house where the children had disappeared.

"He never offered to help you?" he asked with a frown and a quick glance at her baby belly. "But you're—"

Meeting his gaze, Lucy gave him a small smile as she settled a hand over her pregnant belly. "He never knew. I was only a month along, and I didn't even know."

"I'm sorry for your loss."

She looked momentarily startled but then nodded.

Gabriel climbed down and drew a calming breath. Trying to control his increasing anxiety, he tied up his horse and looked around. Horses grazed within the white-fenced paddock. The weather vane on top of the red barn pointing east moved gently with the light breeze. In the distance, he noted a windmill, the blades spinning in slow motion. He circled the buggy and extended a hand to her.

Uncertainty flickered in her expression as, mindful of her injuries, he carefully helped her down. He immediately released her and turned his attention briefly toward the house.

"Would you like to wait here while I get her?" Lucy asked.

"I will if you want me to."

She exhaled slowly then nodded as if coming to a decision. "I don't mind if you come in with me." She bit her lower lip. "I'd like that, actually."

"Oll recht." Adjusting his hat, he studied the house before turning to Lucy. "Your *dochter* will be happy to see you," he said with a small smile. But not him. More people than not were frightened by his looks. Lizzy, his own betrothed, had broken up with him while he was in the hospital, trying to recover. She'd taken one look at the bright red burn across his face, then at the horrible mass of red, blistered and raw skin along the length of his left leg, and decided that he would never be able to provide for her. He was too injured and damaged to ever farm as planned.

The fire and subsequent breakup had changed him. Mistrustful of love and damaged physically, Gabriel had given up the hope of having a future that included a wife and family. Still, the longing lingered.

Her eyes bright, Lucy approached the house, clearly eager to see her daughter. The door opened again and the two girls he'd seen earlier exited the house, chuckling as they glanced over their shoulders. When the boy appeared at the door, the girls shrieked and raced into the backyard. Gabriel stopped, feeling ill at ease as he waited for Susie to notice them.

The door swung open, and the woman who must

be Lucy's sister-in-law stepped outside with a smile. "Susie will sleep *gut* tonight. They've been running all day." She frowned slightly when her gaze settled briefly on Gabriel until the children came back into the side yard, shrieking and running in circles with the boy chasing the two girls.

"Nancy, this is Gabriel Fisher," Lucy said, turning toward him with a smile that warmed him. "He lives down the street from us."

"Gabriel." Nancy glanced away from his scar to meet his gaze before looking with curiosity at Lucy.

"Nancy, it seems like Lucy's daughter has been having a *wunderbor* time," Gabriel said, drawing Nancy's attention.

The woman softened her expression and smiled. "*Ja*, she's been having fun."

"*Mam!*" Seeing Lucy, Susie grinned and threw herself into her mother's arms. Gabriel saw Lucy wince as her daughter hugged her hard. "I missed you!"

"I missed you, *dochter*," Lucy murmured. "The *haus* is not the same without you." She shifted her daughter to keep her close in a one-armed hug. Her gaze fell on her niece and softened. "*Hallo*, Sarah." The older girl nodded in greeting. "It was nice of you to spend the day with your cousin," she said, her lips curving up with warmth.

Susie jerked away from her. "You come to take me home?"

"*Ja*. Are you ready to go?"

Susie bobbed her head as a boy approached and stood by his mother. She turned and spied Gabriel standing beside Lucy. "*Hallo*," she greeted, gazing at him with curiosity. She smiled. "Did you come with my *mudder*?"

"He did," Lucy said, her expression soft. "This is Gabriel and he's our new neighbor." She smiled in his direction before turning back to her daughter. "Did you have a nice time?"

"*Ja!* Sarah and I played horse, and I got to pick wildflowers in the fields." The little girl grinned. "And then we played tag with Caleb being it!"

"It sounds like you had fun."

"I did, *Mam*. Caleb thought he'd catch me when I ran, but he couldn't!" Susie flashed her cousin an impish look. "Maybe next time." She lowered her voice as she faced them. "I think he is tired, *Mam*. Maybe that's why he can't run as fast as me."

Her gaze gentling, Lucy turned to Nancy's son. "*Hallo*, Caleb."

"Lucy." A little quirk of Caleb's lips told Gabriel that the boy had been humoring his little cousin. Caleb met his gaze, and Gabriel was pleased when Caleb didn't reactive negatively to his facial scar.

Lucy returned her attention to her daughter. "I'm glad you had a *gut* time today." She met Nancy's gaze as she placed her left arm around Susie. "*Danki* for keeping her, *schweschter*."

Nancy didn't answer, because her gaze had settled on Gabriel again before she dragged it away, back to Lucy. "She's a pleasure to have. My *kinner* certainly enjoy when she's visiting." She followed as Lucy and Gabriel moved toward his buggy. "Say *hallo* to Joseph for me," Lucy said.

Susie stared at Gabriel a long moment, then she reached for his right hand. Touched by the child's gesture, Gabriel allowed their fingers to entwine while Lucy did the same with her little girl's other hand. Once close to his vehicle, Gabriel let go of Susie's hand to lift her onto the buggy seat. Then he held out his right hand to Lucy, who grabbed hold and allowed him to help her in, as well.

Susie waved vigorously to Sarah and Caleb. Gabriel noticed that Nancy didn't wave or say a word as he picked up the leathers. She was too busy eyeing them thoughtfully.

"I'll see you at service!" Lucy called out the window.

Nancy smiled. "Bring your upside-down chocolate cake! 'tis Joseph's favorite."

"I will!" Lucy replied loudly.

With the click of his tongue and a flick of the reins, Gabriel steered his horse onto the road. Lucy went silent beside him. He chanced a glance at her and their gazes met. He couldn't tell how she was feeling.

"*Mam*, I'm hungry," Susie said, drawing their attention. "Can I have ice cream?"

Gabriel met Lucy's gaze and whispered, "Brubaker's Creamery isn't far. I'll buy."

"Ice cream sounds *gut*," she murmured, "but I can pay." She hesitated. "I owe you."

He opened his mouth to object, but then closed it again. He didn't argue. There was no point. He'd only upset her, and she'd already suffered a trying day. She shifted in her seat as if she was hurting. "It won't take long," he said, sympathetic to her pain, his pleasure dimming with his concern for her.

She nodded then looked over her shoulder at Susie.

"Gabriel is going to take us to a *gut* place for ice cream. We'll get it and bring it home to eat."

In response, Susie clapped her hands and bounced in her seat. "We're getting ice cream!"

"Sit still, *dochter*," Lucy scolded. "You mustn't distract Gabriel's attention from the road. We don't want to have an accident, *ja*?"

"Ja, Mam." Susie sat still, but the grin on Lucy's face as she turned to the front told her that Susie was happy as well as obedient.

Her grin vanished as Lucy locked gazes with him. The memory of her accident earlier hung heavily in the air between them. Gabriel offered her a kind, understanding smile. Recalling her fear and injuries— and the way he'd felt when he'd found her—made the accident a harsh reality, one they wouldn't forget anytime soon.

Later that night Gabriel entered his workshop and set his battery-powered light on his workbench. He loved the smell of wood, sawdust and varnish. He loved working with wood, felt like he was born to woodcraft, and he would never have thought to make a living from a hobby if it hadn't been for the fire. He was supposed to take over the family farm, but the loss of his family, the destruction of the farmhouse and the physical impracticality of farming because of his damaged leg had changed all that. It didn't matter that he couldn't farm. He liked what he did now. *Gott* had gifted him with a skill he enjoyed and the means to earn a living.

Gabriel thought of Susie Schwartz, Lucy's daughter. Her innocent acceptance of him had tugged at his heart. He wanted to make something special for the little girl, and he needed better light than the diminishing daylight. Despite all that had happened that day, he'd enjoyed his time with her and Lucy when they'd eaten ice cream earlier. Susie had chosen the creamery's triple chocolate flavor, and he loved the way chocolate had lined her little mouth while she ate. He'd chosen rocky road, and Lucy had eaten chocolate chip mint. Several times he and Lucy exchanged smiles over Susie's antics. Lucy's daughter was a warm, loving child, and it made Gabriel happy yet sad for himself, that he'd never enjoy one of his own.

He picked up a piece of basswood and eyed it carefully then set it down. Catching sight of a block of birch, Gabriel knew what he wanted to do. He'd make Susie a waddling duck toy from birch, pine and basswood.

Suddenly, a shooting pain hit his thigh, and he cried out. Gasping, eyes tearing, he grabbed onto the stool near his workbench and sat down. He rubbed the scarred flesh, hoping for relief. He knew he'd overdone it today with Lucy's rescue and then remaining constantly on the move. It had been six months since the pain had been this bad.

In the first months he'd been released from the hospital after the fire, he'd suffer an attack in the evening or middle of the night after too much activity. For the last six months, he'd no longer suffered the unbearable stabbing pains that wore him out, enduring only paresthesia—the sensation of pins and needles that felt more manageable to him. The progress had made him sure that his leg was improving. Until now.

When the sharp pain didn't subside, Gabriel gave up trying to work and gingerly got down from the stool, stumbling as his pain worsened. He fumbled for his lantern and staggered out of his shop then hobbled, crying out with each step he took until he finally reached the house. "Emily!"

His sister looked up from the kitchen table where she was mending one of his shirts, her frown immediately turning to an expression of concern as she saw him through the screen door.

"Ach nay, bruder!" She sprang up to open the door and helped him into a chair, then grabbed a second chair to prop up both of his legs. Without another word, she went to a cabinet and pulled out a bottle of over-the-counter medication.

"That's not going to help," he said through gritted teeth.

"Take it anyway, Gabriel," she cried, her green eyes filling with tears. "*Please!* It certainly can't hurt." She shoved two pills and a glass of water at him, watching as he took the medicine. "What else can we do?"

"I don't know," he gasped. Gabriel rubbed his thigh, grimacing as he massaged the scarred tissue. Rubbing it didn't help this time, but he didn't know what else to do.

Emily spun and grabbed two dish towels from a drawer. She wet the tea towel under cold water from the faucet, then hurried back to Gabriel. "Do you want me to cut your pant leg?" she asked, clearly upset.

"Nay, I don't want to ruin them."

After a nod, his sister lay the wet tea towel lengthwise over the tri-blend fabric covering the worst area of his damaged leg, from his thigh to his knee. "I don't know if this will help," she murmured.

With a groan, he released his leg, leaning forward

to bury his head in his hands, praying for the pain to stop. Because it hurt so badly now, he knew his muscles would continue to be sore afterward. His leg was scarred and ugly under his clothes, but he could live with the way it looked. It wasn't as if anyone would see it anyway. But this type of pain was unbearable— a reminder of everything he'd lost during the fire that had stolen family from him and Emily. A reminder that he was a damaged man. The fire still gave him nightmares, although those had gotten a little better since they'd moved to New Berne.

"What else can I do?" Emily eyed him with concern.

He opened his eyes, leaned back in his chair. "Nothing. You know how it is. It will eventually ease on its own." And praise the Lord, it was easing. The sharpness of the pain had morphed into a dull throb and then the familiar burning sensation of pins and needles.

"I thought you were over this," Emily said. "Maybe we should ask the doctor for pain medicine—"

"Nay." Gabriel knew the pills wouldn't help. By the time the medicine got into his system, the pain usually had diminished already. He'd needed the pills during his second-degree burn treatments and again after his surgeries, and the medication had helped then. "'Tis *oll recht*, Em. 'Tis getting better."

Emily closed her eyes briefly, and when she opened them again, he saw relief in them, but it was mingled with deep concern. Her expression was one he knew only too well after seeing it enough times after he was released from the hospital.

"Maybe you need to see the neurologist," she said. "There could be a new treatment available."

He nodded. "I'll stop by to make an appointment in the morning."

She jerked a nod. *"Gut."* She picked up the wet towel and placed the dry terry cloth one over the area to soak up the dampness. "I know it didn't help much, but I had to do something," she said quietly. "And maybe the ibuprofen will help with your sore muscles now that the worst has passed."

Gabriel reached out to grab her hand. "I appreciate what you did." He managed a small smile. "We'll both sleep well tonight," he stated, hoping that it was true.

"Ja." She squeezed the wet tea towel over the sink. "I can take you to Dr. Jorgensen's office to schedule your appointment tomorrow morning if you'd like."

"Nay. I'll be fine by then. If I'm not, I'll let you take me."

Emily smiled weakly. "Make sure you do."

He gently eased his leg off the chair. "I think I'll head to bed." He struggled to rise and was glad to find the worst of the pain was gone.

"You'll sleep downstairs tonight," she told him.

He nodded. He didn't want to do anything that might aggravate his leg. He started toward the great room and the small bed he'd made. He slept downstairs whenever he was too tired or sore to go up to his bedroom.

"Gabriel?" Emily's voice stopped him. "I think you've been doing too much, making those deliveries yesterday. Maybe 'tis time to think about opening your own shop. You've been wanting to. Why wait? We still have some of the money from selling the farm, *ja?"*

"Ja, but—"

"No buts, it's time to look for a place. Or you could sell your things right from the *haus?* Think about it, *ja?"*

"I'll think about it," he promised. Since he'd turned his woodworking skills into making money for them, he'd envisioned eventually opening his own shop. Emily's suggestion that he sell his crafts right from home might work. It would certainly help with the problem of having to make deliveries to area merchants. But he didn't want strangers in his home, nor did he want them in his shop. Which meant he'd have to build a separate building or convert part of his barn where he and Emily could handle customers.

Working and selling close to home would be ideal for him, but he wasn't sure he was ready to invest the rest of the money they'd gotten from selling the farm property. There wasn't much. It was a blessing that he had any of it left. His Amish community in Ohio had been wonderful in helping with his medical bills, but he'd still paid a good share. Would it be wise to use the rest of the money? What if something went wrong with his leg again and he ended up in the hospital? It throbbed painfully, reminding him of the horrible weeks of burn care and failed surgeries until finally, months later, the skin grafts had taken.

As his mind tried to settle into a dark place, Gabriel forced himself to remember this morning when he'd helped Lucy. If faced with the same situation, he would carry her from the buggy again. Some things were worth suffering for afterward.

The next morning, he drove to the medical center and made an appointment. There'd been a cancellation, and he'd be seeing Dr. Jorgensen next Monday.

As soon as he got home, Gabriel returned to his workshop. He was feeling better, but the dull ache in his leg reminded him to take it easy. He set the supplies he needed on his workbench then pulled his stool closer so he could work. When he'd delivered Lucy's bakery items yesterday, both store owners had asked for more of his wooden toys and crafts.

Putting the idea of Susie's toy aside for now, he sat down and got to work. He decided to build two toy rocking horses, using the wood he'd brought home from the lumberyard yesterday. The rocking horses were popular with English customers. He cut out pieces for the heads, the bodies and the curved rails that would make them rock. He then sanded each piece of wood until he was pleased with their smoothness. Two hours later, he finished putting both horses together with dowels and wood glue. Tomorrow he'd paint on the eyes and mouth and add small pieces of leather for the ears and yarn for the mane and tail.

Gabriel looked around the workshop for material to decide what else to make. There was enough wood for a couple of birdhouses and a small shelf or two. He climbed off his stool and carefully reached for the wood, grabbing hold of one plank of pine. The muscles in his leg protested and stiffened to the point of pain. He huffed out a groan and straightened with wood in hand. He set it on his workbench and closed his eyes as he took a moment to focus on relaxing his seized leg.

"Gabriel!" His sister burst into the room, startling him, nearly making him tumble over.

He gasped and righted himself. "Emily! Can't you enter a room without scaring me to death?"

Emily frowned. "I'm sorry."

He softened. "What's wrong?"

"Nothing. I wanted to let you know that I've invited someone special to supper Thursday evening."

Two nights from now. He frowned. "Who?"

"His name is Aaron Hostetler, and I like him. A lot."

He hesitated before replying. His sister had a beau? He knew that someday Emily would marry and leave him, but he didn't want to think about that now. He told himself to stop worrying. He was getting ahead of himself. "How long have you known him?"

Emily blushed. "A few weeks?" She blinked. "*Oll recht*, almost a month."

Gabriel raised his eyebrows. They'd only moved here two months ago. He drew a calming breath. It was just supper, he reminded himself. He managed a smile. "I look forward to meeting him."

"What shall I cook?" she asked, suddenly looking agitated. "I don't know what to cook!"

He closed the distance between them and reached for his sister's hands. "If this man is interested in you, then he will love anything you make because you made it for him." He eyed her with affection as he released her. "I'm partial to your chicken potpie."

Tugging on her *kapp* string, she brightened. "Do you think he'll like it?"

"Your chicken potpie is the best I've ever eaten. I think you have nothing to worry about."

"I'll make that, then," Emily said with a smile. She spun and started to leave his workshop then halted. "And I'll bake lemon cake for dessert."

"Em!" he called as she ran toward the door. "What time is it?"

"'Tis half past two," she said.

Gabriel frowned as he watched Emily leave. He'd

been so involved with the work he was unaware of how much time had passed.

Thursday afternoon Emily would want his help before her beau's arrival. He knew his sister well enough to tell she was worried that he and her new beau wouldn't get along. But Gabriel was prepared to look kindly on the man as long as Aaron didn't mistreat his sister and his feelings for Emily were genuine.

Emily was his only surviving family and she meant the world to him. Since they'd moved here, he'd been content to earn a living so he could take care of his sister.

But something odd had happened to him since Lucy's accident. He felt…drawn to the pretty widow. He'd made a friend. He should stop in to see how she was doing.

It bothered him that he missed seeing her after only one day. His leg was a problem for him, but that didn't mean he couldn't enjoy a friendship with her and her daughter. Being friends was fine, he decided. He could avoid friends when his pain—and his nightmares—got out of hand.

Thinking about mother and daughter had him eager to check in with them. Lucy was pretty, a wonderful mother and someone with a good heart. And Susie was a delight. Clearly unbothered by his face, Susie had smiled at him frequently while they'd eaten ice cream. He was glad to know they were his neighbors. He could head over to see them. If they were busy, he'd leave.

Friendly neighbors, he could do.

Chapter Four

"*Mam*, why is that on your hand?" Susie asked as Lucy re-pinned her child's long blond hair after a busy morning of Susie playing outside. The little girl's prayer *kapp* had long been tossed aside during her daughter's antics. She'd stood and spun until she got dizzy and fell, only to do it all over again. Was it any wonder her dress had become soiled and her hair a mess? *"Mam?"*

Last night Lucy had rewrapped her wrist after her daughter had gone to bed. She'd managed to make breakfast without the Ace bandage, but her wrist had started to ache afterward. "I hurt it, but it's getting better. This keeps me from bumping it again."

Her child glanced up at her, her blue eyes filled with concern. "I'm sorry you got hurt."

"I know you are, *dochter*," she said with affection. She tugged playfully on a lock of Susie's hair.

"When did you bump it?"

"Yesterday."

Susie looked puzzled but didn't ask how. Lucy was relieved.

"Turn around, *dochter*, so I can finish fixing your

hair." With the bandage wrapped around her wrist more firmly, she could more easily manage a few chores. Lucy continued to brush her daughter's golden locks, then pulled her hair into a bun and secured it with hairpins. She didn't bother with Susie's head covering. Today was wash day and she would wash her daughter's *kapp* and dress with the rest of their garments before she hung them to dry on the clothesline in her backyard. She decided to throw her *kapp* in the wash as well and took it off, replacing it with her black kerchief.

"Can we see Gabriel today?" Susie asked as she descended the stairs slowly, her bare feet silent on them.

"I don't think so, Susie. He is probably busy today," Lucy said as they reached the bottom. She was amazed how quickly her daughter had taken to Gabriel.

"He's our neighbor. If he's not busy, he can come over?" Her little girl gazed at her hopefully as they entered the kitchen.

"*Ja,* if he's not busy, but we can't expect him." Lucy settled her daughter in a chair and pushed her closer to the table. "Do you want a sandwich?"

Susie wiggled in her chair. "Can I have cornflakes for lunch?" She grinned while Lucy fixed her cereal with milk and set it before her. "Can we visit Gabriel if he doesn't come here?"

"I don't know, *dochter.*" She had mixed feelings about seeing Gabriel again. She'd missed him since he'd left last evening, but she couldn't expect him to visit just because she wanted him to. *He is my neighbor,* she reminded herself. *And I'm grateful for all he's done.* What if she made him a treat to thank him? They could stop briefly by his house and deliver it. "Shall we make him a pie?"

"*Ja!* A chocolate pie!" Susie exclaimed, smacking the table in her excitement. "And we can bring it to him!"

Lucy nodded. "We can bring it to him, but that doesn't mean we'll stay." She knew where Gabriel lived. He'd pointed his house out to her as they passed it when he'd taken her and Susie home after ice cream.

While Susie ate, Lucy checked to see if she had everything she needed for the pie. Thankfully she did, so there was no reason to go to the store.

Three hours later, Lucy pulled a pie shell from the oven. She had sent Susie upstairs an hour ago to play quietly in her room after her child had become whiny while rolling out the pie dough. She'd checked on Susie a half hour ago and found her asleep in her bed, and Lucy had completed some household chores.

With the pie crust cooling on the rack on the counter, she assembled the ingredients for the filling, added them into a saucepan on the stove and stirred them together as they heated.

A loud knock on her door drew her attention. Lucy widened her eyes when she saw her late husband's best friend, Aaron Hostetler. "Aaron."

"*Hallo*, Lucy," he greeted with a smile. "May I come in?"

"*Ja.*" She pushed open the door and stepped back to allow him entry. He tugged off his hat and set it on her kitchen table. "Susie's fallen asleep," she told him. "She spent the day running with her cousins yesterday, and she's still tired."

Aaron's expression softened at the mention of her daughter. "I'm sure Sarah and Caleb kept her busy."

Lucy averted her gaze as she nodded. "*Ja*, they did."

The mixture in the saucepan on the stove started to boil. She rushed to turn off the burner, stirring the contents several times, and decided it was thick enough. She removed it from the stove and set it on a hot mat on the counter. "I'm in the middle of making a pie."

"Smells *gut*," he said. She turned, startled that he stood so close behind her. She must have gasped because he instantly stepped back.

"Special occasion?" he asked as she faced him.

"I'm making the pie for my neighbor." Lucy turned back to stir the chocolate cream before she dumped it into the baked pie shell. "Is there something you needed?"

"I just wanted to stop by."

"And so you did." She hoped her smile took the sting out of her reply.

He grew quiet, and she realized that something on the counter caught his attention. Her elastic bandage. She'd taken it off to work with the pie dough and forgotten to put it back on.

"What's that?" Aaron asked, his eyes widening.

"It's an Ace bandage. I use it for support while I'm doing chores."

His face turned pale. "It's not because of…"

She gaped at him. *"Nay."* She knew he was remembering the scar on her left arm.

Aaron looked relieved, which made her wonder why. "I should go. Will you tell Susie I stopped by?" He suddenly seemed anxious to leave.

Lucy managed a smile. "I will."

He grabbed his hat from the kitchen table and pulled open the door. "If you need anything…"

"I won't, but *danki*."

After taking two steps out the door, he turned to face her. "Lucy—"

"I am fine, Aaron. You need to stop feeling responsible for me—for us."

As soon as he'd left, Lucy released a sharp breath. Aaron had been a good friend during the weeks after Harley's death, she thought as she poured the chocolate cream into the pie shell, but she needed him to stop his worrying and move on with his life. She and Susie were fine.

It was late afternoon when Gabriel drove his buggy the half mile to Lucy's. If it weren't for his leg, he'd walk. It was a beautiful day for it. With each click of horse hooves against pavement, he felt his heart lighten at the prospect of seeing her again.

He frowned when he saw a man in a wagon leaving her property up ahead. Gabriel slowed his gelding. Who was that? he wondered, a sinking sensation setting in his chest. Probably the husband of a friend or neighbor. As he reached her driveway, he stepped on the brake before making the turn. After parking his vehicle close to the barn, he tied up his horse. Doubts crept in as he approached the house. He worried about being welcome—after all, they'd only met the day before. *But seeing if she is oll recht is the neighborly thing to do*, he reassured himself.

Heart racing, Gabriel raised his hand to the side door and knocked softly. His first thought as he waited for her to notice him was to ask her about the man, but he wouldn't because it was none of his business if she had a male visitor.

The interior door was open, leaving only the screen

door between him and inside. Shifting slightly, he leaned in and saw Lucy putting dishes in the sink. She hadn't heard him.

"Lucy?" he called softly as he knocked again.

She stiffened and faced the door. Her expression brightened when she saw him. "Gabriel, I didn't expect to see you today." She wiped her hands on a patchwork cooking apron as she approached with joy in her pretty blue eyes. "Come in."

"How are you feeling?" he asked, regarding her with concern as he pulled open the door and entered. The rich smell of chocolate permeated the air, making his mouth water.

"A little sore, but I'm managing."

He studied her carefully. "You're not overdoing it, are you?"

"*Nay,* I'm just doing what needs to be done."

Gabriel nodded. *"Gut."* He paused. "I just wanted to see how you were doing."

She gestured toward the kitchen table. "Have a seat. Susie's been napping but I need to wake her. If she sleeps too long, she won't when it's bedtime."

He took off his hat and hung it on a wall hook.

After a glance toward the counter, she met his gaze. "I'll be right back. Can I get you something to drink first?"

Gabriel shook his head and then watched as she left the room. He absently fingered the raised scar on his cheek as he listened to Lucy's soft footsteps on the stairs. Within moments, he smiled at the sound of a little girl's excited voice accompanied by the calm tone of her mother's as they came down the stairs.

Susie burst into the room ahead of her *mam.* "*Ga-*

briel! You're here!" Her pale blue eyes lit up as soon as she saw him.

"*Hallo*, Susie." He flashed her a grin. "It's nice to see you again." Narrowing his gaze, he studied her thoughtfully. "Have you gotten taller since I last saw you?"

"*Nay!*" She laughed. "I can't grow in one day!"

Amused, Gabriel arched an eyebrow. "Are you sure?"

The child bobbed her head. Susie sniffed the air, her little nose wrinkling as she faced her mother. "I smell chocolate. You finished it?"

Her gaze settling on him, Lucy nodded. "Gabriel, I made you a pie. I haven't had a chance to chill it yet. I hope you like chocolate cream."

Stunned, he could only look from her to the pie on the kitchen counter and back again. "You made me a pie?"

Her eyes sparkling with happiness, she inclined her head. "It's a thank-you for…" She blushed then looked quickly at her daughter. "You know."

"Lucy, you didn't have to do that. You don't owe me anything—" He stopped when he realized that Susie watched their exchange with curiosity.

"Don't you like chocolate pie?" Susie asked, her pale blue eyes wide with innocence.

"I love it, especially chocolate cream pie," he said, his lips curving.

"*Gut!*" the little girl cried. "'Cause it's *de-lish-us!*" She turned to her mother. "*Mam*, can I have a snack to hold me until supper?"

"*Ja*, if you'd like." She turned to Gabriel. "Would

you like some tea and cookies?" she asked, her lips twitching with amusement.

"I would. *Danki*," he said, surprising himself. He'd only planned to stay a few minutes, but the only place he wanted to be right now was here in Lucy Schwartz's house, enjoying a snack with her and her daughter.

She placed the pie in the refrigerator. When she reached into the pantry, probably for the cookies, Gabriel got up and put on the teakettle.

Her eyes widened when she saw what he had done. "Gabriel—"

"'Tis fine, Lucy." The teakettle whistled. He poured the hot water into two mugs and added tea bags while she opened a container and put cookies on a plate. Gabriel added sugar to the mugs then brought them to the table.

Lucy poured Susie a glass of milk. She raised her eyebrows when Susie grabbed a cookie and dunked it in her milk.

Her daughter shrugged. "I saw Caleb do it, and I wondered if it tasted better." Susie took a bite. "It does," she mumbled through a mouthful of cookie.

Gabriel snickered; he couldn't help himself. Lucy locked gazes with him, her expression filled with good humor.

He ate bites of cookie between sips of tea. The cookies were tasty. Chocolate chip, his favorite.

Susie talked nonstop. "When did you move here? Do you have family living with you?"

He managed to keep calm although personal questions usually alarmed him, but this was Susie, an innocent child with no bad intentions. "I moved here two months ago, and my sister Emily lives with me."

"I don't have a sister, but I might soon! Or a *bruder*. I don't care which one we get."

She drank from her milk and ate another bite of cookie, swallowing before she continued asking questions. "Do you have any animals? A dog or a cat? I like dogs and cats," Susie said.

"Dochter," Lucy said firmly. "That's enough questions for Gabriel."

Susie nodded, clearly unoffended. She finished two cookies silently and drank all of her milk. She wore a milk mustache when she set down her cup. Lucy chuckled as she wiped her daughter's mouth with a napkin. "Can I get down?" Susie asked.

Her mother nodded. "Where are you going?"

Her little girl smiled secretly before she approached Gabriel and crawled into his lap. She patted his cheek. Susie's fingers moved to caress his scar. "You hurt yourself."

He stiffened, but only for a second, as the child looked at him with genuine concern. *"Ja."*

"I can fix it," she said sweetly. To his astonishment, she leaned forward and kissed his scarred cheek. When she pulled back, she was smiling. "There! Now it won't hurt so much. *Mam* always kisses my boo-boos better."

Emotion rolled over him in thick waves. He fell instantly in love with Lucy's daughter. *"Danki*, Susie."

"You're *willkomm*," she replied breezily as she climbed down from his lap. She kissed her mother. "Can I play outside for a little while?"

Lucy gazed at her daughter as if surprised by Susie's kindness, but she looked happy that her child was open and loving to a man she barely knew yet obviously cared about. "Why don't you play in your room? We'll go outside together after supper."

The child nodded. "I'll see you later, Gabriel. I liked eating cookies with you." Susie scampered from the room.

Silence fell once Susie was gone. Averting her gaze, Lucy rose and awkwardly piled up their plates.

He stopped her with a gentle touch on her arm. "Lucy?"

She seemed to freeze but she met his gaze head-on.

"Danki." Wondering if she could read his thoughts, he quietly studied her. "Your *dochter*…she has a beautiful *hartz*."

Lucy blinked rapidly but managed a smile that looked genuine. "I am blessed to have her in my life."

He nodded. "I can understand that," he whispered, holding her gaze. The tension in the room was thick. It wasn't an angry tension but an awareness between a man and a woman. Worried by the feeling, Gabriel stood. "I enjoyed the snack and…" *the time we spent together.* "I should go and leave you to your afternoon."

She rose. "I'm glad you stopped by," she said as he grabbed his hat from a wall hook and settled it on his head. She stopped him with a touch on his arm as he opened the door to leave. "Gabriel, your pie." She retrieved it from the refrigerator and brought it to him.

He gave her a wry grin as he took it from her. "Can't leave it behind when it's my favorite."

"Be careful with it or it may spill. Another hour in the refrigerator will help."

As he left her house, Gabriel felt as if his heart had taken a wallop. He liked Lucy and he liked her daughter. Maybe too much. He set the pie carefully on the front floor of his buggy before he climbed in.

He was touched by Lucy's gesture. Closing his eyes, he thought of the young widow and her daughter and felt a longing for something he would never have. He couldn't allow himself to be vulnerable again. He was a broken man and he had to keep some distance between them. With a sigh, he reminded himself that he and Lucy were neighbors and possibly now friends, but he could never allow them to become anything more.

Chapter Five

Two days after Gabriel's visit, Lucy sat at the table with Susie, watching her daughter drawing pictures with crayons. "Why don't you draw a picture of a duck like the ones we saw last week in the pond?" she asked when her daughter seemed to struggle with what to draw.

With the tip of her little tongue showing between her lips, Susie concentrated on her drawing for several minutes. She stared at what she'd drawn and frowned. "*Mam*, can I draw in my room? This is going to take a while."

Lucy hid a smile. "*Ja, dochter.* Don't get crayon on the floor or furniture," she warned and grinned as Susie grabbed the crayons and all the paper Lucy had given her and ran from the room.

"*Hallo!*" a feminine voice called through the screened door.

"*Hallo?*" Lucy was startled to see a group of three women she recognized from church, although she couldn't remember their names. "What a nice surprise." She opened the door wide to allow them inside, stepping back as they entered. These women had never visited before, not that she'd enjoyed interaction with the community women while Harley was alive. He'd never allowed them to stay for the midday meal after service or to visit anyone but his sister's family.

"Tea?" she asked. Each woman wanted a cup, so Lucy put on the teakettle then turned to face them.

"We'd like to invite you to my *haus* on Visiting Day," a young woman with red hair and blue eyes said. She looked as if she was in her midtwenties. "I'm Rachel King."

"Are you related to the Kings of King's General Store?" Lucy asked.

"My in-laws." Rachel pulled out a chair at the kitchen table.

The other women shifted the table out from the wall and they sat down. The teakettle whistled. Lucy removed it from the burner and poured out four cups of hot water, which she brought to the table. She set out the fixings for tea and a plate of cookies for the women to snack on.

"I'm Margaret Troyer," a slightly older woman said once Lucy took her seat. "But everyone calls me Maggie. My husband is church deacon."

While she didn't know many church members well, Lucy was aware of each of the elders. "Deacon Thomas."

"Ja." A small, secret smile curved her naturally pink lips.

"'Tis nice of you to visit," Lucy said, wondering why they had.

Rachel chuckled. "We're widows. Well, we were, but not anymore." She pulled the sugar bowl closer and put a spoonful into her tea. "We'd like you to join our 'widows who aren't widows' group, Lucy. We know things have been hard for you, but we'll help you find a better life. There are other men out there. Like us, you will marry again one day to someone who will make a *gut* husband, who will care for you and Susie—" she gestured toward Lucy's belly "—and your little one."

"I appreciate your visit, but I don't know if I'm ready," Lucy admitted, dreading their reaction. She wasn't sure she'd ever be ready.

Each of three women smiled. "We're here," the third one said, "because there's been talk about the other women in our community insisting you need a husband since you have a little one on the way. We're here to support you." She grinned. "I'm Hannah Brubaker. My husband and I own Brubaker's Creamery."

"We understand that you're still grieving," Maggie said before Lucy had a chance to respond to Hannah. "You have time. We remember what it was like after losing our husbands. There's no reason for the others to press you to wed." She exchanged looks with Rachel. "We'd like to be your friends." She paused to take a sip from her tea. "Service is at our house on Sunday. We're hosting."

Lucy hesitated, deciding that it would be nice to have their friendship even if she never married again. "I can make dessert."

"Wunderbor!" Hannah exclaimed. "Bring that for Visiting Day at Rachel's, too. We've tasted your desserts." She grabbed a cookie from a plate Lucy had put on the table. "I recently bought one of your cakes. It was delicious." She took a bite of the cookie. "This is tasty! I wish I could bake like this. I'm a terrible baker."

Her eyes widened at the woman's admission. Lucy didn't know how to respond.

"Your desserts have been selling well," Rachel said. "Mary will get in touch with you soon to ask for more."

Lucy smiled, pleased.

Now that they'd made their intentions known, the churchwomen chatted about their families and the community as they drank their tea and ate cookies. After an hour, they stood and took their leave. Lucy stood on the stoop, waving, and watched as the women left together in Hannah's buggy. After the vehicle disappeared from sight, she turned toward the house. The sound of carriage wheels behind her made her stop and turn around.

"Lucy." Gabriel's familiar voice made her smile. She waited as he tied up his horse before he headed in her direction. Seeing Gabriel Fisher gave her a thrill and made her realize how much she liked his company.

He approached, his expression serious as he reached her. "I heard from Eli Lapp about your buggy. He left a message at King's General Store. He wants to talk with you about it."

"Did he say how much?" When he shook his head, she asked, "When does he want me to call?"

"As soon as possible. I have his number. We can go whenever you're ready." He pushed back his hat brim, and she could see into the shiny depths of his dark brown eyes. "Where's Susie?" he asked.

"Playing in her room." Feeling suddenly breathless, she pressed a hand to her throat. "Are you sure you have time?"

He tugged on his left earlobe. *"Ja."*

Hearting beating wildly, she turned to open the door. "Come in while I get her."

He held on to the doorframe and waited as she entered first. Lucy was conscious of him behind her, his nearness, his scent and the even sound of his breathing. She was drawn to Gabriel as she'd never been drawn to another man. It somehow felt right to be in his company. She caught her breath as she locked gazes with this kind, striking man.

"Have a seat," she said, and then hurried upstairs to Susie's room. Her heart thundered in her chest when she reached the top landing, but not because of the run. Her racing heart was her reaction to the attractive man downstairs in her kitchen.

Lucy smiled as she entered her daughter's room. "Gabriel is here—"

"Gabriel!" Susie didn't wait to hear any more. She flew out of the room and thundered down the stairs in her eagerness to see him.

Susie had left the drawings she'd done on the floor. Lucy picked them up and set them on her daughter's bed. She went downstairs to find her daughter at the table talking a mile a minute with Gabriel intently listening to everything she had to say.

"I drew a duck," she told him. "*Mam* gave me paper and crayons so I can draw things. *Ach nay!*" With a frown, she climbed down from her chair. "I drew something for you, Gabriel, but I left it in my room!" She saw her mother standing in the doorway. "*Mam*, do I have time to get his picture?"

Lucy met Gabriel's amused gaze. "Does she?" she asked him with a little twitch of her lips as she hid a smile.

"*Ja*, we have time."

With a relieved cry, Susie ran up the stairs, and seconds later, they heard her little feet clopping down again. She approached him, clutching a sheet of paper. "Here, Gabriel. I hope you like it." She thrust the paper at him then climbed onto the chair next to him.

Gabriel spread it carefully on the tabletop. Lucy leaned close to get a look and saw a house with three people in the yard—a man, a woman and a little girl. She saw him blink and swallow hard several times as he studied it, as though deeply moved. Lucy, understanding what the drawing meant, was shocked.

"Do you like it?" Susie asked worriedly. "It's you, *Mam* and me outside."

Smiling, he reached out to touch her cheek. "I love it. It's *wunderbor*."

She grinned. "*Gut!*" She got down from the chair. "Where are we going?"

"King's General Store," Lucy said as she straightened her daughter's *kapp*. "I need to make a phone call."

Susie pulled away. "Can I get a candy bar?"

"Susan Schwartz! *Nay*, you may not have a candy bar," she scolded. "You don't get one every time we go into a store."

Her daughter made a face. "Why not?"

"Because it's simply not done!"

"Just this one time, *Mam*?" Big light blue eyes pleaded as Susie looked up at her, her lower lip quivering after her mother's scolding. "I won't ask next time."

Lucy sighed, hating to disappoint her daughter. "This one last time. You're not to ask for any again."

Susie grinned, displaying little white teeth. She turned to Gabriel. "Do you like candy bars?"

Gabriel nodded, and there was laughter in his brown eyes. She shook her head but soon found herself silently laughing along with him. Apparently, he didn't think her a terrible mother for giving in.

"Let's go, *dochter*, before it gets too late."

"It's still light outside," Susie said. "There is plenty of time."

Gabriel coughed into his sleeve, and Lucy knew he was trying to control his amusement. Finally, with a straight face, he stood and held up the drawing. "Do I get to keep this?" he asked Susie gently.

"*Ja*, I drew it for you."

"*Danki*, Susie."

The child nodded. "You're *willkomm*." She opened the door and skipped outside toward Gabriel's buggy.

Silence filled the room after Susie had left the house. "You are truly blessed, Lucy," Gabriel said, his voice filled with emotion. "You have a beautiful, loving child."

"I know," she said, unwilling to look away from the raw pain she suddenly glimpsed in his expression. She resisted the urge to reach out to comfort him.

He gave her a small smile and opened the door, allowing her to leave before he followed. "You have your key?" When Lucy nodded, he turned the lock then pulled the door shut behind him.

Her throat was tight as Lucy walked with him to his vehicle. Susie had already crawled inside. Gabriel offered his hand and she clasped it firmly as he helped her in. How could she not like him? Gabriel was kind and considerate, a genuinely caring man. And he seemed to adore her daughter.

After a short journey to King's General Store, Gabriel got out, tied up his horse and helped her then Susie out of the buggy. He gave Lucy the note with Eli Lapp's phone number. She entered the store ahead of Gabriel, who followed with Susie holding his hand. Lucy was amazed at the easy way her daughter gravitated toward him. Lucy hadn't needed the peek at Susie's drawing to realize how much her daughter adored him.

She thought of Rachel, Hannah and Maggie. Would she find happiness with another man like her new friends had?

Lucy greeted Mary King with a smile before she went to the pay phone in the back of the store. Pulling several coins from a money purse stashed beneath the waistband of her apron, Lucy dropped them into the slot and dialed Eli's number. The phone rang three times before he picked up.

"Lapp's Carriage Shop. Eli speaking."

Gabriel could see Lucy on the phone. Her brow was furrowed as she listened to whatever Eli was saying. Eventually, she hung up the phone then looked around as if searching for him and Susie. She found them in the candy aisle. It was no surprise that Susie had grabbed an entire pack of chocolate bars.

"So we can share," Susie said as she held up the package to show her mother.

"Did you talk with Eli?" Gabriel asked softly while Susie sorted through the other candy on the shelf.

Lucy nodded. "He said he could have it finished for me by the middle of next week."

He studied her, noting her distress, and shifted closer. "Does it cost too much?"

"I have enough," she assured him. "Although I have a few places I need to go before Eli will have it ready for me. As long as it doesn't rain, I'll be fine taking my wagon."

He hesitated. "I'm not sure that's a *gut* idea, Lucy. Not with your sprained wrist." He scratched above his left eyebrow with his finger. "Where do you need to go?"

"Church is this Sunday. The Troyers are hosting. I can't miss it."

Gabriel stayed silent as he debated whether or not it was time for him to become an active member of this Amish community. He could go, as long as his leg held up. "I'll be happy to take you to church service."

She raised her eyebrow. "You will?"

He inclined his head. "I haven't attended church here yet. If you and Susie don't mind riding with me, it will be my pleasure to take you."

Her gaze softened. "*Danki.* I'd appreciate that."

"*Gut.*" He glanced over his shoulder and smiled as he faced her again. "Your *dochter* can't make up her mind about the candy she wants."

"And why did I tell her she could have any?"

Gabriel chuckled. "Because she knows exactly what to say to convince you."

"I'll take care of this," she said. "It's getting late and we haven't had supper yet." She marched toward her daughter and grabbed the bag of chocolates Susie had chosen first. "Time to go, little one. These will have to do." Catching Susie by the hand, she went to the front register and paid Mary for the candy. When she was done, she turned and saw his anxious look. "What's wrong?"

"I forgot we're having company to supper. I need to get home."

Lucy blushed. "I'm sorry. It's not that far. Susie and I can walk."

He frowned. "*Nay*, your *haus* is on my way home."

He followed as she hurried Susie to the buggy and waited for her to get in. Gabriel got to Susie first, picked her up and set her in the back seat. He frowned when Lucy didn't wait for his help. She climbed into the front seat and he got in beside her. "I'm sorry it took us so long."

"It didn't, Lucy. I was having a nice time. And I simply forgot my sister invited a guest to supper."

Gabriel pulled into her driveway a few minutes later. Worried about being late, he jumped out to help her and Susie climb down and was back in the driver's seat within seconds. He waved before he picked up the leathers. "I'll see you soon, Lucy. Be a *gut girl* for your *mam*, Susie."

"I will, Gabriel." Her daughter tore open the pack of chocolates and pulled out four candy bars. "Wait!" Susie cried when the carriage rolled forward. Gabriel immediately drew back on the reins. "Here. For after supper," she told him.

His eyes were soft as he accepted the candy. "*Danki*, Susie." He turned to Lucy. "Have a nice night."

And then with a wave and a flick of the reins, he was heading home, feeling bad that he had to leave them too quickly.

Chapter Six

Hurrying home, Gabriel urged his horse into a trot. He'd wanted to stay with Lucy and Susie, but his sister wanted him home before Aaron's arrival. It was probably just as well. He had enjoyed his time with Lucy more than he should as a friend.

He guided his buggy onto his property, tied up his horse and hurried toward the house. There wasn't another vehicle in the yard. Relieved that Aaron hadn't arrived yet, he entered through the back, expecting to see Emily bustling about the kitchen as she made the final preparations for supper. Instead his sister sat, elbow on the tabletop, her chin propped up on her hand.

The wonderful aroma of chicken filled the air, and she had set the table for three people, except one place setting had been shoved aside. Emily didn't say a word.

He frowned. Something was seriously wrong. "Em?"

She blinked. "Gabriel." She gazed at him, her eyes dull and filled with unhappiness. "Aaron's not coming."

Her response sparked his anger as he pulled off his

hat and hung it on a wooden peg by the door. Covering her hand with his, he sat down beside her. "Why not?"

"I don't know," she said, blinking back tears as she straightened in her chair. "He canceled at the last minute. He didn't tell me why. *He sent his bruder.*" She rose and moved toward the stove. "You must be hungry," she said, her voice flat as she turned on a burner to reheat the meal. "I made fresh bread if you want any and lemon cake for dessert." She faced him, her eyes awash with unshed tears. "I worked hard to make him a meal, and he cancels!" She grabbed bowls off the dining table.

Gabriel gently extracted the dishes from her hands. "Sit, Em. Let me get supper on the table, and then we'll talk, *ja?*"

She sniffed. "I'm not hungry."

"You have to eat, *schweschter.* Are you going to let him keep you from taking care of yourself?" He hesitated. "Maybe he has a *gut* reason why he couldn't come."

Emily plopped onto a chair. "What should I do?" she asked as he took the bowls to the stove.

Gabriel had never seen his sister so upset over a man before. He ladled out chicken potpie then gave her a steaming bowl and kept one for himself. He poured each of them a glass of iced tea and took a seat.

"Try not to judge Aaron, not until you know why he didn't come." He spooned up a taste of the chicken dish. "He may have had a family emergency."

Staring at her supper, she used her spoon to play with her food. "I guess."

Rubbing his chin, he studied her. "You like him, *ja?*"

"Ja." She set her spoon on the table. "But what if he doesn't like me the same way?"

"He agreed to come, didn't he?" He smiled. "You need to trust your feelings. What are they telling you?"

Emily blinked. "You're giving me relationship advice," she said with awe. Suddenly, she narrowed her eyes and stared at him. "You look different, happier. Where were you earlier?"

Gabriel opened his mouth then closed it, unsure what to tell her.

When he didn't immediately answer, she gasped. "You have a sweetheart! You didn't buy the chocolate cream pie!" she exclaimed with surprise. "A woman made it for you!"

"I don't have a sweetheart." His neck burned with discomfort as his sister studied him. "I might have helped a neighbor with a couple of things," he admitted, rubbing a hand across his nape. He sighed. "And *ja,* she made the pie for me as a thank-you for helping her."

Emily looked thoughtful. "The fact that you've spent time with any woman…"

"'Tis nothing," Gabriel said, wondering if it was true. "She's just a neighbor."

"A pretty neighbor?"

He stared at her. "Have you forgotten about Lizzy?"

"Ah, an older one, then."

"Emily, have you forgotten this?" He gestured toward his left leg.

"Gabriel, you deserve to be happy. Lizzy wasn't the right one. Someone else—this woman—might be."

Gabriel didn't comment. He was relieved to see her eat several spoonfuls of her potpie without forcing words from him that he wasn't ready to give. He froze when she stopped eating and met his gaze. He didn't want to talk about Lucy.

"I want to know why Aaron couldn't come," she said. She worried her bottom lip. "What if he changed his mind about me?"

He relaxed at the change in subject. "I doubt that's the reason. You've been seeing him for what? Almost a month?" She nodded. The man had better have a good explanation why he'd canceled on his sister. Gabriel eyed her thoughtfully. "When will you see him again?"

"We didn't make plans, but I should see him on Sunday. He attends church service faithfully. The change in our friendship is fairly new. No one knows that we have been seeing each other, except for you."

"What about his *bruder*? He must know something."

"I doubt it." Sadness filled her expression. "Nathaniel didn't appear to think anything other than Aaron being invited to a dinner at a neighbor's *haus* he couldn't attend."

Gabriel realized that he had to confide his Sunday plans to her. "Em, I offered to bring a neighbor and her *dochter* to church service. I hope you don't mind riding with them." He fingered the raised scar on his cheek. "I thought I'd stay. It's about time I came back to church."

Emily perked up. "Gabriel, I'm happy you're coming! This isn't Ohio. The people here are different. I like this church community. I've found comfort in the Lord here. I know you will, too. I understand you've been struggling since you got out of the hospital. It's been extremely difficult for you, especially after living with *onkel* Reuben. He made it very clear he didn't want either one of us."

After the house fire that killed his family, when Gabriel had been hospitalized for weeks, Emily had lived with their uncle, their mother's older brother. After he was released, he'd endured living temporarily with Uncle Reuben, as well. The man, an old bachelor, had considered him and Emily a nuisance. As soon as he was well enough, Gabriel had used the money from the sale of the property that had been their family farm, then he and Emily had moved to New Berne in Lancaster County to make a fresh start.

Here he and his sister had found a measure of peace. Emily had healed from the loss of their family. While his scars remained a constant reminder of the fire, he, too, was on the road to getting over his painful past. The nightmares he'd suffered since the fire came less frequently now. It had been months since his last one. He found himself in a better mood lately, and he thought that might have something to do with meeting and getting to know a certain young widow and her daughter.

Gabriel frowned as he studied Emily, who continued to eat quietly. Aaron Hostetler's absence this evening had upset her. If he found out the man was playing with his sister's affections, he'd have to do something. What, he had no idea.

He dug into his own supper. "This is *wunderbor gut*, Em," he said after swallowing some of her chicken potpie.

She gave him a small smile. "I'm glad you like it. I…" Blinking several times, she stared into her bowl. "I thought I knew him."

"Emily," he said, placing his hand over hers. "Let's see what Aaron has to say first, *ja*?"

She nodded, and her smile became more genuine.

A short time later, they had finished their meal but hadn't enjoyed dessert yet. "Emily, do you mind if I run a quick errand? I'd love a piece of lemon cake when I get back."

His sister gazed at him hard. "You're going to stop by our neighbor's *haus*," she guessed correctly.

He shrugged. "Maybe."

"What's her name?"

"Lucy."

"That doesn't sound like an old neighbor lady's name. Or is that her *dochter*?" she teased with a grin, and he was glad to see her good humor, even if it was at his expense. "Don't be gone too long," she said, "or I'll be forced to eat the whole cake."

Gabriel smiled as he left the house, relieved his sister was fine with him cutting their meal short. He was eager to get back to Lucy. He feared his quick departure earlier had seemed rude to her, and he wanted to make sure she wasn't upset with him.

He was one mile from her house when the pain hit again. Crying out, he steered his buggy to the side of the road to park. The stabbing pain below the skin grafts on his thigh was excruciating. Gasping, he clutched at the limb, rubbing to relieve the agony. His entire leg tensed up. His foot cramped in an extension of his tightening leg muscles, and he breathed harshly, hoping and finally praying that his suffering would stop. Gabriel sat in his buggy for a good while before the sensation started to ease. When it finally left, he was exhausted and discouraged. This second attack this week reminded him that the fire had made him a damaged man.

He waited for a few minutes more until the pain let up. Then, with the memory of his former betrothed Lizzy's claim that he'd never be man enough to take care of her or any woman, Gabriel turned his buggy around and headed home.

The day after she'd seen Gabriel last, Lucy flipped the last of the pancakes and placed them in a stainless bowl, which she covered with a plate to keep them warm.

"I love pancakes for lunch." Susie sat in her chair, swinging her legs while she waited. "Can I have butter and lots of syrup?"

"Lots of syrup?" Eyeing her daughter, she cracked a smile as she forked two pancakes onto Susie's plate. "You may have syrup, but I'll pour it for you." Susie looked adorable in a bright green tab dress covered with her black apron. She wore her white prayer *kapp* over her blond hair, and her cheeks looked red from excitement and the touch of sun she'd gotten earlier while she'd played in the backyard.

Susie immediately reached for the butter dish, pulling it closer.

"Don't use too much, *dochter*." Lucy watched with satisfaction as her daughter added a small spoonful to her pancakes then spread it around. She poured out Susie's syrup then sank wearily onto her chair. She added a pancake to her plate. She wasn't hungry, though she knew it would be better for the baby if she ate. It had been a while since she'd eaten a decent meal. Her stomach had been bothering her, and since the accident she'd only managed to snack and nibble at her food while Susie ate with gusto.

"Hallo?" The door opened and her sister-in-law stepped in.

Lucy smiled as she stood. She'd expected Nancy to show up earlier in the week after seeing her with Gabriel when she came for Susie. "Want some pancakes? Tea?" she asked.

"Just tea," Nancy said as she approached Susie and rubbed a gentle hand across her niece's shoulder. "How are things?"

"Fine," Lucy said as she poured hot water and fixed tea. "It's been quiet."

"Any visitors?" Nancy asked casually.

Lucy shot her a glance but didn't answer as she carried the tea to the table.

"We saw Gabriel yesterday," Susie piped up, making Lucy inwardly groan.

"Is that right?" Nancy gazed at Lucy with raised eyebrows.

"Ja. And on Monday we went out for ice cream after we left your *haus,"* her daughter said. "It was *gut!"*

"He's our neighbor," Lucy said. "I had some trouble with my buggy and now it's in the shop."

Her sister-in-law frowned. "What kind of trouble?"

"Something with the axle," she murmured as if she didn't know.

"Gabriel is nice. He took us to the store yesterday, too." She ate the last of her pancakes.

"Susie—"

"He did! And I shared my candy bars with him before he left." Susie grinned at her aunt. "He lives with his sister, and I gave him enough for both of them."

"That was nice of you, Susie," Nancy said, her gaze moving from her niece to Lucy.

"Susie? Why don't you go outside to play? But stay in the backyard, *ja*?"

"Ja, Mam." Susie got up and wiped her mouth with a napkin. *"Endie* Nancy? Can Sarah and Caleb visit us soon?"

Lucy nodded, and Nancy smiled. "I'm sure we can arrange that."

"Danki!" She grabbed her dirty dishes and brought them to the counter next to the sink. Then she ran outside to enjoy the day.

As soon as they were alone, she expected Nancy to question her. Nancy didn't disappoint. "Tell me about Gabriel Fisher."

Lucy shrugged. "He's our neighbor. He lives down the road."

"How did you end up getting a ride from him the other day?"

Lucy shifted uncomfortably. "I had some trouble with my buggy and he stopped to help me. We knew immediately that the buggy needed work done on it. I told him that Susie was at your *haus* and he offered to bring me to get her."

"Hmm," Nancy said noncommittally.

"What?"

"He's a *gut*-looking man despite the scar on his face."

Mention of the scar got Lucy's back up. "You can hardly notice the scar."

"Is there interest between the two of you?" Nancy took a sip of her tea.

"Nay!" Lucy exclaimed, her heart beating hard. "He's my neighbor and a nice man."

"That's too bad," her sister-in-law murmured.

Stunned, Lucy blinked. *"What?* Why?"

"You need a man in your life, Lucy."

"Nay, I don't. I'm not ready." After Harley, she didn't know if she'd ever be ready.

"You're having a *bubbel.* You need a husband."

"Nancy—"

"If not Gabriel, what about Aaron?"

"Nay, not Aaron. I don't feel that way toward him."

"People marry for reasons other than love."

"I won't. Not ever again."

Nancy's expression softened. "I know things were hard on you. Harley wasn't an easy man."

"He still loved Susie's *mudder.*"

"You are Susie's *mudder* in every way that counts." Nancy drank the rest of her tea and stood.

"Danki," Lucy whispered as she watched Nancy place their cups in the sink.

"Hallo!" A masculine call came from out in the yard.

Lucy froze. Nancy looked out the window then smirked at her. Lucy opened the door and stepped outside.

"Gabriel!" Susie cried from the backyard. She raced in his direction and gave him a big hug. "I missed you!"

"I missed you, too, little one." His gaze captured and held Lucy's over Susie's head. "I wanted to see you again and to talk with your *mudder.*" Her daughter released him, and he smiled at her.

Nancy joined her on the steps. Gabriel saw her and blinked, looking suddenly wary. *"Hallo,* Nancy."

She nodded, crossing her arms and narrowing her gaze at him. "Gabriel."

"Nancy," Lucy whispered warningly. Her sister-in-law grinned at her.

"Come inside, Gabriel," Lucy invited. He entered the house with her and Nancy following.

Susie raced past and climbed onto her chair. Gabriel stood awkwardly in the kitchen.

"Have a seat, Gabriel," Nancy said before facing Lucy. "I've got to get home. I'll see you on Sunday."

"It was nice of you to visit," Lucy said, making Nancy chuckle before she left.

Susie looked from Gabriel to her mother then scrambled from her seat. *"Mam,* I'm going outside again. Gabriel, don't leave without saying goodbye," she told him.

Lucy smiled when she saw him nod. "Be careful and stay in the backyard, *dochter."* She sat down with a tired sigh.

"Are you ill?" Gabriel asked as he studied her closely. He noticed dullness in her normally bright blue eyes. As soon as Lucy's sister-in-law left, he had found himself relaxing, less guarded.

"Nay. I'm just tired."

He pulled off his hat and set it on the chair against the wall. His expression filled with concern. "You didn't finish your lunch. You need to eat," he urged softly.

"I know." She stared down at her pancake. "Do you want some pancakes? I'll get you a plate." She started to rise, but Gabriel pushed her gently into her seat.

"Nay, I already ate." He watched her until she cut the pancake and took a bite.

"What are you doing here? Do you need something? I just saw you yesterday."

"I just wanted to stop by to see how you're feeling."

"I'm *oll recht*. Well enough to use my wagon to run errands."

He wasn't happy with her driving so soon after the accident. "I thought we talked about this. I don't think you should be handling a horse." He leaned in close to her. "You've still recovering. Your wrist may feel better," he said quietly, "but I bet the rest of you isn't completely healed."

He knew he was right when she grimaced as she shifted in her seat, as if sore. Lucy sighed and put down her fork.

"What's wrong?" He reached across the table to place his hand over hers, enjoying the warmth of it.

"You've done too much already," she said, staring down at their hands. She looked away and he saw her swallow hard.

He gave her left hand a gentle squeeze. "'Tis not a problem."

"You've been kind to us, Gabriel."

"But?" It was difficult for him to resist her. She was his neighbor, but a lovelier woman he'd never met. He was in danger of feeling something more than friendship, but he wouldn't give in to it.

"Are you certain you don't mind taking us to church?" she asked.

"*Ja*, I'm sure." He withdrew his touch as he sat back. He wanted to get back to church although he knew it would be different meeting new people, seeing their reactions to him. Would the congregation stare at his scarred face and make comments? "What time should I come for you Sunday morning?"

"Service is at nine, so eight thirty?"

"I'll be here then." He stood and reached for his hat. "I should get home."

Lucy frowned. "It was kind of you to stop by," she said politely.

Susie entered the house, saw that he held his hat. "Do you have to go?" she asked, her blue eyes filled with sadness.

His eyes grew warm. "I'll see you again soon, little one."

"I wish you didn't have to leave."

He circled the table and touched Susie's cheek. "Be a *gut maydel* for your *mam*."

She grinned up at him. "I will."

Settling his hat on his head, he met Lucy's gaze and remembered the real reason he'd come. He hesitated. "I was wondering… I know 'tis Saturday tomorrow and you probably have a lot to do, but would you and Susie like to go shopping with me?" he asked, hopeful. "At nine thirty? I thought we could look at cell phones."

A little furrow appeared between her eyebrows. "For me?"

Gabriel nodded. "*Ja.* I thought I'd get one, too. For emergency calls, and I think they'll be helpful with our consignment businesses." His smile faded when she didn't immediately give him an answer.

Lucy stared at him as if debating whether or not to go. She finally nodded. "*Ja,* we'll go. I guess having a phone is a *gut* idea."

"*Gut.*" He relaxed. "I'll come for you tomorrow morning at nine."

"Oll recht." Standing on her stoop, he could feel her watching him as he headed toward his buggy.

"Gabriel!" Susie called as she opened the screen door.

Gabriel halted and the child raced to him. She flung herself at him and hugged him about the waist. The movement hurt his leg and he winced before hugging her back. "I wish you didn't have to go," Susie whined.

"I know, little one. I'd like to stay, but I have to get home. But I'll see you tomorrow, *ja*?"

Susie squeezed him again before releasing him and stepping back. He was surprised when Susie tugged on his shirtsleeve, urging his face closer to hers. He bent his head, tilting it as he listened carefully while she whispered in his ear, "I love you, Gabriel."

He felt stunned as he straightened, feeling his whole world light up. He grinned.

As Susie skipped back to her mother, Gabriel captured and held Lucy's gaze. He was surprised to find himself teary-eyed. He had to get out of here before he said something he shouldn't. He doffed his hat, dipped his head and, with a smile, put it on again. Gabriel climbed into his buggy, picked up the leathers and guided his horse onto the road toward home.

As she urged Susie into the house, Lucy wondered what her daughter had said to Gabriel. It looked as if something was bothering Gabriel, but what? He'd looked a little sad until he'd bent down and listened to Susie. She couldn't forget Gabriel's expression after the girl had whispered in her ear.

"What did you tell him?" Lucy asked.

Susie shrugged. "I told him I loved him."

Lucy inhaled sharply. *"Susie,"* she breathed, moved by her amazing, loving child.

"It's true. I love him, *Mam.* I wish I could see him every day."

Gabriel was taking her cell phone shopping, Lucy thought as she washed the breakfast dishes. Maybe they could exchange phone numbers.

By the time Susie was ready to head up to bed that evening, Lucy's wrist ached fiercely. Once Susie was settled, she'd come downstairs and ice it. And try not to think too much about Gabriel Fisher.

The next morning Lucy made potato salad and a chocolate upside-down cake for the meal after Sunday service well before Gabriel was due to arrive at nine. Susie had slept in. When she awoke and found out Gabriel was coming for them, she was excited. Her child loved the man, and Lucy understood why. She should be leery of Gabriel's relationship with Susie, but how could she deny her daughter the influence of a good man? And to see the joy on Gabriel's face was a priceless gift, a blessing from the Lord.

After she stored her homemade potato salad in the refrigerator, she put the cake into a plastic container and set it on the counter. Lucy grabbed her pocketbook and made sure she had her checkbook. She'd opened the account after she'd received the settlement money, and having no idea how much cell phones cost, she figured she'd bring checks just in case.

Susie sat in the great room, looking adorable in a pink tab dress with black apron, white sneakers without socks and her little white prayer *kapp* covering her golden-blond hair. Lucy was back to wearing her dark purple mourning dress but she wore a white apron instead of black. On her feet, she wore sneakers.

It was only eight thirty, and Gabriel wasn't due for another half hour. Lucy was excited to see him again. She knew it was crazy to like someone this much after knowing him such a short time. But how could she forget the way he'd come to the rescue, his calming voice and his inherent ability to make her feel as if everything would be all right? He was a man worth having as a friend. But each time she saw him she liked him more. She'd never expected to be involved with another man, but his kindness and caring made her glad they were friends.

Promptly at nine, she heard the sounds of a buggy through the screen door. Gabriel was right on time. She smiled as Susie ran to open the door.

"Gabriel!" her daughter cried.

Lucy grinned, pleased to see him. She reached the door just as Susie swung it open wide and raced down the steps to meet him. She suffered a moment's fear that her visitor might not be Gabriel, but Susie's cry of happiness quickly put it to rest. She followed in her daughter's footsteps. Gabriel got out of his buggy and smiled, ready for Susie's hug. Her heart leaped as she witnessed the affection between them.

"I'm so glad you came, Gabriel," Susie gushed. "*Mam* said we're going shopping. I'd like to go with you and *Mam*. Do you know where we're going? Do you need to buy something? What is it?"

Her daughter's discourse was nonstop as Lucy approached. Gabriel's gaze captured hers and a warm light flickered in his dark eyes, causing her heart to race and a tingle to start down the entire length of her spine.

"*Hallo*, Gabriel."

She watched him heft Susie into his arms. "*Gut* morning, Lucy. I see you two are ready for our outing."

Susie had put her arms around Gabriel's neck. She removed one to pat him on his right check, the uninjured one. "*Ja*, we are," Lucy murmured as she continued to watch their easy relationship. *I trust him,* she thought, *more than I've ever trusted another man.*

"Susie," she said, looking down at her child's bare feet. "What did you do with your shoes?"

"I took them off," she said.

"Go and get them. You can't go to the store barefoot."

"*Ja, Mam.*" Susie wiggled until Gabriel set her down. While Susie ran inside to get them, Gabriel and Lucy gazed at each other.

"It's nice of you to take us. The more I think about it, the more I realize that having a cell phone is a *gut* idea."

With a small smile reaching his eyes, he nodded. He glanced at her mouth before looking away.

She drew in a sharp breath. "Gab—"

"I got them, *Mam*!" Susie cried, interrupting the tension-filled moment. "Can you help me put them on?"

She dragged her gaze from Gabriel to her daughter. "Sit on the top step, *dochter*, so I can reach better."

Susie kept moving her feet, making it hard for Lucy to tie her shoes.

"Little one," Gabriel said, "stay still so your *mudder* can do your laces."

To Lucy's surprise, her daughter immediately

obeyed. Soon they were all in Gabriel's buggy, heading toward the store. Susie sat on the bench between them. "Where are we going?" Lucy asked, curious.

"There's a cell phone place next to King's." He flashed her a smile. "I thought we'd try there."

She nodded, familiar with the store. Her spirits rose as Gabriel seemed more relaxed, happy, the tension between them gone.

He guided his horse into the lot next to a small store that sold cell phones and other items Lucy was unfamiliar with. After maneuvering his buggy to a hitching post, he secured his horse as Lucy climbed out of the vehicle and helped Susie.

He held out his hand to Susie. "Come, little one. Let's see what's inside."

Following behind them, Lucy realized that she was beginning to care a lot for this kind, sensitive man—and she wasn't sure what to do about it.

Chapter Seven

"You're going to love this one," the saleswoman said as she held up a cell phone.

Gabriel made himself focus on the phone to keep from staring at the woman helping them. She had short purple hair and a nose ring.

"Look!" The young woman turned the phone on and shifted the screen to where Gabriel and Lucy could see it. "You can surf the net, do email and take photos. There are any number of apps you can download."

Gabriel exchanged a brief, horrified look with Lucy. "That's too fancy for us," he said kindly. "Do you have anything simpler?"

The lady, whose name tag read Bett, stared at him for several long seconds. "You mean like a flip phone?"

"What's a flip phone?" Lucy asked. Her daughter was getting antsy, and Gabriel watched as she calmed Susie with a tender touch to her shoulder.

Shaking her head as if she didn't understand why anyone would want a simple phone, Bett rummaged inside a display case. Within seconds, she straightened, holding a small black-and-white box.

Gabriel watched carefully as she worked to open it. He looked at Lucy and saw amusement curve the corners of her pretty mouth. Susie tugged on her dress hem, drawing her attention. *"Dochter,"* Lucy scolded gently. "Just a little while longer."

He hadn't known Lucy long, yet he found himself wondering what it would be like to have more than friendship with her. She was a sweet and caring woman and an amazing mother. He enjoyed the way she expertly handled her four-year-old daughter. She didn't raise her voice or pull her up by the arm after Susie sat down on the floor when she got tired of waiting.

"You need to be a *gut maydel* for a bit longer. I know you're tired and want to go home, but this shopping is important." She paused, bending to caress Susie's cheek with her fingers.

"We've never owned phones before," Lucy told Bett. "Will they cost a lot?"

The saleswoman stared at her hard then, as realization dawned, her face brightened. "You want a phone with no monthly fees. Ah." She grinned. "You want a burner phone!"

"A burner phone?" Gabriel wasn't sure what that was, but anything with the word *burn* in the name couldn't be good.

Bett chuckled. She grabbed two boxes from beneath the counter after putting the other one away. "I think these might be the ones for you. They're burner flip phones. There is a very small service fee each month that will give you thirty minutes of talk time. If you run out of minutes, you can purchase a card to add more." She showed them what she meant. "And you can buy battery packs that can charge them six or more times.

The packs will be charged after they run out, but you could stop here to do that. Unless you know someone with electricity."

Lucy leaned closer to him. "What do you think?" she whispered.

He gave a little nod while he grinned at her. He was sure that Mary King would allow them to charge their battery packs when they needed to. Gabriel turned to Bett. "We'll take two of the burner phones." He gestured toward the boxes. "We'll get the phones and two battery packs. I'll help whenever you need it," he added to Lucy.

She gave him a soft smile, and he felt his heart thump hard.

"Mam?" Susie tugged on her mother's dress hem. "Are we almost done?"

"Ja, dochter, we're almost done," she said, holding his gaze.

He grinned at her. While Lucy was busy with Susie, Gabriel completed the transaction and paid for a year's service fees in advance. He asked Bett to put his phone number in Lucy's phone and his in hers.

"I'll put you both on speed dial. You'll only have to press a two on your phone to call each other."

Minutes later, they left the store with Gabriel carrying the bag with everything. "Now, where would you like to go to lunch?" he asked, and Susie cried out with joy.

"Can we eat ice cream?"

"Susie Schwartz!" Lucy scolded. "What did I tell you about asking for treats?"

The little girl gazed at her mother with a look of innocence. "I didn't ask for candy, *Mam*."

Gabriel had to stifle a chuckle. "*Mam*, she has a point there," he whispered in her ear when Susie couldn't hear.

Lucy slid him an irritated sideways look. "Don't encourage her, Gabriel Fisher."

"I wouldn't do something like that," he said, but his huge grin said otherwise. "Well? What are you hungry for?"

"It's too early to eat," she said. "I should get home."

"Mam!" Susie whined but she stopped immediately after one stern look from her mother.

"Susie," Lucy said firmly, "'Tis time to go home."

Gabriel was disappointed that he wouldn't get to spend more time with her. "Come on, then, and I'll take you back."

Lucy gazed at him with a furrowed brow. "I'm sorry, but I have things to do," she said. "Tomorrow is Sunday." She was silent as he lifted Susie onto the buggy seat.

When he faced her, he saw worry in her expression, and he knew it was because her buggy would be in the shop for some time.

"Gabriel..." She sighed.

"I understand, Lucy. Besides, I'll be picking you up for service tomorrow morning, *ja*?"

She looked relieved. "You really don't mind?"

"Not at all." He felt encouraged that he hadn't suffered another episode of leg pain since the other evening. If he stayed careful, it was possible it wouldn't happen again. And it gave him hope. The realization that he'd be seeing Lucy again soon was enough to lighten his spirits, even if it was just taking her to church service tomorrow morning.

He helped her into his buggy and a short time later pulled up close to her door. He carefully climbed down and hurried to the other side to help Lucy and her daughter out.

"Here's your phone," he told her as he handed Lucy a box. "Bett put our numbers on speed dial. We just have to hit the number two to call each other." He patted Susie's head. She had pulled off her prayer *kapp* during the trip home. "Be *gut* and I'll see you both in the morning."

"How much do I owe you?" Lucy asked.

Gabriel named the cost minus the battery pack. He could buy his friend a battery pack if he wanted, couldn't he? "I paid for a year's service, too. You can pay me later." He turned to leave then stopped to look back, watching as Lucy unlocked her door and entered the house with Susie.

When the door closed behind them, Gabriel climbed back into his buggy. As he rode down the lane, he tried not to think about church service in his new community. The devastating loss of his family after the fire and his lengthy recovery from his burns plus the complications had made it impossible for him to attend service back in his Amish community in Ohio.

And if truth be known, he'd been more than a little angry at what had happened. By the time he'd moved here, his anger had dissipated enough to make him realize that the fire wasn't anyone's fault. Things happened in life that challenged people, and he needed to face his challenges and do what was right. Then Lucy had entered his life and made a huge impact. God had given another sign that it was the right time for him to attend church service again and be grateful that while he couldn't save his other family members, he'd been able to get Emily out not only alive but unharmed. And he was blessed to now have Lucy and her daughter in his life.

While he felt ready to go back to church, it didn't mean he wasn't nervous. He'd never gotten used to people staring because of his facial scar. But because of Lucy—and Susie—he was beginning to feel better about his situation. As long as his leg didn't continue to be a problem, Gabriel could allow himself small hope that he might be able to have a life where he didn't focus on the failures of being unable to save his parents, two brothers and his youngest sister. Could he have a future filled with love, something he hadn't trusted or believed in since Lizzy had abandoned him? The flare-ups in his leg seemed constant reminders that he'd basically become disabled after the fire.

Lizzy would have made a terrible wife, he realized when he thought back to their relationship. Any woman who could abandon her future husband in his time of need clearly hadn't loved him to begin with.

Gabriel never thought he'd find joy in living again. But his new friendship with Lucy made him feel good. He enjoyed spending time with her. He was glad he'd been the one to help her after her accident. Something had shifted inside of him when she'd looked to him for support. It was as if the Lord was reminding him that there were wonderful things worth living for.

Like Susie. What a precious little girl! Lucy's daughter had taken one look at him and immediately accepted him. He couldn't remember the last time he'd felt that comfortable with anyone other than his sister.

And Lucy? His heart leaped. She accepted him, too.

If he wasn't a broken man and Lucy hadn't lost her husband recently, he might have had a chance with her. God had given him Lucy as a friend, and he would treasure and keep the relationship safe. As he drove closer to home, Gabriel prayed that nothing would ever ruin their friendship.

Sunday morning dawned bright and clear. Dressed in their Sunday best, Lucy and Susie waited for Gabriel on the front porch. It was a lovely spring morning. Birds chirped, filling the air with their beautiful song. Sunlight on the grass made the lawn look greener. A soft breeze rustled the leaves in the trees and slipped under the porch roof, bringing with it the scent of the flowers she'd planted along one side of the porch.

Unbidden came thoughts of her late husband. For the most part, their marriage was as she'd expected it to be between two strangers marrying for convenience and the love of a child. Harley had been quiet at first, grieving for his dead wife. Lucy had understood. She was grieving in her own way for the loss of her mother—and the loving man she'd mistakenly thought her father was while *Mam* was alive.

She and Harley had settled into married life. He hadn't been unkind but he'd kept himself distant from her. She'd taken care of Susie and kept house while Harley had worked and done all the things that men were supposed to do. By the second year, Harley had been friendlier. He'd begun to smile more often, and Lucy had felt content with her marriage and life. If Harley got in a bad mood every once in a while, Lucy didn't let it bother her. She'd figured he would get out of it on his own time.

Now, with Harley gone, Lucy wasn't afraid to be alone, but it was nice to know that she had a new friend in Gabriel. The buggy accident had made her realize that life could be frightening, but if she continued to pray and trust in God, she would be fine. For it was God who had sent Gabriel to help her when she most needed someone she could trust.

Her father's selfishness had hurt her deeply. Lucy knew that marriage arrangements happened within Amish communities. But for her father to arrange her marriage because he wanted to get rid of her so that he could take a young wife? And then not have any contact with her after she and Harley moved to New Berne?

Her father's lack of love and warmth was devastating to her. She prayed daily to ask for God's help in forgiving the man who'd sired her. It had been a struggle but she'd finally forgiven her father.

Lucy shoved thoughts of her father from her mind and sought peace instead as she rocked in a white wooden rocking chair on the porch. She had a lot to be grateful for and she would continue to focus on her blessings.

Susie sat next to her in the other chair, looking tiny in the adult-sized seat, her feet swinging above the porch floor.

"Is Gabriel still coming for us?" Susie jerked her body backward hard against the shoulder rest of the chair, throwing her feet up and then down in an effort to move it.

"*Ja*, he'll be here." Smiling at her daughter, she shook her head. "Susie, come and sit with me. I'll rock the chair for you."

"I can do it, *Mam*," she insisted firmly.

"I'm sure you can, but let's sit together for a while, *ja*?" Lucy patted her lap. "I'd like to hug my *dochter*."

Susie grinned and bent forward, tipping the chair until her feet touched the porch floor. She got down from her chair and climbed onto her mother's lap. "I like my Sunday-best dress, *Mam*," her daughter murmured. "We look the same. You wore your blue dress today, just like mine. And you put on a black apron, too."

Her daughter settled herself onto Lucy's lap and stretched out her legs to peer at her shoes. Like many others in the community, Susie often went barefoot during the warmer months, but on church Sundays she wore her black stockings and shoes. Lucy wore a royal blue dress like her daughter's, and each wore matching white organza, heart-shaped head coverings, familiar and identifiable to Lancaster County, Pennsylvania.

Lucy enjoyed wearing something other than her drab purple mourning dress she'd worn for over five months now and was more than ready to give up for good. She didn't think anyone would say a word about her dress today. Even Nancy had been telling her that she should think about marrying again. And she would eventually. She smiled as she recalled the group of women who'd come to visit, widows who'd remarried and now enjoyed a happier life. Life was too short not to live it to the fullest, she decided. Maybe Rachel and Hannah were right and she shouldn't dismiss the idea of finding a new life with a man she could love.

Gabriel's image came to mind...his smile, the warmth in his brown eyes, the kindness and compassion in his expression. Since meeting Gabriel, with his good humor and affection for Susie, she wondered if he could possibly be the man she could build a life with—if, over time, their friendship could turn into something more.

A buggy entered the yard and drove toward the house, drawing her attention.

"Gabriel!" Susie cried as she sprang from Lucy's lap. "We're over here!"

As if he'd heard her cry, he rolled up to the front porch rather than the side door where he often parked. Lucy rose to her feet slowly as he climbed out of his vehicle and approached. She smiled at him as he drew near. "*Gut* morning, Lucy. Susie," he greeted each of them with a nod.

"Are you ready to go, Gabriel?" Susie asked sweetly.

His smile for Susie was soft. "*Ja*, little one." Gabriel searched for Lucy, finding and holding her gaze over Susie's head, his expression warm as he watched her closely.

"*Mam*, don't forget the cake!" Susie cried as she ran down the porch steps and rushed to give Gabriel a hug. He lifted her into the back seat then waited to help Lucy into the front. Minutes later, they were on their way, Gabriel turning onto the street.

Lucy faced front, gazing at the pavement through the buggy's windshield.

"You look *nice* in your Sunday best dress, Lucy," he said, drawing her attention.

Feeling flustered, she blushed, unsure what to say. She averted her gaze, looking through the side window. "I appreciate the ride, Gabriel."

"You are *willkomm*, Lucy."

She saw amusement in his eyes when she looked at him again. Embarrassed, she stared ahead and realized they were going the wrong way. "Gabriel, this isn't the way to the Troyers."

"I know, but my sister wasn't ready, and I promised to go back for her."

He pulled onto the driveway to his house. A pretty woman with red hair and green eyes waited for him. He got out to help her in.

She waited patiently as Emily climbed into the back with Susie, carrying a plastic container. *"Hallo,"* she said to her little girl.

"Hallo," Susie said cautiously. "Gabriel? Who is this?"

Emily laughed. "He isn't *gut* with introductions. I'm Emily, and Gabriel is my *bruder."* She shifted to the middle of the seat, closer to Lucy's daughter, and tapped Lucy on the shoulder. "Lucy, right? Our neighbor and Gabe's friend?"

"Ja, and the little one next to you is Susie, my *dochter."* Lucy felt more than a little relieved. Turning sideways to better see Emily and Susie, she flashed Gabriel's sister a genuine smile. "Nice to meet you, Emily."

The woman's expression warmed. "Same here." She leaned back in her seat. "What have you got in the dishes, Susie?"

"Chocolate cake and potato salad." Susie tilted her head thoughtfully as she looked at the plastic container in Emily's hands. "What are those?"

"Lemon squares."

"I love lemon squares," Susie said, her eyes lighting up.

"My *dochter* loves sweets," Lucy said.

Emily chuckled as she jerked a nod at her brother's head. "She's not the only one."

Lucy was amused to see red rise to Gabriel's cheeks. She'd have to remember that and make sure she made him baked goods often. He never did say whether or not he'd enjoyed the pie she'd given him.

As Susie and Emily chatted in the back, Lucy and Gabriel rode quietly in the front as he drove them to Sunday service. He looked over and met her gaze. They exchanged smiles, but she saw something in his expression that told her he was nervous. Without thought, she touched his arm briefly to comfort him. When he looked at her with surprise, she felt the sudden, strong awareness between them.

Heart racing, Lucy quickly looked away. Her attention didn't leave the road until he guided his horse onto the Troyer property and parked his buggy at the end of a long row of gray family vehicles parked side by side. Only then did she look in Gabriel's direction. Their gazes locked for several seconds before he broke away to get out and tie up his horse, then he reached in to help Susie from the back. Lucy scrambled down on her own and collected her food offerings from the back while Gabriel gently lifted his sister down.

Lucy didn't know what to think as they headed toward the yard, where church members chatted while waiting for service to begin. She saw Aaron across the lawn, talking with three older men. He glanced and nodded in her direction. She gave him the briefest nod and joined the group of young women who had visited her recently. Hannah and Rachel grinned as they spied her.

"Mam," Susie said with a tug on her shirtsleeve. "Can I go over and see Sarah and Caleb?"

Her attention followed Susie's to where her sister-in-law stood with a group of women on the side lawn. "You may say a quick *hallo*, but then come right back. Service will be starting soon."

With a bob of her head, Susie ran to her cousins.

She glanced back, saw Gabriel and Emily near the house, waiting for service. Pulled by emotion, Lucy headed in their direction. When her daughter joined them moments later, she felt complete.

Sensing someone's stare, she glanced back to see Nancy. Her sister-in-law looked in Gabriel's direction with raised eyebrows.

Lucy felt her face heat. Her world seemed to spin in all directions whenever she was in Gabriel's company.

Chapter Eight

❦

Service was about to start. Lucy and Susie sat in the women's section with Hannah Brubaker, Rachel King and their girls in front of them. Gabriel's sister Emily sat next to her with Nancy and Sarah behind her. Gabriel was near the back of the men's area, looking uncomfortable, and Lucy wished she could reassure him somehow that he was welcome within their community.

Maggie Troyer's husband, Thomas, church deacon, entered the preaching area and welcomed everyone to service. It opened with a song from the *Ausbund*, the Amish book of hymns. After that, everyone turned to "Das Loblied," "Hymn of Praise"—the second hymn always chosen for church service. The singing went on for a half hour or more before the preacher, David Bontrager, rose to speak.

Susie was good during service. Attending regularly since she was a baby, she was used to behaving—and being reverent—during worship. Lucy stole frequent glances toward Gabriel and was glad to see him join in the hymns and listen carefully to the preacher. At one point, Gabriel's gaze locked with hers, and Lucy felt her face redden before she hastily looked away.

Service lasted three hours, then everyone stood to get ready for the community meal that followed. The men immediately went to work moving the church benches outside to use as seats. The tables were made of plywood over sawhorses. Capturing Susie's hand, Lucy took her into Maggie's kitchen where the church-women collected and carried the food outside. Their church district was actually small compared to others.

Rachel King smiled at them. "I'm glad to see that you're staying. We're eating outside today since it's sunny and *warum*." The woman picked up two plates of cold meat and carried them out into the yard.

The hostess, Maggie, leaned into the refrigerator to pull out food containers, which she set on the counter. "What can we do to help?" Lucy asked her.

Maggie held Lucy's bowl of potato salad. "Would you take this outside?" She smiled. "Susie, would you carry out the paper plates and napkins?"

Susie bobbed her head and was handed a package each of paper plates and napkins. "When you come back, I'll give you something else to carry," Maggie said.

Lucy followed her daughter outside. "Just put them on the first table," she told her daughter. She carried her salad to the table and found a place for it. "Let's go back inside and see what else we can help with."

Minutes later, she watched Susie carry a box of forks toward a table. Gabriel approached Susie and, smiling gently, he helped her find the right spot for the forks.

Her heart melted when she saw Gabriel's soft expression as her daughter walked to the house. He was quickly winning her over with his kindness and caring concern for Susie and her.

Her daughter ran to the group of children in the backyard. Lucy could hear their laughter through the window screen.

"Susie is growing up too quickly," a feminine voice said from behind her.

Lucy turned and saw Rachel King, who must have been watching her daughter. "*Ja*, she is." She sighed. "Hard to believe she'll be five soon. It seems like yesterday when she was a tiny *bubbel*."

"Susie needs a father," Rachel said. "Maybe Aaron?"

"Nay," Lucy answered quickly. "I don't think of Aaron in that way." Her gaze sought and settled on Gabriel Fisher, who was now chatting with Jed King.

"Lucy, who is that with my Jed?"

Lucy blinked and felt heat rise to her cheeks. "That's Gabriel Fisher. He and his sister Emily are my neighbors. They gave me and Susie a ride this morning."

Rachel studied Gabriel with the intensity of someone who wanted to learn more about him, before she met Lucy's gaze. "He is a *gut*-looking man even with that scar."

"Ja, he is," Lucy agreed, slightly upset that Rachel had mentioned it until she realized that her friend had never met Gabriel before today.

"Maybe a better man than Aaron?"

She averted her gaze. "I don't know him that well."

"But you'd like to," Rachel said, drawing Lucy's glance. There was a spark in the woman's eyes that made her uneasy. Maybe because Lucy did find Gabriel attractive.

"I should check on Susie," Lucy said, wanting only

to escape. She slipped outside into the yard and watched as her *dochter* ran back to Gabriel. Susie stopped and grinned up at him, her little arms reaching out to him. Gabriel looked happy to have her near.

Emotion tightened Lucy's throat until she could barely swallow past the painful lump—something akin to love intermingled with joy, satisfaction…and hope. They were on the far side of the lawn. Lucy started in their direction when a hand on her arm stopped her. She halted and glanced back to see Aaron Hostetler, his expression earnest and caring.

"Aaron!"

"We need to talk, Lucy." Aaron glanced past her and frowned, then quickly pulled her toward a shade tree.

"Why?" she asked, resisting his touch. "What do you want?"

"I worry about you," he said, his voice thick.

She softened her expression. "I know you do, but I'm fine. You need to stop worrying about me and live your life."

"Lucy, what if I want to make you my life? What if I want to marry you?"

She gaped at him with horror. "*Nay*, you don't want that. *I* don't want that." She made it several steps before he caught her arm.

"*Please.* Let me talk to you for a minute."

Lucy sighed. "What is it?"

"I feel responsible for you."

She frowned. "Why?"

"Because if it wasn't for me, Harley would be alive!" he whispered urgently.

"What are you talking about?" Lucy stared at him. "He died in a truck accident."

"Harley wasn't supposed to be in that truck—I was."

Lucy's expression softened. "You didn't send him to his death, Aaron. He died because it was his time."

"But that's not all." Aaron looked miserable. "That night he came home after drinking? I brought him home."

"I'm glad you did—"

"*Nay!* I brought him home and I should have gone inside to make sure he was *oll recht*, that *you* were *oll recht*."

"Aaron, there was no reason for you to come inside that night. Harley was fine. He fell asleep in a chair."

"But not before—" His gaze settled on her arm, and she knew that he was referring to the slight mishap with a knife when her husband had been a bit vigorous trying to get her attention while she'd been making supper.

"Is that what this is all about?" she asked him. "You feel responsible for that?"

Aaron's blue eyes held sadness and remorse. "Lucy—"

She sighed heavily. "Aaron, you had nothing to do with my little injury or my late husband's death." She softened her expression. "*Gott* has a plan for each of us, and what happened was part of it. Now go and find yourself a sweetheart. You deserve to have your own life—not become part of mine because of something you had no control over."

His expression brightened with hope. "You really feel this way?"

Lucy grinned. "I do."

Aaron gave a jerk of his head as if he finally understood and walked away with a small smile.

Feeling much better, Lucy planned to enjoy the

shared meal. She looked for Susie and found her eating with Sarah and Caleb. She filled a plate and looked around to see if Gabriel and Emily wanted to join them, but they were already seated with Mary and James King. The bishop and church elders often allowed families to eat together when the meal was shared outside, forgoing the normal practice of the men sitting down to eat first and the women and children eating after the men were done.

Lucy smiled, glad that Gabriel was feeling comfortable enough to join other community members. She took a seat at the table next to Nancy while Susie and Sarah sat on Nancy's opposite side. Nancy's husband, Joseph, and Caleb sat across from them.

"*Mam*, I'm going to eat my meat and vegetables before I have dessert," Susie said.

"I told her it's the best way to stay healthy and get big," eight-year-old Caleb interjected before Lucy could say a word.

"*Ja*, that's *gut* advice, Caleb. Susie, I'm glad to see you eating like you should."

Susie nodded before she ate another bite-size piece of cold roast beef. "*Mam*, where's Gabriel?"

"He's eating with the Kings."

"How come he didn't want to eat with us?" her daughter asked with a frown.

"*Dochter*, Gabriel is making new friends. That's *gut, ja?*"

"*Ja*, as long as he doesn't forget us."

Gazing at her softly, Lucy rubbed a hand over Susie's shoulder. "He won't forget us."

"*Nay*, he won't forget you," Nancy agreed with a smirk.

A half hour later, Lucy felt sick. She didn't know if it had to do with her pregnancy or something she ate. "I think I need to go home and lie down," she told Nancy as she stood. Susie had run off to play with her cousins and other children. Judging from the shrieks and wild laughter, they were all having a great time.

"Do you want us to take you home?" Joseph asked, having overheard.

Swallowing against bile, Lucy shook her head. "*Nay*, I came with Gabriel. I'll ask if he'll take me. Will you take Susie home if she wants to stay?"

"*Ja*, of course we will," Nancy said, her gaze filled with concern.

Lucy saw him in a gathering of men talking near the barn. He broke away from the group when he saw her approach.

"Gabriel," she said, hands resting on her belly as she reached his side. "Do you know what time you want to go?"

He frowned as he gazed at her. "You're not feeling well."

She nodded.

He eyed her thoughtfully with concern in his expression. "I'll tell Emily that we're leaving."

Lucy hugged herself with her arms. "Your sister shouldn't have to leave."

His gaze softened. "I wasn't going to ask her to," he assured her. "I'll come back for her later."

Lucy breathed a sigh of relief as Gabriel reached his sister's side. Searching for her daughter, she saw that Susie had stopped playing and was now seated with her cousin on a bench close to the food table. Both girls were eating a piece of her chocolate cake. She hurried over and pulled Susie aside.

"I'm going home to rest, little one. Do you want to come? If not, *Endie* Nancy and *Onkel* Joseph will bring you home later."

Susie frowned. "I can stay?"

"*Ja*, you can stay. Run and tell *Endie* Nancy that you want to stay and play." Lucy smiled as she watched her daughter run off.

"I'll watch out for her," Sarah said, rising as if to follow Susie.

Lucy managed a smile, despite the roiling sensation of being sick to her stomach. "I know you will."

A few minutes later, she waited for Gabriel near the Troyers' barn where families had parked their gray buggies side by side in a long row. Gabriel's was on the farthest side from the house.

Gabriel headed her way, and Lucy felt an overwhelming sense of relief. Aaron stood in the yard, chatting with another group of young men.

A wave of nausea hit her, and she swallowed hard and cradled her abdomen. And prayed she wouldn't get sick before she reached home.

"Lucy?" Gabriel's voice was now soft, filled with concern, and she blinked back tears as he held her gaze.

"I'm *oll recht*." Although she wasn't.

Gabriel studied her for several seconds. "Do you need to get anything from inside the *haus*?" he asked gently.

Lucy shook her head. As the movement settled in, she started to tremble. "Come. Let's get you home."

There was silence in the buggy during the ride. Lucy stared out the side window at the passing scenery, eventually becoming aware of Gabriel's frequent worried looks in her direction.

When they reached the house, he hurried to help her out of his vehicle. Averting her gaze, Lucy thanked him for the ride and started toward the house, unaware that he followed her until she opened her screen door and her hands shook so badly that she nearly dropped her house key. He gently took the key from her and unlocked the door, holding it open for her. Lucy turned to thank him again, but he shook his head while gently urging her inside, following her in.

"Gabriel," she whispered.

He smiled at her with a tenderness she'd never seen from a man before. "I won't stay long. Lucy, sit down before you fall." He pulled out a chair for her. "I know you need to rest, but I'd like to make you a cup of tea before I leave."

Lucy felt in no shape to argue, and maybe the tea would help to settle her queasy stomach. "I wouldn't mind a cup," she finally said.

His slow smile before he turned to grab the kettle from the stove made her neck tingle and her face warm. He filled the teakettle with tap water and set it on a hot burner.

She closed her eyes, breathing deeply and praying that she wouldn't get sick in front of Gabriel.

The teakettle whistled, startling her. She shot a look toward the stove and watched as Gabriel made her a cup of tea. "Black with sugar?" he asked, drawing her attention to his handsome features.

She shivered under the focus of his watchful brown eyes. *"Ja. Danki."* She felt slightly better.

Gabriel stirred in the right amount of sugar, and

Lucy realized with surprise that he'd paid close attention to how she drank it.

"Would a cracker help to settle your stomach?" he asked.

She shook her head. "I don't think I should eat anything right now."

He watched her take a sip of tea. "Is there anything else I can do?"

"*Nay*. This is *gut*."

He seemed hesitant to leave, but her nausea was returning.

She swallowed hard. "Gabriel."

She saw his eyes widen with understanding. He opened two cabinets before he found a large bowl that he set close to her just in the nick of time. She was sick several times while Gabriel gently kept her *kapp* strings out of the way. She was humiliated, knowing she would no doubt see horror and disgust on the man's face.

She leaned back with her eyes closed, feeling a little better. She braced herself to face him, but before she did, she felt a dry paper towel dab across her mouth before a damp cloth settled on her forehead, and he wiped every part of her face with it. Lucy opened her eyes and saw Gabriel, a man who cared enough to stay and take care of her, someone who didn't seem put off by her getting sick. He went to pick up the dirty bowl.

"*Nay!*" she gasped and lay her hand on top of his.

He froze and locked gazes with her. The feel of his warm hand beneath her fingers felt too good. It seemed in that moment that they might be more than friends. Until he released the bowl and stepped back. Then she felt so embarrassed. How would she ever look at him again without remembering this? She didn't want him to clean up after her. The thought mortified her.

With a silent nod, he headed toward the door. "Take care and rest."

"*Danki*, Gabriel," she said as she got up to follow him. She stood at the door and watched as he climbed into his vehicle and left. Lucy turned back to the table to drink her tea, her thoughts filled with Gabriel Fisher and his kindness and her growing feelings for him. As she sipped her tea, Lucy thought about what it could be like for someone like Gabriel to love her and be a permanent part of her life.

Gabriel guided his horse back to the Troyer house to pick up Emily. He felt bad for Lucy. He knew she was embarrassed, but she had no reason to be. He was actually glad that he could help her.

He saw Emily waiting near the barn for him as he pulled onto the property. He frowned at her unhappy expression. He pulled up close to her and started to get out to help, but she was already climbing into the front seat. "What's wrong, Em?"

His sister took a deep breath then released it. "I spoke with Aaron."

"And?" Waiting patiently for her to answer, he steered the buggy back toward the road.

Emily didn't respond immediately. "I know why Aaron didn't come to supper."

Gabriel frowned. "Why?"

She blinked back tears. "Lucy Schwartz."

"*What?* How do you know?" He didn't like the sinking feeling that settled in his stomach.

"I saw them talking together earlier, so I asked him

about her. And you know what he said?" She closed her eyes and breathed deeply. "That her late husband was his best friend and she is important to him," she burst out.

He saw her rapidly blinking back tears. "Emily, if her husband was his best friend, then she would be important to him." But just how important? Gabriel wondered. Had Aaron been the one he'd seen leaving Lucy's driveway the other day? How close were Aaron and Lucy? His stomach burned at the thought that they might be closer than friends. "So he didn't come to supper because of Lucy?"

"*Nay*, not exactly," she admitted. "I didn't get to ask him about that. I saw him with her this at service, and I had to know what she meant to him."

"And you're upset by what he told you." Gabriel decided he wouldn't get upset until after he'd spoken with Lucy. Then he remembered that they were only friends, and he had no right to be upset. And yet, he cared for her as more than a friend. And that wasn't good. Maybe he should avoid her for a while until he could think things through. If only he could make himself stay away from her...

Chapter Nine

Gabriel sat on the exam table in his neurologist's office in a hospital gown and looked up as the doctor entered the room.

"Gabriel," Dr. Jorgensen greeted him. "Since you're here, I'm guessing that your leg is bothering you."

"Yes," Gabriel said. "Twice in the last week, I had stabbing pains in my thigh. I haven't had any like those in months."

"Let's take a look at your leg." The doctor examined it, pressing several areas of the grafted and scarred skin. "Does this hurt?" He probed a little more, asking questions with every area he touched. When he was done, he sat down on a stool and typed into a computer. He turned to face Gabriel. "I'd like to run a blood test to make sure there is nothing else going on. I don't think there is, but we have to make certain. Let's talk about your options. Have you tried ibuprofen?"

"It doesn't usually work," Gabriel admitted.

"It may if taken regularly. You should take ibuprofen or naproxen. I'll write down the dosage of both, but only take one kind as they are both NSAIDs. I could prescribe some patches for you to try, but the ones over-the-counter work well and are less expensive. Try those with the NSAIDs and we'll see how you do." He turned back to his computer, added entries then faced him again. "There are a number of other things we can do if you continue to experience this type of neuropathic nerve pain without relief."

"Will it ever go away?" Gabriel asked. "The pins and needles? The stabbing pains?"

Dr. Jorgensen, a gray-haired man with green eyes that were filled with compassion right now, gazed at him for a long moment. "It's hard to say. I can't tell you for sure. It's possible, but it's also possible that your pain may be chronic."

Gabriel felt his chest tighten. "So I have to learn to live with it."

"It's possible. Only time will tell. I can say that sometimes it just takes a little longer for nerves to heal. You suffered burns severe enough to require skin grafts, and from your records, I know you had problems with infection with the burns and after your first skin grafting that required you to undergo more surgery." The man stood, offering a reassuring smile. "Try not to worry. I'll help you manage your pain so that you can enjoy your life. And with time you may find that you no longer feel any pain, except for the occasional paresthesia—the pins and needles sensation. Even that could go away." He smiled and walked Gabriel to the front desk to check out. "I'd like to see you back in two weeks for a follow-up." He wrote on a pad, ripped off the sheet of paper and gave it to him. "Instructions for the NSAID and patches." He studied Gabriel thoughtfully. "Have you had physical therapy?"

"After my surgery."

"It's something else to consider if your pains continue. There are other methods we can try to manage your pain. If your pain worsens after we've exhausted all other avenues, we may want to consider surgery as a last resort."

Gabriel nodded. He didn't ask more about what surgery could do for him. He didn't want to be operated on. Although he wasn't sure physical therapy would work, he was willing to give it a try first. He'd try anything to stop his leg from hurting except surgery. The thought of another hospital stay and weeks if not months of recovery chilled him to the bone. He'd spent too much time in the hospital recovering from his burns and skin-graft surgeries to forget the horrible experience.

Minutes later, he left his doctor's office and headed for home, stopping once along the way to pick up naproxen and the pain patches his doctor wanted him to use. He hoped they worked. If not, he would have to try something else.

Chronic pain. That wasn't what he wanted to hear. But he wouldn't give up hope. Pins and needles he could live with. That sensation could be uncomfortable at times, but it was the stabbing pain that stole his breath and made it nearly impossible for him to walk that he feared most. He hoped it wouldn't become chronic. He had things to do and a life to lead.

An image of Lucy came to mind, and he had to wonder why it suddenly seemed important that he get better fast. For her. Until he remembered Aaron Hostetler. He needed to ask Lucy about the man.

* * *

The following morning bright and early Gabriel sat on his stool at his workbench and carefully eyed the piece of basswood he held. He was finally going to make the toy for Susie. If he was going to ask Lucy about Aaron, he needed another reason to go over as well, and he planned on gifting Susie the toy. The duck toy would be made from three types of wood: birch, pine and basswood. Using a carpenter's pencil, he sketched out the head, body and legs and used a hand-held coping saw to cut out each part. He then sanded the edges smooth before he assembled them together.

An hour after he'd started, he was done with the toy except for the finish. He tested it, watching as the wooden duck easily waddled down the elevated wooden track. He smiled as he envisioned the child who would be playing with it. He brushed on a clear coat of varnish and set it aside to dry.

He left the workshop then and headed toward the barn area he'd decided could be sectioned off and renovated for his wooden crafts store. Sunday after they'd gotten home, he'd brought Emily into the barn and told her of his plans, hoping to distract her from Aaron. He'd asked if she would help him by working in the store with him once it was ready.

Emily had smiled at him. "You're going to do it!"

"'Tis time, don't you think?"

"*Ja*, and it will be *wunderbor*."

"What are you going to call it?" she'd asked with a thoughtful smile. "Your store?"

"I don't know. I haven't given it any thought."

"I'll think of a few names and you can choose."

Now Gabriel studied the space that needed to be

renovated. His first order of business was to section off an area with the addition of a new wall and an entrance door. After that, he'd cover the walls with Sheetrock and layer over the concrete floor with linoleum. He would need a sales counter where they would wait on customers. He could do the work himself, but not without suffering afterward. Which meant he had to find someone who worked in construction.

Still, Gabriel was excited. Having his own store would be worth the extra cost. He wouldn't have to make early morning deliveries anymore, nor would he have to share his profits with another store owner.

He smiled as he envisioned how the store would look after the work was done. He had no idea why but he had the sudden urge to tell Lucy about his plans. It was Tuesday, and he hadn't seen her since Sunday afternoon when he'd brought her home. He wondered how she was doing. Thoughts of her brought with them thoughts of Aaron Hostetler, and he didn't want to think about the two of them together.

Forcing his thoughts back to his store, Gabriel decided to ask Jed King, who worked with his parents at King's General Store, whom he should hire. He'd recently learned that Jed had previously worked in construction.

He went back to his workshop where he'd left his cell phone. After a quick check on the drying status of Susie's waddling duck toy, he made the call to Jed King.

Seated at the kitchen table, Lucy wrote a check for the repairs to her buggy. It was late morning Tuesday, two days after church day and the last time she'd seen

Gabriel, and she still felt embarrassed that she'd gotten sick in front of him. Rachel King had stopped by an hour ago with a message that had been left by Lapp's Carriage Shop at the general store for her. Eli Lapp had fixed her buggy and the vehicle was ready to be picked up. Staring at the check, she cringed at the amount that would be taken from her bank balance. It was a large chunk of the settlement check from her late husband's employer. Thankfully, though, her baked items had sold well at King's and Peter's Pockets.

She still owed Gabriel for the cell phone and accessories—and that wasn't all she owed him. She knew why he was staying away. No one wanted to see their friend get sick, although Gabriel had been sweet about it. She knew she should call him or go over to his house to pay him, but she was still too humiliated.

She missed him, she realized. Lucy wondered when she would see him again. *If* she'd see him again. Even Susie had asked when Gabriel was going to visit them.

At least Lucy was feeling much better than she had been on Sunday afternoon.

The windows were open to allow fresh air to filter in throughout the house. Susie sat on the floor with crayons and paper. Her daughter had already drawn several pictures, which Lucy had placed on the refrigerator with magnets.

It didn't matter what her little girl was doing, Susie always made her feel better. Lucy would have been content to watch Susie all day, but she needed to get baking. Mary King and John Zook both needed more cakes and other bakery items from her. She hoped to expand her business to other stores, and Gabriel had offered to help with that, but they'd never actually discussed it. The next time she saw him, she'd have to ask.

She liked the idea of opening her own bakery, except she didn't want to spend the cash needed to rent a storefront right now. Besides, once her baby was born in two months, there'd be no time to run her own bakery. Maybe she'd open one after her children were old enough to be on their own. It was more important to be there for Susie and her baby, so selling on consignment was the best way for her to make a living right now.

She felt a flutter of life inside her as her baby moved, something her child was doing more and more each day. Lucy stood, her hand on her pregnant belly. She was nearly seven months along, and it seemed as if the baby was growing by leaps and bounds now. Soon, she feared, she'd be unable to get up without assistance. Of course, with no husband to help, she'd have to manage, wouldn't she?

"Time to put your drawing materials away, *dochter.* We have errands to run."

Susie looked up. "Where are we going?"

"To the bank and then to shop for baking supplies."

"You're making money like *Dat* did," Susie said with a little furrow between her brows.

"Something like that," Lucy said, "except I can bake, make money *and* stay home with you."

Her daughter grinned. "How about cookies, *Mam*?" She stood and placed her crayons and paper into a plastic bin on the table. Then she brushed off her knees and the back of her dress. "You can sell your chocolate chip cookies. And I can help you make them. We can make sugar cookies and snickerdoodles, too."

Lucy grinned. "You like my cookies, little one?"

"Gabriel calls me 'little one.'"

"He does." She felt a pang in the area near her heart.

"Ja." Susie crawled onto the chair next to her mother. "Why hasn't he come to see us?"

She tore out the check and closed her checkbook. "I'm sure he's busy," she said. "Probably making wooden things."

"Like what?" Susie climbed to her knees and leaned over the kitchen table, turning her head to lie against the wood to face her mother.

"Toys and vegetable bins." Lucy laughed and stood, urging her daughter to sit properly in her chair with gentle hands. "He sells them in stores on consignment. Like how I sell my baked goods."

Lucy put the check with her checkbook in her purse. "We'll take the wagon to the bank, then we'll come back to make cookies, a couple of apple pies and a chocolate cake."

Susie scrambled down from her chair. "And we can make whoopie pies! I like whoopie pies."

Lucy's gaze dropped to her daughter's bare feet. "Can you find your sneakers for me, please?"

Susie ran off then returned with her sneakers and handed them to her mother. She sat in a chair and extended her legs to make it easier for Lucy to put them on.

Lucy slipped the shoes on her daughter's feet and tied them. "You need to practice tying your laces, *dochter.*"

"Ja, Mam."

When they were ready to leave, Lucy went to the paddock fence to coax Blackie closer with a carrot.

Blackie looked in her direction then went back to eating grass. She sighed and tried again.

"Blackie!" Lucy raised the hand with the carrot. Her gelding turned its head and moved in her direction. "Thunder," she murmured. "I wasn't calling you." She smiled as Thunder came up to her. "But you'll do." She watched the horse take the treat like a gentleman. "Ready to take us to the bank, boy?" She rubbed his nose then grabbed hold of his halter and tugged him toward the barn, grimacing when the movement hurt her arm. As much as she wanted to, she couldn't hitch up her horse, not when the simple action of leading him inside had caused her arm to ache and her wrist to throb again. Frustrated, she took Susie by the hand and headed back toward the house. "We're going to wait to do errands, *dochter*."

Susie looked up at her mother. "How come?"

"It's better if we go later," Lucy told her.

She saw her cell phone on the counter as she entered the house. Gabriel had told her to call him day or night. Should she? Lucy hated the idea, especially after she'd embarrassed herself on Sunday by getting sick in front of him.

After an inner debate, she called him. Her heart raced as the call went through.

He answered on the first ring. "Lucy, are you *oll recht*?"

"I'm fine, Gabriel, but…" She paused. "I could use a little help. I don't need it right away. I need to hitch my horse to my wagon, but with my arm I can't manage—"

"I'll be right there."

"*Nay!* You don't have to come just now!" she exclaimed with dismay, but he had hung up the phone.

Within minutes, Lucy heard the sound of buggy wheels in her driveway. She hurried outside and watched as Gabriel parked his vehicle and hopped out, then headed toward the house.

"I could have waited," Lucy said with a scowl.

"Morning, Lucy," Gabriel greeted with a nod. "'Tis nice to see you, too."

"*Gut* morning," she mumbled, but he noticed the moment she couldn't contain her grin.

Susie ran out of the house. "Gabriel!"

He crouched to the little girl's level. Excited, Susie flung herself into his arms and wrapped her own around his neck.

"*Hallo*, little one," he said with a smile. Pain shot down his leg as he tried to lift her and stand. Resisting the urge to rub it, he gave up, giving her one more hug before he rose stiffly to his feet. Thankfully for him, the pain dissipated to a bearable ache. "How are you?"

"I've been drawing pictures. Want to see?" Susie grabbed his hand and started to tug him toward the house and Lucy.

"Wait," Gabriel said, halting. "I have something in my buggy for you."

Susie's eyes widened. "For me?"

"*Ja.*" He reached into the back of his buggy and pulled out a wooden toy.

"What is it?" she whispered, enthralled.

"It's a waddling duck toy."

He moved the two pieces of the toy closer and set up the wooden track. "See this duck?" he asked, watching her closely, loving the look on her face. The child nodded vigorously. "You can make him waddle down this ramp." He met Lucy's gaze with a smile before turning his attention back to Susie and the toy. "Watch, little one." He placed the toy on the front seat of his buggy and showed her how it worked. The little girl cried out with delight as the wooden duck waddled down the track.

"Can I try?" Susie asked, her pale blue eyes glistening with excitement.

"*Ja*. It's yours to keep and use whenever you like."

Lucy's adorable daughter set the duck at the top of the track with her little fingers and laughed as it waddled down its entire length. "See, *Mam*? I made him do it!"

"I see, *dochter. Wunderbor gut*." Lucy gave him a look of gratitude as her child continued to play with her new toy.

Gabriel felt his stomach flutter when she smiled at him. She silently mouthed, *Danki*, and he grinned at her, pleased.

Susie continued to play with the toy, expressing her delight each time the duck waddled from the top of the track to the bottom. Suddenly, the child stopped and looked at him with love in her eyes that floored him. Scar or not, stranger or not, Susie accepted him for who he was, not how he looked. He felt overwhelmed by emotion as he picked up the duck and sent it waddling down the track again. "I'm going to put this in the *haus*," she said as she grabbed it before running inside.

Gabriel turned to Lucy as soon as Susie was inside. "Where do you need to go?"

"I'm fine to drive," she told him. "If you'll hitch up my horse for me, I can run errands."

He eyed her with disapproval. "Lucy," he said with great patience, "where do you need to go?"

She sighed heavily. "Just the bank…and the store. I need baking supplies." She hesitated. "I sold everything on consignment."

"That's *wunderbor*." He smiled at her with approval. His gaze captured and held hers a long time, making him feel warm and giddy. "I'll take you wherever you need to go."

"What I really need is my buggy. Eli from the carriage shop left a message at King's that he finished fixing it."

He frowned as he pushed back the brim of his black-banded straw hat. "Are you going to send him a check? We can have Bert's friend pick it up and bring it back for you."

"That makes sense," she said.

Gabriel waited for Susie to return. "I'll take you to the bank and store." He sighed heavily when she didn't answer him. "Lucy."

"Fine." She looked tired, and he realized she didn't have the energy to argue. "I should go to the bank first."

He nodded, gazing at her with tenderness, and the look in her eyes gave him pause. "You used your cell phone."

She blushed. *"Ja."*

He was pleased. "I'm glad you called." He gazed at her carefully. "You look much better. Your color is *gut*."

Lucy averted her gaze. She was likely embarrassed remembering their last time together.

Susie came outside again. She reached her mother's

side then glanced curiously between the two adults. "What are you talking about?"

Lucy flashed him a look. "Gabriel is going to take us shopping."

Susie groaned. "Not for cell phones."

Gabriel laughed. "*Nay*, we already have our phones."

"When are we going?" her daughter asked with raised eyebrows.

"As soon as I get my purse." After one last look at Gabriel, who smiled at her reassuringly, she hurried into the house.

When she returned with her purse over her left arm, Gabriel was deep in a conversation with Susie, but they immediately stopped talking when they saw her.

Lucy narrowed her eyes. "What's going on?" Her daughter wore a cute little smirk. She switched her attention to Gabriel with raised eyebrows. Gabriel shook his head but continued to smile. "What are you two planning?"

"Are you ready to go?" Gabriel said, unwilling to answer.

Susie tugged on her arm and grabbed Gabriel's with her other hand. "Come on before it's lunchtime and I get hungry." She pulled them toward his buggy.

Lucy exchanged amused looks with Gabriel. He felt eager to spend the day with her.

"Do you have your phone?" Gabriel asked softly.

"In my purse," she said, patting it.

He nodded in approval as he allowed Susie to pull him toward his vehicle.

"*Mam*, can I sit in the front?"

"I think you should sit in the back, little one," Gabriel said with a smile.

"Listen to Gabriel, *dochter*. It's his buggy."

"Oll recht," Susie said with a little pout. She obeyed and climbed into the back, then tugged on the back of Gabriel's shirt. "I love my duck toy. *Danki*, Gabriel."

"You're *willkomm*, little one." He climbed into the driver's seat.

Danki, she mouthed, and the look in her eyes made his heart trip.

The mailman stopped and put mail in Lucy's mailbox. "Can we stop so I can get my mail?" Lucy asked.

"Ja, of course." He stopped the horse before the buggy was close to the road. "I'll get it," he said, before getting out and retrieving her mail.

"Gabriel." She shook her head as he handed her the small bundle of mail.

"It was no problem, Lucy. You're *willkomm*," he teased and chuckled when she blushed.

As Gabriel drove her to the bank, Lucy looked through her mail. She flipped through the stack easily, then paused a long moment to stare at an envelope.

"Something wrong?" he asked her with concern, feeling her sudden tension.

She shoved the envelope between the others. *"Nay*, everything is fine."

He frowned, suspecting there was something that was not fine, but he couldn't make her tell him.

In the bank parking lot, Lucy climbed out at the front door of the brick building. "I won't be but a minute," she said before she headed in.

Gabriel waited patiently with Susie for Lucy to return. He felt fortunate to have this time with her and Susie. He turned to see what Susie was doing, and she smiled at him. He grinned back and then watched through the windshield as Lucy left the bank and approached. The sight of her warmed him from the inside out. He started to move to help her, but she climbed in before he had a chance.

She slid onto the seat next to him and handed him cash. "For the cell phone and fees," she said.

He frowned. "Luce, this is too much money."

Lucy shook her head. "Take it, Gabriel. I'm only paying my fair share. Friends don't take advantage of other friends."

Gabriel sighed. He couldn't argue with that.

Chapter Ten

Unlike the tense ride home from church on Sunday, the drive from the bank to the store to pick up groceries was filled with Susie's laughter and chatter with the man in the driver's seat. Though finding a letter in the mail had shaken her. What could her father possibly want? She hadn't heard from him in over four years.

A male chuckle drew her attention. What a lovely sound, Lucy thought. She found herself relaxing as she glanced at the man beside her. Gabriel looked wonderful in his spring green shirt, black tri-blend pants with black suspenders and shoes. The color of his shirt brought out the warm rich tones of his stunning brown eyes, now filled with amused fondness for her daughter.

It was a beautiful June day. A warm breeze wafted in through the sides of the vehicle, teasing his face and Lucy's *kapp* strings. He kept his attention on the road, but she felt it when he stole quick glances at her.

They visited King's General Store first. Lucy entered the store and went to grab a market basket but chose a shopping cart instead. She started down the baking aisle with Susie and Gabriel following closely. She grabbed flour, sugar, vanilla, baking powder, chocolate chips and unsweetened baking chocolate. She heard her daughter chatting nonstop and she thought she heard Aaron's name. Or was she mistaken? Susie wouldn't have mentioned him unless Aaron was here. Lucy looked around the store and was grateful when she didn't see him.

"Do you need eggs or milk?" Gabriel asked quietly a few moments later as he came up to stand beside her.

She smiled at him. "Both."

"I'll get them for you," he said before he walked away.

The smile left Lucy's face as she watched him go. It seemed as if something was bothering him. Had he guessed that she'd been upset by the letter she'd received in the mail? She studied him when he returned with the eggs and milk and put them in her cart. "Gabriel?" He looked at her without expression. "Is something wrong?"

"What could be wrong?" he said without expression.

She frowned. "You tell me."

He shook his head. "Not now."

She felt something hard sink in her chest. Gabriel had seemed fine when he'd picked her up. In fact, he'd appeared so fast after she'd called him that she'd been startled. So maybe it did have to do with the letter. Or was it something else?

Lucy took a calming breath then finished her shopping and paid for her purchases.

Soon they were on their way back to her house.

"You're *orrig* quiet," Lucy commented for his ears

only minutes later as he drove his buggy onto her property. "Are you going to tell me what's bothering you?"

He shrugged as he parked close to the hitching post near the house. "Stay where you are please." He got out and tied up his horse then came around to help Lucy get down from the carriage.

She braced herself with her hands on his shoulders for support as Gabriel lifted her down. While he reached for Susie, Lucy grabbed her mail from the floor of the buggy and clutched it against her.

"*Danki* for coming to my rescue again," she said.

"You're *willkomm*." He studied her without smiling. "If you need anything else, please let me know. Would you like me to call Bert to arrange for his friend to get your buggy?"

Lucy nodded. "That would be *wunderbor*." She didn't want him to leave, but she needed a private moment to read her father's letter. She could tell him later, when she was ready, after supper. She debated as she stared down at her shoes, before looking up and locking gazes with him. "Would you like to come back for supper? At five thirty?"

He didn't immediately respond. "That would be nice."

She felt instant relief. "Do you like fried chicken?"

"I do, but I don't remember the last time I had it." He smiled at Susie with warmth. "Be a *gut* girl for your *mudder*, little one." His smile for Lucy was less warm. "I should get going. I'll see you at five thirty." He paused. "If you're sure you want me to come."

"Of course I want you to come." She lowered her voice so that Susie wouldn't hear her. "I wouldn't have invited you if I didn't."

His expression softened as he nodded. He reached inside his buggy to get her groceries and carried them into the house for her. He set them on her kitchen table then turned to leave. "I'll see you later," he said softly.

"*Mam?* Where is Gabriel going?" Susie asked as Lucy watched him leave.

"Home, Susie. But he'll be back later to have supper with us."

"Bye, Gabriel!" Lucy's daughter called out through the screen.

"I'll see you later, little one," he said with a wave.

When he was gone, Lucy ushered Susie farther into the house and closed the door. "Why don't you lie down for a little while? I'm going to rest, too, after I put away the groceries and read the mail," she said as she started to unpack the grocery bags. "We can eat something later."

"Can I lie down with you?" Susie asked, pleading with her big blue eyes.

"Go ahead and lie in my bed. I'll come up soon. I have to do something before I join you. You'll have to try your best to sleep, *ja?*"

"I will." Susie grabbed the duck toy from the kitchen table. "I'll just put this in my room first."

After making sure the house was locked, Lucy sat at the table and stared at her father's handwriting on the envelope. Her heart raced as she wondered what he had to say. She was afraid to open it. He had hurt her badly, and couldn't imagine why he'd felt the need to write to her. Had he recently read about Harley's death in *The Budget*, the Amish newspaper? Maybe he had sent condolences. She shook her head. *Nay*, that wasn't something her father would do. He didn't care enough about her to worry over her as a widow. Which meant he wanted something from her.

She tore open the envelope, pulled out the letter inside. She felt sick to her stomach as she hesitated to unfold it and read what her father had written. Lucy drew a sharp breath, unfolded the letter and began to read.

> Lucy,
> *Mari is pregnant. I need you to come home to help her. Harley can take of his dochter or you can ask that sister of his to watch the girl. I'll expect to see you soon. I am your dat. Do not disappoint me.*
> *Your vadder*

"Nay, *Vadder*, I'm not coming. I'm pregnant, a widow, and I have a *dochter* who I love and appreciate, unlike you do your *dochter*—me," she muttered. "You didn't care when I left. You may be my *vadder* but I don't owe you anything." She tried to block out the guilt. "I did everything I could for you, and it wasn't enough until I left like you wanted me to." She shook her head. "You should have known about Harley's death, but apparently, *Vadder*, you don't care enough about anyone else to read our Amish newspaper, *The Budget*."

In the past, Lucy would never have thought she would disobey her father, but his actions and his coldness toward her had changed all that. Her life was here now, and she was staying. He'd have to find someone else to help his young pregnant wife. The only person she missed back in Ohio was her little brother. Was

Seth well? Was their father being good to him? Did he care for his son? She hoped so. He'd never cared for her.

She had written to her brother several times over the years with no answer. Seth had been only nine years old when she'd left. He would be thirteen now, almost a man. She'd wanted to visit Seth, to make sure he was all right, but Harley hadn't allowed it. She was not to interfere with a man's raising of his son, Harley had hold her. Still, Lucy had remained worried about leaving her sweet little brother in the hands of her father and his new wife.

She refolded her father's letter and slipped it back into the envelope. She would write back to him later, after she rested. With her mind made up to reject her father's offer, she felt relieved as she climbed the stairs. She was tired and more than ready for a nap.

When Lucy woke up from her nap, she felt more rested. She looked at her watch and saw that she'd slept for an hour and a half. She sat up and smiled to see Susie still sleeping beside her.

She got up carefully and went downstairs. She told Gabriel that she'd make fried chicken for supper, and there was plenty of time before she'd have to cook the chicken. It was best if it was freshly fried and hot right before eating it.

Lucy made herself a quick cup of tea and ventured into the great room to enjoy the quiet for a few minutes. Her mind settled on her father, and she forced her disappointment with him away. As she sipped from the hot brew, she thought of Gabriel. Something had been bothering him even before he'd given her the mail. What?

Lucy was intensely curious about him. She wanted

to ask how he had gotten his facial scar. About his family. And his sister, whom she'd met briefly. Emily had been pleasant, although Lucy hadn't spent much time in her company since she'd left early on Sunday the way she had.

Where were Gabriel's parents? Did he have other siblings? Where did Gabriel and Emily live before coming to New Berne? Did they like living here?

She'd only known the man a short time, but she felt extremely comfortable in Gabriel's presence. She liked him. A lot. Gabriel was the direct opposite of Harley. Nor was he like Aaron. And he most definitely was not like her father.

Gabriel Fisher was someone special.

Lucy took a sip from her tea, allowing its warmth to slide down her throat and soothe her wayward thoughts. She carried her tea as she went through the kitchen and stepped outside. The afternoon sun was warm and felt good against her skin. The scent of the flowers she'd planted along the side of the house and up to the porch reached out with their perfume. She loved spring and early summer, which started next week.

Lucy finished her tea then got to work. She took the chicken out of the refrigerator and cut it into frying-size pieces. Then she grabbed some potatoes from the pantry closet and scrubbed them in the sink, then cut them into small chunks and covered them with water in a pan. After setting it aside to boil later, she dumped a jar of sweet and sour canned mixed garden vegetables into a bowl and put it into the refrigerator. Then she assembled the ingredients for the cobbler crust before she opened the jar of peaches, drained the juice into a bowl and stirred cinnamon and sugar into the fruit.

As she prepared the dessert, someone knocked on her side door. She glanced through the glass, surprised to see Aaron.

"Lucy?"

She opened the door but didn't let him inside. "What are you doing here, Aaron?"

"I just wanted to check up on you."

She sighed. "I understand that you and Harley were best friends, but your checking up on me has to stop. We talked about this on Sunday."

Aaron nodded. "I know, but—"

"I think you need to stay away," Lucy said, interrupting him. First her father's letter and now this visit. She'd had enough. "You can see Susie on Sundays after church service."

"Lucy." When she remained firm, he sighed. "I'm sorry."

"Don't be sorry, Aaron. Just go."

She watched him leave with a new sense of freedom. She was done being manipulated by the men in her life. It was time to fully take charge of herself, to do what she wanted and needed—within the bounds of the Amish community.

She felt a sudden sharp longing for Gabriel, wishing he'd come early. He never made her feel anything less than who she was. Lucy realized with a shock that she felt safe and loved with him. Did he feel it, too? If she could figure out what was bothering him, then maybe they would have a chance at more than friendship. Unless what was bothering him was that he'd guessed she had feelings for him and he didn't return them.

She put the peaches in the refrigerator and the ingredients for the crust away. She would serve peaches with ice cream and forget the cobbler.

"Mam?"

"Did you have a good sleep?" Lucy asked softly when her daughter entered the kitchen, rubbing her eyes.

Susie bobbed her head. "What time are we going to eat?"

"Soon. Gabriel is coming to supper."

She suddenly looked excited. "I forgot! Can I set the table?"

"I'd like that." Lucy put plates, napkins and forks within her reach. She watched with affection as Susie folded the napkins set them next to each plate.

"Is Gabriel here?"

"Not yet," Lucy said. "I have an idea. Why don't you get your duck toy and play with it in the great room until Gabriel gets here? I think he would love to see you play with it."

"Oll recht." Susie went upstairs to get the duck from her room.

A second buggy appeared in her driveway. Gabriel's. He stepped down from his vehicle and approached the house. Her gaze took in every aspect of him, from his black-banded straw hat to his royal blue shirt with black pants held up by black suspenders.

She felt a jolt when he locked eyes with her. She was suddenly afraid. She was starting to fall for this man and didn't know how he felt about her.

As he reached the house, Gabriel saw the door open. Lucy stood, a breathtaking sight in a bright blue dress with her white prayer *kapp* covering her dark hair. Her eyes were a vivid blue, and they were filled with emotion. He halted and froze. It looked like she might have deep feelings for him. He was afraid to hope, because despite the way he'd felt earlier when he'd left, he'd done a lot of thinking. And the only conclusion he'd come to was that Lucy meant much more to him than his former betrothed.

He smiled and continued until he reached her. She held the door open and he stepped inside. "*Hallo*, Lucy," he greeted softly, pleased by the look in her eyes. He stepped inside the house and dared to take her hand, interlocking his fingers with hers. He knew she didn't mind when her eyes brightened as he gave her fingers a gentle squeeze before releasing them. "How are you, Luce?"

"Better now that you're here," she murmured as she led him through the kitchen.

"Are you going to talk to me this evening?"

She nodded. "After Susie's in bed. Can you stay?"

"I can stay," he said, pleased that she wanted him to.

"Susie's in the great room," she explained. "She couldn't wait for you to get here."

Gabriel grinned. "She is a special little girl," he whispered, his heart full.

Her expression warmed as she took him into the other room where her daughter was. "I'm going to put on the chicken," she said. "It won't take long."

Joy settling in his chest, Gabriel gazed at her with tenderness. "Lucy—" he began.

"Gabriel!" Susie exclaimed happily, interrupting, drawing his attention. Lucy's daughter sprang to her feet and ran to him. "You came!"

He grinned at her welcome. "I did. You seem glad to see me."

"I am! I've been waiting all afternoon for you to come." She gestured toward her toys on the floor. "Look! I'm playing with my duck! See?"

"I'm happy you like it, Susie." He could feel Lucy observing them closely. He met her gaze, saw her blush and look away. He couldn't remember a time when he'd felt this kind of excitement, this hope.

"Gabriel, do you want to play with me?" Susie asked.

"*Dochter*, Gabriel just got here," Lucy told her. "Let's go into the kitchen and you can play on the floor where he can relax and watch you."

Minutes later Gabriel alternately watched Susie play and Lucy put on supper. She turned on the heat under the potatoes and warmed oil in a frying pan. The kitchen was soon filled with the scent of the fried chicken. His stomach grumbled as he watched Lucy turn the chicken in the sizzling grease until each piece was crispy. When the chicken was ready, she removed the pieces from the pan and placed them on a paper towel to remove some of the grease before setting them on a large plate. She finished mashing the potatoes, then spooned them into a bowl before she set everything on the kitchen table.

They sat down to eat, and he thought of how much they were like a family, eating together, talking about ordinary things. After dinner, Lucy got up to clear the table and Gabriel rose to help her.

"You don't have to do that," she said with surprise.

"You don't want my help?" He stiffened and met her eyes.

She looked stunned and grateful. "It's not that," she explained hesitantly.

"Then what is it?" He softened his expression as he stood close to her, holding the dish of leftover mashed potatoes. He lowered his voice. "Your husband didn't…"

Lucy stole a glance at Susie, who had climbed down from her chair to help. She took the dish from Gabriel and reached up on her toes to put it on the kitchen counter.

"Lucy, why are you surprised by my help?"

"*Dat* never helped her," Susie said matter-of-factly as she turned and went back to the table to collect the paper napkins.

"Susie," she began, looking horrified at what her daughter had said—and feeling even more surprised she had noticed at such a young age—until she realized that Susie didn't think anything less of her father for not helping. It was just the way he was. She'd felt so uncomfortable under Harley's scrutiny that she'd wanted only to escape. Like many Amish men, her late husband had adhered to a strict division of duties within the household.

Gabriel hadn't moved. Lucy saw his face had become unreadable as he waited for her to explain. *Can I tell you later?* she mouthed to him.

He nodded, then picked up the meat platter and placed it next to the bowl of potatoes. They cleaned up after dinner in silence.

"It's a nice night," Gabriel said after the dishes were washed and put away. He had dried after she'd washed. Lucy had been amazed at his willingness to help with "women's work." He smiled at Susie, who was cuddling her doll on the linoleum floor. "Shall we sit outside on your front porch?"

Lucy nodded. *"Oll recht."*

She gazed at her daughter lovingly. "Susie, would you like to play on the front porch for a while before bed?"

"Gabriel, are you coming, too?" She sprang to her feet.

He lifted her into his arms. *"Ja,* I wouldn't have it any other way."

Susie grinned at him, displaying little even teeth, as she patted his right cheek. "I like it on the porch. We don't sit there much." She struggled to get down, and he released her. Susie picked up her doll, clutching it to her. "You used to sit outside with *Vadder* sometimes, didn't you, *Mam*?"

Lucy froze. Had Susie heard her and her father talking? "Sometimes," she admitted, afraid that she'd heard Harley's loud, hurtful voice complaining about her mother.

"We don't have to sit outside," Gabriel said quietly, watching her closely as if he'd sensed her unease.

She made a genuine effort to smile. *"Nay,* 'tis a beautiful evening. We can enjoy dessert outside. Are you ready for peaches and ice cream?"

"Ja!" Susie cried as she raced to her mother to hug her. "I can't put my arms around you, *Mam*. Your belly is getting bigger and bigger."

Blushing, Lucy stole a glance at Gabriel. "I love peaches and ice cream," he said.

"When is the baby coming?" her daughter asked, still holding on to Lucy.

"Not for a while yet." She saw him stifle a smile.

A few minutes later, she and Gabriel sat side by side in porch rockers, eating dessert, while little Susie sat on the top step, enjoying hers, as well.

"Can I have more?" Susie asked, turning to show a mouth covered with vanilla ice cream.

"Tomorrow, after you eat all your lunch," Lucy said.

"Can Gabriel come over and have more, too?"

"He's always welcome." Lucy stole a glance and was pleased to see Gabriel's smile.

"This dessert is too *gut* to not come back for more," he said with amusement.

"Susie, *dochter*, time for bed. Go upstairs and wash up. I'll be up shortly to help you get ready."

After handing over her plate to Lucy, Susie rushed to open the door, pausing after she swung it wide. "I'll see you tomorrow, Gabriel."

He nodded. "Sleep well, little one." His voice was soft, his expression tender. He captured Lucy's gaze and she exchanged smiles with him while Susie entered the house and ran upstairs.

"I'll get her into bed and then…" Her voice trailed off. She felt suddenly nervous at the prospect of the conversation they were bound to have.

He reached for her and Susie's plates. "I'll wash these for you."

"You don't have to," she objected but stopped and relented when she saw his face. *"Danki."*

Gabriel couldn't remember the last time he'd enjoyed himself more. Before the fire, he realized with amazement. Mother and daughter were beautiful and precious, and he hoped that Lucy returned even a fraction of what he felt for her. Still, there was the matter of Aaron Hostetler. He needed to know how big a part of her life Aaron was, if Emily's fears that Aaron cared too much for Lucy were valid.

He washed and dried the dessert dishes, then put them away where they belonged. Lucy came into the kitchen as he was putting the leftover peaches into the refrigerator.

"Gabriel," she breathed.

He reached for her hand. "I enjoy helping you, Luce." He ran his gaze over her pretty features, appreciating her as he so often did. Today, her bright blue dress matched the azure color of her captivating eyes. "Would you like to sit outside?" he asked quietly.

Soft, silky eyelashes flickered against her cheeks, drawing attention to their rich dark color. Her nose was small and slightly pointed at the tip. Her mouth, a dark natural pink, was perfectly shaped with a lovely dip in the center of her upper lip. "We can sit on the front porch," she agreed. "Susie is already asleep, despite taking a nap this afternoon."

He continued to study her, fascinated with her face, the color of her eyes, the way she came up to his chin when she stood. "Lucy…"

She blushed. "Did you want something more to drink? Coffee? Tea?"

He curved his lips slowly upward. "*Nay.* You?"

Lucy shrugged. "Not really."

Gabriel shook his head. "Let's just sit for a bit, then."

At her nod, he took her hand and led her outside, releasing her to sit before he took the other chair. She stilled when he shifted his rocking chair closer.

"I have to ask you something, and I don't want you to take this the wrong way," he began.

She nodded. "What is it?"

"Aaron Hostetler."

She froze. "What about him?"

Tension radiated from her, increasing his. "Are you and he…"

Lucy jerked. *"Nay!"*

"My sister Emily cares for him. They've been seeing each other for weeks now, but she thinks that he canceled supper with her because of you."

She grew quiet and looked reflective as he studied her. "Aaron was my husband's best friend. After Harley died, he was there for Susie and me. It was fine, at first, but then he wouldn't stop coming around, worrying about me. I told him to stop but he wouldn't. I couldn't understand why. Until Sunday."

He could tell she was upset. "What happened on Sunday?" he asked quietly.

"He told me he needed to take care of me. That I should marry him. I told him I wouldn't. I didn't need him, and he needed to live his life."

Gabriel frowned. "He said he wanted to marry you."

"He did, at first, but then I found out why. It's not because he wants to marry me. It's because he blames himself for Harley's death. Apparently, Harley took his place in the truck that had the accident, while Aaron stayed on the job longer and went home with another crew."

"So he felt responsible for you." He glanced away, his thoughts processing what she'd said.

"And there was more," Lucy said, drawing his glance. "About six months ago, Harley came home from the job drunk. He'd gone out with the English crew. He'd been upset since the night before. He was upset with me." She stopped, looked away.

He reached out, captured her hand. "Why?"

"Harley loved Susie's mother. He—" He could feel her embarrassment.

"Six months ago," he echoed. He blinked in sudden understanding. Her baby. "He felt guilty after being with you."

She wouldn't look at him, wouldn't answer him, but he knew it was true. "So Aaron…" he prompted, hoping to move them forward. She should never be embarrassed with him.

"Ja," she said. "Harley came home drunk. I was making dinner. Fried chicken." Her smile for him was wry. "He wanted my attention and in his eagerness, he grabbed the knife I was using and—"

Gabriel gaped at her. "Did he hurt you?"

"It was an accident. The slice on my arm was just an accident, and Harley felt terrible. He was so sorry, he cried like a baby. After that, he retreated to the way he was when I first married him. Alone and distant. Only with Susie did he show any warmth."

He reached out, touched her cheek and stroked it with his finger. She briefly closed her eyes. "I'm sorry." He withdrew his hand.

"Why? You didn't do anything wrong."

"I'm sorry that you had to go through that." It bothered him.

"I got Susie out of my marriage so I consider everything I went through worth it." She smiled. "May I ask you something?" When he nodded, she said, "Where did you move from?"

"Ohio."

"You and Emily." She tilted her head as she considered him. "What about the rest of your family? Your parents?"

He stiffened but answered her. "Dead."

She gasped. "*Ach nay*, Gabriel. I'm so sorry. I didn't know."

He gave her a weak smile. "How could you?"

"How?" she breathed, almost as if she was afraid to ask.

"House fire. They all died in a house fire."

Lucy eyed him with a soft expression. She reached out and touched his facial scar. "Is that how you got this?"

He nodded. "That and worse," he admitted. He had to tell her, if he ever wanted a future with her. For some reason, it felt like she was the only one he could tell.

"Where?" she asked, her voice soft, her eyes glistening. When he didn't immediately answer her, she shifted in her chair. "Your leg," she guessed. "I saw the way you limp sometimes. 'Tis your left leg, *ja*?"

"*Ja*, it was—is—bad."

Lucy saw the pain in Gabriel's eyes as he talked about his leg. She suspected there was more he hadn't told her yet, and she wanted to know. Not because it would make a difference in how she felt about him, but because she wanted—needed—to make him feel better, if she could. "Was Emily hurt in the fire?"

"*Nay*, I got her out first."

"You tried to rescue the others," she said, watching as his expression mirrored his pain.

He nodded. "I brought my little *bruder* out next, but David was dead. Smoke inhalation, they told me."

"Oh, Gabriel…" She shifted her chair closer, slipped her arm around his. He tried to withdraw from her, but she wouldn't let him.

He shuddered out a sigh. "I tried to go back in for the others, but the fire department had arrived and wouldn't let me. My pant leg was on fire. I didn't realize—didn't care. I only wanted to save my parents, my older *bruder* and *schweschter*, and my *mam* and *dat*."

She stood and moved behind him, slipped her arms around his shoulders, leaning in close so that she could listen closely to the sound of his harsh breathing.

"How long were you in the hospital?" she asked, closing her eyes.

"Weeks. It was…"

"Terrible," she supplied for him.

"*Ja*, I had third-degree burns on my thigh and second-degree burns from my knee to my ankle. The burn treatments were…bad," he admitted. "The second-degree burns wouldn't heal and ended up needing skin graft surgeries to replace the damaged skin on my leg. Not all of them took, and I had to go in for another one."

She felt his pain and found herself silently crying. "I'm sorry."

He pulled forward and glanced back at her, seeming stunned by the sight of her tears. "Lucy…"

"I care for you, Gabriel. I know we haven't known each other long, but I've never felt this way about anyone before."

He stared at her. "You do?" When she nodded, he briefly closed his eyes. "I feel something, too, Lucy."

She stepped back and returned to her chair. She gazed at him with love, feeling happiness beyond anything she'd ever known. He had shared something painful, which made her feel closer to him. She wiped her eyes. "Gabriel, I…what can I do to help?"

His brown eyes glistening, he cracked a small smile. "I could use a cup of coffee."

Chapter Eleven

Minutes later, Lucy sat with him on the front porch as they sipped coffee.

Gabriel was silent as he drank from his mug in the chair beside hers. The brew had eased the lump in his throat that had risen as he'd recalled the terrifying moments of the fire. It was a lovely night, and he felt... refreshed. He'd told her about the fire and his leg, and she had been supportive, loving. Lucy was a woman he could take a chance with, he realized. He closed his eyes briefly before opening them to focus on her.

"Gabriel..."

"Tell me about the letter you received today."

She stiffened but then relaxed with a little sigh. "It was from my *vadder*."

He frowned. "Why did a letter from your *dat* upset you?"

"Because it was the first time I've heard from him since I married Harley over four years ago."

His expression went soft, his brown eyes filled with compassion. "Tell me why."

"He arranged my marriage to Harley. My *mudder*

died only a few months before, and he wanted me out of the way so that he could marry again."

Gabriel furrowed his brow as he studied her. "I don't understand."

"Because his new wife didn't want me there." Lucy stared into the distance. "His wife, my stepmother, was only a year older than I was."

He gazed at her with shock. "I see why that's upsetting." He reached out for her hand again. "Do you have any *bruders* and *schweschters*?"

"One *bruder*. Seth. He was only nine when I left. Apparently, Mari didn't have a problem with him living in the *haus* with them." Her tone was filled with such pain that he longed to take her fully into his arms and hug her.

"Lucy."

"I'm *oll recht*," she assured him. "I didn't want to marry Harley, but my father told me I had to." She stopped, as if unwilling to discuss the pain of her only living parent's betrayal. Releasing a sharp breath, she shifted in her chair to face him. "If I didn't, I'd have to fend for myself. I was too embarrassed to tell anyone. So I married Harley for Susie. She was a beautiful, tiny *bubbel* when I first saw her. Only two weeks old. Harley had come to Indiana because his wife Fannie was originally from our Amish community. He wanted to show his in-laws their *dochter's* baby. Only Fannie's parents were no longer living there. His brother-in-law Abe was, however, and Abe suggested that Harley marry quickly so the baby would have a mother. Harley couldn't earn a living *and* take care of his child. Abe knew my *dat*, and he met with him to discuss the idea of marrying me to Harley. My *vadder*…was receptive."

Gabriel frowned. "I bet his was."

Lucy looked away. "The marriage was beneficial to everyone."

"You, too?"

"Only because I became Susie's *mam*."

"Let's stand a moment," Gabriel said. He stood, held out his hand. When she placed her hand in his, he smiled and pulled her to her feet. He led her to the porch railing to look out over her front yard and the trees on the other side of the lawn that concealed her house from the road.

She relaxed as she leaned against the railing with a sigh. The scents of late spring were more noticeable this evening—the rosebushes along the front had bloomed, filling the evening air with the white, red and bright pink blossoms' sweet smell. Gabriel shifted to stand behind her and rested his hands on each side of her on the railing, caging her within the circle of his arms. She inhaled sharply but didn't try to break free.

She caught a faint whiff of Gabriel's soap and the pleasing scent of the outdoors that emanated from him. The sun had dipped low in the sky, casting a glow as it made the transition from day to night. The light played over the porch, surrounding them with soft golden light. She could see clearly the tiny hairs on the back of his arms below his short shirtsleeves.

"Why did your *vadder* write to you, Lucy?"

She stiffened. "He wants me to come for an extended visit."

"Are you going to go?"

"Nay."

"Why not?"

Lucy tensed, stiffening, before she looked at him briefly over her shoulder. "Do you think I should consider it?"

"*Nay*, unless you want to."

"I don't." She tried to move away, but he soothed her with a soft touch on her shoulder.

"I only ask because he's your *vadder*, your only living parent," he pointed out gently. "It would be natural for you to want to see him, mend the rift between you." He trailed his fingers down her nape. "I know he hurt you."

"He doesn't want me to visit him to fix our relationship, Gabriel. He wants me to come home to work. To take care of his pregnant wife."

She heard him inhale sharply. "That's…"

"Wrong," she said. Her throat tightened.

"*Ja.*" He turned her to face him. "*Ja*, that's wrong." He regarded her with brown eyes filled with regret. "I'm sorry. I lost my parents, and they were wonderful people who loved all of us. I can't imagine parents who aren't the same."

Lucy relaxed against the railing. "I understand. But you need to know that while my *mudder* loved my *bruder* and me, I didn't see, didn't realize, until after her death, that my *vadder* loves only himself. He is the head of the family so everything he says must be obeyed." She spun back to face the front yard. "I did obey him time and again, like a dutiful *dochter*. But I won't now. This time I will listen to my heart. This is my home. My *vadder* doesn't know Harley is dead, and it wouldn't make a difference to him if he did. In his mind, it would be more of a reason for me to come 'home.' But Indiana is not home. New Berne is."

Lucy took a moment to breathe deeply and evenly before continuing. "Do you know what else he told me? That if Harley wouldn't watch his daughter, then I should get Harley's sister to watch the girl. All my *vadder* cares about is that I come to help his pregnant wife, the same wife who supposedly didn't want me around before now. I don't think he even likes me. If he liked me at all, he would never have treated me the way he did."

He leaned close to whisper in her ear. "Lucy, I like you." She could feel his breath on her nape. "I like you a lot."

She jerked with surprise and tried to face him again, but he kept her in place then lowered his chin to her shoulder. Leaning against the railing with Gabriel at her back, she softened against him. "I like you a lot, too," she admitted in a whisper. She was quiet for several moments. "Gabriel?"

"Hmm?"

"Will you let me see your leg?" She wanted to know more about him, including the times he suffered. How could she understand fully otherwise, if she didn't know?

She felt him tense up. "I…it's bad, Lucy. I'm not sure you're ready to see it."

"Oll recht." She cared deeply for him and wouldn't push him until he was ready. And eventually he would have to be if he wanted a future with her. If that was what he intended when he'd told her he liked her. Unless it was to comfort her when she'd confessed that she didn't think her father loved her like a father should. Gabriel would love his children, she thought. He was

kind and affectionate with Susie. He would make a wonderful father.

"Let's go for a walk," he suggested.

"Are you sure you want to?" She hesitated. "Susie—"

"I'm fine." He smiled at her. "And we won't go far. We'll be able to hear her if she wakes up."

"Let's walk, then," Lucy said and reached for his arm, her fingers gripping his bicep.

They descended the porch steps into the yard. The sun had dipped lower in the sky, and he could see lightning bugs by the evergreens that lined the roadway in front of her house. Gabriel directed them to the side of the house and Lucy easily followed his lead. He stayed on her left. Reaching for her hand, he interlocked their fingers. The warmth of her hand against his heated her from the inside out. She loved spending time with him, eating and sharing secrets. He had shared something painful with her, and she had told him about her father's letter.

"Gabriel?" she asked, her voice reaching out to him in the dusk.

Thanks to Gabriel, Lucy had begun to understand that *Gott* had a plan for her, a life that had included heartache but would also give her joy.

She stepped back and held his hand, leaning against him slightly as they continued their evening stroll. They walked around, not straying far from the house. As night descended, the pain of their pasts seemed to linger in the air between them. Gabriel gave her fingers an affectionate squeeze and she felt a lightening within her heart.

She wanted to hold on to these moments with him

until they reached the point where they both felt secure with one another.

"You've become quiet," she said as they neared the porch after circling the house twice.

"Just thinking."

"About?"

He halted, touched her cheek. "You." She felt the warmth of his hand as he caressed her face before he withdrew his touch. "I should go. It's getting late."

"Ja," she breathed.

"I don't want to go, but I'll come back tomorrow... if you want."

She gave her answer by leaning into him. "I'd like that," she said.

They stood close, and he seemed as reluctant as she for the night to be over. When Gabriel kissed her cheek, she nearly swooned. *"Gut nache*, Lucy. I'll see you tomorrow afternoon. I have a delivery to make in the morning. If I get done early, I'll come sooner."

"I'll look forward to seeing you again." At his gentle urging, she climbed the steps. "Until tomorrow, Gabriel."

Gabriel carried the sweet memory of the evening with Lucy all the way home.

Emily was surprisingly awake and reading by oil lamp when he entered the house fifteen minutes later. "You've been gone a long time," she said accusingly. "You were with her again, weren't you?"

"Do you have a problem with my spending time with Lucy, *schweschter*? I thought your problem was with Lucy and Aaron together, not with her and me."

With a heavy sigh, she closed her book. "It is with

her and Aaron, but it's been hard since Aaron has stayed absent."

He pulled out a chair and sat next to her. "Em, Lucy doesn't care for him. She told me that Aaron was her husband's best friend and he keeps trying to help her, but she doesn't want or need his help." He waited until she met his gaze. "Are you sure Aaron is the right man for you?"

Tears filled her eyes. "I don't know. I love him, but I'm beginning to wonder if he ever had feelings for me."

"You are a warm, *gut*-hearted woman. If not Aaron, then you will meet some other man deserving of your affections." He studied her bent head. "You look exhausted. Why don't you go to bed? Tomorrow is another day and things may look different."

Nodding, Emily rose and reached for the oil lamp. "Are you coming up?"

"In a few minutes." He stood and took a flashlight from a kitchen drawer. "Go ahead up. I've got my light to see." He switched on the light. After watching his sister leave, Gabriel poured himself a glass of milk and sat down again, his thoughts lingering on his day with Lucy, the woman he cared about. And he smiled.

After Gabriel left, Lucy was too excited to head up to bed. His friendship, his caring, made her feel good about herself. She made herself a cup of hot milk, sweetening it with sugar, then she sat in the kitchen and wrote back to her father. She didn't mention Harley's death in her letter. Her father would have pushed it as an excuse for her return to Indiana.

Dear Vadder,
I won't be returning to Indiana. My life is here
in Pennsylvania. I have a daughter to raise and
soon I'll have another baby of my own. My life
and my friends are here, and I'm not leaving.
You will have to find someone else to help Mari.
Lucy

With her letter done, she finished her warm milk, headed up to bed and fell asleep with thoughts of the wonderful evening spent in Gabriel's company.

The next morning at 5 a.m., she woke up refreshed and ready for the day. The first thing she did after dressing was to put a stamp on the envelope addressed to her father and put it in the mailbox by the road. Susie was still in bed when she returned. After a quick check on her daughter, Lucy went to work, baking cakes, pies, muffins and bar desserts to replace her stock at King's and Peter's Pockets. Her buggy would be arriving today, and she wanted all of her bakery items ready for delivery. She allowed everything to cool before she wrapped each treat and labeled them for sale.

The sun shone through the kitchen windows, which she opened to allow in the fresh air. Susie came downstairs at eight, and with a warning to stay put, Lucy gave her a muffin to eat on the front porch. Basking in the warmth and joy of the day, Lucy ate a bowl of cornflakes then enjoyed a second cup of tea. She wondered what time this afternoon Gabriel would get here.

Suddenly, she heard the rumble of a truck coming up her driveway. Lucy opened the side door just as the large flatbed tow truck carrying her newly repaired buggy pulled up alongside the house and parked.

"*Mam*, a truck is here!" Susie cried, running from the porch through the house to reach her.

"*Ja, dochter*. It's our buggy," Lucy told her, pleased with how Eli had made the vehicle look brand-new.

"It looks shiny!" Susie pushed to get past her, but Lucy grabbed her before she could run out to the truck.

She watched the men roll off her buggy. "Where to?" one asked.

Lucy gestured toward her outbuilding. "Could you put it close to the barn?"

The truck left a short time later. Lucy wanted to hitch up her horse, but she knew it would be better if she waited for Gabriel to do it for her. She couldn't stop the warm happiness that filled her up in knowing the wonderful man whose company she enjoyed so much would soon be there. They'd shared a lot with each other recently, even confessed that they liked each other. He meant a lot to her. She trusted the feeling was mutual. For a heartbreaking moment, the thought that he didn't care for her as much as she cared for him entered her mind, worrying her. Until she remembered the way he'd looked at her and held her hand as they walked together near her house, and her concern disappeared.

It was up to God to decide. If their relationship was meant to be, it would happen.

Chapter Twelve

At noon, Gabriel parked his buggy next to Lucy's. He'd woken up this morning with a painful twinge in his leg and had been quick to put on a lidocaine patch. The patch seemed to work, and thankfully the pain had dissipated as if it had never been. He got out and walked around Lucy's repaired vehicle, pleased with how wonderful it looked, almost brand-new.

Eli Lapp had done a good job. He'd have to keep the carriagemaker in mind if he ever needed work done on any of his carriages or if he wanted to purchase a new one.

He left the buggy to head toward the house then changed directions when he saw Lucy sitting outside with Susie on a quilt spread out on the grass. Mother and daughter looked beautiful with the sun shining on their smiling faces. He was overwhelmed with joy as he headed their way.

"You're here!" Susie cried when she saw him. She jumped up from the quilt and ran to meet him.

"How are my two favorite girls today?" he asked as he dared to pick up Susie, hefting her into his arms for a brief hug before setting her down. His leg didn't feel the strain under Susie's weight. The NSAIDs and the patch he wore under his pants leg did wonders for him. He'd begun to feel, to hope, that he could continue to live a pain-free life.

Studying the woman before him, he saw a beautiful soul behind a lovely face. The memory of last evening with Lucy made him happy and warm whenever he looked at her. And he said a silent prayer of thanks when he saw that delight in her bright blue eyes as they locked gazes. She was as pleased to see him as he was to see her.

With her in mind, Gabriel had dressed nicely in a bright spring green short-sleeved shirt with navy pants. He tugged off his hat and laid it along with his cell phone on the quilt before he sat down on the edge. Susie didn't join them. She ran around the backyard with excess energy. The child was a whirlwind of motion, an adorable, loving whirlwind of joyful, youthful motion.

Gabriel watched Susie for a minute before turning his attention fully to Lucy. He leaned close to her. "*Hallo*, Lucy," he murmured into her ear.

"Gabriel, you're just in time for lunch. I made extra sandwiches in case you stopped by earlier than expected."

He gave a slow smile. She jerked. "Oh!" She cradled her abdomen and laughed. When Gabriel tilted his head with curiosity, she grinned. "The baby moved." He became startled when she grabbed his hand and placed it on her belly. Her unborn daughter or son moved for him, and he widened his eyes. "Lucy," he breathed in awe.

"I know. It's amazing."

He dipped his head and didn't move his hand, startled by the intimacy and wonder of feeling the ripples that were her baby's movements. The warmth of her beneath his fingers felt alive and comfortable. They locked gazes, and with a little grin of embarrassment, he sat back, taking his hand with him.

"Gabriel, a baby isn't easy," she began as if it was something that she needed him to consider. "Not like Susie. A baby cries a lot and needs twenty-four-hour care."

"I know," he said with a small smile. "You think I've never been around a baby." He grew quiet and pain flickered across his features. "My *bruder* David," he said, "He was two years old when he died. I remember what it was like to have a *bubbel* in the *haus*."

She looked stricken. "I'm sorry."

"I'm not sorry that you're pregnant, Lucy. If we… I'd easily love your baby because the child will be yours. Don't think you having a baby will make me change my mind…you, because nothing can do that. Nothing." He paused. "Do you understand?"

Her eyes filled with tears. "I understand," she whispered.

Gabriel never expected to love again, but Lucy Schwartz turned out to be a woman he could see himself falling for. His feelings for her were stronger than what he'd ever felt for Lizzy.

Watching her, he was overwhelmed with emotion. He'd never felt a baby move inside a mother before. Some might be shocked that he and Lucy had gotten so close, but they had been through so much—in the past, before they'd met, and together. They hadn't actually exchanged words of love. Perhaps it was too soon for that, but he was falling for her.

"Susie, are you ready to eat?" Lucy called as her daughter continued to race around the yard.

Watching her with amusement, Gabriel figured she'd wear herself out and be ready for a nap not long after eating. Susie ran to the quilt and beamed at him as she sat down close to him.

"Are you going to eat with us?" she asked.

Gabriel met Lucy's gaze before he answered her daughter. "*Ja*, little one."

"Peanut butter and jelly for Susie," she declared. Lucy handed him a sandwich. "And for us, chicken salad with lettuce on white bread."

Gabriel unwrapped the sandwich and took a bite. "Best chicken salad ever," he said, closing his eyes briefly as Susie had done. "*Ja! Wunderbor gut!*" He was delighted when Lucy laughed outright.

"*Danki.* I'm glad you like it." Her lips curving, Lucy handed him a bottle of water.

"I like everything about you," he whispered out of Susie's earshot.

Her bright blue eyes lit up. "I feel the same…" she stole a glance at Susie, who was watching two tiny birds scuttling through the grass while she ate "…about you," Lucy breathed. "But Gabriel…"

He sighed. "I know. We've known each other only a short time."

"*Ja.*" She looked cautious, wary, but he knew she felt the same way. She showed how much she cared about him from the look in her eyes to the warmth of her smile. They would be together, he thought. He just had to be patient.

After finishing lunch, Lucy gave out the cupcakes she'd made. Gabriel experienced a deep feeling of contentment as he ate a cupcake with Lucy and Susie. "Your buggy looks *gut*. Eli did a nice job," he said after he swallowed a delicious bite of cake.

Lucy chewed and swallowed her own bite of cake then ran her tongue over the frosting that had stuck to her upper lip. "*Ja*, they brought it this morning."

"You didn't hitch up your horse," he observed.

"*Nay*, I was waiting for you."

He grinned. *"Gut maydel!"*

She returned his grin. "I'm hardly a girl."

"That's true," he admitted. "You must be old enough to be my *grossmudder*. You're seventy-five, *ja*?" He couldn't control his smile.

She balled up her sandwich wrapper and threw it at him. "Hardly."

He regarded her with affection "How old, Lucy?"

"Twenty-three." She raised her eyebrows. "And you?"

"Twenty-six." He cracked a smile. "The perfect ages."

He heard a rumble from the street. "Mailman," Lucy said and watched as the man stopped and took something out of the mailbox before he drove on.

He felt her relax as the mailman drove away. "Do you want to go for a ride next week?" he asked.

She spun to face him. "Next week?"

"*Ja*, I have to spend some time in my workshop and making deliveries, but mostly, Jed King and some others are coming to work on my new store."

Lucy widened her eyes at his news. "You're going

to open your own store! That's *wunderbor*, Gabriel!" She smiled.

He grinned. "'Tis something I've always wanted. I'm doing well, and while I haven't lived here long, I've made good contacts. I know what people—both Amish and English—like to buy. It will be easier for me to sell my merchandise in my own store, and I won't have to share the profits."

"Where will you build it?" she asked.

"Right on my property. Jed is going to help me convert part of the barn into the wooden crafts store." His eyes were full of excitement, and she loved seeing him this happy and pleased. "It will work best until I can move to a bigger space someday. The cost of renting isn't something I want to invest in right now. Maybe after my business expands enough for it to be an easy move."

Lucy nodded. "I understand. Someday when my children are grown, I may open my own bakery."

"You're doing well at King's and Peter's Pockets." He reached into his hand and pulled out a small sheet of paper, which he handed to her. "A few other shops who might be interested in selling your bakery items."

Lucy beamed at him. *"Danki,"* she breathed with an awed look in her pretty blue eyes. "Gabriel, I have a delivery to make in the morning, so I was wondering..." She bit her lip. "Would you hitch up my mare to my buggy?"

"You don't have to ask. I'll be by in the morning early and do it for you first thing."

Early the next morning, Gabriel returned to hitch Lucy's mare to her buggy. He grabbed the tack he'd need from inside the barn, then he went into the paddock with a chunk of apple that Lucy had given him to lure Blackie in. The mare was close to the outbuilding, so the apple worked well. As he held it out for the horse to eat, he grabbed onto her halter with his other hand. The mare munched happily and remained docile as he moved her from the paddock through a gate to the front of the buggy. Within a short time, Blackie was hitched to it, ready for Lucy to take later this morning.

Gabriel wished he could drive her where she needed to go, but he had things to do that could provide a better future for him…and anyone else he wanted to include in his life.

He got into Lucy's buggy and maneuvered it to where he could tie up the mare. He was finishing up when he sensed Lucy's presence. He turned and smiled at her. "You're all set."

"Danki." She regarded him warmly, and he felt her look clear down through him. She handed him a wrapped package. "Chocolate upside-down cake, a favorite of my brother-in-law and others within our community."

He smiled and touched her cheek. *"Danki,* Luce. I know I'll enjoy every bite." He wasn't ready to leave her, but he knew he had to go. "So next week? Will you and Susie take that ride with me?"

"Where are we going?"

"No place. Every place. Just for a ride to enjoy the sun and changing scenery. It will be the first week of summer. Will you come with me?"

"I'll come," she agreed. "What day?"

"Tuesday?"

She nodded, although she looked disappointed.

"*Gut.* Be ready early. By eight. I plan to make a day of it."

Her expression brightened. "We'll be ready."

Gabriel left, eager to see her again, but he had to make sure he could provide for his future. And for the woman and two children he wanted in his life.

Tuesday seemed like a long way from now, Lucy thought as she and Susie got into her buggy that morning. She would take her daughter to Nancy's first. She would normally have Susie come with her, but this was the first time she'd driven since the accident, and she was nervous. It wasn't too far to Nancy's. Her sister-in-law, she knew, would be happy to keep Susie for the couple of hours she'd need to make her deliveries and do some shopping. Thankfully, her wrist was feeling much better, and she no longer needed to wear the Ace bandage at all.

Nancy was outside as Lucy pulled onto the lane that led to the Joseph Yost house. "*Hallo*, Lucy! Susie! What a lovely surprise!"

Lucy stepped down and waited until Susie climbed out after her. "I was hoping you wouldn't mind keeping Susie for a couple of hours. I have a few errands to run, and I think she'd enjoy being with you here more."

Nancy's smile was warm. "We'd love to have her. Susie, why don't you go inside? Sarah is in the kitchen eating breakfast. I made chocolate chip muffins this morning!"

Susie grinned. "Bye, *Mam*! See you later!" she cried and ran into the house.

After gazing after her for a few moments, Lucy met Nancy's eyes. *"Danki."*

"Are you *oll recht*?" Nancy asked, looking at her thoughtfully.

"*Ja*, I'm fine. Why?"

"I don't know. You seem off. Nervous."

Lucy gave her a wry smile. "My buggy just came out of the shop. It's been a while since I've used it."

But Nancy was shaking her head. "That's not it." She looked toward her buggy. "It looks brand-new."

"*Ja*. Eli Lapp did an amazing job fixing it." Lucy gasped. She should have kept silent.

"Did you have an accident in your buggy, Lucy?" Nancy walked over to Lucy's vehicle and examined it from all sides.

"Maybe a little one," Lucy admitted grudgingly.

She heard Nancy's sharp inhalation of breath, saw the concern on the woman's face. "What happened?"

"A car hit me from behind, spooking Blackie and sending my buggy into a ditch."

"Lucy!"

"I'm *oll recht*. I sprained my wrist, but it's fine now." Lucy bit her lower lip, debating. "That's how I met Gabriel. He stopped to help me."

"Praise the Lord for Gabriel." Nancy grew quiet. "How is he?"

"He's well, I think." Lucy wasn't ready to talk about her feelings for Gabriel Fisher. "I should get going. I won't be long. I need to deliver these cakes and pies."

"Are you coming over for Visiting Day?" Nancy asked.

"I...actually, Rachel King invited me to her and Jed's *haus*."

"*Gut.*" Nancy grinned at her. "We've been invited, too. We'll drive you."

Relieved, Lucy smiled. "That would be nice. *Danki*. I should get going. I'll see you in a little while." She climbed into the driver's seat of her buggy and guided her horse around toward the road. She waved to her sister-in-law, who waved back but was gazing at her with worry. *I'll be fine*, she thought. *I'll always be fine no matter what happens in the future.*

She thought of Gabriel as she drove toward her first destination, Peter's Pockets, and felt happy. When she was done, she'd consult Gabriel's list and stop to talk briefly with the store owners.

It had been less than five hours since she'd seen Gabriel last, but she missed him all the same. Gabriel had business to take care of and so did she. Lucy concentrated on doing what needed to be done with the warmth and joy she felt in knowing that she'd be seeing him again in less than six days.

"I don't know, Gabriel," Jed King said as he examined the space Gabriel had selected for his store in the barn. "The existing walls aren't in the best shape. It might be better if you build a separate building. How big do you need it? Sixteen-by-sixteen?"

Gabriel frowned. He didn't want to hear that he couldn't use the barn, but Jed would know best, and if building his store there wasn't a good idea, he would listen to the former construction worker. "*Ja*, sixteen-by-sixteen would do."

"You could build it closer to the road for exposure. You own that strip of land on the other side of the barn?"

"*Ja*." Gabriel studied the land in question. "Why? You think the store should be built there?"

"I do. Why don't I work up a price for you for material, then you can let me know. There'll be no cost for labor, as you're one of us now." Jed grinned. "I'll ask Aaron Hostetler and a few others to help me. Aaron is particularly *gut* at this kind of work. With the group of us, it won't take but two days at the most to get it done."

Gabriel arched his eyebrows. "That fast?"

"*Ja.* 'Tis only sixteen feet. And don't you worry, we'll make it look inviting like any of the shops on Main Street. Will you need a stockroom?"

"No need for one. I'll keep extra stock in my workshop." Gabriel was excited. The prospect of the new store construction sounded wonderful. And it wouldn't take deep pockets to get it done.

Jed leaned against the picnic table in Gabriel's backyard and made a sketch of the building. "Something like this," he said as he showed it to Gabriel when he was done. "You can put a counter here. Have a window on each side wall for daylight. The front door will have glass in it and will give you more light. You can put shelves along here and here, and you may want glass in the counter where you can display your smaller wooden craft items."

Gabriel liked what he saw. "That looks *gut*. Let's do it!"

Jed gave him a smile that lit up his blue eyes. "It will feel *gut* to build something again." He paused. "I miss working in construction, but I do enjoy working in my family's store." He folded up the paper and placed it on the front seat of his vehicle. "Are you coming on Sunday? We're having friends over for Visiting Day. You and your sister are invited and most *willkomm*."

"I appreciate that."

"I'll have the list of material and the cost ready for you."

"I'll see you then," Gabriel said as he stood back while Jed climbed into his vehicle. "What can we bring?"

"Yourselves," Jed called out before he drove away.

Gabriel would have to ask Emily to make something. He wondered if he'd see Lucy there with Susie. He smiled at the prospect of seeing her sooner than their planned Tuesday outing.

Chapter Thirteen

Visiting Day at the Kings' was going to be a large event with friends and extended family. On Saturday morning, Lucy set about making two of the promised chocolate upside-down cakes that Nancy's family and others within their community had told her was their favorite dessert. Susie sat on the floor playing with her wooden waddling duck toy as Lucy measured the ingredients and set them in two separate bowls.

She was getting ready to mix up the first cake when she heard a car in the driveway. Curious, Lucy went to the door and stepped outside. She didn't recognize the car as belonging to one of her English neighbors. The rear door of the sedan opened and a tall man stepped out. He grabbed a satchel, paid the driver then watched as the car drove away. The man turned and Lucy gasped. It was her younger brother.

"Seth?" She ran toward the young man, who was actually a boy of thirteen, and skipped to a stop in front of him. *"Bruder?"*

Seth looked at her with dull eyes. "Lucy. *Vadder*

told me I had to come." He glanced down and saw her pregnant belly, and his bright blue eyes widened.

Lucy smiled. "*Willkomm!* I'm so glad to see you." She reached for his arm, gazing at him with warmth and love as she led him toward the house. She'd missed her brother and always wondered if he was happy with their father at home. "Come in!"

Susie appeared at the door. "*Mam?* Who's that?"

"That's my *bruder*—and your *onkel*." She climbed the two steps to the stoop and opened the door, pulling Seth inside the house with her. "His name is Seth."

Her daughter grinned. "*Hallo, Onkel* Seth. Are you going to live here now, too?"

Looking uncomfortable, Seth averted his gaze.

"*Ja*, he is," Lucy said, deciding immediately. "Isn't that *wunderbor!*"

Seth looked at her then with a glimmer of hope in his blue eyes so like her own.

"We've got lots of room *Onkel* Seth! Sit down. You must be hungry. Did you come from far away?" Susie asked. She turned to Lucy. "Where did he live before now, *Mam?*"

"Indiana, where I grew up."

Susie nodded and pulled out a chair for Seth, gesturing for him to sit. "I think you'll like it here better, *Onkel* Seth. We love it here. And you'll get to meet Gabriel. He's our friend. He can be your friend, too."

He took a seat silently. He hadn't said a word since he'd arrived, except to tell her that their father forced him to come. Lucy wondered—and worried—about what had happened to make Seth so quiet.

"*Mam*, can we give *Onkel* Seth some cake? *Mam* made a lemon cake yesterday. She bakes a lot," Susie said. "She bakes and sells her cakes and other things in stores. But she always makes some for us to keep. The cake has lemon frosting. Do you like lemon cake with lemon frosting?" Her daughter was talking like a chatterbox.

Seth gazed at Susie as the little girl talked, and Lucy caught the beginning of a smile on her younger brother's face.

Lucy couldn't believe that Seth was here. He was a teenager now, a young man. She hadn't seen him since he was nine years old, and he was the only person she missed since leaving their Amish community in Indiana.

"Seth," Lucy said softly. "*Danki* for coming. Our home is now yours."

He stared at her a long time, and she was shocked to see tears form in his eyes. "I… *Danki*," he whispered with gratitude, and Lucy smiled.

It was only later that she realized what Seth's arrival could mean for her and Gabriel. She had Susie and her baby on the way, and now she would be raising her thirteen-year-old brother. They'd never confessed their feelings in definite terms, although it had certainly been implied between them. Lucy sighed. Would Gabriel be willing to take on all of them as his family?

"Where's your husband?" Seth asked quietly that evening after dinner and Susie had left the room. Lucy was glad to see that her brother was now relaxed enough to feel comfortable. She'd cared for him after their mother had passed on, before her father had made her marry Harley and leave. She was overjoyed to have him here.

"*Dat* died," Susie said, having overheard, as she slipped back into the room. "A long time ago."

Seth's gaze locked with Lucy's. "Nearly six months ago now," she told him.

"I'm sorry," he said. "I didn't know. *Dat* didn't know."

"He didn't care," Lucy said without heat. "He's only concerned with Mari."

Her brother nodded. "I don't want to be a burden," he said.

"Seth, you could never be a burden. You're my *bruder*, and I love you. I've missed you. I was worried when you didn't write back to me."

"You wrote to me?" he asked, looking stunned.

"*Ja*, of course I did. I didn't want to leave you. When I didn't hear back, I wanted to visit, but Harley…was against it." She smiled to show him how happy she was that he'd come. "I can't believe how much you've grown."

Seth's lips twitched. "I don't remember you being this short. And I never expected to see that," he said with a gesture toward her baby belly. His expression sobered. "Are you happy about it?"

"About the *bubbel*? *Ja*," she replied with a soft smile. "I love Susie—she's my daughter, and I want nothing more than to give her a baby *bruder* or *schweschter*."

Susie climbed up onto her uncle's lap, shocking him. "I don't care what we have, do you? As long as our baby's healthy."

Seth took one long look into Susie's eyes and grinned. "'Tis a *gut* thing I'm here to help your *mam*, then, *ja*?" He tugged on her *kapp* string. "She's going to need all the help we can give her."

"Ja," Susie agreed. "You, me and Gabriel, too."

"Gabriel?" her brother asked.

"Our neighbor."

"And *Mam*'s *gut* friend. We love him," Susie said, making Lucy blush.

Seth suddenly looked worried. "I don't want to intrude."

"You're family, Seth. You belong with us." Lucy could never turn Seth away. If Gabriel didn't like it, there was nothing she'd be able to do about it.

Lucy sent up a silent prayer that Gabriel would understand that if he wanted a relationship with her, then he would have to accept everyone who came with her. Her stomach burned at the thought that she could lose him, but there was nothing she could do to change her situation or her life.

Visiting Day turned out to be a large event on Jed and Rachel's property. Nancy and her family came for her and Susie—and with the added surprise of Seth—and brought them to join in the gathering. When they arrived, Joseph parked with the other buggies on the far side of the barn. Lucy noted there were ten buggies, if not more, as they drove up next to the one on the far end and got out. Caleb climbed out after his parents and helped Susie down, followed by Sarah, Seth and Lucy. Lucy and Seth each carried one of her requested chocolate upside-down cakes. As they entered the yard, Lucy looked around to see how many people she knew.

Rachel broke away from a group of women to meet them. "Lucy, you made your cakes!"

"Ja," Lucy said with a smile. "How are you, Rachel?"

"Fine. Fine. Nice gathering, *ja*?" Her gaze scanned the yard as if taking in the sight of all her guests. Her attention settled on Seth. "Who's this?" She smiled. "Wait, I can tell. You're Lucy's *bruder*."

Seth blinked. "How did you know?"

"We have the same color eyes," Lucy said. Eyes they'd inherited from Emma Troyer Graber, their mother.

"Come and I'll introduce you around." Rachel waved for them to follow her.

Lucy felt Seth looking at her and smiled. "'Tis fine. They are *gut* people here."

She started to trail after Seth, who was following Rachel, when she spied Gabriel at the far end of the backyard. He and Rachel's husband, Jed, were deep in a discussion. To Lucy's shock, Aaron Hostetler and several others were part of the group. She couldn't help wondering what they were talking about.

Emily Fisher approached her with a smile. "Lucy."

"*Hallo*, Emily. 'Tis nice to see you again." Lucy had trouble keeping her gaze from straying toward Gabriel.

"Are you looking at my brother or Aaron?" There was tension in the girl's voice.

"Gabriel."

Emily smiled. "I thought…" She exhaled loudly. "Aaron and I were seeing each other but then he pulled away, and I thought it was because of you."

Lucy was horrified. *"Nay!"*

Gabriel's sister laughed. "I can see that."

Gabriel happened to glance in her direction at that moment. After murmuring something to the other men, he left them and quickly headed her way. His expression was soft, his eyes warm, until he stumbled and she saw him grimace. He slowed his pace until he finally reached her side. "*Hallo*, Lucy. I'm happy to see you here." A small smile hovered on his lips.

"Don't mind me. I'll find someone else to talk with," Emily said with a chuckle.

To Lucy's astonishment, Gabriel's face turned red. "Sorry, Em. It's just that I haven't seen her in forever."

Emily's expression softened. "I'll leave you to her company, then," she said softly and left them alone.

"How are you, Lucy?" Gabriel asked, his eyes warm and affectionate. "I've missed you."

"I saw you talking earnestly with Jed and Aaron and some other men. What is that all about?"

"My store. I was going to convert part of my barn into the store, but Jed convinced me that it wasn't the best idea. He drew up plans for me. He, Aaron and a group of men from our community are going to do the work. They assure me that it won't take more than two days."

"That's *wunderbor*, Gabriel," she replied, sincerely happy for him. She glanced past him to see her brother headed her way. "Gabriel, something has changed at home," she said urgently. "There's something I need to tell you."

"Lucy!" Seth said with a grin. "They love your cake. They want to eat it before the meal!"

Lucy laughed. "Tell them to wait or I won't bring any next time."

"*Oll recht.*" Her brother left her then to return to a group of young people near the food table.

She turned back to Gabriel with a smile that quickly died when she saw the expression on his face. "Gabriel?"

"Who is that?" he asked as he reached down to rub his thigh.

She looked at his hand, and he immediately stopped what he was doing. "The someone I need to talk with you about—"

"Who is he?" he asked, his expression taunt.

Lucy gaped at him. "He's my *bruder*," she breathed, hurt by his tone. "Gabriel, what's wrong? Aren't you feeling well?"

"I'm fine."

But he didn't look well to her. She'd seen how his features had contorted briefly with pain before he regained control of it. "You don't look fine."

"I said I'm fine. So, your *bruder* has come to live with you?" he asked.

"That won't make a difference, will it? For us?"

"Lucy..." he began then stopped, looked away.

"You changed your mind about me."

He didn't meet her gaze.

"Listen, Lucy, we have to talk." He looked pained, regretful. "But not here."

Drawing a deep breath, Lucy studied him. "Something *is* wrong."

"I'll come by your *haus* this evening."

"Nay, if you want to talk, we'll talk now." She had to know what was bothering him.

"Fine."

Lucy felt a terrible sense of impending loss as she followed him toward the front of the house and around to the other side where trees separated the view from the backyard and no one was within earshot.

He halted abruptly and turned to her with pain in

his expression. "Lucy, I know we thought there was a possibility of a future with you but…"

"You've changed your mind."

"Ja." He looked away as if it was too painful for him to see her humiliation.

"Because of Seth—"

Gabriel stared at her then. "I have my reasons."

"Which doesn't mean *nay*."

"I'm sorry."

She spun, eager to leave him. It hurt too much to spend time in the company she cared for too deeply to ever get over him. Without glancing back, she hurried away but then something made her stop when she was several yards away. What she saw made her inhale sharply. Gabriel was hunched over, staring at the ground while he rubbed his thigh. He looked so dejected that her heart thumped hard. But then his head lifted and he locked gazes with her. His hard stare made her realize that she'd been mistaken. She walked away, knowing that she'd left a huge chunk of her heart behind with Gabriel Fisher.

Since she had come with Nancy, she'd have to stay and keep her distance from Gabriel. She was falling for him, and she'd been so sure he had feelings for her too.

Lucy recalled the look in his eyes when he'd seen her across the yard and immediately broken away from the men to meet her. He'd seemed happy to see her. Gabriel had appeared ready to accept her and her two children, but adding a teenage boy into the mix had been too much for him and he'd ended their relationship.

He didn't once look at her at all as he rejoined the men's discussion in the yard. Needing time alone to think, she started to walk in another direction. She didn't want anyone to see her cry.

"What's wrong?" Emily Fisher asked from behind her.

Lucy froze then faced her, unable to control her tears. "'Tis nothing." She wiped a hand under each eye to wipe away the moisture.

The girl looked beyond her to where Gabriel was probably standing. Lucy didn't know for sure. "Gabriel," she said with a *tsk*. "Did you two argue?"

"Not exactly."

Seth came up to her and Emily then. "Hey, Lucy, some of the others want me to join in their baseball game. Is it *oll recht*?"

Lucy managed to control her hurt feelings to give her brother a genuine smile. "Of course. Have fun."

"Who's that?" Emily asked.

"Seth. My *bruder*."

Gabriel's sister stared a moment in the other direction and laughed. "Lucy, he's jealous! Of Seth!"

"*Nay*, Gabriel knows he's my *bruder*. I told him." Lucy continued to wipe her cheeks, making sure there was no lingering trace of her tears.

Emily narrowed her gaze. "I wonder what's bothering him. Maybe 'Tis his leg."

Lucy shook her head. "He said we needed to talk We did, and he broke up with me." *As if we were a couple instead of friends, although we were heading to become more.*

"He didn't!" The young woman was stunned.

"*Ja*, and I think I know why. 'Tis because Seth will be living with me now. I come with a young *dochter*, a *bubbel* on the way and now a thirteen-year-old boy. Too much for any man."

"*Nay*, Lucy. I don't think that's a problem for him. You mean something to my *bruder*, and no woman has meant anything to him since the fire. I could tell by the way he talks about you that you are someone special to him, more so than Lizzy, his former betrothed, ever was."

"Lizzy... I got the feeling that she hurt him badly," Lucy said.

"She devastated him," Emily explained, "breaking off their betrothal when he was at his most vulnerable. He was injured and needed her support but she only cared that he was a broken man who could no longer take care of her."

A tingle along the back of her neck made Lucy turn to find Gabriel staring at her, but when he saw her glance he turned quickly away. "Our friendship is new, and while I'd hoped we'd become more than friends, Gabriel doesn't want the same thing. I don't think he's ready for an instant family, and I understand. I really do, but I love Susie and Seth, and I already love my unborn baby."

"And Gabriel?" Emily asked, her expression serious, her voice quiet.

"I'll always care about Gabriel, Emily, but I know that he deserves better than all this responsibility."

"And what about me? Am I a complication you don't need?"

"*Nay*, Emily! You would always be a part of our family." Lucy clapped a hand over her mouth. "Oh."

Emily's expression softened. "Lucy, Gabriel has always wanted a family. Do you think having four new people in his life won't make him happy?" Emily shook her head. "If you think that, then you're wrong. He loves you but he's afraid. He wants you but feels he is too damaged to have you."

Lucy shook her head. "He's not the damaged one. I am," she said.

"He's the one who suffered the loss of his family. He's the one with the scarred leg," Emily pointed out. "Not you."

She knew Emily was right, but she still kept away from him. She remembered how he'd rubbed his thigh until she caught him at it. Had he been in pain? What that why he'd pushed her away? It didn't matter, she decided. She wanted to leave but she couldn't ask her sister-in-law to go. While Lucy felt miserable, Nancy and her family were having a wonderful time.

She ate and engaged in conversation with her new friends Rachel, Maggie and Hannah. If they noticed that she was sad, they didn't comment. Lucy hoped they couldn't tell how bad she felt inside.

At least twice, she saw Gabriel head in her direction, and she fled to avoid him, pretending an eagerness to join in a conversation with a group of women.

Finally, people began to leave. Lucy, more than ready, waited with Susie and Seth near the buggy for Nancy and the rest of her family to come and take them home.

She could feel Gabriel's gaze on her but she refused to acknowledge him.

Minutes later, she was headed home and couldn't be more relieved to reach the privacy of her small house.

"I'll see you soon," Nancy called out after Joseph had dropped off her family, before they'd left.

"Lucy?" Seth asked as she climbed the steps and unlocked the door. "Are you *oll recht*?"

Lucy managed a smile for him. "I'm fine. Does anyone want a snack and a drink? I have some homemade chocolate chip cookies!" she said cheerfully, although she didn't feel happy.

"*Ja, Mam!* Seth, can you get *Mam*'s cookie tin! I'd like milk with my cookies. What about you, Seth?"

Lucy heard Seth tease her daughter, and she finally managed a genuine smile. She might have lost Gabriel but she still had Seth, Susie and her unborn baby. She'd somehow find comfort in her little family.

Gabriel was tense as he and his sister drove home from the Kings'.

"You are an idiot," Emily said.

He glared at her. "Excuse me?" His thigh ached something terrible and he stifled the urge to rub it. It had started to cramp up when he'd approached Lucy. In fact, it had hurt so bad he'd nearly stumbled and fell. Right then and there, he should have turned around and stayed away from her. It wasn't good for a man to snap at the woman he was falling in love with. But loving her didn't change the fact that he was too much of a damaged man to be good for her.

"You love Lucy yet you're ready to give up your relationship with her." She shook her head. "You're a fool, Gabriel Fisher. I thought you were a smart man, but you're not."

The truth of her words hit him hard. He hadn't told her how the stabbing pain had returned frequently and that he'd been hiding it so that she wouldn't worry. He hadn't confided in her about the surgery he might have to undergo that might help with the pain. He still had other options, but he feared that none of them would work. He still wasn't sure he could ever agree to another operation, but he might not have any choice. "Emily, you don't understand—"

"I understand that you are too willing to give up a chance at happiness with the woman you love. Lucy is *gut* for you, Gabriel. I've never seen you this happy before."

Gabriel stayed silent. He didn't know what to say. "I'm broken, Em."

"Broken? What, physically?" Emily said. "*Nay!* Broken inside, maybe. How do you think Lucy feels? She has a father who doesn't love her enough to keep her at home. *Nay*, he had to marry her off to get rid of her so he could wed a pretty young wife. Then she had a husband who gave her a sweet daughter, but did he care for her? Love her? *Nay*." She placed her hand on his arm to draw his attention. "I don't know what is going through that thick head of yours, but you need to think long and hard about your relationship with her."

"I have been." And he'd done the right thing—the best thing—for Lucy.

He'd thought he'd gotten over the worst of the pain. He'd lived a couple of days pain free since he'd seen the doctor. And then the pain had returned, its intensity worse than before. Maybe he should see Dr. Jorgensen again, he thought. Did he really want to lose Lucy forever? No, he didn't. Maybe he needed to find out more about the surgery he eventually could be forced to have.

Gabriel said in a strangled voice. "My leg's been bad, Em. Really bad. Nothing seems to be helping."

"*Ach nay, bruder.*"

He closed his eyes. "I can't be a burden to her."

She studied him with sympathy. "She cares about you, too, you know."

"What if she no longer does because she's tired of having to deal with me as I am?" He faced her, feeling vulnerable. "My leg, Em. The doctors said that if nothing else works, I might need surgery."

"Oh, Gabriel…" Emily said softly. "You can't let your leg rule your life. Lucy isn't Lizzy. She's a better person. She's strong and the right woman for you. She will understand that you'll have *gut* and bad days. All you have to do is explain and convince her you love her and want her in your life."

He huffed out a laugh. "That's all?"

Emily snickered. "*Bruder*, I didn't say it would be easy."

Chapter Fourteen

Gabriel had messed up with Lucy. He loved her desperately, but because of his fears and unwillingness to share all of his pain with her, he had hurt her badly. His sister was right, he knew. Lucy had become important to him, and he'd driven her away before she could leave him. His leg had been hurting, but that was no excuse. It was possible that it would always hurt him. He couldn't let it stop him, not if he wanted to live again. Perhaps she would forgive him after he explained. But what if he needed the surgery? He didn't want to put Lucy through the worry of the procedure and his recovery afterward. He realized with sudden clarity that he'd been afraid she would leave him like Lizzy had. But as Emily reminded him, Lucy wasn't Lizzy. Lizzy had been weak, while Lucy was strong. He had never loved Lizzy the way he loved Lucy. He gasped. *Ja*, he loved Lucy! He couldn't give her up, but would he be able to convince her to give him another chance.

Lucy Schwartz was a loving, wonderful mother and a sweet woman, and he could easily envision her as his wife and the mother of his children. He wanted Susie and her baby for his own, and Seth… He would enjoy raising Lucy's brother. The boy needed a man who cared about him, who would stand by him and teach him things that a man needed to know.

He realized he'd never gotten over the trauma of the fire, the loss of his family compounded by the rejection from the woman he'd thought he'd loved. He should have gotten help, but instead he'd suffered in silence, and had been afraid and acted foolishly because he hadn't been able to get past what had happened to his family, to Emily. To him.

He should have spoken openly with her about his feelings. That would have done more for him than any doctor ever could.

Lucy meant more to him than Lizzy ever had. Would he be able to fix things with her? Would she ever forgive him for being *doom-kop*?

Before Visiting Day, Lucy had agreed to go for a ride with him on Tuesday. He would visit her then and convince her to go on that ride. But first, he needed to talk with Seth. What if the boy didn't want him in his life? He understood that Seth would come first. Gabriel wanted her even if he would always be last. He loved her that much. And Seth? If Seth was all right having him as part of the family, then he would ask for the boy's help.

Gabriel left the house for the new store building that Jed, Aaron and two other men were building for him. He liked Jed, but he didn't know how he felt about Aaron. His sister had liked him, but he'd disappointed her because of Lucy—although Lucy had told him that she didn't want the man in her life. He'd believed her. He still did.

He should trust her. He *did* trust her. He was his own worst enemy, and he knew it. He had to change, or else lose all chance of happiness with the woman he had fallen in love with.

It was Tuesday morning, and his store building was nearly done, with windows and two doors. Jed and Eli Brubaker were whitewashing the exterior walls. Gabriel heard hammering inside and wondered what Aaron and Matthew Bontrager were doing.

"Looks *gut*," he said after he'd greeted Jed.

Jed stopped what he was doing to smile at him. "Told you it wouldn't take us long. We started it on Friday and we'll be done with it by the end of today. Aaron and Matt are inside working on your counter and your shelves." He paused. "What color do you want your door and trim? Something other than white, *ja*?"

"What do you think?"

"How about blue?"

Gabriel nodded. "Sounds *gut*. I'll let you pick the color." He stood back and gazed at the building with a good feeling. "May I look inside?" he asked.

"'Tis your place," Jed said, brushing on another swipe of white paint. "Go on in."

He opened the door and spied Aaron without a hat, his blond hair damp with sweat as he worked on the store counter. Three sides had been nailed together, leaving an opening in the front. The Formica top for the counter was leaning against the far wall. "What's that for?" Gabriel asked, gesturing toward the open end.

"For glass or plexiglass or whatever you want to put there to create a display case." Aaron barely looked him in the eyes. The man was clearly uncomfortable after learning that Emily was Gabriel's sister.

"Where's Matt?"

"He went out to pick up some wood screws and brackets for the shelves. We thought we had enough but we don't."

Gabriel chewed the inside of his mouth as he watched the other man work on his knees, checking measurements and driving nails in deep to hold the counter together. "Are you in love with Lucy?" he asked Aaron.

"What? *Nay!* She was my best friend's wife. I was worried about her."

"You don't need to be. I'll take care of Lucy from now on if she'll let me. I messed up with her but I intend to fix it."

Aaron glanced up at him with surprise. "You know Lucy?" His face lit up as the truth dawned on him. He smiled. "You know Lucy," he said softly. "Well, now I understand." He put down his hammer and stood, wiped the dampness from his brow. "Does she feel the same way?"

"I thought so, but I'm not sure," Gabriel admitted.

"I wish you all the best," Aaron said, sounding sincere. "Lucy tries to be independent."

"I know she does." He smiled. "And I like that about her, as long as she still allows me to help her." Gabriel needed to know what the man thought of his sister. "What about Emily? How do you feel about her?" He paused. "She's my sister."

The man's expression softened. "I like her."

"You canceled supper," Gabriel pointed out.

"Got hurt on the job that afternoon. Was in the emergency room."

"Why didn't you tell her?"

He crouched down to pick up his hammer. "My *bruder* was supposed to tell her."

"He didn't. He just told her that you weren't coming."

Aaron scowled. "No wonder she won't talk to me." Setting down his hammer, he rose to his feet. "I'll need to have a talk with her. I won't leave until she listens to me."

Gabriel chuckled. "I wish you all the best in that. Emily tends to be independent, like Lucy."

The other man cracked a smile. "That's what we love about them, *ja*?"

"Absolutely." He looked around the interior of the store, pleased with how it was shaping up. "This will work perfectly. *Danki* for taking the job with Jed and the others."

With a nod and a smile, Aaron bent down to get his hammer. "We'll be done today."

"So I hear. I appreciate it." Gabriel left the store and went to his workshop. Last night, he'd worked long into the night on something special for Lucy. She might not want it, but he'd put his heart and soul...and love... into this gift for her. He'd stained and varnished it last night, and he knew it was ready.

The cradle was well constructed, sanded smooth and stained, and it was just the right size for a newborn to use until he or she was several months old. Gabriel had debated whether or not to paint a design on the sides but then decided not to, not without Lucy's permission. Besides, he had no idea if she was carrying a boy or a girl.

He could use the cradle as an excuse to see her, but he didn't think it was right to do that. Besides, he wanted to talk with her brother, Seth, first, explain what he wanted—a life with Lucy, Susie, the baby and Seth. Would the boy accept him into his life? Would Lucy decide he wasn't worth a second chance with her time, her friendship…or her love?

Gabriel left the workshop and let his sister know that he was going out, before he got into his buggy to make the drive down the road to Lucy's house. If he could find Seth alone outside, he might be able to initiate a man-to-man talk with him. If he could make Seth understand how he felt, then maybe, with the boy's help, he'd have a chance at forever with the woman he loved.

Despite that he'd long given up the hope of a forever life with any woman before he met Lucy, he didn't want to live without her. He needed her and she needed him, but mostly he loved her and he thought she returned his love. If she did, maybe he'd have his forever after all.

He'd start with Seth and then go from there, for if the teenager didn't want him in Lucy's life, then Lucy wouldn't want him either. But he prayed that wouldn't be the case.

Tuesday morning Lucy felt listless. She was tired. She hadn't slept well since Sunday, after she and Gabriel had had words. He'd hurt her, and she'd become angry. Anger was a sin, and she felt terrible about it, repentant. She'd prayed to the Lord since he'd discarded her friendship. She still didn't have an idea of what the Lord had decided where she and Gabriel were concerned.

She missed him. With every breath she took, she missed him, and she wished they could redo Visiting Day and that things had gone differently. She should have asked about his leg, pushed to know the truth of why he had rejected her.

The more Lucy thought about that moment, the more she realized that there was more Gabriel hadn't told her. That he hadn't been scared off by the prospect of a ready-made family.

Gabriel has always wanted a family, Emily had said. *Do you think having four new people in his life won't make him happy? If you do, then you're wrong. He loves you but he's afraid. He wants you but feels he is too damaged to have you.*

And she had told Emily that she was the damaged one. She recalled Gabriel's concern with how people would react to him. She hated that he often felt that way. He was an attractive man who just happened to have a burn scar on his left cheek.

He had a severe one on his leg, too. Gabriel had admitted as much and said he wasn't ready to show it to her. Was it because he was afraid that she wouldn't want him, love him, if she saw it? And exactly how much did it bother him?

"Oh, Gabriel," she whispered. "Don't you know there is nothing that will ever make me stop loving you?"

How was she going to fix this? Should she go to his house to talk with him? It had only been one day. Maybe she should wait another day or two to give him time for clarity. Then she would approach him for a calm discussion during which she'd demand to know the truth, because the more she thought about it, the more she realized that he hadn't explained why he thought they should stop seeing each other.

Lucy tried to keep busy, and her baking helped to

keep her mind occupied. Still, thoughts of Gabriel lingered. As she made a chocolate cake, she remembered how much he loved her chocolate cream pie. When she made lemon squares, she recalled the first time she'd met Emily. Every ingredient she picked reminded her of Gabriel in some way. When she finished her baking, she gazed at the vast number of sweets that covered her countertop and kitchen table. And still thought about Gabriel as she looked at them.

She laughed without humor. It wasn't the ingredients, nor was it her cakes and pies that made her think of Gabriel. It was the fact that her love for him was lodged so deeply inside of her that she couldn't let it go. She didn't want to let it go. She'd never let it go.

The door behind her opened and slammed shut as Seth entered the house. "Lucy, do you need any help with anything?"

"You've driven a buggy before, *ja*?"

"I'm thirteen years old, not three, *schweschter*," he said with a teasing roll of his eyes. "Of course I have."

Lucy nodded. "If I give you a list, would you pick up a few things at the store for me?"

"*Ja*, I'll be happy to go for you."

"Where's Susie?" she asked as she jotted down several items with a pencil on paper.

Seth moved to peek out the window. "She's outside in the yard. Do you want me to take her with me?"

"*Nay*, I'd like her to come inside and rest for a while." Lucy felt terrible, for she'd sensed that Susie noticed a change in Lucy's relationship with Gabriel. Like Lucy, her daughter had slept badly ever since.

Seth took the list Lucy handed him, looked it over. "Where can I find these things?" he asked.

"King's General Store. Just make a left from our property and continue straight until you see the store on your right. Think you can find the way?"

Her brother nodded. "I'll get Susie for you before I go."

Lucy smiled and touched her brother's cheek. "*Danki*, Seth. Have I told you how much I love having you here?"

Seth smiled. "I never get tired of hearing it. And you should know that I love living here with you." Her brother exited the house and returned within minutes with Susie. "Here she is."

"You wanted me, *Mam*?"

"*Ja, dochter.* I'd like you to lie down with me. Will you do that?"

Susie tilted her head as she met Lucy's gaze. "With you?"

"*Ja.*"

"*Oll recht.*"

Seth hadn't left yet. "We're going to take a nap," Lucy told him. "Would you mind putting away the groceries for me after you bring them home?" Her brother nodded and left, and Lucy headed wearily upstairs with Susie, where they both lay down on her bed and rested. Her new resolve to talk with Gabriel again eased her mind a little, allowing her to fall asleep.

As he neared Lucy's property, Gabriel saw her buggy leave her driveway. He realized immediately that it wasn't Lucy who was driving. It was Seth. Recognizing a good opportunity when he saw one, he followed the vehicle until it turned into the parking lot of King's General Store and pulled all the way around to the hitching post in the back instead of using the one on the side of the building. He pulled in and parked beside Lucy's buggy, got out and tied up his horse as Seth secured Blackie.

Gabriel circled his vehicle. "Seth."

The teenager stiffened as he turned. He was tall for his age, an attractive boy with dark hair like his sister, and he also had Lucy's bright blue eyes. He wore a royal blue shirt and black tri-blend pants held up with black suspenders. His black-banded straw hat had a smaller brim than Gabriel's. "How do you know my name?"

"My name is Gabriel Fisher," he introduced himself pleasantly. "I live down the road from your sister."

Seth stared at him, narrowed his eyes. "You're Lucy and Susie's friend."

"Actually, Lucy and I had a bit of a disagreement, which I'd like to talk about, if you'll let me."

The boy looked uncertain. "I don't know." He glanced around the parking lot to see if anyone was watching them. "I'm not sure that Lucy would want me to."

Gabriel inhaled and went for it. "Seth, I love your sister. I want to marry her and I want you, Susie and the baby to be my family. Will you help me? I messed up and I could really use your help."

Seth blinked. "You want to marry my sister?"

Relieved that Seth didn't appear to be against the idea, Gabriel nodded. "*Ja*. But I… I need to talk with her, and I would like to talk with her alone. Do you think you could take Susie over to see her cousins, Sarah and Caleb, tomorrow morning? About nine?

Last week Lucy agreed to go for a ride with me today, but…"

Seth cracked a smile. "I get it. I'll help, if you're sure this is what you want." His smile disappeared. "I don't want Lucy hurt. My *vadder* hurt her enough to last a lifetime."

And hurt you as well, Gabriel thought, recognizing pain when he saw it in the boy's eyes. "I have never been more sure of anything in my life." He bucked up for what he had to say next. "And if she doesn't want me to be in her life, I'll respect that. The last thing I want to do is hurt or bother her." He shifted from one foot to the other. "What do you say?"

The boy grinned. "I'd say *willkomm* to the family, but you'll have to convince her of that first, *ja?*"

Gabriel laughed at the boy's teasing. "*Ja*. What are my chances?"

Seth tilted his head while he seemed to give it some thought. "*Gut,*" he said. "More than *gut*, I think."

He saw the list in the boy's hand "Do you need a hand with shopping?"

Lucy's brother looked at his list. "*Nay,* 'tis a short list."

"Don't always expect it to be so with your sister, Seth," Gabriel said as he headed toward his buggy and was gratified to hear the boy laugh.

The next morning, Gabriel was up and dressed early while it was still dark. To say he was nervous was putting it lightly. His future with Lucy depended on his apology and his convincing her to give him a second chance. They'd never talked about a future together, but he'd certainly thought about one from the first moment he'd laid eyes on her. He'd denied it, but he knew it was true. He had an ugly burn scar and persistent trouble with his leg. Would Lucy really want a man who was that damaged? He'd have to explain that eventually he might have to undergo surgery. He would upfront and honest. He prayed that it would be enough to win her love.

Then he thought about his feelings for Lucy, how Susie, her unborn child and now the newest member of her family, Seth, hadn't changed his love for her. Her family members only enhanced his love. She was everything he'd ever wanted in a woman. He could see them years from now, working side by side in the house, in their store. His new store might not be big enough for Lucy's bakery items, but it would do until they found a bigger place, a bigger house, for he wanted more children with Lucy.

At eight forty-five, Gabriel put the cradle he'd made for Lucy's baby into the back of his buggy then headed toward Lucy's house. If she rejected him, he'd leave the cradle and go. He wanted her to have it. He'd planned to give her something special, and the baby cradle seemed like a good thing for an expectant mother. And if she accepted him into her life, then the cradle would hopefully get a lot of use, he thought with a smile.

He saw Seth leaving the property with Susie, the boy driving the buggy with expert hands. Seth was going to make a fine man, he thought. And if he had anything to do with it, Seth would never doubt that he was loved and wanted in his sister's home—which would hopefully be his, too.

When the buggy was but a spot in the distance, Gabriel turned onto Lucy's property and parked close to the road. He hoped that Lucy hadn't heard him arrive. He wanted to surprise her, catch her off guard. He left the cradle in the buggy and walked the rest of the way toward the house. His leg tightened up, but he breathed through it. He wasn't going to allow his pain to keep him from the woman he loved—this new feeling was also giving him a new determination.

He continued until he reached the top of her stoop and knocked.

"What did you forget, Seth?" he heard Lucy say as the door opened. She gaped at him. "Gabriel!"

"*Hallo*, Lucy," he ventured shyly. "May I come in?"

She wouldn't look away. *"Ja."* She stepped aside as he entered.

He pulled off his hat and hung it up as he usually did on the wall hook. "Yesterday, we had plans for a ride."

Lucy frowned. "I thought they were canceled."

"I understand why you thought that," he acknowledged with a nod. "May I tell you something?"

Lucy's blue eyes filled with wariness. "What is it?"

"I love you. I'm sorry for the way I acted. I love you so much and I want to marry you, if you'll have me." He held up his hand and rushed on when she opened her mouth to speak. "I want you and Susie and your baby…and Seth. I want all of you to be my family. I'm not an easy person to live with. I can be irritable when my leg hurts. And, Lucy, my leg…it's ugly. It's ugly and sometimes I feel terrible stabbing pains while other times I feel pins and needles. I've seen my neurologist, Dr. Jorgensen, and he's working with me to help with the pain. And the pain gets bad sometimes. I may need surgery if my doctor doesn't find another way to manage it. I didn't want to put you through the worry, but I can't live without you. You don't deserve someone as damaged as me, but I'm asking for a second chance anyway. I've never met anyone like you. I've never loved anyone as much as you." He closed his eyes in silent prayer before he continued. "Be my wife, my love, and the mother of not only the children we have already but our future children. We can own a store together. We'll sell my wooden crafts and your cakes and pies. I don't expect an answer right away," he said. "I'll give you all the time you need, but please give me a chance at loving you…at loving our ready-made family."

He turned, picked up his hat and reached for the door.

"Where do you think you're going?" Lucy said softly.

Gabriel turned, faced her. The light in her blue eyes and the softness in her expression gave him hope. "Lucy?"

"*Ja*, Gabriel. I will marry you. I decided I'd never marry again unless it was for love. And I do love you, Gabriel." Tears filled her eyes as she gazed at him. "Just do me a favor? Talk to me when something bothers you so we work things out when there is a problem, and I promise to do the same."

He eyed her with joy. "I promise," he said as he hung up his hat again. He went to her, pulled her into his arms and kissed her on the forehead. "I love you, Lucy."

"I love you, Gabriel."

"And now we wait until Seth gets home with Susie so we can tell them both."

Lucy frowned. "How did you know that Seth left with Susie?"

His lips twitched. "I may have had a little help so that I could get a few minutes alone with you to apologize and propose."

"You talked with Seth?" she asked with raised eyebrows.

"I did, and he is *oll recht* with it, as long as this is something you want."

Lucy grinned and leaned her head against his chest, and he instinctively tightened his arms around her.

Gabriel pulled back to look her in the eyes. "Lucy, I want you to see my leg before we wed. It's not a pretty sight, and I'll understand if you want to change your mind."

"Nay."

"Nay?" He gazed at her in shock. "You don't want to see it?"

"Nay, I'll never change my mind. I love who you are and everything about you, including your left leg."

"Wait here, then."

"Gabriel—"

"I'll be right back, Lucy."

He went outside to his buggy, which he drove closer to the house. He tied up his horse then reached into the back of the vehicle to pull out something long, wooden and familiar.

She gasped as he brought it into the house.

"I wanted to make you something special," he said as he set it down.

"Gabriel, 'tis beautiful." She bent down to touch it, running her fingers over the smooth, polished wood.

When she straightened, she had tears in her eyes. "I love it. I love you. *Danki*."

They sat at the kitchen table eating pie and making plans while they waited for Seth and Susie to come home. A little while later, Gabriel insisted on showing her his leg, and he rolled up his pants leg as far as it would go so she'd get a hint of what lay underneath it.

"You can't see the worst of it," he told her, watching her closely.

She smiled. "I don't care. I love you, and that's all that matters." She seemed unaffected by the scarred tissue, the discoloration. "And, Gabriel, if you need surgery, I'll be there for you. We'll get through it together. All of us as a family, because that's what we do when we love each other."

"Lucy," he whispered, his expression filled with love.

"You've nothing to worry about," she assured him.

"I have other scars, too. They had to harvest some of my own skin for grafting. I'm a scarred, broken man. Are you sure you're ready to take me on? For all of it?"

"I'm positive." Lucy gazed at the man across from her and her heart melted. She loved him so much. Her baby moved, and the flutter made her smile. In two months, she and Gabriel would welcome a baby son or daughter.

"I'd like to get married soon, if that is *oll recht* with you," Gabriel said, his gaze settling on her belly where her hand lay.

"How soon?" She shifted in her chair.

"I thought as soon as I get permission from the church elders. I'll talk with the bishop after I leave here.

We don't have to wait until November since you're a widow. But we will have to wait for the banns to be read."

"So next month?" Lucy asked with a smile.

"*Ja*, that's what I was thinking."

She nodded. "I like that idea." She grew thoughtful. "Where will we live?"

"We can live here if you'd like until we can buy a bigger place. The store is on my property but that's only a half mile from here, an easy commute. The counter will have a glass case in it, Lucy. The others thought it would be good place to feature small items and toys, but I think it will be a great place to sell your cookies and cakes."

Lucy smiled. "I like that idea—"

The side door slammed open, and Susie ran inside first. "Gabriel!"

"*Hallo*, little one."

"You didn't come before now," she said with a frown.

He nodded gravely. "*Ja*, I know, little one, but that's going to change."

Seth entered moments later. He looked first to Gabriel then to her. "Lucy?"

"*Ja*, Seth. We're going to be a family."

Susie gazed at the two of them and frowned. "Who is going to be a family?"

"You, Seth, the baby, and Gabriel and me. Gabriel and I are going to get married. Is that *oll recht* with you?"

"*Ja!*" Her daughter jumped up and down in her excitement. "We love him, and we want him to be our family."

Lucy laughed. "*Ja*, we do." Her gaze went to her brother, who remained awfully quiet. "Seth? Are you *oll recht* with having Gabriel in our lives?"

He nodded. "Are you sure you want me?"

Gabriel rose, went to Seth and grabbed hold of the boy's shoulders. "Seth, you belong here, more than I do, but I'd like to be part of your family, if you'll let me."

"*Ja?*" Lucy was surprised to see Seth blink back tears. Her eyes welled up with her own as she watched the man she loved reassure her brother.

"*Ja*," Gabriel said, squeezing Seth's shoulders lightly before releasing him. He turned toward Susie. "Susie?"

With a cry of joy, Susie flew into his arms and hugged him hard. Lucy saw him wince slightly where her daughter grabbed him but his expression never changed. "I love you, Gabriel," her child said.

He settled his hand on her head affectionately. "I love you, too, little one."

Epilogue

Winter, New Berne,
A year and a half later

"Gabriel."

Lucy's voice nudged him awake. He must have fallen asleep. They had been relaxing in upholstered armchairs side by side in their great room. Gabriel opened his eyes and smiled at his wife. They were married well over a year now, having wed six weeks from the day they'd first met. He loved every moment of their life together. Their family was like a never-ending adventure with excitement and love. Being her husband and a father, he was the happiest he'd ever been. He stretched and shifted in the chair. His leg was stiff, but the new medication his doctor had put him on was working. Surgery might be an option for the future but for now his leg had improved without it.

Gabriel reached out to run a finger across Lucy's cheek. "I must have dozed off."

"Me, too," she said with warmth in her pretty blue eyes.

They had been sharing a quiet moment together this afternoon. Susie and Jacob were spending the night with Rachel and Jed King. Nancy had offered to take them, but Susie wanted to spend time with her new friend Bess, Rachel's daughter. Rachel was also good with their son Jacob, a toddler who needed a younger woman like her to take care of him. The Jed Kings had become a close friends with him and Lucy, and he was grateful for the couple they trusted with their children.

Worried because his sister's time was near, Seth was outside, shoveling snow off the walkway and driveway. He had been a big help with Susie and Jacob, always lending a hand, keeping an eye on both children. He also helped out in the store whenever Gabriel needed him. Seth had gone with the children to the Kings' in the hired car earlier before the driver had brought him back to the property where the boy had immediately started to work.

Gabriel thought highly of the boy. Seth had finished eighth grade, his last year of school, and he was happy, healthy and glad to be a part of their family.

They'd had one terrible day when Lucy had received a second letter from her father, requesting Seth's return. Seth was happy here and had refused to go. Lucy had written her father back to tell him. That was six months ago, and they hadn't heard a word from the man since. If he wrote again, he and Lucy would handle his demands together. Seth belonged to them, and no one, especially not his own father, would take him away or make him feel less than he was ever again.

He and Lucy were enjoying these rare peaceful moments together that didn't come often with two young, energetic children—and with their third to arrive any day now—in the household. With the blustery, wintry weather outside, Gabriel had closed Fishers' Store, their successful toys and treats shop in the building on his old property that now belonged to his sister Emily. No one would be venturing outside on a day like today, and he was glad, for he loved spending this quality time with his Lucy.

The snowfall blanketing the ground made the countryside beautiful. It was the perfect day to spend inside with his beloved wife in their new home. They had sold Lucy's house and bought another one large enough for their growing family, property with a paved driveway and sidewalk. Emily was living in their old house, and she was seeing someone new.

Gabriel gazed at his wife with a smile until he saw pain move across Lucy's features and he became immediately concerned. Alert now, he straightened. "What's wrong?"

"'Tis time."

"The baby?" He felt a little nervous flutter in his chest as he studied her.

She sat up, straightening her back, and groaned. *"Ja."* She rubbed her hands across her belly in its advanced stage of pregnancy. Apparently, their *bubbel* was ready to face the world.

Gabriel had planned for this time. If he hadn't, he would be more panicked than he already was at the thought of getting her to the hospital on snowy streets. "What do you need?"

A sound at the door heralded Seth as the boy entered the house. He stomped snow off his boots before he took them off. He pulled off his woolen hat, revealing a mop of unruly dark hair. He removed his jacket and gloves then grinned at them. The grin fell off his face when his gaze landed on his sister.

"Seth, here is my cell phone," Gabriel said. "Call the doctor by hitting number three and let her know we'll be heading to the hospital soon. Then if you'll dial for me, I'll call—"

"Bert," Seth finished for him, already grabbing the phone to make the first call.

Gabriel remained calm while Seth called Lucy's obstetrician and then Bert Hadden, their English friend who had stopped to help them after Lucy's accident. The man was waiting to spring into action and drive them to the hospital in his four-wheel-drive vehicle that easily handled the snow.

This wasn't the first time Gabriel had been with Lucy when she'd delivered a baby. While Seth remained with Susie at home, he'd waited anxiously in the waiting room when she'd gone into labor less than a month after they'd married. Finally allowed into his wife's hospital room after Lucy had endured a C-section, Gabriel had looked at the baby boy in his mother's arms and fallen instantly in love. Their son, Jacob, had his wife's blue eyes and her late husband Harley's blond hair. And soon she would give birth to a third child, the one they'd created together, a child they'd love like they did their other children. He was nervous but eager to meet the newest addition to their family.

Seth put the phone on speaker and handed it to Gabriel. "Hello?" Bert said.

"Bert! This is Gabriel," he said. "It's time."

"I'm on my way," the gruff man said and immediately hung up the phone. Gabriel grinned, knowing the man would get there in record time and that he would get them safely to the hospital on the increasingly snowy roads.

"Are you *oll recht*, Lucy?" Seth asked with concern. He hesitantly approached his sister.

"I'm fine, *bruder*, just having a baby," Lucy assured him with a grin, reaching up to give the boy's arm a squeeze, making Gabriel love her all the more.

With loving hands, Gabriel helped his wife to rise and bundled her into her heavy woolen coat. Lucy was a vision of loveliness with her bright eyes, big belly and the smile she reserved for him. The knock came minutes later, revealing Bert, who had left his vehicle idling and ready to go.

"Do you want to come?" Gabriel asked Seth.

The boy blinked. "You don't mind?"

"You're family. Come with us."

Seth shook his head. "I would, but I should make sure the *haus* stays warm."

Gabriel nodded in understanding.

Barely an hour later, Lucy gave birth to a daughter. Gabriel gazed through eyes filled with tears at their precious baby girl with her fine wispy dark hair the same color as his and Lucy's. He knew Susie was going to be so happy to finally have a sister.

"She's *wunderbor*," he told his wife. "Every day, every month and every hour, you never cease to amaze me. I love you, Lucy Fisher, and I love our baby girl. I never thought I'd ever be this happy."

"Gabriel," she whispered, "you have made me feel loved, and I'm so grateful to have you as my husband and the father of our *kinner*. *Gott* has surely blessed

our marriage and our family. *Danki* for loving me…
and our little ones. For loving Seth."

"I love you. I love our family, Luce, and with you
by my side, I will love and guide our children for as
long as we are on this earth together."

"Are you ready for life to get noisier and a bit wilder
with a six-year-old, a one-year-old and a newborn?"

"*Ja*, I'll always be ready for life with you, dear wife."
He grinned. "Besides, we have Seth. He's becoming
a man."

Lucy smiled tiredly. Their daughter's birth had gone
well, but she was still exhausted. "What shall we call
our *dochter*?"

Gabriel leaned over to kiss his wife's cheek. "We
could call her Miracle, for she, like Susie and Jacob,
is a precious gift given to us by *Gott*."

His wife shook her head but continued to smile.
"Let's call her Grace."

He was infused with warmth, like he'd been kissed
by the summer sun. "Our *bubbel dochter* came to us
by the grace of *Gott*." He blinked back tears. "I love
that," he said. "I love you." He leaned down and kissed
her sweetly.

"I love you, Gabriel," Lucy replied. "You and our
family."

"Not as much as I love you." He grinned and she
laughed. Life was good.

* * * * *

Get 4 FREE REWARDS!

We'll send you 2 FREE Books plus 2 FREE Mystery Gifts.

FREE Value Over $20

Both the **Love Inspired®** and **Love Inspired®** Suspense series feature compelling novels filled with inspirational romance, faith, forgiveness, and hope.

YES! Please send me 2 FREE novels from the Love Inspired or Love Inspired Suspense series and my 2 FREE gifts (gifts are worth about $10 retail). After receiving them, if I don't wish to receive any more books, I can return the shipping statement marked "cancel." If I don't cancel, I will receive 6 brand-new Love Inspired Larger-Print books or Love Inspired Suspense Larger-Print books every month and be billed just $5.99 each in the U.S. or $6.24 each in Canada. That is a savings of at least 17% off the cover price. It's quite a bargain! Shipping and handling is just 50¢ per book in the U.S. and $1.25 per book in Canada.* I understand that accepting the 2 free books and gifts places me under no obligation to buy anything. I can always return a shipment and cancel at any time. The free books and gifts are mine to keep no matter what I decide.

Choose one: ☐ **Love Inspired**
Larger-Print
(122/322 IDN GNWC)

☐ **Love Inspired Suspense**
Larger-Print
(107/307 IDN GNWN)

Name (please print)

Address   Apt. #

City   State/Province   Zip/Postal Code

Email: Please check this box ☐ if you would like to receive newsletters and promotional emails from Harlequin Enterprises ULC and its affiliates. You can unsubscribe anytime.

Mail to the Harlequin Reader Service:
IN U.S.A.: P.O. Box 1341, Buffalo, NY 14240-8531
IN CANADA: P.O. Box 603, Fort Erie, Ontario L2A 5X3

Want to try 2 free books from another series! Call 1-800-873-8635 or visit www.ReaderService.com.

---

*Terms and prices subject to change without notice. Prices do not include sales taxes, which will be charged (if applicable) based on your state or country of residence. Canadian residents will be charged applicable taxes. Offer not valid in Quebec. This offer is limited to one order per household. Books received may not be as shown. Not valid for current subscribers to the Love Inspired or Love Inspired Suspense series. All orders subject to approval. Credit or debit balances in a customer's account(s) may be offset by any other outstanding balance owed by or to the customer. Please allow 4 to 6 weeks for delivery. Offer available while quantities last.

Your Privacy—Your information is being collected by Harlequin Enterprises ULC, operating as Harlequin Reader Service. For a complete summary of the information we collect, how we use this information and to whom it is disclosed, please visit our privacy notice located at corporate.harlequin.com/privacy-notice. From time to time we may also exchange your personal information with reputable third parties. If you wish to opt out of this sharing of your personal information, please visit readerservice.com/consumerschoice or call 1-800-873-8635. Notice to California Residents—Under California law, you have specific rights to control and access your data. For more information on these rights and how to exercise them, visit corporate.harlequin.com/california-privacy.

LIRLIS22

Cowboy and veteran Yates Trudeau returns home to his family ranch bruised and battered and carrying a life-changing secret. When he bumps into Laurel Maxwell, the girl he left behind, she might just set him on the path to healing that his body—and his heart—so desperately needs...

Keep reading for a sneak peek at
The Cowboy's Journey Home,
part of the Sundown Valley series by
New York Times *bestselling author Linda Goodnight.*

Had he really come to the woods before going to the ranch house? She had a feeling she was right and that he had. She wondered why—another habit of journalists. She needed to know everything, especially motives.

Yates's gaze seemed glued to her face, and she fought off a blush that would let him know he still affected her on some unwanted, visceral level. People say you always remember your first love. Yates had been her first and only.

She'd spent the better part of a year waiting to hear from him and another year getting over him.

Now here he was in the flesh, stirring up old memories. At least for her.

The annoying blush deepened. Laurel turned her attention toward the children and the dog. With a smiling

Justice in the center, they formed a circle of petting hands and eager chatter.

"Those aren't all your kids, are they?"

A small pain pinched inside her chest. "Sunday school class." To turn the focus away from her, she asked, "Was he really a military dog? Like a bomb or drug sniffer?"

"Explosives."

"Did something happen to him? Why'd he retire?"

Yates's face, already closed, tightened. "Stuff happens. Soldiers retire. Look, I should go. Enjoy your picnic."

With a snappy military about-face, he started to walk away.

"Yates, wait."

He paused, gazing back over his shoulder.

"After you get settled, come by the *Times* office. I'd love to interview you and the dog for the paper." She put her fingers up in air quotes. "'Hometown Hero Returns' would make a great feature."

"No interview. We're civilians now. Nothing heroic about that." Turning away, he gave a soft whistle. "Justice, come."

Before she could say more, Yates and his dog disappeared into the foliage.

Don't miss
The Cowboy's Journey Home *by Linda Goodnight,*
available August 2022
wherever Love Inspired books and ebooks are sold.

LoveInspired.com